Northwest Vista College
Learning Resource Center
3535 North Ellison Drive
San Antonio, Texas 78251

THEATER
IN THE
AMERICAS

A Series from
Southern
Illinois
University
Press
ROBERT A.
SCHANKE
Series Editor

D1519214

Other Books in the Theater in the Americas Series

THE
HUMANA
FESTIVAL

THE

THE HISTORY OF NEW PLAYS AT

HUMANA

ACTORS THEATRE OF LOUISVILLE

FESTIVAL

JEFFREY ULLOM

Southern Illinois University Press
Carbondale

11 10 09 08   4 3 2 1

Permission to use quotations from interviews was granted
by Lee Blessing; Christen McDonough Boone, Director of
Development, Actors Theatre of Louisville (A.T.L.); Julie
Crutcher; Michael Bigelow Dixon, former Literary Director/
Associate Artist, Guthrie Theater; Liz Engelman, Dramaturg;
David Jones; Trish Pugh Jones, Manager of Patron Relations;
Marilee Hebert Miller, former Associate Director, A.T.L.;
Jeff Rodgers, General Manager, A.T.L.; James Seacat, Com-
munications Director; Val Smith, former Associate Literary
Manager; Alexander Speer, former Executive Director, A.T.L.;
and Roanne Victor. These interviewees retain copyright of
their contributions to this volume.

Library of Congress Cataloging-in-Publication Data
Ullom, Jeffrey, 1971–
The Humana Festival : the history of new plays at Actors
   Theatre of Louisville / Jeffrey Ullom.
      p. cm.
Includes bibliographical references and index.
ISBN-13: 978-0-8093-2849-9 (pbk. : alk. paper)
ISBN-10: 0-8093-2849-6 (pbk. : alk. paper)
   1. Actors Theatre of Louisville. 2. Humana Festival.
3. Theater—Kentucky—Louisville—History—20th century.
4. Theater—Kentucky—Louisville—History—21st century.
I. Title.
PN2277.L62A38 2008
792.09769'44—dc22   2007038541

To my wife, Megan, and to my parents

CONTENTS

ACKNOWLEDGMENTS

This book has been made possible thanks to the contributions of the many colleagues and friends who offered me sage advice and constant encouragement throughout the years. I am indebted to not only those listed below but also many unnamed students and family who offered a kind word or unconditional support during any moments of toil.

My journey with the Humana Festival began when Michael Bigelow Dixon hired me to work at Actors Theatre of Louisville as his intern. His guidance proved invaluable, and his willingness to grant a former employee his time, advice, and assistance is greatly appreciated. Without him, this book would not have been possible. Even though the staff of the Actors Theatre literary office has changed over the years, I have received invaluable support for my work, especially from Valerie Smith, Liz Engelman, Amy Wegener, Michele Volansky, and Steve Moulds. The many staff and associates of the Louisville theatre also deserve thanks for their help in providing a complete history of the annual event. In addition to applying my unique perspective from having worked on a festival, I assembled the history by corroborating facts and developing opinions from a wide variety of resources. A final note for the staff who oversaw my work in Louisville: because I was an intern at Actors Theatre, I have made certain not to betray any confidence entrusted to me during my time of employment.

I have been extraordinarily fortunate to benefit from generous and accommodating colleagues throughout the years, beginning with those at the University of Illinois, especially Robert B. Graves and Peter Davis, and now those at Vanderbilt University, namely Holly Tucker, Edward H. Friedman, Kassian Kovalcheck, and John Sloop. My most heartfelt thanks go to my friends and colleagues in the Department of Theatre at Vanderbilt University, including Terryl Hallquist, Jon Hallquist, and my chair, Phillip Franck. Also, I enjoyed overwhelming support from my friends in the Playwrights Program of the Association for Theatre in Higher Education.

The enthusiasm for the project demonstrated by Robert A. Schanke has allowed for the completion of the book, and I thank him, as well as Les Wade, Kristine Priddy, and all others at Southern Illinois University Press for making this book a reality. I also thank Mark Pilkinton for his willingness to read my work and provide astute criticism.

As for my friends and family, I owe them an enormous debt of gratitude for their affection and support for this endeavor. Megan Alban Ullom and her family, Bob and Peggy Ullom, Noel and Vaughn Ullom, James Ullom, Peggy Juergens, Jerry Portele, and Fabio Serafini have my never-ending thanks.

THE
HUMANA
FESTIVAL

INTRODUCTION

At the beginning of every semester, I introduce myself to my students in a calculated attempt to seem personable and friendly in advance of the inevitable difficult tests and bad grades. Detailing my expertise, I list my qualifications for teaching a theatre class, most notably my educational background and my experience working in professional theatre. Naturally, students ask where I worked, expecting to hear New York or some other major city, but when I respond that I interned at one of the most respected theatres in the country, which happens to be in Louisville, a puzzled or disappointed look appears on their faces. One student bluntly asked, "Louisville? Seriously?" Possessing the commonly held perception that Broadway is the mecca of American theatre, my family gave the same confused response when I announced my intention to work in Louisville, compelling me to explain why that city would be my destination (not to mention having to describe what a dramaturg does).

I must admit that I too was surprised when I first learned the annual new play festival at the Actors Theatre of Louisville was a national phenomenon that transformed a small theatre in Kentucky into one of the leading regional theatres in the country. Every spring, theatre professionals, artists, and critics from around the world converge on Actors Theatre of Louisville to view the premier new play festival in the United States and to predict which play will be the favorite to appear on the Great White Way or Off Broadway. In his review of the Twentieth Annual Humana Festival of New American Plays in 1996, Greg Evans of *Variety* explained why he and so many other critics attended the annual event: "First-rate productions, even more often than not acted and directed with a professional quality that smug New Yorkers too often assume only exists east of the Hudson River." He added, "That's not to say that the smuggest of the smug won't point out that during the run of the festival, Louisville virtually becomes a second home for many Gotham theatre professionals."[1] Although the event certainly has not been consistent in its artistic and commercial success, the Humana Festival remains the most influential new play festival of the past thirty years and the most successful one in American theatre history.

Perhaps the most surprising aspect of the Humana Festival of New American Plays is its location. Created by Jon Jory and his staff at Actors Theatre of Louisville, the festival thrived in conditions where few would have expected any arts festival to prosper. For example, the Alley Theatre in Houston—at 4 million people the fourth-largest city in the nation, behind only New York, Los Angeles, and Chicago—produces twelve or thirteen shows a year. In Louisville, however, the sixtieth-largest city in the nation, Actors Theatre produces between thirty and thirty-six plays annually in twenty to thirty productions. Rivaled by local opera, orchestra, children's theatre, and other theatre companies, Actors Theatre of Louisville manages, in a town with a little over a million people, to accomplish every regional theatre's and artistic director's dream: to provide audiences with quality entertainment, to push the limits of its own theatre artistically, and to keep the institution financially solvent.[2]

The bread and butter for Actors Theatre's success certainly is the Humana Festival of New American Plays, and without the festival, the Louisville theatre would not merit special recognition. However, given the institution's reputation as a "playwright's theatre" due to its commitment to the development of new works, the Humana Festival provided Actors Theatre of Louisville with an international reputation for supporting established playwrights, discovering new talents, and presenting America's best new plays. From its humble beginnings in 1976, when it produced only two plays, to its twenty-fifth anniversary, when it featured fifteen new works by twenty-nine writers, the Humana Festival endured many changes under the guidance of Actors Theatre's producing director, Jon Jory.

The key to understanding how the Humana Festival survived and thrived during this twenty-five-year period is to analyze the many managerial decisions of Jory and other personnel at Actors Theatre of Louisville. Not only did Jory's personal initiatives and the administrative support he received help his institution survive in a Kentucky city with limited audience potential, but also his choices concerning play selections, subject matter, audience tastes, and experimentation spoke to the broader context of the status of American regional theatre. His deft ability to garner local support while also producing an annual event that reflected national trends (and frequently challenged practiced conventions of professional theatre) amazed theatre producers around the country. With each success, as theatre critics and producers turned their attention away from the coasts and looked to the banks of the Ohio River for a showcase of the latest in American playwriting, theatre professionals admired Jory's ability to remain relevant in the landscape of American theatre yet often misattributed his many achievements to luck.

Early in my yearlong internship in Louisville, at a welcoming session for new staff, I first heard a concise explanation for the theatre's surprising success. A bevy of new interns gathered in the boardroom on the second floor of the administrative building, and the brief meeting began when Jon Jory walked into the room. Personable and confident, Jory introduced himself to the awaiting staff and thanked them for their commitment to the theatre. During the short discussion, Jory quipped that he enjoyed great luck in establishing the festival, and he repeated this coy response on numerous occasions throughout his thirty-one years in Louisville.

This work concedes that good fortune and good timing certainly played roles in establishing the annual new play festival, but analysis of the decisions made by Jory and his staff reveals that luck is too simplistic an answer for how the festival found success. The history of the Humana Festival, in fact, is one of calculated risks, dogged work ethics, and artistic vision. In fact, Jory's managerial decisions created the conditions that allowed his luck to occur; his success derives not from luck but from his talents, showmanship, and determination. Once Jory established the festival and it received international acclaim, the producing director used his clout to enact changes he deemed necessary and to pursue artistic endeavors that he supported. With financial stability, quality productions, access to the best playwrights, and a staff that believed in their leader's vision and abilities, Jory skillfully managed to appease the tastes of local audiences while making sure that his festival not only reflected national trends (as a means of maintaining relevance) but also became a home for experimentation by contemporary playwrights.

To turn his annual event into a nationally recognized festival, Jory and his dedicated staff directed the Humana Festival through a variety of phases to maintain its success. By charting these shifts in the festival, three essential questions can be answered: First, how was the festival established? This book explores how Actors Theatre of Louisville became interested in producing new plays, how it built an audience, and how it formed a symbiotic relationship with the Humana Festival. Second, how has Actors Theatre utilized its fame to help further the growth of the festival and influence trends in American theatre? Since other regional theatres created new play programs to compete with the Humana Festival, Actors Theatre endeavored in several ways to ensure that the festival remained the premier new play program in the country. This work details how Actors Theatre overcame institutional constraints by adapting the festival to guarantee its commercial and critical success. Third, how has the annual event changed in format or in reputation since Jory's departure?

Providing an answer to these questions is the purpose of this work. Even though Actors Theatre of Louisville received international acclaim for its Humana Festival of New American Plays, as well as numerous awards (including

Tonys, the Margo Jones Achievement Award, and the Shubert Foundation Vaughan Award) for its efforts in regional theatre, very little has been written about the theatre itself.[3] While several books are about specific regional theatres, none focuses solely on Actors Theatre of Louisville or highlights the festival's artistic successes and failures in a year-by-year analysis. Because of the overwhelming success of the Humana Festival, the history of Actors Theatre and its festival remains a unique and necessary study.

Instead of providing a simple history that details significant events but fails to discuss how the institution operates and adapts to achieve its goals, this work explores the decisions, achievements, experiments, and failures of the Humana Festival of New American Plays and the Actors Theatre of Louisville by dividing Jory's twenty-five years with the festival into phases. Each period is defined not by a certain number of years but by specific agendas that Jory followed as he chased good fortune and exploited its success. The phases reflect the ways in which Jory pursued a variety of goals that dictated the play selections and managerial decisions of the period, and the shifts in focus illustrate how the festival reflected national trends in professional theatre. When applicable, this work emphasizes a particular production in each phase as a representation of the struggles faced by both the Humana Festival and the American theatre at large. Issues involving these productions provide an opportunity to discuss other events in the festival's and Actors Theatre's history, as well as trends in both regional theatre and New York theatre.

The first two chapters focus on productions and events that occurred before the establishment of the Humana Festival yet proved instrumental to the theatre's development. The first production, a dreadful performance of *The Importance of Being Earnest*, symbolizes Actors Theatre's struggles in the context of the development of regional theatre across the country, as well as the current trends on Broadway. The representative production for the second chapter, Jory's *Tricks*, described as "one of the greatest failures of the decade," determined the future relationship between Actors Theatre and New York, especially in its founding years.[4]

During the first two phases of the Humana Festival, Jory pursued agendas that involved the discovery and expansion of good fortune. For the first three years, 1976–79, Jory's determination to establish a national reputation for the festival led to his discovery and presentation of *Crimes of the Heart*, the representative production of the third chapter. Chapter 4 articulates how Jory built on the event's surprising success during 1980–82 to exploit and expand his festival's newfound fame and garner an international reputation. These two chapters also detail how, with the success of *Crimes of the Heart* and other productions, Jory's agendas altered the relationship between nonprofit theatres and Broadway producers looking for commercial successes in regional theatres.

During the next two phases, Jory relished his festival's success and, for the first time, felt free to exploit its achievement by initiating widespread changes in the operations and artistic choices of the festival. For the "from product to process" phase, described in chapter 5, the activities and productions of the Humana Festival mimicked the events occurring in regional theatres around the country. And the sixth chapter, "The Exploratory Years, 1986–93," highlights how regional theatres and Broadway producers desperately searched for new dramatic voices.

During the final two phases under Jory's leadership, the festival mirrored the trends then current in regional and Broadway theatre. The fifth phase provokes a discussion of the formulaic works of the festival during the mid to late 1990s and its counterpart of "corporate theatre" on Broadway. Jory's sixth and final phase with the festival details the variety of changes theatres made to stay in the limelight. Jory yearned to rediscover his good fortune, and the festival endured many shake-ups that revitalized the event and prepared the festival for the future, actions that helped separate the Louisville theatre from other regional theatres and from Broadway productions.

The chronicle of these six phases charts the changes in artistic and administrative policies that occurred during Jory's tenure and provides a framework through which the reader can both view developments in the Humana Festival's history and evaluate the context for each production. Because Jory left Actors Theatre in 2000, this book also examines Marc Masterson's handling of the festival and answers key questions about his ability to maintain the success of the event. Through exploration of the motivations as well as the accomplishments and failures in each period, a complete history of the festival is provided. Furthermore, from this analysis of the festivals and the critical responses to the Humana Festival plays, one can easily trace the trends in American playwriting, analyze the artistic tastes of the Humana Festival artists, and provide a comparison between festival years to explore how the festival itself changed, becoming a proving ground not only for playwrights but for Jory and Masterson as they established, adapted, and improved the festival to maintain Actors Theatre's reputation as a "playwright's theatre." Throughout the book, the reader is taken inside the festival by means of descriptions of the working environment, the festivities of a "VIP Weekend," and the variety of personnel that help made the festival successful. In addition to serving as a guide for regional theatres interested in producing new plays, it is hoped this work provides a model for future studies of both regional theatre and play festivals.

Finally, the purpose of this work is neither to bury nor to praise Jory and Actors Theatre but to supply an analytical record of the festival and its endeavors. Throughout the long history of the festival, mistakes have been made and astonishing accomplishments have been achieved, and this work explores the reasoning behind the important events and decisions to evaluate their effect. Without delving into gossip or personal lives, this work charts the development of America's greatest new play festival by examining the motives, decisions, and desires of one of the most important figures in contemporary American theatre while also demonstrating how Jory's choices represented trends that were occurring across the country, making the annual event a truly national festival.

In other words, this work corrects the ignorance that I possessed many years ago, before I knew of the far-reaching influence and impact of the new play program at Actors Theatre of Louisville. According to the theatre's Web site, "over 90 million Americans have seen additional productions of the many plays originated in the Humana Festival, not including film audiences who have seen Humana plays adapted for the screen."[5] With its worldwide reputation and its national influence, the Louisville institution became a national theatre and served as a leader through its artistic choices. However, to entice both local and national audiences, the festival and the theatre also mimicked the administrative and financial practices executed by many regional and New York theatres. Just as the Humana Festival and Actors Theatre developed a symbiotic relationship, so have Actors Theatre and the American theatre at large. With this analysis of Jory's creation and utilization of his perceived luck in the context of other events that were occurring in American theatre, a critical study of the Humana Festival becomes more complete and relevant.

1   THE FOUNDING OF A DIVIDED THEATRE

The journey of Actors Theatre of Louisville to success and international acclaim was not an easy one. In fact, its early struggles typified the experiences of many regional theatres around the country. Exhaustive pains to secure financial support, difficulty in maintaining audiences and locating performance spaces, and clashes over artistic vision plagued numerous regional theatre producers across the country during the 1950s and 1960s, and for the leaders of Actors Theatre of Louisville, the path was no different. The establishment of the small company in Louisville is a tale of rivalry, stubbornness, and egotism, yet the determination of community leaders to support theatre in Louisville helped the institution survive until a truly visionary leader could salvage the failing theatre. Through its many trials and tribulations, the founding of Actors Theatre epitomizes many of the struggles that most regional theatres endured, as the Louisville company underwent several changes in management and artistic vision in its first few years.

The establishment of any regional theatre in America owes much to the vision and determination of Margo Jones, considered the creator of the regional theatre movement. Jones's efforts symbolized the beginning of the decentralization of the American theatre from the East Coast (specifically New York City) to "a new basis of theatre not dependent on Broadway."[1] Her book, *Theatre-in-the-Round*, traces the history of her Theatre '47 and provides a worthwhile study for any historian or regional theatre director. Published in 1951 and initially received as a how-to for developing regional theatre, the book contains methods and suggestions that seem outdated and impossible owing to changes in economic conditions and to the variety of entertainment options for contemporary audiences. Nevertheless, the ideals championed in Jones's book represent the goals and motivations behind the endeavors of both old and new regional theatres in America: "A permanent repertory theatre with a staff of the best young artists in America; a theatre that will be a true playwright's theatre; a theatre that will provide the classics and the best new scripts with a chance for good production; a theatre that will enable Dallasites to say twenty years from now, 'My children have lived in a town where they could see the best plays of the world presented in a beautiful and fine way.'"[2]

The realization of Jones's dream certainly demanded a great amount of time (approximately eleven years) and effort, because of the difficulties she encountered in cultivating interest in a permanent regional theatre and maintaining an audience. Developing and sustaining local support have been the burden of regional theatres over the past fifty years, and the failure to do so caused the downfall of numerous institutions in spite of their locations in thriving cities.[3] A case in point is the turbulent history of Jules Irving and Herbert Blau's Actor's Workshop in San Francisco, established in 1952. After presenting classical plays and newer works to mostly critical praise, Irving and Blau expected to see a surge in audience attendance; however, Actor's Workshop enjoyed only miniscule growth, a result of poor decisions involving its artistic, economic, and administrative endeavors. First, the co-producers failed to educate the community about the value of their artistic accomplishments, even though many San Franciscans had postulated that citizens would not accept a regional theatre purely because of their trendy demands (the theatre's lodgings were described as "shabby") and a popular resistance to anything established, including theatres, as well as classical play productions. The two leaders' artistic offerings also suffered from bad financial decisions. Irving and Blau made no overtures to the various San Francisco communities for public relations purposes or to the local corporate powers for financial backing and security. With little funding, the Actor's Workshop remained in a dingy building that kept certain clientele away. Further damaging their relationship with the city (as well as ruining their fund-raising potential), Blau often wrote scathing newspaper articles that ridiculed their audiences and implied an antiestablishment holier-than-thou attitude, thus disenfranchising many traditional patrons.[4]

Actor's Workshop suffered from administrative failings as well. The theatre staff underestimated the importance of marketing, as they never attempted to retain their loyal audience members. According to Joseph Zeigler, author of *Regional Theatre*, Actor's Workshop's audience base dropped sharply from twenty thousand to sixteen thousand in 1963–64 partly because whenever patrons moved or changed addresses, staff members simply discarded the names and addresses instead of finding their new residences and retaining support for the theatre. In retrospect, the Workshop provides a glaring example of how not to launch or manage a nonprofit theatre. Thankfully, most institutions in the regional theatre movement established themselves by pursuing support from a wide range of sources while adjusting their artistic, economic, and administrative goals to accommodate the tastes of their local community.[5]

At the numerous regional theatres that managed to avoid the missteps of Actor's Workshop, producers still faced an abundance of challenges and obstacles in determining which path to follow to success.[6] Divisive issues plagued many upstart theatres, as directors, producers, audiences, and boards of directors often used different standards to define success. Boards of directors often favored commercial fare to ensure substantial box office, while directors and producers frequently argued for greater aesthetic adventurism or progressive work. These debates questioned the very nature and purpose of regional theatre—did it exist simply to bring theatre to the masses or did these institutions have a responsibility to challenge their audiences and present culturally relevant work? Ideally, a regional theatre would accomplish both goals, and thus the lesson learned by most regional theatres in their earliest years was the value of balance. This crucial quality applied not only to the selection of plays in the context of local audience preferences but also to the establishment and designation of institutional administrative responsibilities.

In his book *New Broadways*, Gerald M. Berkowitz provides four different models to demonstrate the numerous methods for the establishment of regional repertory theatres across America. Berkowitz's models also yield four examples of an achieved balance and how each compromise helped define the inner workings or purpose of a given theatre. The most widely recognized and copied of these models is the Alley-Arena model named after Zelda Fichandler's Arena Stage in Washington, D.C., and Nina Vance's Alley Theatre in Houston. Much like Margo Jones's Theatre '47, these theatres were created by a "charismatic leader of an amateur company that graduates to professional status."[7]

The Alley-Arena model, as first articulated by Jones, recognized the financial difficulties in trying to operate as a profitable business while maintaining a resident company and presenting a repertory season. Jones realized that she needed to discover an appropriate balance between her personal artistic inclinations and having to cater to the community for financial support. Hoping to alleviate some of the economic demands, Jones incorporated her theatre as a nonprofit organization monitored and supported by a board of directors. This group of citizens and local business leaders provided beneficial ties to various communities, as well as guaranteeing corporate help and continued support for the theatre. Furthermore, with the nonprofit label, the theatre could apply for governmental grants and tax-deductible gifts from private foundations.[8]

The transformation from a small, amateur theatre to a larger, repertory institution was not an easy process for many theatres, as evidenced by the struggles of the Alley Theatre. Nina Vance, who worked with Jones in

Dallas, announced the formation of an amateur theatre group in Houston and initiated a campaign to obtain financial support. Vance sent postcards to supporters of local arts groups, inviting them to attend an informational meeting, and approximately one hundred people attended. Of these one hundred guests, thirty-seven pledged twenty dollars each to provide capital for the first shows. Six weeks later, the Alley presented the first of its six presentations for the 1947–48 season, *A Sound of Hunting* by Harry Brown.[9]

Trouble beset the Alley Theatre the following year when the fire marshal condemned their building, forcing administrators to find a new home for the theatre. Their solution helped set an example for the regional theatre movement, especially Actors Theatre of Louisville: claiming any space as a viable theatre. Jones's "pattern setting" adaptability turned an abandoned building on the Texas State Fairgrounds into her performance space, while the Alley Theatre moved into an abandoned fan factory that could be reached only through a back alley. Soon after, both Margo Jones and Nina Vance faced a new challenge: resolving the problem of amateur actors and their often-questionable reliability and quality. Jones was the first to make the official change and hire professional actors, but Vance encountered a backlash of criticism by hurting "the feelings of the many community talents who had worked for five years to make the Alley a success."[10] At a crucial meeting, Alley Theatre's board members gave Nina Vance artistic control of the theatre, a decision that became the standard in regional repertory theatres, as it reflected the necessity of one person to dictate the artistic vision of a theatre. Also, the balance struck by Vance and the board of directors not only defined the limits of the artistic director's control but also legitimized the value and power of a theatre's governing body.

Communities or governmental agencies that dictated the need for a theatre constitute a second model, often labeled the Lincoln Center model. Numerous theatres resulted from the tireless efforts of community leaders, not theatre artists, who believed that having a regional repertory theatre was essential to their city. For instance, a committee in Seattle claimed an abandoned building from the Seattle World's Fair for the purpose of creating the Seattle Repertory Theatre in 1963, and in Pennsylvania, William Ball, an Off-Broadway and regional theatre director, established the Pittsburgh Playhouse after being hired by a board of directors. Given that these institutions derived from a community dictate, several of these theatres function under a compromise by which the theatre is beholden to cater more to public tastes than to the artistic director's aesthetic inclinations.[11] With such institutions offering more popular fare, it is not uncommon to see rival theatres attempt to offer a balance to the community (the most obvious example being Seattle's A Contemporary Theatre, whose name blatantly defines how it differs from Seattle Repertory Theatre).

Universities and colleges helped develop a smaller number of regional theatres, resulting in a third model for establishment. Recognizing the potential and support within the university system, W. McNeil Lowry of the Ford Foundation stated, "The future of professional training in the arts depends, first, upon a radical shift in the university atmosphere surrounding students considered potential artists, and, second, upon the provision of postgraduate opportunities for professional apprenticeship."[12] Perceiving universities as cultural centers ripe for the arts, numerous amateur (and, later, professional) theatres aligned themselves with academic institutions for financial and creative support, accepting lessened financial risks at the expense of often working with amateur actors or educational mission statements. The most notable theatres to thrive under this formula are the McCarter Theatre (associated with Princeton University and becoming Equity in 1972), and Yale Repertory Theatre (obtaining professional status in 1972 also).[13] For Actors Theatre, the limited number of colleges in Louisville and their small theatre departments prohibited the use of this model.

The final model for establishing a regional theatre in the 1960s depended on the efforts of individuals who used their clout to attract support. Bored with the routine of directing in New York and London, acclaimed director Tyrone Guthrie, Broadway producer Oliver Rea, and stage manager Peter Zeisler established a professional repertory theatre far from the East Coast. They selected the city of Minneapolis for its remote location from other theatre centers, as well as the extensive support for the arts given by the community. Guthrie and company dazzled the Minneapolis civic leaders and enticed them to build a $2.25 million theatre complex. In 1963, with a professional resident company complete with stars, the Guthrie Theater opened to immediate success and a renowned reputation. Under this model, the balance utilized is one where the community gives the artistic director substantial power in executing his or her own artistic vision in exchange for an increased awareness of the city's cultural offerings and potential national attention and acclaim for its local theatre.

Other theatre artists followed the Guthrie model on a smaller scale: a Yale graduate, Harlan Kleiman, successfully ran a summer stock theatre group in a town near New Haven, Connecticut, with a fellow Yale graduate student, Jon Jory, the son of the famous Hollywood actor, Victor Jory. The two men together dreamed of organizing a repertory theatre in New Haven, but both realized their disadvantages: their inexperience (Kleiman was twenty-four, Jory was twenty-six) and their lack of funding (neither had any capital nor any reputation to borrow money).[14] Mirroring the actions of Nina Vance, they met with several people in the community and made "connections," constantly trying to build an audience base and secure financial support. From the fall of 1964 to the spring of 1965, the partners "talked to 250 or 300 people . . . telling them about their plans and asking them questions: 'Can we use your name?' and 'Will you give us names of other people who might be interested?'"[15] Finally, a building was chosen: the cinderblock Long Wharf Terminal market. Community leaders initially considered this location, sandwiched between the Connecticut Turnpike and railroad tracks, to be a horrendous choice for a theatre. Nevertheless, audiences flocked to the theatre, and the inaugural summer season played to more than 99 percent capacity.[16]

The establishment of Actors Theatre of Louisville derived from several of these models, including socialites using their connections to elicit support, confrontations with the theatre's board of directors, debates over Equity actors, and even condemned buildings. The story of the tumultuous founding of Actors Theatre of Louisville began with four classmates from Atherton High School in Louisville, two of whom led diverse lives until they returned home. The ensuing battle between these two over the founding of a local theatre led to public feuds and even a back-alley brawl. Although their individual strategies were short-sighted and lacking in other ways, their stubborn personalities allowed these two men to create the theatre that would eventually bring Jon Jory to Louisville.

The first person to begin establishing a regional theatre in Louisville was Richard Block. Tired of enduring the life of an unsuccessful actor and songwriter, Block left New York and returned home to Louisville in 1962 with the idea of establishing a repertory theatre. Frustrated by the lack of opportunities afforded to him in the northeast, he realized that his dream of producing and directing quality theatre productions could be accomplished only in a repertory setting: "I never wanted to be a producer, but I discovered very quickly that the only way that I was ever going to get anywhere was to be a producer."[17]

Block considered several cities, including Indianapolis and Atlanta, but he finally decided on Louisville for the single reason that he could live at his parents' house while working to establish the theatre. Known to be a meticulous planner, Block mimicked Nina Vance by organizing an informational meeting for community leaders at which he proposed his idea for a repertory theatre. The immediate response was substantially supportive and provided the motivation to proceed with fund-raising for the new institution. Following Margo Jones's model, Block incorporated Theatre Louisville on May 15, 1962, as a "nonprofit, cultural, and educational organization" and publicly declared a one-hundred-thousand-dollar fund-raising campaign. Hoping to begin production on theatrical works, as well as a new playhouse, within a year, Block favored a methodological approach that emphasized financial security: "I felt it was vitally important that it be done properly, and that we have enough support so that we could truly guarantee the people of Louisville that this was not a flash in the pan, that this was going to go forward, and it was going to last."[18]

To help attain his desired financial security, Block quickly secured sizable grants from the Ford Foundation, as well as public support from two notable Louisville figures: Barry Bingham Jr., a member of a prominent philanthropic Louisville family, and William Mootz, an arts critic for one of the local newspapers, the *Courier-Journal*. Bingham agreed with Block's argument for a regional theatre and generously offered his financial and social support.[19] The two continued to meet with community leaders but also realized the need to inform the public of their plans through coverage in the local newspapers. While attracting the attention of the local press might be a daunting task, the fact that the Bingham family owned both of the local Louisville papers made the challenge less difficult. Furthermore, Block sought out Mootz to gain his support for the development of a regional theatre, and the two began a friendship that lasted for many years. In fact, Mootz later admitted aiding Block's cause by reviewing numerous regional theatre productions in other cities as a means of promoting the value of a resident theatre to Louisville readers.[20]

With interest in a resident theatre rising, Bingham and Block organized a larger informational meeting, hoping to persuade Louisville citizens to support their bold endeavor. Although the events of the gathering had been meticulously planned (a credit to Block), the young director was worried because of torrential storms that pushed into Louisville that evening. "It poured down," Block recalled. ". . . There was water everywhere. I was a wreck [and thought] nobody is going to show up." In spite of the tempestuous weather, the meeting received "a good turnout" and "a considerable amount of enthusiasm."[21] To elicit support from the attendees, Block arranged for presentations to be given by architect Jasper D. Ward III, who unveiled his concept for redesigning a space within the Arts in Louisville building, and by the president of the Cincinnati in the Park theatre group, Morse Johnson, who discussed the hardships endured and efforts needed to establish a resident theatre in smaller cities. By the spring of 1964, thanks in part to the excitement generated by the organizational meeting, Block's plan began to show fruit: "His systematic approach, dogged determination, sixteen months of work and research were paying off. He had assembled supporters and induced them to expend time, energy, and resources. Theatre Louisville Inc. appeared to be on the way to forming a permanent resident theatre."[22] Ironically, the only obstacle to Block's approach would come from a former classmate at Atherton High School.

Serendipitously, the challenge of founding a regional theatre in Louisville became a two-man race when another native, Ewel Cornett, returned home in 1964 with a touring production of *Camelot*. While visiting Louisville, he met with his friend, Dann C. Byck, a member of another philanthropic Louisville family and a former schoolmate of both Block and Cornett. Like Block, Cornett was a disenchanted actor looking for new avenues to explore in expressing his artistic desires: "My life as an actor was an unhappy one. . . . I was disgruntled with . . . the way things were happening [in the business]."[23] The two men discussed the possibility of establishing a resident theatre company, and Byck agreed to support the endeavor. Cornett quickly abandoned New York City and arrived in Louisville with plans for hurriedly establishing a repertory theatre.

Contrary to Block's slow and cautious approach, Cornett hastily assembled an amateur acting company, which he officially titled Actors Inc., and began looking for a performance space. Like Vance, who transformed a factory into a theatre, Cornett and Byck decided to turn the former Gypsy Tea Room, a second-floor loft, into a performance space despite the many columns that obstructed the view of patrons. Some supporters expressed serious doubts that the space could be transformed into a theatre, but Byck described the cramped performance space as crude but acceptable: "It was not a theatre; it was just a room. You had to crawl up steps to get to it. . . . The playing area that would be called the stage was about twelve or fifteen feet square. We had a small room for dressing rooms, and then I had a closet for an executive office suite."[24]

Cornett's decision to quickly mount plays led to a piecemeal transformation of the performance space. Spalding University, a small Catholic school a few blocks south of the new theatre, provided rows of black-canvas seats that were tied together, and the lighting was makeshift at best. Actors Inc. board member and former Atherton High School classmate Roanne H. Victor recalled that the lighting instruments were "made out of Number Ten tomato cans painted black."[25] By May 1964, Cornett announced his summer season of four plays, while Block continued to organize financial support for his theatre. Competition and comparisons between the two factions became frequent and heated.

Ironically, Richard Block and Ewel Cornett met before establishing their competing theatres in Louisville. The two men were in the same class in high school but did not reestablish ties until they bumped into each other in New York City. According to Karl Victor—another native Louisvillian and friend of Cornett—the two men were not friends in high school because each played different social roles: Cornett was the popular "big jock," and Block was "puny," studious, and artistically inclined. When Block and Cornett met accidentally in New York, both men were researching resident theatre companies at the offices of the American National Theatre and Academy. The two acquaintances casually discussed establishing a resident theatre in Louisville, both as partners and as separate organizations. This chance conversation was the full extent of their discussion before descending on Louisville, but both men knew that they operated with opposing philosophies. In describing Cornett's approach, Block explained, "Ewel's idea was a theatre not of a producer or of a director, but a theatre of actors. It was an interesting, a very appealing, and a very legitimate idea. One that has a lot of power to it. Not an institutional kind of theatre, but a theatre where the actors are the theatre, and the actors create out of themselves. . . . That's why he called it Actors Inc."[26]

Although a few successful theatres began as quickly organized groups determined to produce plays regardless of the cost or environment—Barbara Gaines's Chicago Shakespeare Theater first offered productions on the roof of the Red Lion Pub yet now resides in a $24 million facility on Navy Pier—history favors institutions utilizing Block's methodological approach. Still, in an age when few models for successful regional theatres existed, Block and Cornett represented two opposing philosophies concerning the purpose of a resident theatre and how to go about establishing such an institution. Whereas Block's apprehensions concerning financial stability led to a lengthy fund-raising period, Cornett and his backers believed that successful productions would lead to financial rewards. Dann Byck, in fact, harshly criticized Block's methodology, labeling his approach "wrong" versus Cornett's vision and agenda: "The idea, just the name of theatre that Ewel came up with was all of it right there as far as I was concerned. He called it Actors Incorporated, [and it] had nothing to do with monuments; it had to do with what you saw on stage. Dick's was Theatre Louisville, which is a monument. It is really significant, terribly significant."[27]

Unable to compete with Block's fund-raising endeavors and growing financial security, Cornett had no choice but to gather fellow out-of-work actors to quickly begin production on shows and, it was hoped, steal press from Theatre Louisville. Cornett contacted an old friend, *Louisville Times* critic Dudley Saunders. Just as Block had gained the support of *Courier-Journal* critic William Mootz, Cornett sought counsel from Saunders, and the conflict between the two theatres became constant fodder for the press. With battle lines being drawn, it became clear to many involved in the arts in Louisville that the competition between the two rival companies eventually would result in a harsh defeat for one group.

Animosity, however, intensified and became personal when the impetuous Cornett refused to contact Block. Instead, in hopes of promoting his own theatre, Cornett criticized the slow, methodical procedures of Block and his Theatre Louisville. In retaliation, members from Theatre Louisville bad-mouthed Cornett and his organization to the press, complaining about Cornett's brash methods and the questionable merits of the actors whom Cornett had assembled. Actor Jack Johnson, one of the first performers to work for Actors Inc., did not refute Theatre Louisville's allegations when he said that Cornett's impulsive and energetic ways represented the entire group: "The actors who were in that first company were real rebels. . . . For instance, a couple of them one night went to a key club where there was illegal gambling. They lost this money. They went outside, and they saw police officers going in to take their take, and they got in the police car, out of anger, and drove it around town. Then, [they] took the keys and threw them on top of a building. That's the kind of actors that were there."[28] Block's supporters argued in the press that such people were not worthy representatives of the arts in Louisville and that Actors Inc. was not a professional theatre, because it did not employ Equity actors. Both Block and Cornett quickly became resentful, and the rivalry between Theatre Louisville and Actors Inc. intensified as both companies realized they could not coexist in a town of Louisville's size.

With tensions mounting, both companies eagerly anticipated Actors Inc.'s summer season in 1964. While Cornett needed successful productions to provide a foothold in the long climb toward financial stability and growth, Block was faced with a paradox of desires. On the one hand, he wanted the rival company to fail so that all the support would fall behind his Theatre Louisville. On the other hand, worried that Actors Inc. might fail too much, Block claimed that he "became very frightened. I felt that Actors Inc. could do exactly what I was organizing to prevent. Open, go broke, close, and kill professional theatre in Louisville."[29]

The summer season of Actors Inc. was ambitious in scope and impressed both critics and audiences. William Mootz labeled the first production, Christopher Fry's *The Lady's Not for Burning*, as the best of the season. The production (which opened May 29, 1964) also proved to be a financial success. During its three-week run, 1,655 customers paid over $3,940, bolstering Cornett's hopes and the rivalry between the two theatres. Unfortunately, the remainder of the summer season failed to live up to the expectations set by the first production. Mootz described the second Actors Inc. presentation, Friedrich Dürrenmatt's *The Visit*, as "a noble attempt" despite his fierce criticism of every aspect of the production. Mootz and Saunders offered more praise for Cornett's efforts in the final two productions, O'Neill's *Desire under the Elms* and an evening of Albee one-acts, *The American Dream* and *The Zoo Story*. In both cases, Mootz and Saunders complimented Cornett's ability to provide an engaging and emotional experience, as well as his inventive utilization of the small space.[30] In spite of the mixed reviews, Louisville critics labeled the summer season a critical success; however, Saunder's and Mootz's objectivity can be questioned, since they both admitted their intentions to gather support for a local regional theatre through their reviews.[31]

With a total attendance of 7,655 persons, Cornett's summer season was enough of a financial success to be deemed a legitimate threat to the future of Theatre Louisville. The constant rumors of a merger, however, quickly tempered the elation of Cornett and Actors Inc. Both leaders knew that a merger was inevitable and that each company needed what the other had—Block needed artists and a performing space, while Cornett's company needed financial support. Even before discussions began, Block exhibited his "abrasive personality," as well as his resistance to a proposed merger, when he refused to even consider the union unless all of Actors Inc.'s debts were paid, further complicating any negotiations. Fortunately, Karl Victor's mother willingly donated the money in the interest of helping theatre thrive in Louisville, allowing the two theatres to initiate talks. Regardless of the logical arguments in favor of uniting the two companies, the two men dreaded the possibility of working together.[32]

In July 1964, the boards of the two companies grudgingly agreed to meet in the Arts in Louisville building for discussions about the possible merger. Unfortunately, just as the rivalry between Block and Cornett had been rooted in a distant relationship, tensions and arguments between the two boards resulted from their distinct social circles within the Louisville community. "We knew a lot of the same people," Karl Victor explained, "[but] we didn't socialize with them."[33] As the artists and board members filed into the meeting room, the divisions were clearly evident: two feuding artistic directors with two different approaches to theatre, each supported by a board that did not associate with the other. Nevertheless, they all understood that the city of Louisville would not sustain two local theatres and that a merger was necessary.

Those involved with the merger discussions remember them as being bitter, angry, difficult, and extremely tense. Following the Alley-Arena model, they agreed to form one company with a new board to be assembled from the two existing boards, but a problem quickly arose, in that each board selfishly believed that the new board should consist of more of their members than of those from the other theatre. Since the Actors Inc. board was smaller, all of its members were placed on the new board—a decision that angered Theatre Louisville supporters and added to the animosity between the two groups. After Block's theatre was allowed an equal number of board members, bickering erupted over who should become the first president of the theatre. After further contentious debate, they finally reached a solution: The first president would be Actors Inc.'s Dann Byck, who would be followed by Theatre Louisville's Barry Bingham Jr. Thus a pattern was established whereby the role of president would continue to alternate "sides," meaning that the appointment was based on the old rivalry between Actors Inc. and

Theatre Louisville. The prominent animosity from everyone involved—Block, Cornett, and the new board—stunted the growth of Actors Theatre of Louisville and overshadowed many accomplishments of the young theatre. These divisions would not be mended until the Louisville theatre found a leader with the charisma and experience to make them unite behind a single vision and cause. Unfortunately, neither Block nor Cornett would be that person.

With the decision to merge, even in spite of the protestations of Block and Cornett, the newly formed Actors Theatre of Louisville found itself briefly operating under the community-driven model—a new organization with a board of directors yet no producing director. The combination of the two rival groups forced the new board to make a difficult choice in selecting either Block or Cornett as their leader. Although institutions like the Seattle Repertory Theatre thrived under the direction of its local citizens, the decision made by the new board members to hire Actors Theatre's first artistic director proved disastrous. It is not surprising that when it came time to elect either Block or Cornett as the director of the new company, the two factions reached an impasse. In spite of their ability to compromise on prior issues and because of their exhaustion from the tense meetings, board members attempted to strike a balance that, in the end, failed to resolve the long-standing conflict. Although the two artistic directors dreaded the idea of a combined company, the new board officially agreed to retain both Cornett and Block on two-year contracts as coproducers and co–artistic directors.

The name of the new theatre, Actors Theatre of Louisville, was simply the combination of the two names, and the logo adopted for the new group featured a large *A* with a *T* and an *L* underneath. More symbolically, a coronet topped the ATL logo (representing Cornett), and the entire drawing was ensconced in a colored square (a block for Block). Once again, board members and actors pettily took sides, with some members of the new theatre continuing to disparage the other group through trifling arguments, boasting that Actors Inc. "won" because the "A" was bigger. Others argued that Theatre Louisville won because more of its name was in the final title. Even though the board of the new theatre was optimistic about the future and proud of its new logo, the outcome of the merger—a theatre with coproducers and codirectors—appeased no one on the theatre staff, especially Block and Cornett. According to Cornett, "It was folly to think that Dick Block and I could work together, because we were so different."[34] Tensions persisted, as each company believed that the other was benefiting more from the merger. Block argued that his organization had "much more to lose. Because they really didn't have anything," but Cornett countered, "When we merged, then he came into *my* theatre."[35]

The new board's decision to retain both Block and Cornett as coproducers placated no one; the organization's artists and staff found themselves struggling with competing aesthetics and management styles. In spite of their disagreements and animosity, the two leaders began planning for the upcoming season. Although critics eventually considered the first season at Actors Theatre of Louisville (1964–65) an artistic success, the newly merged company struggled both economically and administratively. For example, Block and Cornett endured the casting process together but failed to discuss the financial burden of employing out-of-town actors before their casting trip to New York. After numerous actors were cast and brought to Louisville, insufficient funding forced Actors Theatre to fly the actors back to New York and to postpone the opening of the season, greatly embarrassing Block and Cornett.[36]

The coproducers quickly rescheduled the season for a December opening but quarreled over the size and scope of the season, as well as every aspect of production, from play choices to casting. They not only expounded differing methodologies but also embodied the very struggle that regional theatres endured. Block, having worked tirelessly to secure financial backing, resisted presenting confrontational and controversial work that might alienate audiences. Cornett, however, was less inclined to cater to audience preferences, preferring to provide socially relevant and progressive work in his theatre.[37] As the season progressed, the widening rift between the two producer-directors led to frequent verbal fights and, eventually, physical violence. According to Roanne H. Victor, "There was a fistfight. Ewel beat the shit out of Richard one night behind a bar on Bardstown Road."[38]

As the season progressed, the tension between the coproducers became unbearable. Neither Block nor Cornett was happy under the current employment conditions, but neither considered sacrificing or compromising his vision for the theatre. In spite of their differences, Block and Cornett "were doing their best to keep up a smiling face inside the theatre and not show any friction" between them, but, as tempers flared, most of the acting company sided with Cornett, while some administrators supported Block. Block blamed his troubles on the actors, who knew Cornett first and resisted working with "a very strong director with very strong opinions. Not only about the plays, but how they should be performed."[39] While Block's explanation certainly supported his perception of his talents, several actors attributed the cool reception toward Block to his "academic" approach to directing. While cast members were charmed by Cornett's passionate and energetic approach to acting, they often criticized Block's directorial style as humorless and uninspiring. Granted, some of the actors' biases in favor of Cornett resulted from their previous involvement with Actors Inc., but Block's inability to engage his actors reflected more on his personality than the actors' refusal to work with a pragmatic director.[40] Block's relationship with Cornett's actors never improved.

Although Block's productions received mild to generous praise, the actors involved expressed great dissatisfaction with him, both personally and professionally. Resident ATL actor Jack Johnson provided the actors' perspective: "There was a lot of hostility toward Richard. . . . The actors said to Ewel, 'We can't work any more with Richard. You must go in and tell the board that. . . . Just see what you can do.'" The rising tension resulted in a strike by the actors, forcing the administration to listen to their criticisms and complaints. Once again, the board divided along prior sides. With the actors sitting on one side of the theatre aisle and the administrators on the other, the company-at-large discussed whether Block and Cornett were "going in different directions." At the end of the lengthy meeting, actor John Seitz summarized the actors' frustration, childishly claiming, "We want to be loved, that's all. . . . We're not getting loved if you guys are fighting."[41]

After listening to the actors' public dissatisfaction with the structure of the dual leadership, as well as their private criticisms of Block, everyone agreed that a problem existed, but the board could not reach consensus on how to solve it. Since the two sides of the board each supported its former leader, the only proposal that received unanimous support was to hold another meeting, and both Block and Cornett separately sought counsel from friends and other professionals, including the local critics. Cornett met with Saunders, and the critic remembered how Block and Cornett handled the pressure: "Each was saying, 'How long can I put up with this? This can't go on.' Ewel's impatience, I think, broke first. Block was capable of being more patient with things. Block was, I think, looking down the road and saying, 'Alright, I can do this as long as I've got to.' Ewel was looking and saying, 'I'm not sure how long I can stand this.' His patience began to wear thin."[42] According to friends, Cornett was tormented by having to work with Block and by having to listen to the constant complaints of his devoted actors. The impulsive and embattled director decided that action was the only way to resolve the unbearable situation.

When the second meeting convened, Cornett surprised the board by issuing a bold ultimatum. At the request of the actors, Cornett took an aggressive stance and demanded that the board of directors choose either Block or him, because, he said, the current situation was unacceptable.[43] To decide which of the two men would become the sole artistic director, the board invited both to plead their cases at a third meeting, this time at the Pendennis Club, an elegant, private social gathering place downtown. As the day of the final meeting approached, Block stopped by Mootz's home to discuss the upcoming decision. The Louisville critic remembered fearing the worst for the former Theatre Louisville producer: "I said to him, because I was so convinced that he was going to lose [and] that Ewel was going to win, 'Well, after it's over, stop by, and let's have a drink.' I think at that point, Richard, if he thought that he had no chance to win, he didn't admit it. . . . I said to a friend 'Dick Block is going to be by here around ten o'clock, and, you know, we have to have the crying towel ready and the drinks out.'"[44]

The atmosphere of the meeting was extremely tense as the two men waited their turn to enter the closed room and speak before the board. Cornett, an admittedly uncomfortable public speaker, found himself speechless in front of the board yet was able to make a simplistic plea. Cornett recalled the meeting: "I just said, 'If you want a good theatre, you'll take me.' One of the board members—I don't remember which one—said, 'Yes, and Hitler also said just give me Poland.' I'll never forget that. I laugh about it now, but that really hurt me."[45]

Block, whom Cornett described as "very articulate," made the more persuasive argument, declaring that voting was inappropriate and would be a breach of contract. Block presented his case: "When we merged last year, you made a commitment to the two of us for two years, and if Ewel does not wish to stay his two years, then let him leave. But you cannot tell me to leave because you have a commitment to me. . . . If he chooses not to fulfill the commitment, his part of that, that's up to him. But it's not up to [the board of directors]."[46]

Once Block finished his speech, the two men departed, leaving board members with the dreaded task of ending either Block's or Cornett's career at Actors Theatre of Louisville. Most of the members believed that Cornett was a better theatre artist and nicer person, but Block presented a more valid argument. Even though the board voted mainly along prior loyalties, several Actors Inc. members found no legal reason to fire Block, since he was keeping his end of the initial agreement. In the final tally, Cornett lost by only two votes; the board, therefore, rejected Cornett's ultimatum and accepted his resignation. Although the final voting margin was narrow, the verdict to release Cornett from his position as coproducer represented one of the first steps toward unity within the theatre. By not yielding to an ultimatum and by disregarding personal and emotional biases, the assertiveness of the new board eliminated a major obstacle to the institution's growth.

The reactions of the two men were predictable. Block received the news while standing in Karl and Roanne Victor's kitchen, and he proceeded to Mootz's home to deliver the good news. Mootz answered the door with a long face and greeted Block with apologies for his defeat. According to Mootz, Block corrected his friend and informed him of the voting results, explaining how the "critical issue" brought about Cornett's dismissal: "Ewel was breaking faith. If Mr. Cornett breaks faith with us this way, can we [ever] trust him?"[47]

Understandably, Cornett was devastated by the board's decision. Karl Victor described the aftermath: "The man was absolutely bananas. He was so upset. Roanne, I know, received calls [from Ewel and others]. I received calls. Everybody on the old Actors Inc. received calls that he couldn't believe this had—you know—that this kind of thing was happening."[48] Block and Cornett huddled with their respective support groups, with the Theatre Louisville faction celebrating and the Actors Inc. contingent in disbelief about their leader's removal. Once again, the theatre was divided along sides, but now it was clear which side had won.

In retrospect, Cornett's ultimatum was a regrettable miscalculation. If he had waited another year, the board likely would have released Block and given Cornett ultimate control of the theatre. In fact, when Cornett spoke to Saunders before the blowup, the critic cautioned him not to issue an ultimatum. Saunders remembered advising Cornett not to be brash: "I said, 'Ewel, don't do it. If you do this, you're out. You do not issue ultimatums to Barry Bingham Jr., to Dann Byck, [and] to Karl Victor. . . . If you issue an ultimatum, you're going to lose. If you wait, you'll get it. Just stick it out right now . . . even before your season begins next fall, you'll have it.'" Even though Mootz was a supporter of Block, he too agreed with Saunders's assessment of Cornett's miscalculation, stating, "Ewel had moved too early. If he had sat quiet until the end of that initial agreement, Ewel would have gotten the theatre."[49] Unfortunately for Cornett, his stubborn pride and impulsive decision led to his greatest blunder.

Immediately after the board announced the voting tally, the acting company, as well as several board members, privately begged Cornett to withdraw his resignation. But he refused, proclaiming, "I have said what I have to say. I have been voted out. I am leaving because I have made that stand."[50] Cornett left Louisville for West Virginia, where he enjoyed a self-described successful career as an actor, composer, stage manager, playwright, director, and producer until his death in 2002. Nevertheless, he considered his brief tenure at Actors Theatre a learning experience, and he admitted that he wished he could have altered his actions. Cornett also stated that if he could, he would have changed his relationship with Block. Both men eventually apologized to each other for their hostilities during the merger and the first (and only) Actors Theatre season with coproducers and codirectors.[51]

With any competition now eliminated, Block proceeded to fulfill his vision for a regional theatre in Louisville, solely responsible for all the theatre's achievements and failings. He endured hostility from former Actors Inc. members who lamented Cornett's removal, but Block wisely made a concerted effort to heal any rifts between the two groups. "Block mended a lot of fences after the blowup," Saunders reported. "There were some people who told me that Block would be gone by the end of his first season by himself, but apparently he put things together."[52] In spite of his attempts to unite the theatre, Block's own actions soon created another divide in the theatre—one that he could not repair.

Just as Actors Inc. converted a loft to launch its theatre, Block attempted to reestablish Actors Theatre in a different building. Faced with a performance space that allowed only one hundred seats and offered no street recognition to passersby, Block began his tenure as sole producer-director with the challenge of finding a larger facility for the theatre. Block and the board of directors searched for a downtown building with easy access and high visibility. After an extensive search, a limited number of options forced the board to select a curious choice: the Illinois Central Station Railway Terminal, at Seventh Street and River Road, alongside the Ohio River. Although the building allowed for greater visibility, its proximity to the river led one critic to label Actors Theatre the only regional theatre with a potential flooding problem. To complicate matters, because the board deemed the need for expansion so important, Actors Theatre selected the abandoned railway station in spite of its having been scheduled for demolition to make way for an interstate highway.

Again employing the talents of architect Jasper Ward, the company began renovations for the 350-seat theatre in September 1965, only a few weeks before its official opening of October 14.[53] To highlight the achievements of the new Actors Theatre of Louisville and put the Block-Cornett public feud behind them, the board organized a celebration for the grand opening of the new theatre. That evening the audience gathered at the Tenth Street Depot, rode a train to the new space on Seventh Street, and, unfortunately, had to endure a disastrous performance of *The Importance of Being Earnest*, overly staged as low farce.

Despite the poor showing onstage, Actors Theatre's grand opening was a turning point for the young institution in its effort to reestablish itself, as it now enjoyed the stability of a new performance space and a single leader supported by a board of directors, both staples of the Alley-Arena model. The Louisville theatre, however, was not alone in its quest for a new beginning. Also in 1965, several theatre professionals attempted to reestablish themselves with new companies. After being hired by a board of directors and providing one year of service to help guide the Pittsburgh Playhouse to success, William Ball spurned the new company for "political, aesthetic, and temperamental" reasons, only to form his own rival company in Pittsburgh, the American Conservatory Theatre (which moved to San Francisco two years later). Also, following the dismantling of the Actor's Workshop, Irving and Blau moved to New York to establish a new company at Lincoln Center with the help of several of their former actors.

The 1960s saw an astonishing number of theatres being founded (or refounded) across the country, and the events in Actors Theatre's brief history that led to the production of *The Importance of Being Earnest* certainly reflected this trend. While Actors Theatre and the American Conservatory Theatre enjoyed reestablishment, theatre patrons in 1965 also witnessed the founding of several notable regional theatres, each of which strove to provide a desired balance for its community. A Contemporary Theatre sought to fulfill a perceived void by presenting new plays (compared with the classical repertoire of Seattle Repertory Theatre), and El Teatro Campesino began catering to a certain demographic not represented by mainstream theatres. Both Long Wharf Theatre and the Roundabout Theatre Company attempted to provide the chance for local citizens to view classic plays where few such opportunities existed (New Haven) or where newer work received the majority of patronage (New York).[54]

With the reestablishment of Actors Theatre of Louisville, the national press began to acknowledge it as a legitimate regional theatre when articles about the new space appeared in the *Chicago Tribune*, the *New York Times*, and the *Nashville Banner*. Furthermore, interest in the new building helped to increase subscriptions sharply, and the theatre began to receive both state and federal grants. The first season in the new building featured, in addition to *The Importance of Being Earnest*, a balance of classic and contemporary offerings, namely *Waiting for Godot*, *A Doll's House*, *The Tavern*, *Death of a Salesman*, and *School for Wives*. The season, however, was not a critical success. Julius Novick, the outspoken author of *Beyond Broadway: The Quest for Permanent Theatres* and a former critic for the *Village Voice*, visited Actors Theatre of Louisville and described his experience: "The production I saw there of George M. Cohan's *The Tavern* was so ponderously overdirected by Mr. Block . . . that it was hard to discern whether the actors had any talent. The performance I saw had been entirely sold out to a local high school, but the house was half empty: an ominous sign."[55]

In addition to growing criticisms about Block's directing, another event typified the difficulties that the young producing director faced in his first year. The production of *Death of a Salesman* marked the return of Ned Beatty, a Louisville resident, to acting. Beatty worked at a local record store, but Block encouraged him to leave his job and take the role of Willie Loman. Beatty, whose performance drew rave reviews, failed to arrive for one performance, forcing Block to go onstage, reading from a script. Block later found Beatty walking along Dixie Highway, so distraught about his wife having just left him that the future film star had to be hospitalized. In spite of the challenges faced during that year, Block's first season was a financial success, playing to 38,898 people (compared with the previous season's total of 15, 533).[56]

After completing his first season as sole producer-director, Block received a one-year renewal on his contract. The following season (1966–67) involved several achievements for the theatre, most notably the incorporation of a policy in support of color-blind casting, a teacher-training program, the first tour of the state, and a more ambitious season, featuring *All My Sons, Slow Dance on the Killing Ground, Miss Julie, Charley's Aunt,* and *A Streetcar Named Desire.* Unfortunately, problems between Block and the board of directors overshadowed many of the season's artistic achievements.

The season-opening production of *All My Sons* received notoriety because Block's director's notes in the program proposed a parallel between the action of the play (a man knows of faulty machinery yet fails to act) and the actions of car manufacturers. Furious with Block's inferences, automobile dealers who advertised in the program threatened to pull their advertising.[57] Seemingly unconcerned with the potential loss of advertising revenue, Block surprisingly refused to remove his director's notes, arguing that few patrons read the program and that removing the pages would simply call attention to an issue that normally would be overlooked. Ignoring Block's pleas, the board of directors asked the printers to cover the offending paragraphs, but that effort failed, as most of the text was still legible. The standoff turned serious when the board eventually demanded that Block remove the notes from the program or offer his resignation. Block eventually compromised and conceded that the pages should be torn out, claiming that his change of heart came in consideration of the theatre's best interest (and not from a fear of being fired). As a result, every night before the show, the ushers were charged with tearing pages 17–20 from 250 programs. This controversy clarified the rights and freedoms of the director, as well as the responsibilities of the board of directors, concluding in the assertion that "the board is in a position of final authority in cases of disagreement with the producer-director, communications between the producer-director and the board of directors [having] been very poor, [and] a distinct element of distrust [existing] on both sides."[58]

Communication between Block and the board disintegrated further, though, throughout the 1967–68 season, beginning with Block's statement to the press that Actors Theatre of Louisville hired "three Negroes." The lack of racial integration was a widespread problem in the 1960s South in every aspect of life, as only 15.9 percent of black students attended integrated schools and only 52.8 percent of blacks in southern states were registered to vote. Integration was also a problem in theatre; in his essay for *The Theatre of Black Americans,* Tom Dent explains that black community theatres became widespread in the South during the early 1960s, but African American actors often struggled to make the transition into the major nonprofit theatres. As the decade progressed, however, Broadway and regional theatres in major cities began casting minorities with greater frequency.[59] In Louisville, Actors Theatre's board of directors fiercely objected to Block's announcement concerning the hiring of the African American actors—not to Block's politics but to the unfortunate timing of the announcement. Block chose to make the declaration during the week of contentious civil rights marches for open housing in Louisville, giving the appearance that the theatre took a progressive stance in the midst of a civil-rights debate in a conservative town. Block failed to inform the public relations committee about his announcement, and, as a result, the board demanded that he inform the board in advance of any new policy changes.

As Actors Theatre prepared for its next season, play selection was a point of contention between Block and the board. Even though attendance had steadily increased—over fifty-one thousand patrons attended the 1966–67 season—expenses outweighed ticket sales, and board members questioned Block's choice of plays. Furthermore, during the previous season, only four of the eight plays were considered by school boards to be suitable for children (meaning that sold-out matinees for schools were not offered for half of the productions). The long-standing discord between artistic choices and economic demands emerged when board members argued that plays like *The Hostage* and *The Firebugs* were too avant-garde and not appealing to the "tired businessman." According to the minutes of several board meetings, "spirited debates" took place over Block's choices of plays, ending with the decision that play selection was solely Block's responsibility. The end of the season was marked by the election of a new board president, Ian Henderson, and the realization that subscription sales declined because of "disappointment in [the] plays."[60]

The continuing conflict between the board of directors and Block caused further distractions during the 1968–69 season. The budget problems were so severe that board member Bernard Dahlem removed radiators from the lobby and sold them for scrap. Board members continued to criticize Block for driving away patrons with his esoteric selection of plays and for refusing to participate in fund-raising activities. Block explained his resistance to pressure from the board in terms of his own artistic desires:

> I came constantly under more and more pressure for two things: one, to lighten the season and two, to spend less time directing and more time writing grant proposals and going to Washington and going to Frankfort [the capital of Kentucky]. You know, be more of a producer and fundraiser. I had to insist that the reason I had started Actors Theatre was to direct, to be able to direct plays. . . . I had this conflict with the board almost every spring when I came up with the plays we were going to do. They always wanted me to do more popular things. . . . It got to be, to a certain extent, me against them.[61]

The strain of the job was taking its toll on Block, and his increasing resistance to the board's wishes and demands created a rift that could no longer be bridged. Any sense of balance achieved by the selection of Block as sole producer had faded, as he frequently challenged the board, pushing the theatre in a direction of his own interest without consideration for the community or the financial stewards of the institution. Just as Block and Cornett had represented opposite ends of the spectrum in the purposes and goals of a regional theatre—serving the artists versus favoring the community—Block now frequently stood in opposition to the board's demands and requests. While Block enjoyed the ability to articulate the theatre's artistic vision, the board retained the ultimate power to determine whether that vision was appropriate for the community.

Board members unanimously agreed that the theatre was on a decline, both artistically and financially. The board blamed Block for "imposing his view of life" and his politics onto the stage and for demanding too much of the city (in expecting citizens to support his productions). While other nonprofit theatres successfully produced socially progressive work—most notably the Public Theatre's *Hair* (1967), the Arena Stage's *The Great White Hope* (1968), and Chelsea Theatre Center's *Slave Ship* (1969)—Saunders recalled that the conservative Louisville audiences were "unhappy with being preached to" and that board members grew more concerned with Block's negative affect on the financial health of the institution: "They [the board] were looking ahead, and they were seeing huge deficits. They were beginning to say, 'What are you going to do next year?' and not liking what he was beginning to say."[62] According to board president Ian Henderson, Block "was so immovable in his principles, theatre-wise, about what he was going to do."[63]

Hoping to resolve their differences, Block and the full board met on January 15, 1969, but the result of the meeting was that he would not continue in his role as producer-director of the theatre. Block claimed that he had planned to take a yearlong leave of absence after the 1968–69 season, because he knew that the environment at Actors Theatre of Louisville was not right for him. He declared his decision to leave was necessary, both professionally and personally, asserting, "I was committing so much time and energy to the theatre that I had very little life. I was producer-director, and what I really wanted to be was the artistic director. . . . I knew that I was not what they needed anymore. What they wanted was a more popular theatre . . . It was hard for me to walk away." Block righteously dismissed the notion that he was fired: "The truth is that I did resign, but I never made my resignation known to them."[64]

In spite of his assertion that his decision to leave Actors Theatre was his own, the truth is that Block was forced out as producing director. With the subscription rate declining and concerns about the public perception of the theatre increasing, members of the executive committee voted not to renew Block's contract. Barry Bingham, Block's partner in founding Theatre

Louisville, argued that Block might have been in over his head and that the establishment and management of the Louisville theatre was a "longer and tougher economic struggle than he expected." William Mootz also cited Block's failing as a financial steward as well as a director, lamenting a falling off of Block's work and arguing that Block's productions exhibited a desperate attempt to be controversial. This criticism is ironic, given that Block initially dismissed Cornett's season selections as being too progressive and not accommodating enough to the tastes of Louisville audiences.[65]

After expressing his regret and disapproval of the board's decision, Block graciously offered to help monitor and facilitate the transition into a new leadership. Local newspapers carried the story, citing economic difficulties and a difference of artistic vision as the official causes for the separation. The reports also stated, ironically, that the next leader of Actors Theatre would be concerned solely with artistic matters while nonartistic and producing duties would be relegated to someone else.[66]

Even with the agreement that Block would no longer remain in charge, many board members expressed sympathy for their former leader, especially those who had supported Theatre Louisville. According to Henderson, "That was an emotional thing to have to tell a person, [that] he's going to have to give up his creation and go on and do something else." During Block's brief tenure as artistic director, however, he had not only alienated himself from the public and their tastes but also disenfranchised the board to such an extent that the members would have refused to help raise money to cover the theatre's mounting debts (between thirty thousand and forty thousand dollars).[67]

In spite of their best efforts, the leaders of Actors Theatre established a theatre with clear divisions and tensions between its two producers, between the two sides of its board of directors, between its producer and the Louisville community, and between its producer and its board. With Cornett departed and Block "resigned," the board of Actors Theatre ventured into what could have been dangerous territory. In the search for a new producing director, the theatre had little to attract major candidates: massive debts, a falling subscription rate in a city of limited population, a board rife with infighting, and an audience that demanded to be catered to in terms of play selection and accessibility. The young Louisville theatre survived a tumultuous beginning that threatened to kill any possibility of professional theatre thriving in the small Kentucky city, but thanks to Cornett's dogged determination to produce plays, Block's methodical efforts to secure financial stability, the growing confidence of the board, and assistance from the local press, Actors Theatre survived its early trials. Attempting to capitalize on the growth of the regional theatre movement, Actors Theatre searched for a new leader, someone who would build audiences and produce quality work. Little did the board members or the city know that the person they chose would not only change the direction of professional theatre in Louisville but also alter the landscape of regional theatre and new play production across the country.

2 The Education of Jon Jory

By the end of the 1960s, Actors Theatre was a small participant in a larger revolution: a revolt against "a direful trend—the contraction and imminent death of the art of theatre."[1] Recognizing Broadway's limited employment opportunities and its frequent emphasis on financial reward over artistic expression, more and more theatre artists explored creative prospects available in resident theatres around the country, leading *Variety* to report in 1966 that more professional actors found employment outside New York than on Broadway. In spite of the increasing decentralization of American theatre, regional theatre artistic directors still looked to Broadway for the best new plays, thus presenting the same playwrights and plays in city after city, year after year. In hopes of discovering new talent, legendary New York producer Joseph Papp and other resident theatre artistic directors began to augment their institutions by developing new plays. However, these theatre professionals and producers succumbed to the widely held belief that success was defined by Broadway—a myth that an upstart producer in Louisville would attempt to challenge.

With the January 15, 1969, dismissal of Richard Block as its leader, Actors Theatre began the arduous task of finding a new artistic director (with the new title of producing director). Realizing that many smaller regional theatres faced the "uphill, never-ending struggle against poverty and slow acceptance," the board members of Actors Theatre of Louisville knew that to succeed they needed to hire someone with good public relations skills who would understand and cater to the tastes and personality of the city.[2] The board assigned the task of interviewing and selecting the new producing director to a search committee composed of the three past presidents, namely Dann Byck, Barry Bingham Jr., and Karl Victor. In total, "five or six" men were interviewed for the position. As board member Bernard Dahlem jokingly recalled, "I don't know why they were interested in being the producing director of Actors Theatre. We were broke . . . but they interviewed anyhow."[3]

Certainly the most memorable interview took place at a unique location: the Louisville airport. Even though Jon Jory expressed interest in the

Louisville position, his directing schedule prohibited him from taking an extended trip to Kentucky for the sole purpose of interviewing. Instead, Jory scheduled a two-hour layover in Louisville between directing jobs. During this brief meeting, he stunned the search committee by admitting that he recently led the Long Wharf Theatre into bankruptcy. After clarifying that the theatre's financial troubles were not solely his fault, he avowed that he would never allow a theatre to fall into bankruptcy again, and he argued that his Long Wharf Theatre experience taught him to accommodate the tastes of the community. He expressed his desire to push the theatre and community artistically, but only to the point where both would jointly benefit. According to Barry Bingham, "Jon clearly came to us with a concept that you've got to have a break-even budget or you're going to lose your theatre."[4]

After wowing the three past presidents with his honesty and charisma, the search committee recommended Jory for the producing director job on February 19, 1969, and the board quickly invited Jory to Louisville on March 9 to present his ideas for the future of the theatre.[5] Hoping to counter the widely held perception that the Louisville theatre suffered from poor production values, Jory again surprised the board by arguing that he did not think a seven-show season of quality productions was possible under the theatre's current budget of approximately two hundred thousand dollars.[6] In addition to proposing a $227,000 budget, Jory showed confidence in his vision by boldly refusing to sign a contract unless the board approved his financial plan. Board members debated the merits and financial figures of Jory's budget, which featured "small cast shows, higher-paid actors, good plays . . . 5,000 subscriptions at current prices, a ten percent increase in hard tickets" yet leaving a deficit of approximately $28,000.[7]

Even though Jory's inflexibility might have surprised some, given his limited experience in managing a regional theatre, it is easy to see where Jory learned such a trait: his father, Victor Jory. A brief biographical passage about the film actor states that Victor Jory was "supremely confident of his talents, remarking on several occasions that he was 'damn good'—though he was tougher than any movie critic in assessing his lesser performances." On numerous occasions, the younger Jory exhibited these same characteristics, as well as his father's reported generosity with young actors (exemplified by Jon Jory's desire to teach at a university).[8]

Perhaps the greatest attribute that Victor Jory passed on to his son was his extraordinary work ethic, a trait that proved crucial in helping to reestablish Actors Theatre. Jory's childhood in California was likened to an average middle-class existence in which fathers went to work during the day and returned home for dinner, and Jory recalled his father following the same pattern. The only difference was that Victor Jory worked in movies along with his wife. Instead of summer vacations, the Jorys worked in summer stock, with the entire family performing in plays, allowing Jon and his sister to earn Equity cards at a young age. Family remained important to Jory when he applied to college; he wanted to follow his sister to the University of Washington, but his checkered high school career led to his rejection and eventual enrollment at the University of Utah (from which he did not graduate) and later a brief stint in the Army.[9] Theatre later played an important role in Jory's own family, as his first marriage, to actress Lee Anne Fahey, resulted in two children (including one pursuing theatre) and his second wife, Marcia Dixcy Jory, is an accomplished costume designer and dramaturg.[10]

In spite of his divergent path, it was in Jory's blood to work in the theatre. In a recent interview, Jory recalled, "It would never have occurred to me to think about medical school or law or any of those things, simply because in our family we worked in theater or film of TV or radio." Through his father, Jory developed the ethic and the mentality that theatre is *work*. In a discussion about himself as a theatre artist, Jory disputed the label: "I don't know what it is. I think of myself as a theater worker. I think there probably are such things as artists and I think in my field there may be as many as four or five in a generation. The fact that everybody else trots about calling themselves artists I find somewhat amusing."[11] Jory's predilection for work eventually led him to quit graduate school at Yale, opting to work at a regional theatre instead.

With tireless energy and a strong work ethic, Jory defended his budget to the board of directors of Actors Theatre by calming worries about the remaining debts and discussing ways to raise the extra money needed. Whereas Block resisted the board's overtures to dedicate more time to public relations activities, Jory announced that he enjoyed meeting the public, explaining, "I think I can help get subscriptions back up to the 5,000 mark; I think the season will be more popular than you have had; I am not afraid at all to ask people for money. . . . I think you are going to have to face the fact that you are going to have to fund-raise this year, next year, and every year."[12] Jory's new contract also required that the theatre raise the necessary funds to operate the entire seven-show season. If, by October, the board knew that it would not be able to raise the necessary money, then Jory would be released from his commitment and given one-third of his yearly salary.

After the two parties agreed on a contract and the board announced its decision to the press on March 10, 1969, the newspapers heralded the selection of Jory, citing his experience as a founder of a regional theatre, as well as his success with the development of new plays.[13] Several articles recounted his trials, as well as his accomplishments, at Long Wharf, including the creation of an outreach program to bring theatre to local schools, a new play festival that failed to obtain audience or financial support, fierce competition from the Yale School of Drama, and declining subscriptions. Even though extensive fund-raising allowed Long Wharf to reject Yale's proposed absorption, the financial struggles "disaffected" Jory, and he soon resigned to become a freelance director at regional theatres around the country.[14]

Fortunate timing benefited Jory, as he perceived Block's departure from Actors Theatre to be a perfect opportunity. Barry Bingham recalled that Jory viewed the Kentucky theatre as an operation that had not lived up to its potential, boasting that he could turn the theatre around. Jory was exactly right for A.T.L. because of his eagerness to perform the tasks Block was not willing to do, especially meeting with and catering to the community.

Remembering his promise to protect the theatre from financial ruin, Jory worked tirelessly upon his arrival to promote the theatre's new direction. In his earliest days as Actors Theatre's producing director, Jory became a bit of a chameleon by catering to the two factions of the community, termed here "New" and "Old" Louisville. Consisting of transplants as well as younger, middle-class citizens who wanted the city to become more cosmopolitan, the New Louisville demographic appreciated Jory's expressed interest in producing more contemporary plays rather than traditional classics. While conceding that *Oedipus Rex* is worthwhile, Jory argued that numerous contemporary plays provide the same theme and message but in a more direct manner. Furthermore, Jory exhibited his youthful temperament when he later employed kooky promotion ideas in hopes of demonstrating the new energy and excitement at the local theatre, including bumper stickers humorously boasting that "Actors Theatre does Shakespeare in the nude" or "Actors Theatre does Shaw in Yiddish." Apparently, the New Louisville community warmed to these publicity ploys and quickly supported Jory and his lighthearted attitude.[15]

Old Louisville consisted not only of many key donors to Actors Theatre (including the Bingham family) who favored classical works but also of members of the general public who preferred lighter fare and viewed theatre as escapist entertainment. In an attempt to win back these latter audience members, who believed the previous selection of plays to be too avant-garde or political, Jory stressed his desire to produce "fun" theatre, claiming, "My basic love is theatre that relates to what theatre once was—vaudeville and circuses. That feeling you got when you watched jugglers or a high-wire act—I want to recreate that feeling for adult audiences in the theatre." He elaborated further on his view of theatre when asked about the educational responsibilities of the profession: "If the theatre has any educational job to do, it is to broaden people's emotional base, and open new doors on their feelings about what entertainment is."[16] Given that he was raised doing summer stock, this perspective from Jory provides one explanation for why he opted to produce mainstream works in his earliest years, but his favoring popular fare in his play selections also served a practical purpose.

Jory's willingness to cater to the tastes of the community denoted a crucial attribute for any successful regional theatre producer. According to Joseph Zeigler, any leader "must be willing to abnegate himself for his theatre while fulfilling himself through it."[17] A self-described "old-fashioned liberal," Jory wisely recognized that he could not "go around saying what I thought about this or that issue" and kept his political views off the stage in an effort to appease the conservative tendencies of his board of directors and the Louisville community.[18] He understood that his priority was to entice audiences to the theatre but that once his institution became financially secure, he then could take greater risks and follow his personal artistic inclinations (a ploy he utilized when establishing the festival).[19] In the meantime, Jory vigorously labored to endear himself to the entire Louisville community through his selection of traditional plays and his tireless promotional appearances around the city. Jory was an energetic showman who felt more comfortable directing comedic and popular plays, while Block was frequently perceived as somber.[20] Even Block acknowledged that Jory possessed a great gift as a producer and public figure, admitting, "I would have never been able to do what he did. Nor would I have had the motivation to. It's a different temperament. . . . His true contribution is as a producer."[21] Much to the board's approval, Jory was determined to take Actors Theatre on a very different course.

On March 26, 1969, only sixteen days after the declaration of Jory's appointment, Actors Theatre of Louisville announced the first of many successful fund-raising campaigns, beginning with a drive to cover the budget deficit. The theatre's grim financial status worsened when Alexander Speer, executive director of Actors Theatre, reanalyzed the financial records of the institution and discovered that the theatre needed to raise an additional fifteen thousand dollars, bringing their total deficit to thirty-eight thousand. The board members considered releasing Jory from his contract and closing the theatre for a short period. In fact, Jory was so uncertain about the future of the theatre that he did not unpack for the first six weeks that he lived in Louisville. Relief came when the board received the news that the Courier-Journal and Louisville Times Foundation would pay for a large portion of the debt if the board members would cover the remaining twenty-five thousand dollars, allowing the theatre to avoid begging the public for generous gifts. As a result, the board reached the controversial decision that each member would be responsible for raising a specific amount of money, but several board members declared this policy to be unfair, since some were in better financial condition than others. Speer recalled the negative reaction to the new financial responsibility forced on the board, explaining that the members were "divided into three categories: those who simply said, 'Goodbye—this is not my problem'; those who wrote a check and said, 'Goodbye—I don't want to be involved any longer'; and those who wrote a check and stayed on board."[22]

With the debt eliminated, Jory and his new publicity director, Trish Pugh Jones, turned their attention to increasing subscriptions, and like the staff of numerous regional theatres in the 1960s, they sought the advice of Danny Newman. A former press agent for the Chicago Lyric Opera, Newman traveled the country helping resident theatres "hard sell" to specific audiences through mass mailings. According to Newman's approach, "attempts to attract a broad cross section of the population were not only too costly but foolhardy."[23] Instead, he encouraged an intensive advertising campaign to the middle-class, white demographic—a tactic that did not appeal to many theatre producers who wanted to diversify their audiences.

Newman's hard sell to specific audiences succeeded in Louisville during the 1960s, because the city's population had grown (from 369,129 in 1950 to 390,639 in 1960) as a result of increased urban development, suburban expansion, and moves by numerous corporations to the Kentucky city. Newman's philosophy, however, began to falter by the late 1980s, when the exploited demographic shrank and producers believed the approach did not reflect the population at large. The Louisville population had shrunk to 361,472 by 1970 and even further, to 298,451, by 1980. By contrast, the African American population in Louisville increased from 57,772 in 1950 to 79,783 in 1980, representing a rise from 15.6 percent overall to 29.6 percent during the three decades. With the overall population declining and the nontargeted population increasing, Newman's hard sell was of limited practical use to Actors Theatre, which eventually needed to discover a new audience to maintain support.[24] In its inception, however, Newman's campaign helped many theatres, including Actors Theatre of Louisville, quickly increase the number of their subscriptions.[25]

Reflecting on Newman's influence, Trish Pugh Jones, now the manager of patron relations, stated, "He was the P. T. Barnum of the regional theatre movement. His hard-sell techniques were what got the regional theatre movement, I believe, off the ground." Jones explained why and how Actors Theatre engaged in other marketing endeavors besides Newman's controversial tactics: "We brought Danny in that first summer, and of course audiences at Actors had dwindled to an almost alarming level, and so we needed an immediate turnaround. So we did it two ways: one, using Danny's hard-sell techniques, and two, through personal contact."[26]

Reaching out to the Louisville community, Jory and Jones helped to build audiences through numerous speaking engagements, and Jory often invited journalists to attend his speeches in hopes that his ideas and proposals would be printed in the newspaper (and they often were).[27] After subscriptions fell from fifty-seven hundred for the 1967–68 season to thirty-eight hundred for the 1968–1969 season, Jory sought to rebuild subscriptions to the five thousand mark with a campaign that featured mass mailings to 285,000 people, the staffing of promotional booths at fairs and on university and high school campuses, the resurrection and restructuring of the volunteer organization Actors Associates, and speeches by employees of the theatre at more than one hundred coffee or cocktail meetings. Jory proved his ability to connect with the Louisville community when subscriptions for the 1969–70 season increased to 5,017, a remarkable rise of more than eighteen hundred over the previous year. The upward trend continued the following year, with subscriptions totaling 8,216, marking a national record for the highest percentage of subscriptions sold in relation to the seating capacity of the theatre (94.7 percent sold through subscriptions). The new subscription total also set another national record due to the 61 percent increase in sales over the previous year.[28]

Jory's impact was evident not only to those involved in sales of subscriptions but also to the board and the entire theatregoing community. Board member Roanne H. Victor described Jory's immediate influence this way: "The whole atmosphere changed because, for the first time, we knew that the theatre didn't just belong to us anymore. It belonged to everyone. There was a much more cosmopolitan feeling. It's a coming of age. It was exciting. And it's good."[29] Victor's statement reflects two impressive achievements: the theatre's record-breaking subscription sales and Jory's ability to end the long-standing battle between the two sides by uniting the board in its support for him. Under Jory's leadership, the people of Actors Theatre finally became a unified group, leaving behind the tensions and differences of the past and looking forward to the future. Furthermore, Jory united a community eager to support the arts. Through his showmanship and his popular play selections in his earliest years at the theatre, Jory enticed the entire Louisville community to support his vision—a necessity if Jory ever hoped to diversify his theatre's offerings through productions of new plays.

With its astonishing subscription rate and growing support from the community, Actors Theatre considered echoing a trend by moving to a larger theatre to capitalize on its success, just as other thriving theatres around the country looked to expand their operations. Joseph Papp, one of the foremost producers in the history of Off Broadway, had such success with the outdoor New York Shakespeare Festival that he explored the possibility of moving into a building to house winter productions and, as a result, offer a year-round season. According to Helen Epstein, author of *Joe Papp: An American Life*, Papp searched for a suitable space in a less trendy neighborhood of Manhattan so that the Festival might inspire efforts for redevelopment. After considering several locations around New York City, Papp settled on the Astor Place Library (the site of the famous Astor Place riots of 1849), a massive building constructed in the 1820s. When supporters cautioned that the structure was too large, Papp responded in his typical boastful fashion, claiming that "in three years it would prove too small." Papp also envisioned a building with enough space for rehearsal halls, administrative offices, and two theatres—a large main stage and a smaller space on a higher level—partially funded by grants from the city. To help prevent demolition of the building by a developer, he pressed city officials to designate the building a historical landmark. Although the renovation costs exceeded initial expectations, the new Public Theatre space established Papp as a major player in the New York theatre scene, allowing him to begin looking north toward the Great White Way.[30]

Papp later seized two more theatres, the Vivian Beaumont and the smaller Forum, in the Lincoln Center. Like Jory, who assumed the helm of a theatre when a dual leadership failed, Papp was approached by a search committee for the Lincoln Center in 1972 after Jules Irving resigned (Herbert Blau, like Cornett, having resigned earlier). Papp, however, became interested in using the two available theatres as an expanded home for his Public Theater/New York Shakespeare Festival. Although his institution enjoyed consistent growth, it amassed debts in excess of $1 million, and he hoped that the Lincoln Center spaces would provide new revenue. Unlike his first expansion project into the Astor Place Library, Papp's second effort foolishly was driven by a need for financial stability. When Jory enlarged his operations, he had studied the earlier actions of Papp and expanded because of popular demand for theatre rather than financial desperation.[31]

With audiences growing and revenue increasing, Jory and the board of directors decided that it was time for Actors Theatre to move, especially since the construction of an on-ramp for a new interstate highway along the riverfront was slated to run directly through the theatre. Knowing that the demolition was inevitable, the board had previously petitioned and received a two-year "stay of execution," which allowed them ample time for fund-raising, but a place still had to be found for the theatre. In their search, Actors Theatre considered three factors as necessities in selecting their new home: a downtown location, a space large enough to accommodate all of the theatre's operations, and an economically reasonable purchase price and renovation cost. Like Papp in his search for a new space, the Actors Theatre board of directors considered several possibilities, including renovation of an old high school, taking over a domed structure on top of a parking garage, and sharing a space with other arts organizations in a new complex to be built downtown. (Jory astutely rejected this last proposal, saying he did not want to be forced to share a theatre space.)

Although Jory decided not to renovate the old school, there was pressure on him and the Actors Theatre board of directors to renovate one of several downtown buildings. In the early 1960s, plans to encourage urban restoration were begun by many cities, including Cincinnati, Chattanooga, Baltimore, Denver, and Berkeley. As detailed in the book *Cities and the*

Arts: A Handbook for Renewal, civic leaders in Louisville also pursued urban revitalization through preservation by establishing, in 1966, the Kentucky Heritage Council, which soon was followed by Louisville's Landmark Ordinance in 1973. One of the leaders of the preservation movement was Barry Bingham Sr., who helped "transform Old Louisville" through political action by testifying against new development projects and arguing for federal and local tax assistance to help restore older buildings. Given Bingham's immense influence over the creation of Actors Theatre, as well as his family's continued philanthropy, it would have been extraordinarily foolish for Jory not to have given serious consideration (and eventual support) to Bingham's cause.[32]

Not surprisingly, the board decided to purchase and renovate the historic Bank of Louisville building at 316 West Main Street, Actors Theatre of Louisville's current home. The cost of land acquisition, new construction, and renovation would total $1.5 million, a figure that the board deemed economically feasible, since the new space (like Papp's Astor Place Library) allowed for two theatres, as well as ample room for administrative offices and other necessary rooms (shops, dressing rooms, lobby, bar, etc.). Announcing a fund drive totaling $1.4 million dollars, board president Owsley Brown declared the theatre's intention to move to the new location in time for the opening of the 1972 season. In addition to the campaign, the theatre received a hundred-thousand-dollar donation anonymously, and the city of Louisville applied for a hundred-thousand-dollar federal grant. Also helping bear the financial burden, the Ford Foundation announced a plan to provide one dollar for every three dollars raised by Actors Theatre in support of the new building.[33]

Even though impending demolition forced the theatre from its home in the former railroad terminal, the move to West Main Street exemplified the wisdom of Jory and his board while also mimicking the earlier actions of Papp and his Public Theatre. The community viewed the decision to renovate the former Bank of Louisville as a gracious action, saving a beautiful building and preserving Louisville's history. Once the building was purchased, Actors Theatre successfully petitioned for it to be designated a national historical landmark as "one of the best examples of small-scale Greek Revival architecture in the country."[34]

Furthermore, Jory's decision to renovate an older building instead of constructing a new one illustrated his understanding of the needs and desires of the Louisville community while also reflecting his studied decisions about protecting his theatre from future financial troubles. Jory avoided the mistakes of other regional theatres in designing and building a completely new theatre space by learning from their errors. Many thriving regional theatres risked financial security by constructing elaborate spaces that served "chiefly as an expression of [the artistic director's] artistic ego, out of proportion to the real needs and resources of the institution."[35] Jory cited the failings of

Oklahoma City's Mummers Theatre Company, which constructed a beautiful yet exorbitantly costly $3 million facility in 1970. Although the design of the theatre won architectural awards, the financial demands of the new space, combined with insufficient audience and corporate support, caused the theatre group to close one year later. Instead of housing the Mummers group, the space sat empty except for the few evenings when it was rented by community or university theatres. After studying Papp's successful efforts in transforming the Astor Place Library into the new Public Theatre and learning from other regional theatres' construction endeavors, Jory sensibly listened to the board's financial advice and the preferences of the Louisville community, proving that he understood Louisville by deftly catering to both the theatre's needs and the city's preservation efforts.[36]

Within five years of his arrival, the achievements of Jory and his staff were extraordinary: the theatre's subscription rate rocketed, the annual budget increased from $235,000 to $600,000, the production season grew by two months, to double the number of productions offered, and the company began presenting children's shows. The organization also moved into the new space on West Main Street, with two theatres. The larger space, a six-hundred-seat auditorium, received its moniker after a former Kentucky governor, John Y. Brown, provided a substantial donation to Actors Theatre in the early 1970s. In return for his generous gift, Actors Theatre named its new space the Pamela Brown Auditorium in honor of the governor's sister, who died during her attempt to cross the Atlantic Ocean in a hot-air balloon. The second space, a smaller black-box theatre on the third floor, was named the Victor Jory Theatre in honor of the producing director's father, an actor who often performed in Actors Theatre productions and quickly became an audience favorite.[37]

Just as Papp used his second theatre to present a greater variety of work, Jory expanded the theatre's artistic repertoire by offering two subscription packages to appeal to both Old and New Louisvillians: a "Broadway" season of more conventional works and an "Off-Broadway" season in the smaller theatre that featured avant-garde and contemporary performances.[38] Furthermore, Jory announced that the theatre was capable of and interested in developing new plays. Although Jory's success with the Summer Premiere Festival at Long Wharf won him the Margo Jones Award, his company was not the only regional theatre to attempt to stage new plays. Numerous regional theatres in the 1960s and 1970s found and produced new plays with the help of the Rockefeller Foundation (the Ford Foundation not having funded new play development until the late 1970s), which supported the creation of the Milwaukee Repertory Theatre's "Theatre for Tomorrow" program, the Mark Taper Forum's "New Theatre for Now" series, and new play development programs at many other regional theatres around the country.[39]

With Jory bringing financial stability and audience support to Actors Theatre, the board willingly trusted his decision to produce new plays that previously had been staged at other theatres. Although some of the new plays were not well received, Trish Pugh Jones and Jory spent much time convincing the Louisville community that new plays were worth watching. Jones recalled the public relations campaign that justified Jory's decision to produce new plays: "On the brochures, it would say, 'Nine plays for the price of six equals three plays free.' And we would say to people, 'Now you're getting three plays free, so you can hate one and it won't cost you anything. You can hate two [or] you get to hate three, and it still will not cost you anything. And the chances of you hating three are very slim.' So that's what we emphasized, and that was the beauty of the personal contact that helped us get that message across."[40] Jones's hard sell appealed not only to audiences who were willing to experiment with "free" theatre but also to many New Louisvillians who wanted to feel more cosmopolitan by viewing progressive works.[41]

Jory's catering to public tastes methodically amassed audiences for his productions of new plays. In the summer of 1971, Jory enticed audiences to support new plays with a wise, popular, and safe selection: the first regional theatre production of Woody Allen's successful Broadway play *Play It Again, Sam*. Having studied other regional theatres' efforts to elicit support for new play productions, Jory showed that he understood his community with the selection of Allen's play, which continued an established compromise between play selection (accessible and popular) and audience preferences (expecting nothing controversial or debauched in exchange for continued attendance). With Actors Theatre of Louisville's short history of producing new work, a growing national call by critics for play development, and Jory's previous national acclaim for staging new plays, Jory met little hesitation to his proposal to make the transition from offering second-production plays to staging original works.

Jory decided the time was right to attempt the theatre's first major production of original work during the 1971–72 season.[42] On October 13, 1971, *Tricks*—a musical adaptation of Moliere's *Les Fourberies de Scapin* coauthored by Jory—premiered to strong reviews and interest from other regional theatres. Once again, Jory utilized popular fare to attract audiences, and patrons attended the musical farce in great numbers. *Tricks* was so popular, in fact, that immediately after a run in *Cabaret*, Joel Grey visited Actors Theatre to consider producing the show as a starring vehicle. Instead, the production moved to the Arena Theatre in Washington, D.C., where again it received rave reviews for its "delightful dazzlement."[43]

When producer Harold Levin sponsored *Tricks*'s move to Broadway, Jory agreed to direct the show, even though he preferred directing in regional theatre. In an interview with John Christensen of *The Louisville Times*,

Jory asserted, "What's so nice about regional theater is this: If we were on Broadway, I'd be fighting for my life, and if this show didn't go well, I might not get work for two years. But here, we have established ourselves with our audience, and they know that if the show doesn't work, there will be others that will be better."[44]

Jory also denounced another disadvantage of directing in New York. Directors and investors have long complained about the inflated significance of opening night, when producers anxiously anticipate the review in the next morning's *New York Times*. Jory labeled this ritual a myth because he had nothing to prove to the critics, proclaiming, "I don't see what New York could do for me. The New York critics may teach me something about directing a play, but I don't need them to affirm that I can direct one."[45]

Several years earlier, Joseph Papp had also bemoaned the rituals of Broadway when he transferred *Hair* from his Public Theatre to Broadway in the fall of 1967. Like Jory, Papp exuded confidence about his skills as a producer and director, yet felt helpless against the New York critics. The hippie musical—the first production in Papp's new Public Theatre—received mixed reviews because mainstream theatre critics did not support a shift away from the traditional Broadway musical. Nevertheless, *Hair* was a popular success and sold out its run at the Public Theatre. Papp opted not to extend the run, closing the production to allow for his production of *Hamlet*, a decision he later regretted. Soon after *Hair*'s Public Theatre run, Papp (at the behest of others) considered moving the production to a Broadway theatre, but financial difficulties prevented its immediate transferal. Michael Butler, a businessman from Illinois and a fan of the musical, offered to coproduce *Hair* with Papp, opening the show in a local discotheque. In spite of its sold-out performances at the Public Theatre, the new production struggled to attract an audience and quickly closed.[46] With the rights reverting back to the authors, Papp moved on, but Michael Butler quickly acquired the rights to the musical and mounted another production. When the third incarnation of *Hair* became a Broadway hit in May 1968, Papp gave Broadway another try with an overrated musical adaptation of *Two Gentlemen of Verona* that succeeded with critics and audience members, eventually winning a Tony Award for best musical over Stephen Sondheim's *Follies*.[47] Familiar with Papp's struggles to mount a successful Broadway show and aware of the risks involved in producing new work on the Great White Way, Jory came face to face with the powerful Broadway myth on January 8, 1973.

Tricks opened in the midst of what Jory termed "the worst season in years for musicals on Broadway."[48] By the time *Tricks* premiered, six of the seven new musicals on Broadway had already opened and closed, most notably *Via Galactica* with debts of $1 million. *Tricks* fared no better, opening to one rave, a few favorable reviews, and numerous pans. In his mixed review for the *New York Times*, Clive Barnes praised the performance of René Auberjonois but criticized Jory's directing as hectic and undisciplined. In his book *One More Kiss: The Broadway Musical in the 1970s*, Ethan Mordden provides a detailed yet harsh criticism of the production, labeling it one of the two worst musicals of the decade (*Dude* having received the top honor). While mocking the exorbitant style of the production—noting that *Tricks* contained "more zany posing than in the entire seventeenth century"—he described the exhausting demands of the show: "The staging was very physical, with the cast popping out from behind screens, running offstage into the auditorium (and unfortunately running right back on again), grabbing straw hats and canes for one number, and making a big deal out of a character's fatuously antique wheelchair. At one point, an actor flew across the stage on a rope painted like a peppermint stick, landed on a slide, slid, and jumped to his feet to snap out a single line."[49] Mordden questioned Levin's decision to produce the inflated show, wondering whether the rock score made him believe that he could reproduce the success of *Hair*. Citing Levin's success with *My Fair Lady*, Mordden asked, "Doesn't he know what good music is supposed to sound like? One might call *Tricks* one of the 'why?' musicals: why do something so unnecessary?"[50]

Given the power of the Broadway myth, the negative reviews killed the box-office potential of the show, and *Tricks* closed after only eight performances. Just as Papp retreated to his Public Theatre after *Hair* failed, Jory returned to Louisville. Both men remained undaunted in their efforts to produce quality work, and Jory, like Papp, refused to admit defeat, declaring the process a learning experience. "Actors Theatre profited from *Tricks*," Jory informed the *Louisville Times* on his return to Louisville. "Our cast benefited from it. Everyone involved learned some valuable lessons. A couple of our resident people—Chris Murney and Adale O'Brien—got their first chance at Broadway and did quite well. Everybody knows who and what Actors Theatre is now."[51]

Tricks was a turning point in Jory's career, both professionally and personally. While Papp moved quickly toward his second attempt at Broadway, most people who knew Jory claimed he was angry and frustrated by his Broadway experience. Trish Pugh Jones described the ordeal as "incredibly painful" for Jory, but in recent years, he talked about his *Tricks* experience and the affect the flop had on him. In an interview with the *Seattle Post-Intelligencer*, Jory remembered the response of the press, admitting, "They hated it. It was ten years before I would wear my T-shirt with the *Tricks* logo on it."[52] Papp's experiences with *Hair* led to "the producer's awakening to the possibilities of Broadway," eventually culminating in the creation of the record-breaking *A Chorus Line*. Jory's experience with the Broadway myth, however, resulted in a very different reaction and approach to new work and New York. As a result of the *Tricks* failure, Jory rejected Broadway as the next plateau for his career. Burned by the New York press and the financial pressures of mounting a show on Broadway, Jory instead focused on improving the quality of work in regional theatres and developing plays at Actors Theatre.[53]

The notorious *Tricks* was not the only new musical produced at Actors Theatre. Shortly after *Tricks* left Louisville for Washington, D.C., Jory initiated plans for two more musicals at Actors Theatre: an adaptation of a Georges Feydeau comedy called *In Fashion* to be written by the same team as *Tricks* and a musical by Daniel Stein intended to appeal to local interests, *Kentucky!*[54] The latter show opened first and was rehearsed while Jory was in New York with *Tricks*. He arrived home to Louisville only to see *Kentucky!* receive similar reviews. Even though limited audience support and a faulty production led to the failure of *Kentucky!*, Jory learned something important about Louisville audiences from the show: his patrons were not interested in local history but, instead, increasingly wanted to appear cosmopolitan in their aesthetics.[55]

Ironically, *In Fashion* (which starred future television stars Charlotte Rea from *Facts of Life* and Max Wright from *ALF*) perhaps benefited Actors Theatre more than *Tricks* did because of its production history. After *In Fashion* opened to positive reviews in Louisville, several critics wondered whether Jory would attempt to take it to Broadway. The production did in fact go to New York but only to be taped and broadcast on national television. Presented as part of the WNET/PBS *Theatre in America* series that filmed various productions at regional theatres around the country, *In Fashion* and Actors Theatre reached a national audience, bringing further notice to the Louisville institution. Whereas Papp followed his failure with a determination to succeed on Broadway, Jory rejected Broadway and all its alluring promise. His decision to shun the Great White Way eventually changed the mentality of Broadway theatre as well. Not only would the great work of regional theatre travel to New York, but also Jory's efforts forced New York to travel to regional theatres, forever altering the relationships between Louisville, New York, and the rest of the American theatre landscape.

Concerning the production of legitimate drama, Jory continued to wisely and cautiously entice the Louisville audiences to support new plays, eventually presenting American premieres of plays that enjoyed successful runs in England. After audiences supported these new works, as well as another original musical work commissioned by Actors Theatre (a third Jory musical, *Chips 'N' Ale*, opened in 1974), Jory expressed interest in presenting a series of new plays (which would later become a "festival") for the 1976 season. However, after the failure of *Kentucky!* and only moderate success for *Chips 'N' Ale*, Jory began to question his new play production process, as he identified a problem in locating and producing high-quality new works. "The trouble is finding good plays," Jory explained in an interview, "but we've got to establish a system to seek them out. It's a tricky business, because I can't do all the reading myself, yet other readers must be aware of my tastes."[56]

The assistance came in the form of ElizaBeth Mahan King, whom Jory hired as a full-time script reader to help him correspond and develop relationships with numerous playwrights (as many as seventy-five in the first year), encouraging them to revise their plays for resubmission.[57] Having studied how Papp and other producers enlarged audience support while expanding operations, Jory stepped into uncharted territory with only his instincts and his talents as his guide. With one eye on his conservative audience and the other eye on potential playwrights, Jory embarked on a journey that would change Actors Theatre of Louisville forever. He undertook the challenge of presenting a collection of new plays in the fall of 1976.

3   THE LUCKY YEARS, 1976–79

When Jory became the producing director of Actors Theatre of Louisville in 1969, several regional theatres were experimenting with producing new works. According to James Leverett, a former director of the literary services department at Theatre Communications Group,

> When the Humana Festival began [in 1976] . . . the great movement to decentralize American theatre was well under way. It was started in the early 1960s by no more than a dozen theaters, all striving to become established on the European publicly subsidized model and to provide an alternative to the usual transient fare of Broadway road shows. At first, these institutions sought to stage the standard world repertory of great drama, just as orchestras and museums present their classics. It soon became evident, however, that in order to keep the art truly vital, it would be imperative also to support the creation of new works. Theatre people believed this; they convinced the corporations, foundations, and endowments that fund theaters; soon audiences joined in as well. In fact, it became an economic as well as creative necessity to do new plays—a kind of badge of artistic honor.[1]

Jory perceived new play development as a natural evolution for his growing theatre, arguing that Actors Theatre was duty-bound to produce new work. "It was time for us to stop addressing ourselves to problems we'd already solved—problems of survival," Jory explained, "and consider for once what was outside ourselves. It was time to consider the author."[2]

In the mid-1970s, regional theatres that produced new work hoped to transfer it to Broadway, and a variety of shows—*American Buffalo*, *Streamers*, and *Annie*, to name a few—eventually ended up there after premiering outside New York in nonprofit theatres.[3] With production costs for a Broadway show skyrocketing, producers scouted the regional theatres for new work, often coproducing plays or appropriating a regional theatre's grant money to develop a specific script with plans to transfer the production if it succeeded. As productions of new plays became more frequent, regional theatres followed Joseph Papp's model with *A Chorus Line* by collaborating with commercial producers throughout the production process, often receiving a monetary advance in return for giving a certain producer the first option to transfer a production to New York.

In a 1974 interview, theatre owner and producer James M. Nederlander described this new relationship between Broadway and nonprofit theatres: "The regional theatres have become the tryout ground for Broadway. In other words you try it out with [a nonprofit theatre] and, if it's good, it moves to Broadway."[4] As more and more regional theatres produced new plays, New York simply became a showplace for new work that first had been developed and produced in a theatre far from the lights of the Great White Way. With Jory's passion for developing new plays at Long Wharf, his awareness of play-writing trends across the country, and his rejection of the Broadway myth, it was not surprising that he aspired to position his Louisville organization as a major player in American theatre. Actors Theatre, however, needed a little bit of luck to make it happen.

Just as he methodically built an audience, Jory utilized a formula that proved successful for the first decade of the festival: establishing then exploit-ing a local foundation with an eye toward national visibility. Cognizant of the financial risks in producing new plays yet buoyed by patrons' strong support for *Tricks* and other new musicals, he believed he had built an audience who were passionate about supporting new work. For the transition from new musicals to legitimate theatre, the challenge was twofold: to educate his audi-ence to the aesthetics of new plays and to foster the audience's willingness to support multiple productions. His solution was a festival format that would safeguard his local support (the "establishment" necessary for success) while allowing opportunities for creative explorations. Former literary manager Tanya Palmer described Jory's calculative and effective model: "If Actors Theatre put up a bunch of new work and created an event around that, then audiences who might otherwise be resistant to unfamiliar voices and visions would embrace the *idea* of the festival, and the sense of event that surrounds it, even if the individual plays themselves were not always to their liking."[5]

To secure an audience for new work, Jory wisely incorporated the new plays into the regular season. The price of subscription included entrance to one festival play each year, yet not all subscribers viewed the same work. If one production garnered strong reviews or positive word of mouth, then subscribers often returned to the theatre to see an additional show. By not forcing his audience to see multiple new plays, Jory made his new play festival a low-risk venture, especially given the event's slant toward popular fare in the earliest years of the event.[6]

Disregarding the need for Jory to systematically build audience support for new plays, playwrights and critics chastised him and other regional theatre producers for not presenting newer works or nurturing new playwrights. Critics, in fact, questioned Jory's dedication to the development of new works, since his play choices were perceived as "safe" in comparison with the tasks of nurturing and producing new scripts. Jory finally responded by announcing the creation of his New American Writers Festival in the spring of 1976. Even though the festival featured three new plays recently presented Off Broadway, it included one world premiere and was the forerunner of the Humana Festival of New American Plays. Thus Actors Theatre of Louisville was able to promote itself as the producer of the newest works outside the East Coast.[7]

Once again, local reviewers questioned Jory's strategy for introducing new work to Louisville audiences, who had become accustomed to the lighter fare offered in the regular season. *Courier-Journal* critic William Mootz expressed skepticism that the festival would succeed, arguing that Jory "built his large subscription lists, we heard, by spoon-feeding his audiences facile farces and clever comedy. . . . If he tried to engage them seriously, his audiences, reared on theatrical pap, will rebel."[8] Jory himself echoed Mootz's concerns about the Louisville audience's readiness to accept new plays, but Jory's calculated approach prepared both his institution and his patrons. Jory recalled, "We spent seven or eight years simply building an audience which had a tremendous affection for us. We now trade on that affection by going a little deeper into the bush with the material we're doing. And the audience goes, 'Well, you're a friend of mine. I'll walk with you down this forbidding path.'"[9]

In fact, Jory astutely realized that the festival first would have to be a local success before it could attain national recognition, claiming, "The idea of the festival was for local rather than national or international reasons. Subscribers to A.T.L. might not look forward to new plays, but they would reluctantly put up with one a season. If we grouped the plays, each subscriber would see only one, but we could produce two in rep (and then five, and then seven, and then, God help us, eleven). Thus, the idea of a new play festival was to camouflage just how interested we were in new plays."[10]

Knowing that a more select audience would be interested in new plays, Jory prudently mounted these newer works in the small Victor Jory Theatre. To engage his audience in supporting new work, Jory included a "critic sheet" in each program, allowing playgoers to respond to the production and to feel they are a valued part of the new play development process.[11] Experimenting with his first festival, Jory reduced the risk of critical and audience backlashes by choosing to present second-production plays—plays that already received productions in other theatres—instead of trying to instigate a new play development process in his very first festival. By learning how to successfully operate a festival without the additional demands and risks involved with new play development, Jory cautiously moved ahead with presenting new works to his Louisville audiences.

Unlike the experimental or deconstructionist plays that thrived Off Broadway in the 1970s, the plays in Jory's New American Writers Festival were a sampling of relevant yet mainstream work. Presented from October 12 to November 7, 1976, each of the four festival selections served a dual purpose: to help Jory attract patrons to the event and to reflect contemporary playwriting trends. While Jory could rely on his audience to support his new endeavor, he was concerned about the critical reception of his festival. Support from audiences and reviewers alike was essential if the festival were to continue, and a critical backlash against it could negate all of the hard work Jory and his staff had committed to building their audience.

For the first play, Jory relied on topicality to spark interest in audiences and to satisfy the call from critics for pertinent content. In an interview, the Louisville producer had argued that playwriting trends shifted away from plays of Vietnam disenfranchisement and away from imitations of Sam Shepard, Eugene Ionesco, and Samuel Beckett. However, because Actors Theatre was not accustomed to producing newer works, these contemporary "disenfranchisement" plays had yet to appear in Louisville. While a play about the Vietnam War might have seemed a daring choice, given Louisville audiences' penchant for lighter entertainment, Jory believed that many audience members (especially the New Louisville contingent) would support the first such play presented at Actors Theatre, and Jory's instincts were correct. In fact, Tom Cole's *Medal of Honor Rag*, a haunting story about the horrors of the war, the climate surrounding the conflict, and the demons that people hide within themselves to function in society, was the best-received production of the New American Writers Festival. Theatre patrons attended in great numbers to view the new work about survivor guilt and to seek closure for memories of the destructive war, proving Jory's understanding of his audience and his adroit timing.[12]

While Cole's war drama was topical, Jack Heifner's *Vanities*—a tale of three women who realize the façade of friendship and the loss of individuality as they progress from high school through marriage—supported Jory's notion that new works tended to focus more on characters than on social and political themes. Certainly the most conventional play of the festival, *Vanities* denotes Jory's caution and deliberation in selecting a play with broad appeal that, at the very least, would not offend Louisvillians or dissuade audience members from supporting new work in the future. Once again, Jory's catering to audience preferences paid off, as patrons delighted in the performances even though critics dismissed Heifner's writing. Knowing that Louisville audiences would enjoy this low-risk production, Jory next explored more controversial scripts, hoping to appeal to audiences who supported Actors

Theatre's Off-Broadway series and who grew tired of the lighter fare of the regular season.[13]

Jory's provocative choice for the third presentation in the festival was the only play that asked the audience to go down a "forbidding path." The most notable production and the only comedy in the festival, David Mamet's *Sexual Perversity in Chicago* perplexed critics, who cited the extreme length of the production and the excessive foul language as reasons for reserved audience members to stay away. Jory's choice of Mamet's profanity-laden script appeared motivated by an attempt to break with the formulaic storytelling techniques of the other festival plays. Furthermore, knowing that conservative Louisville audiences shunned plays that featured harsh language, Jory may have selected Mamet's play to promote the small festival as provocative and daring.

The greatest achievement of the New American Writers Festival was its one premiere production, but Jory wisely lessened the risk by producing a smaller play instead of a full-length production. With Mamet's *Sexual Perversity in Chicago* winning an Obie Award earlier in the year, the festival proudly presented the world premiere of another Mamet play, *Reunion*. Performed in repertory with the other three productions, the one-act play presents a meeting between an alcoholic man and his daughter, whom he has not seen in twenty years. This shorter, "unfinished" work delivered only a few moments of insight into the characters and situation, and reviewers faulted the production for dwelling on the seriousness of the moment and overlooking the humor within the script.[14] In spite of the less-than-memorable production, *Reunion* deserves recognition as Jory's first foray into new plays in a festival format.

Thanks to Jory's calculated risks and mainstream play selections, critics and audiences alike praised the new festival, commending Jory "for the deed, acclaiming him and his company as champions of playwrights on their way up in the world of theatre."[15] In fact, Mootz retracted his prognostications, crediting the producing director with filling the Victor Jory Theatre to 80 percent capacity. Actors Theatre of Louisville, however, soon faced new criticism. Mootz now questioned the cautiousness of the Louisville theatre, especially that its festival featured plays that had been "coaxed through the nurturing process" by other theatres. Contrary to his earlier assertions that Louisville audiences would never support a new play festival, Mootz declared, "Until A.T.L. nurses a play through a first reading, then on into a workshop production that will help its author learn its strengths and weaknesses before preparing a final draft for commercial unveiling, the company cannot be called a champion of playwrights."[16]

Jory faced criticism from outside Louisville as well. In a *Courier-Journal* article, a Lexington playwright with a remarkably coincidental name chided the producing director of Actors Theatre for his process of selecting "plays developed elsewhere" and refused to label Jory as a champion of new playwrights. "A new play," playwright Jory Johnson argued, "must be nurtured and tended until it is ready to receive the full sunlight of public and critical scrutiny."[17] The most interesting aspect of Johnson's criticism of Jory is a comparison between Jory and Joseph Papp. Johnson lavished biased praise on the New York producer, for whom he served as a script reader in New York. Johnson unabashedly admired Papp's willingness to take risks with unproduced scripts, arguing that Papp "realizes scripts don't flow to producers in finished form. And [Papp] has this terrific method of encouraging them through various stages of production."[18]

Jory defended his cautious choices and producing record by retorting that while at Long Wharf Theatre, he won the Margo Jones Award for "the most significant contribution to dramatic art through the continued production of new plays."[19] Regardless of Mootz's and Johnson's shortsighted demands, Jory took calculated steps in establishing a play festival. Although Mootz's suggestion had merit, it would have been unwise of Jory to begin a new play festival without first testing the waters. By relying on previously produced plays, Jory and his staff enticed Louisville audiences into supporting new (although not entirely unproven) works. Jory's cautious decision to initiate the play festival with second-production plays helped prepare his staff and audience for the challenge of producing untested scripts.

While Papp and his New York Shakespeare Festival certainly enjoyed widespread support for their many creative endeavors owing to Papp's larger audience base, Jory could not take similar risks in the smaller city of Louisville. However, once Jory received praise for his New American Writer's Festival, he initiated another venture that further helped to silence his detractors. Eager to demonstrate that his institution was ready to handle the increased demands and risks involved with developing new work, Jory responded to criticism in the spring of 1977 by announcing the creation of Playfaire 76/77, a small festival featuring two world premieres for Louisville audiences.

With Playfaire 76/77, Jory seized an opportunity not only to help struggling playwrights but also to make a name for his own theatre. Given Jory's prior success with mainstream works, there was no reason for the producing director to stray from his tried-and-true formula. Jory was comfortable supporting more traditional work, believing that the playwrights he chose served an important role in the development of American theatre. In an interview with Michael Billington of the *Guardian*, Jory justified his play selections: "American theatre is now much more secure in its own voice. I would also say there has been a retreat from the mythical and the phantasmagoric and a return to realism—we've mythed ourselves out of existence. What one does find is that new life has been breathed into the American family play. . . . My feeling is that in America right now people are trying to find ways to respect and enjoy themselves and that some of the traditional values (particularly about small-town and family life) are re-appearing in drama."[20] In his essay "New Realism: Mamet, Mann, and Nelson," David Savran agreed with Jory's assessment about the return of traditional playwriting, citing that the "revolutionary fervour" of the early 1970s largely had subsided. Billington credited this change to America's moving "out of the Johnson-Nixon era towards an optimistic Carterism."[21]

Not only was Jory selecting safe plays to support a trend in American playwriting, but also he was carving out his theatre's niche in the landscape of professional theatre. By catering to audience preferences and a heartland sensibility, the new play festival featured work that could be remounted in any regional theatre around the country. In addition to their widespread appeal, Jory's selections reflected his own preferences, as well as his vision for the festival: "I want to be with my times, not behind them . . . or ahead of them."[22] Given the important role that family played in Jory's life in and out of theatre, it is not surprising that many of the new plays developed by Actors Theatre also focused on familial relationships and other ties that bind. Despite his frequent criticism, Mootz understood and applauded the producing director for his vision and his accessible play selections: "Obviously, Jory is out to provide for the American Midwest what such companies as Joseph Papp's Shakespeare Festival in New York and Zelda Fichandler's Arena Stage in Washington provide for the East Coast."[23] *Wall Street Journal* critic Edwin Wilson noted Jory's ability to develop an identity for the theatre, praising the success that Actors Theatre enjoyed with traditional plays. Jory agreed, boasting, "Every theatre has to find its own voice, and I think we've begun to find ours."[24]

After reading numerous scripts, Jory finally announced the two plays that would begin to establish the festival's reputation. First up would be John Orlock's *Indulgences in a Louisville Harem*, a play that had had a workshop production at Penn State University and been recommended to Actors Theatre of Louisville by a friend of the playwright.[25] When asked whether he chose the play to attract local audiences, Jory quickly denied the charge, responding that it was chosen because of the quality of the writing. Although Jory argued that the title mattered little in terms of its selection, certainly a play with *Louisville* in its title would be easier to promote to local audiences. (In fact, the play has little to do with Louisville per se.) Orlock's script about two spinster sisters who entertain men selected from a catalog served as a metaphor for the growing distrust in appearances and perceived positions in society (a reflection of the Watergate scandal a few years earlier).[26] With its lukewarm critical reception, Jory might have been concerned about the outcome of Playfaire 76/77, but *Indulgences in a Louisville Harem* was overshadowed quickly by the critical and commercial success of the other festival presentation.

When assistant to the producer ElizaBeth Mahan King heard of a small production in Los Angeles of a play titled *The Gin Game* by D. L. Coburn, she requested that a script be sent to Actors Theatre of Louisville for possible inclusion in its new festival. Within three days of receiving the play, Jory committed to mounting the play's first professional production, which received rave reviews.[27] In later interviews, Coburn frequently expressed amazement at Jory's ability to discover his script. While speaking to reporters in Louisville, Coburn remarked, "This far from California, [Jory] is so well attuned that he heard of my play being done by non-professionals in a forty-nine seat room."[28]

It is impossible to overestimate the importance of *The Gin Game* to the early accomplishments of the festival. On several occasions, Jory attributed the successful establishment of the annual event (especially the first year) to his luck in discovering the play, a feat that impressed the Louisville community and raised interest in Actors Theatre. At the very least, the eventual commercial and critical success of *The Gin Game* ensured that the festival would continue for a second year. Given that Actors Theatre did not have an elaborate system in place for script discovery as it does today, Jory was extraordinarily fortunate to have discovered and produced for his very first festival of untried works a play that would later win the Pulitzer Prize for Drama.

The overwhelming critical reception of Coburn's script in Louisville also supplied Jory with a unique opportunity to help promote his new festival. Jory wrote in a recent piece, "We recognized very early on that the Humana Festival could only really serve the playwright if it was highly *visible*."[29] To capitalize on the positive response to Coburn's play and, in turn, receive publicity for the festival, Jory sent the script to Hume Cronyn and Jessica Tandy. The couple, as well as famed director Mike Nichols, traveled to Louisville to see the production, becoming the first stars ever to visit the festival. Frazier Marsh, production manager for Actors Theatre of Louisville, recounted the arrival of the three stars from a unique perspective: in March 1977, Marsh served as a backstage crewperson as a member of the 1976–77 Apprentice Company. Marsh recalled, "One evening at a performance of *The Gin Game*, about ten minutes before places, I crawled backstage and peeked through some black masking just in time to see Jessica Tandy, Hume Cronyn, and Mike Nichols taking their seats. Needless to say I was star-struck. But it began to dawn on me that what I was involved in must be a pretty big deal if these folks would fly to Louisville to see this play. Apparently, I was right and the rest is theatre history."[30] Jory's creative endeavor with new plays not only provided success for Coburn but also garnered immediate attention for the Louisville theatre. Articles about Actors Theatre of Louisville and Jory's festival appeared in newspapers across America, including the *Atlanta Journal-Constitution*, the *New York Times*, and the *Chicago Daily News*.[31] Certainly no one could have predicted that one of the first two new plays produced in Louisville would win a Pulitzer Prize and become a Broadway hit, and several factors that support Jory's notion of "luck" contributed to the festival's success: How successful would the festival have been if ElizaBeth King had not heard of the small production in California? What if Coburn, never having heard of the new festival, refused to allow Jory to produce his play? What if Tandy and Cronyn expressed no interest, so that the play did not travel to Broadway?

Even though the stars did align for Actors Theatre and certain aspects of the Playfaire 76/77's success can be attributed to luck, Jory's skills as a producer cannot be dismissed. Year after year, Jory successfully selected scripts that brought the Louisville theatre national acclaim and greater recognition in the press, and his ability to organize a play development process that allowed these scripts to be discovered and succeed deserved commendation. After the first festival, however, many in the theatre establishment (i.e., judgmental New York critics and Broadway producers comfortable with the modus operandi that allowed them to proclaim cultural superiority) questioned the permanence of the event, refusing to believe that Louisville would continue to be a major source of new plays worthy of recognition. With the increased attention and astonishing success came new pressures, as people wondered whether Jory's great luck would be a one-time occurrence.

Jory knew that if his theatre was to be considered a serious participant in the development of American playwriting, then he needed to validate his achievement by discovering another blockbuster script. The problem was that plays were in short supply. Besides theatre professionals and critics, playwrights also viewed Actors Theatre of Louisville's success with skepticism. Although numerous playwrights desperately wanted their new plays to receive productions, few playwrights took the festival in Louisville seriously. Even with the attention accruing to Actors Theatre because of *The Gin Game*, Jory and literary manager ElizaBeth Mahan King still struggled to locate scripts and persuade playwrights to send their new work to Louisville. Jory attributed some of the difficulty in finding good scripts to the overwhelming power and influence of Joseph Papp. According to the Louisville director, he discovered many promising scripts, but Papp tightly controlled the rights to these plays. This situation became extraordinarily frustrating for Jory, especially when Papp, because of his theatre's reputation, often received the first option for scripts, yet failed to produce most of them.[32]

Even before Playfaire 76/77 opened, Jory began screening newly submitted scripts for the next occurrence of the festival, to be renamed A Festival of New American Plays. Yet he quickly realized the need to find a solution to the "Papp problem"—one that would increase Actors Theatre's access to unproduced scripts and, in turn, bolster the festival's chances for continued success. Determined to fulfill his theatre's commitment to the development of new plays and to enhance Actors Theatre's reputation, Jory initiated a new means for Actors Theatre to obtain scripts by creating a national playwriting competition.

On February 11, 1977, an article appeared in a Louisville newspaper announcing the contest: "The people at Actors Theatre of Louisville are looking for some great, American plays. In fact, they've announced a competition they're calling the Great American Play Contest. New scripts that have not received Equity production are eligible, and there is a $1,000 prize for first place and a $500 award for second."[33] The Great American Play Contest demonstrated Actors Theatre's dedication to developing new plays through its monetary gift and its promise of production in a festival, and the annual competition (and the money associated with it) encouraged hundreds of playwrights to submit their plays to Louisville.[34] Through the contest, Actors Theatre discovered new voices in American playwriting and began to establish its reputation as a "playwright's theatre."[35] Furthermore, given Jory's keen showmanship, it is no mistake that he advertised his festival as an "American" event, in hopes of appealing to both theatre artists around the country and to Louisville audiences. Not only did this qualifier limit the scope of the festival and encourage American writers to pen plays for the theatre, but the label implied a preference for mainstream theatre. By supporting an American (as opposed to avant-garde) event, local audiences could expect plays that presented traditional values or pertinent relationships, or both, works with which they could identify.

Playwrights from around the country submitted approximately four hundred scripts for the contest, and agents from the east and west coasts sent hundreds more for consideration. Now that Jory had a sufficient number of script submissions, the pressure was on him to put together a successful festival. Aware of the national critics' heightened expectations and his patrons' penchant for mainstream fare, Jory wisely altered the format of the festival to increase his chances for striking gold. Although two plays were awarded prize money as cowinners of the Great American Play Contest, Jory pressed his luck with the new festival by featuring six premieres in rotating repertory, a dramatic increase over the previous festival's two productions.[36] Jory proclaimed the 1977 festival one of the most complex, exciting, and rewarding projects ever undertaken by the Louisville theatre. Not surprisingly, the local press supported Jory's claim, describing the festival as "awesome in its scope and ambition."[37]

Jory's enlarged festival required an increase in public support, so Jory made sure to heavily promote his theatre to the local community. Whether it was a calculated choice or simply circumstance, the local press commended Jory's selection of a Louisville native, Marsha Norman, as one of the two winners of the Great American Play Contest. When asked about the odds that a Louisvillian's play would be selected, Jory stated, "If you'd asked me about this a few months ago, I'd have told you that the odds were extremely against it . . . [But] I'm sure that our just being here influenced the author to write for us, and the resulting drama is a fine one."[38] In addition to discovering a new talent, Jory appreciated the publicity opportunity that Norman afforded. Since Jory tripled the number of productions offered for the second festival, selecting a local playwright helped Jory advertise the theatre as regionally specific, encouraging local patrons to come and support the work of one of their own. Given that critics unanimously considered Norman's *Getting Out* to be an exceptional play, few in the national press second-guessed Jory's decision to promote the festival to the community by selecting a local playwright.

The decision to include *Getting Out* was an easy one for Jory because of his role in the creation of the play, and the development of Norman's script exemplified Jory's willingness to take a chance on new writers. Although Jory suggested that Actors Theatre's presence simply "influenced the author to write for us," Jory specifically pursued Norman as a potential playwright. The writings of Norman, a columnist for a local newspaper, appealed to Jory, and he invited her to write a play for Actors Theatre. Jory first suggested a script about busing in Louisville, but Norman rejected the idea. Instead, she proposed writing about the release of a young woman from prison.[39] After six drafts, Norman's *Getting Out* premiered on November 2, 1977; it told the story of Arlene's first forty-eight hours of freedom after serving eight years in prison for murder.

The local press heralded the drama as "a stunning achievement," praising the narrative construction—which presented both an adult and a teen-age Arlene—as "superb."[40] William Mootz recalled the opening of *Getting Out* with great fondness:

> Ask me what I remember as the most electrifying of all theatrical events that crowd my memory, and I have a ready answer. It was Actors Theatre's premiere of Marsha Norman's *Getting Out* on a chilly fall night in 1977. The evening was memorable for a number of reasons. At its end, a thunder-struck audience rose in a standing ovation to salute Norman, a children's columnist who had grown to astonishing dramatic maturity as if before our very eyes . . . and, although many of us might not have been aware of it that night, we were applauding Jon Jory's opening of the door on a new chapter in the history of American theatre. With the success of *Getting Out*, Jory was ready to go public with his plan to establish America's theatrical hinterland as an arena for the nourishment of a new breed of American playwrights.[41]

The national press echoed the sentiments of the Louisville critics and audiences when the production received rave notices from the likes of the *Los Angeles Times*, the *New York Times*, and the *Detroit Sunday News*. After the festival, *Getting Out* quickly became a national success, opening at the Theatre de Lys in New York City on May 15, 1978, and receiving the American Theatre Critics Association's award for best new American play of 1977.[42]

In addition to thrusting Actors Theatre further into the national limelight, the immediate success of *Getting Out* silenced critics who had predicted that the festival's achievement with *The Gin Game* was a one-time fluke. With the overwhelming success of Norman's play, Jory furthered his reputation as a miracle worker of sorts, able to locate, select, and produce award-winning plays that eventually spread to theatres across the country. Within its first two years, both *The Gin Game* and *Getting Out* garnered more than eleven awards and honors for playwriting (not including those given for performance aspects). Furthermore, larger numbers of press and theatre professionals attended the second festival (including writers for the *New York Times*, the *Washington Post*, and the *Los Angeles Times*), helping to promote Actors Theatre's accomplishments throughout the national media.[43] The New York theatre establishment, however, questioned the influence of the festival, as evinced by a dismissive *New York Times* review in which critic Richard Eder disapproved of Jory's efforts to establish Louisville as a major theatre center and ridiculed the Louisville theatre's efforts at producing new plays. "It is understandable that Mr. Jory, trying to make known his laudable intention to sponsor new work, has organized his material into a new festival," Eder chided. "But he is holding a christening party for new life that is still midway along in gestation."[44]

One of the plays most frequently dismissed by the national press, in fact, exerted a long-lasting influence on the history of Actors Theatre's annual event. Besides the discovery of *Getting Out*, the most important event of the festival was the final presentation, *The Louisville Zoo*, a collection of short plays written by anonymous Louisvillians that satirized local political and social personalities. Performed in the Victor Jory Theatre, the production amused local audiences and critics, but the national press dismissed it.[45] Created for local patrons, the inclusion of *The Louisville Zoo* in the festival was (once again) a blatant and calculated attempt to entice Louisvillians into the theatre, yet the short-play collection featured two important attributes that have become staples of the new play festival: Jory's love for experimentation within a festival's offerings (which occurred to a great extent after the fifth festival) and his support for the short-form play. While the content of *The Louisville Zoo* failed to deserve wide commentary, the production marked the first appearance of ten-minute plays in the Louisville festival.

Jory perceived the ten-minute play form as a great opportunity for Actors Theatre to work with a larger number of writers, further illustrating Jory's determination to become a playwright's theatre. As a producer, he encouraged the exploration of the short-form play in response to changing production demands (smaller casts and minimal set). Jory defended his love for the format: "Would we say a play is less complex because it lasted ten minutes? Is a haiku 'less complex' than a narrative poem? It brings us to the matter of distillation, of boiling something down to its essence and thus giving it power and energy through reduction. The best of these plays are irreducible. They don't circle around the point; they are the point."[46] After their introduction in the 1977 festival, short-form plays became a valuable resource, as well as a popular form of entertainment, in all but a few of the annual presentations. In time, Actors Theatre of Louisville became the champion of the short-form play, later spawning play contests and several published collections through Samuel French, the play-publishing company.

At the close of the second festival, Jory's staff thanked their guests by handing out lapel buttons that read "I Survived ATL's New Play Festival."[47] This button's light-hearted humor cloaked a bold assertion—that Actors Theatre was a force with which to be reckoned. To claim that someone was lucky to have "survived" the onslaught of plays in Louisville is to imply that such trials or opportunities are rare. In this sense, the button itself symbolized Jory's badge of honor and his accomplishments with the festival. In two short years, Jory had begun transforming his institution into a playwright's theatre and enticed Louisville patrons to support the festival in large numbers. Granted, the festival's predominance of traditional works appealed to Louisvillians, yet Jory's success with play selections was not out of step with contemporary playwriting trends. Many regional theatre producers recognized a move away from political and controversial themes and toward audience-friendly playwriting that allowed more of such plays to be produced. According to critic William Glover, "There is a shift in the scripts. More sympathetic in theme and better structured, many of the new works reject the avant-garde eccentricities so popular in the sixties and early seventies. . . . Many of the plays seen were about the middle and older generations," evidenced by Jory's selection of *The Gin Game* and *Indulgences in a Louisville Harem*.[48]

While Jory justifiably took pride in his accomplishments, his success also brought increasing pressure on him and Actors Theatre as they headed into their third festival. Jory knew expectations were high for his third festival, as audiences and critics alike wondered (again) whether he could pull another success out of his lucky hat, but he relished the challenge and thrived under pressure. Not only did Jory endure the numerous prognosticators of doom, who refused to consider the festival a legitimate success, but he also faced an administrative nightmare. When ElizaBeth Mahan King and the literary department began searching for the third group of new plays, the influence of the Great American Play Contest was evident: the theatre received more than two thousand submissions. Given the substantial increase, a few critics now *expected* Jory to discover the next great play or playwright—another sign that Actors Theatre was becoming a major participant in the landscape of new play development.

With the added pressures, Jory played it safe by sticking to his proven formula: following playwriting trends and offering conventional play selections that resonated with the so-called heartland sensibility. After combing through the thousands of plays, Jory and King selected six productions and fourteen authors to participate in the new festival. Opening in the spring of the 1978–79 season and coinciding with Jory's tenth year as producing director of Actors Theatre of Louisville, the third edition of the festival once again garnered national attention and praise for its productions and new playwriting talent. The most cherished discovery of the festival was Beth Henley's *Crimes of the Heart*, one of the cowinners of the annual contest. Even though some reviewers likened the simplicity of the script to a TV soap opera, most critics emphasized the play's commercial appeal, and audiences adored Henley's wit, as well as her ear for dialogue and southern rhythms.[49] Signifying the festival's growing influence on American theatre, *Crimes of the Heart* became the first play ever to win the Pulitzer Prize before appearing on Broadway.

Indeed, with the commercial successes of *Getting Out* and *Crimes of the Heart*, Jory carved out his theatre's niche: support of southern drama, especially that by southern female playwrights. Other than plays in the Humana Festival and the failed musical *Kentucky!*, Actors Theatre produced few southern plays. The Louisville theatre toured various productions around the state throughout the 1970s, but these works rarely represented any developing aesthetic of southern theatre, instead offering productions of *Dames at Sea*, *Arms and the Man*, and a collection of works by Chekhov, Brecht, and Pinter. Except for a tour of North Carolina during the 1971–72 season, Actors Theatre primarily presented classics and lighter fare to Kentucky residents in the place of work that reflected the heritage of southern theatre. Instead, Jory used his annual festival to showcase southern dramatists, establishing his legacy with the plays of Marsha Norman, Beth Henley, and James McLure.

In his prologue to *The History of Southern Drama*, Charles S. Watson lists several traits of southern drama, most notably distinctive social types (the belle and the poor white), violence, fundamentalist religion, and rhythms and idioms commonly identified as southern.[50] Historian Sally Burke concedes that the family drama is a staple of the American stage but argues that the South fosters passionate familial relationships. Given Jory's past preference for family drama and his audience's familiarity with southern work (Old Louisville being very proud of its southern heritage), the inclusion of southern drama again enticed local audiences to attend the festival while also allowing Jory to include works that he was comfortable directing and developing.[51]

Recently, theatre historians have studied Actors Theatre's dedication to female southern playwrights in particular. In *Southern Women Playwrights*, Elizabeth S. Bell notes Jory's dedication to promoting southern drama, as well as female playwrights, in the application for and receipt of a twenty-thousand-dollar grant from the Ford Foundation to commission ten female playwrights (including four from the South). Bell describes a determination by Jory and the staff to support female writers by creating a "freeing" environment while also selecting plays with themes often found in southern drama: "strong family ties, a proclivity for violence, [and] women as 'steel magnolias.'"[52] On a larger scale, Jory's support of female writers represented the growing prominence of women playwrights around the country. In his book *Broadway Theatre*, Andrew B. Harris argues that Broadway became a home to female playwrights in the 1980s, thanks in part to the Louisville festival's discovery of Henley and Norman.[53]

The label of "southern drama" also gave Jory more freedom to present provocative material on the stage thanks to the perception that a play was "southern." It seemed that audiences were more willing to stomach any controversial content if the work reflected the audiences' concerns and values and often employed familiar traits (as cited by Watson and Burke). Louisville audiences and critics provided, in addition to overwhelming approval of *Getting Out*, rave reviews for a set of dramas that, if they had not been southern in theme, might have upset conservative Louisville patrons. Further enhancing the theatre's reputation as the leading producer of southern drama, two short works by James McLure, *Lone Star* and *Pvt. Wars*, premiered in Louisville and then quickly transferred to New York. *Lone Star*, an official presentation of the third festival (*Pvt. Wars* having been presented as a workshop production), centers on Roy, a drunken Vietnam veteran (the "poor white") who likes to tell stories about his youth in a small Texas town and brags about his prized possession, his pink Ford Thunderbird. Set in a hospital ward, *Pvt. Wars* presented three Vietnam veterans in a series of quick scenes (involving violent descriptions). The play's deathbed humor is a means to explore the three men's "desperate, lingering lives."[54] Despite the popular appeal of Beth Henley and Marsha Norman with Louisville audiences, critics called McLure one of the best writers discovered in Louisville. With this double bill, Jory had not only matched his festival's prior success but surpassed it, as two festival plays proceeded to New York and received rave reviews.[55]

Not only did attachment of the "southern drama" label to *Lone Star* and *Pvt. Wars* help further the theatre's reputation as a supporter of such drama, but the local patrons' acceptance of these works also allowed the festival to promote its relevance by mirroring national playwriting trends. In his essay "1970–1990: Disillusionment, Identity, and Discovery," Mark Fearnow described the playwriting of the 1970s as a period marked by pessimism. He explained, "The 1960s saw the dismantling of the heterosexual family drama as the home of American theatre and its replacement with a drama of radical questioning and realism. The 1970s flooded those dream estates with pessimism, ushering in what could be called a 'drama of malaise.'"[56] Certainly in comparison with certain works by Sam Shepard, David Mamet, and Edward Albee, plays like *The Gin Game* and *Crimes of the Heart* appeared simplistic and trite. While the festival relied on these popular hits to gather support and ensure the festival's future, many of the other festival's offerings were in line with works being celebrated Off Broadway. Plays like David Rabe's *Streamers* (1976), Lanford Wilson's *Fifth of July* (1978), and Michael Weller's *Moonchildren* (1972) achieved commercial success in New York yet managed to reflect "a level of exhaustion and anger with the failures of the 1960s."[57] Similar works found their way onto the Louisville stage, with *Lone Star, Pvt. Wars, Getting Out*, and *Indulgences in a Louisville Harem* also depicting a growing despair due to societal power structures.

Despite the festival's ability to keep pace with playwriting trends and to accumulate numerous accolades, Jory's creation was not immune to failure. The burgeoning success of the festival was tempered in 1978 when national acclaim came at a price. Marsha Norman returned to the third festival and hoped to repeat her success there with her new play *Circus Valentine*, the story of a traveling circus that loses its main act: juggling Siamese twins. Unfortunately, critics faulted the writing as unfinished, artificial, and containing "only a hint of what it can someday be."[58] The story behind the failure of *Circus Valentine* reveals how the growth of the festival impacted Jory's methods as producer and how *Crimes of the Heart*'s success was, in actuality, a result of the mounting pressure on Jory to repeat his previous success.

In greater numbers than in previous years, the professional theatrical world assembled in Louisville for the third collection. Besides the more than one hundred critics from all major publications in both the United States and the United Kingdom, guests included representatives from the Kennedy Center for the Performing Arts and the Shubert Theatre chain, famous playwrights (Megan Terry and Israel Horowitz), and literary agents and managers from all over the world. According to one reporter, the *Wall Street Journal* critic Edwin Wilson wandered through the bar at the theatre complex and "pronounced the crowd the most distinguished gathering of theatre folk since the opening of Washington's Kennedy Center." Another observer claimed, "My God, they must have closed New York tonight."[59] With the extensive, high-powered guest list, all the critics and professionals looked for Jory to continue his lucky streak.

According to staff members, Jory reacted to the pressure to maintain the festival's success by overseeing all aspects of its production.[60] He feverishly maintained strict control of the plays and productions throughout the rehearsal process. According to former literary manager Julie Crutcher, Jory was "very dictatorial. We had one year where every change that happened in the script had to go to him. He had to see every change. I can't tell you the hours I spent Xeroxing, and the playwrights rebelled like crazy. They're like, 'What the fuck is this? I don't want this guy telling me–' And I said, 'Look, he's just trying to keep control of it, and he has to see everything.'"[61]

Although Jory only jokingly said that he became a producer in part because he liked to tell people what to do, many staff members viewed him, nevertheless, as an intimidating boss. His dictatorial approach in producing these early festivals, however, was certainly understandable. During the early years, the press focused on Jory, making his name synonymous with the festival; one critic simply stated, "This is Jon Jory's show all the way."[62] With increasing national attention because of the transfers to New York and the playwriting awards, Jory quickly met his goal of ensuring continued support for the festival. Its phenomenal growth in such a brief period must have unsettled the normally cautious producing director. Comfortable with controlling all artistic decisions for his theatre, he now faced increased expectations, yet the magnitude of the annual event made it difficult to maintain the festival's high quality. In retrospect, with his professional reputation at stake, Jory's controlling methods were justified and rational, especially considering that as the festival grew, he was forced to hire and delegate responsibility to other artists (directors, stage managers, designers, etc.) whom he did not know well.[63]

To maintain the high standards of the festival and thus ensure its future, Jory occasionally intervened in a rehearsal process. Crutcher cited one instance during the third festival when Jory took over the direction of *Crimes of the Heart*: "He fired the director. Now, at the same time, he was also supposed to be directing Marsha Norman's second play [*Circus Valentine*] which got a horrible production. And I'm not sure Marsha will ever forgive him because she felt very abandoned. But, at that point, he really felt like it was his festival—he took ownership of the whole thing."[64] Jory admitted feeling the pressure to succeed in the early years of the festival, and he justified the few times he seized control of a production by saying that success was hard to achieve because of limited rehearsal time.[65] Still, as one reporter noted, at Actors Theatre "*shrewd* is not a bad word," and given the effect of *Crimes of the Heart* on the festival's reputation, one cannot fault Jory for firing the director and assuming the duties himself.[66] Just as the accomplishments of prior festivals validated Actors Theatre's independence from the New York establishment, the events surrounding the *Crimes of the Heart* production illustrated Jory's determination to maintain that independence.

Despite *Circus Valentine*'s failure, the critical response to the third festival was overwhelming praise for the theatre. In *Time* magazine, critic T. E. Kalem equated the festival's success with the great achievements of theatrical history: "Ancient Greece and Elizabethan England staked enduring claims on the minds and hearts of generations to come through the power of their dramatists. Whatever glories of the U.S. musical, the chances are that the laurel wreaths of posterity will rest upon the brows of dramatists whose stature equals that of Eugene O'Neill and Tennessee Williams. To foster potential successors to such playwrights is the worthiest of theatrical aims. Under the venturesome leadership of Jon Jory, that is precisely what Kentucky's Actors Theatre of Louisville does."[67] In a reversal from its prior review, which mocked Actors Theatre of Louisville's efforts, the *New York Times* praised the festival, claiming, "Soon Louisville may become as famous for nurturing new drama as it is for breeding horses—all because of Jon Jory."[68]

By the end of the Third Annual Festival of New American Plays, Actors Theatre of Louisville had become a major center for new play development in America. It is not surprising that other regional theatres tried to emulate Actors Theatre by incorporating new plays into their seasons. The problem for other producing directors, according to one critic, was that "the blueprint for Actors Theatre might not be easily copied. Its success can be traced to a rare combination of vision, timing, civic pride, foundation support, and the charisma of a producing director."[69] Jory himself repeatedly tried to deflect the awe and fascination, especially when the success of the festival was being compared with the achievements of other regional theatres.[70] For instance, when discussing whether the success at Actors Theatre would be relevant for the Cleveland Play House, Jory once again downplayed his festival's potential influence: "I don't want anyone to hold us up as any kind of model. . . . We are establishing a different tradition [than the Play House]: to find new works with an emphasis on Southern work. We try to find new Southern writers, and that is not Cleveland's business."[71]

Regardless of whether Jory officially labeled his agenda a "formula," his decisions and actions created a model for other producers to follow. By catering to community preferences and building a local audience base, Actors Theatre found financial and creative security. Once Actors Theatre advertised itself as a popular institution, Jory exploited his audience base by slowly and cautiously integrating the new play festival into the regular season. Jory applied the same formula of "establishment, then exploitation" to the new play festival—when the new endeavor quickly thrived, Jory and Actors Theatre not only exploited the annual event to attract national and international attention and acclaim but also capitalized on the festival's success to increase the theatre's grant revenues, helping further ensure continuation of the yearly event.[72]

While many regional theatres followed similar formulas in developing their own new play festivals, the component unique to Jory's success was indeed the luck that brought immediate national attention. The kind of good fortune that Jory enjoyed—finding four award-winning plays in three years—can never be anticipated or predicted, much to the chagrin of theatre producers everywhere. As he jokingly claimed, "It became almost immediately clear that we had unwittingly stumbled over an idea that had national resonance, which we could claim that we foresaw and become 'visionaries,' which in our profession you can then put in your resumé ad infinitum."[73] At the same time, Jory deserves credit for his creation of a system for discovering plays and his willingness to take risks that allowed his perceived luck to transpire.

With the festival's rise to fame between 1976 and 1979, playwrights not only clamored to have a play produced in New York but also hoped to see their work performed in Louisville before a throng of critics from around the world. Instead of Actors Theatre traveling to New York to establish its national reputation, producers searching for new projects came to Louisville. A former literary manager at the McCarter Theatre, Liz Engelman, explained, "Making theatre happen and making it an exciting event so you can't miss . . . that's what Jon did. So you can't just put a new play in your season, so you make a festival out of it. You don't go to New York, so you make New York come to you, and you make all this stuff that people can't miss."[74] Although the critics who predicted the festival's demise had been silenced and the staff of the Louisville theatre took pride in their creative accomplishments, the pressure to continue the festival's success never abated (as Jory's tough decisions about the *Crimes of the Heart* production showed). Even though the festival achieved so much in a short period, the theatre was not allowed to rest on its laurels—instead, Jory and his staff pressed forward. The most important events in the festival's history were about to occur.

4   BECOMING AN INSTITUTION, 1980–82

Even though the 1980–82 festivals featured award-winning plays, including William Mastrosimone's *Extremities*, Wendy Kesselman's *My Sister in This House*, and Lee Blessing's *Oldtimers Game*, as well as works by noted playwrights Athol Fugard, Brian Friel, Wole Soyinka, Shirley Lauro, and John Olive, this second phase of the festival is best remembered for its behind-the-scenes achievements. With the meteoric rise of the festival, the new challenge for Jon Jory was to secure the event's future by transforming it into an institution, which he defined as "a theatre structure so strong that it survives generation after generation." The producing director wanted to seize on the startling success of his festival and make it impervious to the whims and dictates of critics and even local audiences. This new agenda would eventually allow Jory to become more experimental (as he saw fit) and to ensure that the festival would thrive for years regardless of critical responses or local audience preferences.[1]

To fortify his festival for the future, Jory needed to address three problems that resulted from the rapid growth of his annual event. First, he needed to ensure that the festival's reputation and relevance grew beyond the New York establishment, allowing it to become more than a "shopping mall of plays" for New York producers. Second, he needed to perfect his play discovery system, given staff turnover in the literary department. Finally, he needed to secure financial backing to fund the growing number of productions. In addressing each of these problems, Jory seized an opportunity to expand his theatre's artistic, administrative, and financial endeavors while also cementing the symbiotic relationship between the theatre and its celebrated festival.

ENLARGING ACTORS THEATRE'S REPUTATION

Certainly after three years and four New York transfers, the national press was well aware of the festival's accomplishments; now it was the theatre establishment's turn to formally recognize the impact of Jory's event. Within three months after the close of the third offering of new plays, Actors Theatre was lauded with two national awards. In late March 1979,

Jory and Actors Theatre received the Margo Jones Award, one of the most prestigious prizes in professional theatre. Previous winners of the award, given annually to theatres and producers who help encourage and develop American playwrights, include Joseph Papp, Zelda Fichandler, and Edward Albee. The award proved to be a landmark achievement for Jory: he was the first person to win the award twice (also having received it in 1966 while at the Long Wharf Theatre).

In late May, Gerald Schoenfeld, president of the Shubert Foundation, expanded Actors Theatre's collection of trophies when he presented Jory and his staff with ten thousand dollars and the James N. Vaughan Memorial Award. Named after the brother of the founder of the Shubert firm, the award is presented for "exceptional achievement and contribution to the development of professional theatre." Schoenfeld credited the Louisville theatre for its achievements with the festival but also for its involvement with the community. According to Schoenfeld, "Here, in a moderate-sized American city, probably more people attend the theatre than in any other city of its size . . . [ATL] is *really* a part of the community. Louisville, Minneapolis with its Guthrie Theater, and cities like this—to me, they are prouder of their theatre than other cities."[2]

The accolades continued after the Fourth Annual Festival of New American Plays in 1980, when Actors Theatre received the Tony Award for Distinguished Achievement, given to an individual or a theatrical organization that has made a substantial contribution to the profession of American theatre. Usually awarded to one or two regional theatres each year, many professionals assume that all major theatres will eventually be recognized. While other regional theatres received the Tony Award prior to 1980—most notably the American Conservatory Theatre, the Long Wharf Theatre (founded by Jory), and the Mark Taper Forum—Actors Theatre was one of the first regional theatres not on either coast to receive the award, marking a shift in the landscape of professional American theatre and symbolizing the growing influence of the regional theatre movement.

In hindsight, many theatre artists do not express surprise that Actors Theatre received the Tony Award, but few realize the importance of the timing of the presentation. Without the new play festival, Actors Theatre of Louisville was a very traditional regional theatre, providing quality works but nothing worthy of national recognition. Once the festival had garnered many awards and much critical praise, the American Theatre Wing determined that Jory and his company were worthy of the distinguished honor. In fact, the Louisville theatre's contribution was deemed so significant that it received the recognition before many other (and older) regional theatres, including the Alley Theatre, the Cleveland Play House, and the Goodman Theatre.[3]

With the reception of the Margo Jones Award, the James N. Vaughan Memorial Award, and the Tony Award, Actors Theatre of Louisville became the first theatre in the country to receive all three honors, furthering Actors Theatre's reputation as one of the preeminent theatres in the country.[4] Once Actors Theatre had received all of the major theatrical awards that a regional theatre could hope to acquire, it seemed as though the festival had nowhere to go but downhill. By 1979, the theatre establishment and most professionals knew of the Louisville festival's remarkable achievements, and there seemed to be little more that Jory could do to entice them to attend if they hadn't already. Never one to rest on his laurels, however, Jory sought a spark—a larger audience base or a new gimmick—that would keep his festival relevant and create new interest in his event. He pursued two different endeavors to enlarge the theatre's reputation from a national to an international level.

The first solution came through the festival itself, as Jory commissioned playwrights from outside North America. Featuring short one-acts by Fugard, Soyinka, Friel, and seven other playwrights, *The America Project* remains the only production to utilize foreign playwrights in the new play festival. Many critics found the artistic achievement of *The America Project* to be Fugard's *The Drummer*, a short piece without words in which a street bum rummages through a garbage can and finds a pair of drumsticks. Several people within the theatre, however, expressed disappointment in Fugard's one-page work, consisting of a long stage direction and no dialogue, dismissing it as an "afterthought" or a "forgotten responsibility" rather than a sincere effort from the playwright.[5] Jory's decision to expand the festival by inviting respected foreign playwrights to participate in the annual event was a blatant publicity ploy, an attempt to further the reputation of the festival as the premiere new play festival while spending a minimal amount of money (by commissioning ten-minute plays, as opposed to full-length works). None of the *America Project* writers appeared in the festival again, making this project the only expansion effort during this phase not to impact the future practices of the festival.

The America Project, however, did garner the attention of the international press. Few critics from abroad attended the festival, but with the Louisville theatre briefly offering a wondrous array of talents from around the globe, Jory's theatre quickly became a talking point for international critics. Regardless of the hype surrounding *The America Project*, Jory knew that the financial strain of commissioning major international playwrights on a consistent basis was too onerous. Therefore, when a rare opportunity presented itself, Jory quickly decided to further his festival's reputation through another avenue: if the international press wouldn't come to Louisville, then Actors Theatre would go to them.

In 1980, the U.S. government selected the Snake Theatre of San Francisco to serve as the country's ambassador for the 1980 Belgrade International Theatre Festival in September. Tragically, the artistic director of the company suddenly died in the early months of 1980, and due to the resulting turmoil, the Snake Theatre pulled out of its commitments. Given that the Louisville theatre won the Tony award a few months prior, the government offered the touring opportunity to Actors Theatre, a proposal that Jory gladly accepted. Local critic Owen Hardy celebrated the selection of Actors Theatre, dismissing the argument that their signing at the last minute "doesn't mean that A.T.L.'s glory is less deserved. It probably would have come sooner or later anyway."[6]

In addition to performing in Yugoslavia, Actors Theatre opened the Dublin Theatre Festival at the end of the month and performed in Israel, the first time in more than twenty years that an American theatre company received an official invitation to that country. Two of the theatre festivals visited on the tour emphasized avant-garde works, yet Actors Theatre was not considered an avant-garde theatre by any means. Instead of mounting a production outside its proven niche, the Louisville theatre instead decided to celebrate its short legacy and offer a play from its lauded play festival, considered a good measure of current trends in American playwriting and acting.[7]

Marsha Norman's *Getting Out* was the logical choice for the international tour for several reasons. The multi-award-winning play emphasized the theatre's growing influence in American drama through its support of new plays and discovery of new talents, especially since Norman was a playwright-in-residence for the Louisville company in 1979. According to the local press, Norman and Actors Theatre not only represented American theatre but also symbolized the pride and achievements of the Kentucky city. Norman also stood to gain from the selection of her play; after garnering several national playwriting awards, she viewed the international tour as an opportunity for publicity and inclusion in future international theatre events.[8]

Jory's endeavor to develop an international reputation for the theatre and its festival succeeded; the foreign press lavished praise on the Louisville company throughout its tour, providing international recognition rarely given to American regional theatres. Although some critics considered the naturalistic play inappropriate for the avant-garde festivals or dismissed the work as "American realism" with its gritty depiction of prison and Norman's use of slang and heavy dialect that proved troublesome for numerous foreign critics, most reviewers praised not only Norman's script but also the Louisville company, its festival, and its director. In its first stop in Belgrade, critics praised the production's "sharpness and compassion," as well as its "sharp-tasting vitality."[9] In Dublin, Tim Harding and Emmanuel Kehoe of the *Sunday Press* lauded, "It's a great pity that Actors Theatre of Louisville are no longer with us. Their production of Ms. Norman's play, traveling on after only a few days in Dublin, has left standards in performance that will be hard to match throughout the festival. . . . The Actors Theatre of Louisville should be welcomed back. As soon as possible."[10] In its final stop at the Haifa Theatre at the invitation of the mayor of Haifa, Israel, as well as the American ambassador to that country, critics said that Actors Theatre deserved its previous awards and praise because of its superior ensemble of actors. Most important, in addition to wowing the press on its whirlwind tour, Actors Theatre's international exposure also influenced critics from across the globe to attend its future festivals, further bolstering the Louisville institution's international reputation.[11]

In a reversal of its tack with *The America Project*, which brought international playwrights and press to Louisville, Actors Theatre began to send its work to countries around the world. The 1980 tour instigated a long series of international tours, as the company represented (although unofficially) the best in new play development in American theatre at numerous foreign festivals. Actors Theatre accepted invitations from and eventually sent productions to Toronto, Vancouver, Budapest, Warsaw, Okinawa, Tokyo, Sydney, and Perth.

On a more personal level, these international tours provided Jory with invaluable exposure to other directors and production styles. When Jory returned from Actors Theatre's first tour, he reflected on his experience, stating, "I'm forty-two now. If only I had had the opportunity to attend international theatre festivals when I was younger, say twenty-one or twenty-two[;] think of all the time and effort, the trial and error [I] could have saved by watching other directors' styles from around the world."[12] Of course, Jory was not the only one who benefited from the international exposure. With its burgeoning reputation, the Festival of New American Plays was becoming a bigger event, and Jory was determined not to disappoint. Of course, with the increased number of productions came the need for more funding, and the producing director knew that if his festival was to become an institution, he needed to ensure financial security, as well as immunity to critical responses. Capitalizing on their growing stature in American theatre and international culture, Jory and his company moved quickly to address the festival's rising production costs and potential financial instability.

ACHIEVING FINANCIAL SECURITY

In Jory's search for additional funding, one avenue was closed to him. Unlike Papp, whose New York Shakespeare Festival coproduced several shows on Broadway, Jory decided not to work with New York producers to send *Crimes of the Heart* or any other festival show to the Great White Way. Instead, he let the author control the development of his or her play (reinforcing the Louisville theatre's boast that it produced new plays to help playwrights, not to further its own financial interests). Jory said that his rejection of the coproducer's role verified Actors Theatre's dedication to its mission of producing new work: "It takes too much time, and we're too busy. . . . We could involve ourselves in it, but it is such a hassle, and we do such a volume of new work that we finally said, 'Hey, let's just let this go.' And ever since we did that, we feel a lot better about things."[13]

With Jory forgoing money because of his principled protection of playwrights, he needed to tap other resources for funding, especially with expectations raised by accolades for the theatre and its international touring. Actors Theatre already elicited corporate sponsorship for its festival, but rising costs made such donations insufficient. Instead of trying to discover new resources, Jory revisited a current partner to ask for more money. Once again, he exploited the trust that he had established, asking a corporation go do down a forbidden path with him.

It has often been remarked that Actors Theatre was lucky to find the Humana Corporation, as though Jory and Alexander Speer simply discovered a corporation down the street that no one before had noticed. In fact, the relationship between Actors Theatre and Humana began long before the festival in the unlikeliest of places—a popular downtown bar and restaurant frequented by Louisville businessmen. Jory and Speer enjoyed casual lunches with numerous business leaders, including the two founders of Humana, Inc., and a professional relationship between the two businesses slowly developed.[14]

The decision to pursue Humana, Inc., during the first phase of the festival was not a choice made at random or out of desperation but was, instead, a logical progression. With its world headquarters in Louisville, Humana, Inc., sought to increase its involvement in the community, and Jory believed that its support of the new play festival would provide the young corporation an opportunity to improve its visibility both within Louisville and throughout the country.[15]

When Jory first made a proposal for funding in 1979, those in leadership positions at Humana were familiar with the work and leadership of Actors Theatre of Louisville. David A. Jones, a cofounder of Humana, Inc., and a former director of the Humana Foundation, recalled being impressed with Actors Theatre's initial request for funding of its annual festival. According to Jones, "Jory's statement glowed with lucidity and fire. ATL's clear vision, along with Humana's desire to nourish the arts in Louisville, propelled the two organizations to work together."[16] Jones described the initial proposal as "a model of clarity, two pages long, that stated how much he needed and exactly how it would be spent. I took it in to Wendell [Cherry, cofounder of

Humana, Inc.,] and said, 'Look, this guy is a clear thinker. Let's support him.' And that's how it all began."[17] Humana was the only corporation that Jory approached with this proposal, and, luckily, the company accepted. If it had declined to support the festival, Jory might have encountered difficulty in funding his annual event and the festival might have suffered as a result.[18]

With an initial donation of one hundred thousand dollars from Humana in 1979, Jory quickly affirmed the importance of the company's funding, stating that without the corporate grant, "there wouldn't be this festival."[19] Nevertheless, rising costs dictated greater financial support, so Jory, Speer, and the board of directors went back to their leading corporate sponsor, hoping that their long-established trust would result in a substantial increase in support. According to Speer, "I think what had happened is that we asked for either a two or three year commitment initially, but we felt that the money wasn't enough in retrospect, and we went back and asked to renegotiate." As part of the renegotiations, Actors Theatre offered to name the festival in the corporation's honor. "We went back and asked them for a lot more money," Speer recalled, "and then we offered the name."[20] With this expanded partnership, the annual event would now be known as the Humana Festival of New American Plays, a title that would apply to the previous festivals as well.[21]

The impact of this agreement was immediately obvious to the leaders of the Louisville theatre. Speer explained, "The key to the marvel of their support—which is still true today but even more so during the early years—was the three-year commitment, because it allowed the planning time that we needed. We could foresee that there would be a Humana Festival two years from now."[22] To this day, while corporations sponsor individual productions for various regional theatres throughout the country, the Humana Foundation's annual gift to Actors Theatre remains the longest and the largest grant support to any single theatre in the country.[23]

The partnership between Actors Theatre and Humana is both typical and atypical of theatre business practices during the early 1980s. For the first five years of the decade, foundations continued to contribute to professional theatres, but these contributions failed to keep pace with inflation, resulting in a slower rate of growth and less of a percentage in covering a theatre's operating expenses. The new partnership between Actors Theatre and Humana Foundation was astonishing, given that from 1980 to 1983, not only did the amount of donations from foundations to professional theatres fail to keep pace with inflation but the number of contributions actually decreased.[24]

The timing of the festival's new partnership was fortunate, as federal government funding for the arts in the 1980s also took a downward turn under the Reagan administration. Frequent attempts to slash federal funding hurt many regional theatres during Reagan's eight years in office, and these institutions struggled to find compensation from the private sector. In an assessment of the dwindling support for the arts during the Reagan years, Barbara Janowitz Ehrlich wrote, "Federal arts appropriations have remained virtually flat since 1981, rising only 4 percent, while theatre operating expenses have increased by 89.7 percent, resulting in a shrinking percent of costs covered by federal grant subsidies—from 7 percent of expenses in 1981 to 4.3 percent in 1988."[25] With increased support from Humana, Actors Theatre was able to withstand major losses in governmental funding, while regional theatres across the country had to scramble for other sources. Furthermore, with the newly extended commitment for the festival, Jory and Speer could budget for potential financial droughts, giving further stability to the festival and greater freedom for Jory to change the festival as he saw fit.

Although the substantial amount of the Humana donation contradicted corporate giving tendencies, the generous actions of the foundation did mirror a national trend. While some corporations gave to arts organizations through their foundations, many corporations in the 1980s supported regional theatres as part of their marketing strategies. Berkowitz noted, "Corporations are not primarily in the charity business, and to support not-for-profit theatre the relevant executive had to be convinced that a grant was a good investment for the company."[26] Instead of giving money to a theatre's general fund, corporations increasingly offered money to sponsor specific productions or projects. Even though Humana, Inc., and its philanthropic arm, the Humana Foundation (established in 1981), donated additional money to Actors Theatre's regular season, their support for the annual festival certainly represented the growing trend of corporate donations given for the expressed support of a specific project.

Not all producers, however, welcomed potential relationships with corporations, especially if they exerted influence on the art that the theatre produced. Joseph Papp reportedly resisted accepting money from AT&T, claiming that the company would soon demand that he produce plays with phones in them. The Roundabout Theatre also expressed hesitation when American Airlines offered money in exchange for the right to name the institution's new theatre. In Louisville, director of development Christen McDonough Boone reported that Actors Theatre has never encountered attempts by corporations to change the content of a certain production. Since businesses are more likely to support a single production than provide money for general purposes, Louisville corporations may choose which productions with which they want to be associated.[27]

Given this national trend of corporate selectivity in sponsorship, Humana's relationship with Actors Theatre, one in which both the theatre and the corporation strive to make themselves relevant and useful to the community, serves as a model for other regional theatres. Both Actors Theatre and Humana realized that together they could not only help each other's reputation but also engender civic pride (by Actors Theatre's bringing national attention to Louisville and by Humana's supporting local arts groups). The key to the success of this relationship is trust—the Humana Foundation never requested or pursued any form of censorship of the Humana Festival plays. David A. Jones, as chairman of the Humana Foundation, took pride in its hands-off policy concerning the festival: "Our approach has been to support the talented leadership of A.T.L., not to write, edit, or produce plays!"[28]

Ironically, Actors Theatre of Louisville never produced a play that is critical of health maintenance organizations, the business of Humana, Inc. Jory claimed never to have received a well-written play that criticized America's health care system. Although there is no proof to refute Jory's claim, the coincidence is certainly questionable. While a few plays have addressed health care issues (one of the most notable being Margaret Edson's *Wit*), Jory or staff members probably have been more critical of plays dealing with health care issues in an effort to avoid angering Humana, Inc. Although this theory may explain the absence of such topical plays at the Humana Festival, there is no evidence to suggest anything contrary to Jory's assertion.[29]

Jory now had the funding to mount a high-quality festival year after year (at least in terms of production values if not scripts), and the festival was well on its way to becoming the institution that Jory had planned. With an international reputation and sufficient funding, the festival now possessed the ability to persevere regardless of critical reactions. All the festival administrators had to do was select successful plays, yet a problem arose that threatened to keep the event from running smoothly.

SOLIDIFYING A PROCESS

Thanks in part to the establishment of the Great American Play Contest, Jory's festival consistently discovered and produced hit plays. However, contrary to popular belief, Jory and his literary staff still struggled, after three festivals, to find quality scripts, and the pressure to find plays that could travel to Broadway began to take its toll. The correspondence from the literary department of Actors Theatre reveals the great lengths to which ElizaBeth Mahan King and her staff went to locate producible scripts. In a solicitation letter to theatre critics and newspaper editors, King requested, "We wrote nine months ago for suggestions of new plays from your region, and we received many names of playwrights whom we then contacted. Because you were so helpful we are writing again as we are now seeking new scripts for next season." With this letter, Actors Theatre enclosed a self-addressed envelope for the critic to jot down any suggestions.[30]

Letters similar to the aforementioned critic solicitation were mailed to a wide range of professionals in hopes of learning about new and exciting playwrights. King posted letters to university playwriting programs ("We understand that your department offers a unique educational opportunity for playwrights. . . . Are there any students you personally recommend whom we should contact?"), stage managers ("Perhaps there is someone in your company who has not yet been recognized as a writer"), playwriting workshops ("I have heard of your work with new writers; the reports are very good. . . . I would very much like to see any new scripts you respect"), as well as form letters for specific playwrights ("We would very much like to read [left blank]. Jon heard about this (these) script(s) through the National Endowment panel on which he serves").[31]

With the theatre still struggling to locate quality scripts, Jory and King had to explore other options. Thankfully, Jory knew where to turn, and during the next three-year phase, two of the festival's biggest triumphs came from the most unlikely of places. Considered by many to be one of the best plays in the festival's history, John Pielmeier's *Agnes of God*, presented during the fourth festival, resulted from Jory's decision to look within his own theatre to discover potential festival playwrights.[32] Holding an MFA degree in playwriting from Penn State University, Pielmeier first was introduced to Louisville audiences through numerous performances as an actor at Actors Theatre, including *Holidays* in the third festival. More important, he represented one of many Actors Theatre company members who wrote plays for the new play festival, including Ken Jenkins, Patrick Tovatt, and Kent Broadhurst.

Jory justified employing actors to write by claiming that they reduced the risk involved when working on new plays. Because Jory had to hire many out-of-town artists when organizing the festival, the familiarity of these actor-playwrights provided Jory with a greater sense of control over the challenging play-production process. Furthermore, the actor-playwrights were accustomed to Jory's methods and expectations as a producer-director.[33] While a few critics (including Actors Theatre's own literary manager) leveled charges of favoritism, Jory maintained a respectable critical success rate for scripts written by actors, and given the difficulty in mounting six or seven plays, it was reasonable and resourceful of Jory to protect his festival against future failure and unpredictability.

The second unlikely hit play of this phase was also an in-house discovery, yet the mysterious circumstances of its origins led to a lengthy controversy for the theatre and its producing director. Unlike his prior play selections, which resulted from careful consideration and the weighing of risks, Jory's decision to produce a ten-minute play by an anonymous author quickly raised questions as to whether the playwright truly was unknown. Submitted in a plain brown envelope and slid underneath the literary department's door, Jane Martin's *Twirler* presents a one-woman narrative about a "Jesus freak" who draws pictures of Jesus in the sky with her baton. The inclusion of *Twirler* in the fifth festival's *Early Times* collection began the long and controversial relationship between Jane Martin and the Louisville theatre. Since the first festival appearance of a work by Martin, critics assaulted Jory with a barrage of questions, asking whether he was indeed the pseudonymous playwright (or the head of a "Jane Martin committee"), but he consistently denied authorship of her plays. As a result of the mystery surrounding the playwright, the most anticipated play of the Sixth Humana Festival of New American Plays was Martin's collection of women's monologues titled *Talking With*. After critics devoted half of their reviews to guessing the mysterious playwright's identity, they expressed their approval of and appreciation for Martin's mastery of the monologue format and her creation of "fascinating and off-beat" characters.[34]

Even for a festival with critically acclaimed and award-winning plays, the pressure to succeed never abated, and the theatre's continuous struggle to locate scripts, as well as maintain its streak of Broadway transfers (a determinant for success according to critics, not Jory), began to take its toll on certain members of the staff. While the press celebrated Jory's remarkable ability to discover high-quality new plays and playwrights, Actors Theatre faced an internal crisis following the fifth festival: the departure of ElizaBeth Mahan King after five years as literary manager. If Jory was going to turn his event into an institution, he needed to make sure that the theatre's bread and butter—its ability to discover hit plays—did not suddenly falter and counter the growing momentum. King's impending departure meant that Jory had to find someone to organize the theatre's play discovery process—an ingredient crucial to the future stability of the festival. Without effective management of the literary department, the festival might fail to find the hit plays that helped maintain its international reputation.

The problem for Jory was that the duties and demands of the literary manager's job had changed with the growing responsibilities of the festival. The immediate success of the festival compelled Jory and King to search for "production ready" scripts (those that had already been developed in prior readings). Jory sent King to theatres around the world to search for new plays. According to Julie Crutcher, who was a good friend of King's and worked under her for a year before being hired as her replacement, "Jon never does anything half-assed. He had her not only looking for new plays in the U.S.—he had her going to Europe, sending her to London all the time."[35] King's international journeys exemplified Jory's determination (and perhaps desperation) to find other successful scripts to build on the festival's prior achievements with *The Gin Game* and *Crimes of the Heart*.

The impact of the Festival of New American Plays and the demands associated with the theatre's national play contest eventually took their toll on King. "I think she was just burned out. . . . She was tired of it, tired of Jon," Crutcher explained. "When I inherited that office, I had forty or fifty, maybe even a hundred, plays from overseas. Nobody had ever looked at them. They were just sitting in the office. . . . The trunk of her car was full of manuscripts. She was horrible at having a system to get that stuff out of here. . . . Some of the scripts had been there for four years, and the agents went nuts."[36] Although events in King's personal life might have compelled her to leave the position, Crutcher believed that the demands of the festival and the contest became too great for King: "She was wildly creative and not systematic at all. I think it was time for her to move on. . . . I think she's a computer programmer or something; she left the theatre completely."[37]

A change in personnel is common in professional theatre, and the decision to promote Julie Crutcher to the literary manager position resulted in an increasingly efficient literary office, as well as a landmark system for handling new play submissions—one that has been copied by many other theatres and is still utilized at Actors Theatre. At first, Crutcher was overwhelmed by the demands of the job and recalled the impact of the Great American Play Contest on the literary department, claiming, "It really is an administrative nightmare. Because at that time [when Crutcher became literary manager], we were getting 3,000 scripts a year. And you had to have a system to get them in, get them read, get them screened, get them out. It had to be a good system."[38]

Although King and Crutcher employed different management styles within the literary office, Crutcher wisely maintained King's system for script reading, which helped Actors Theatre's literary department process and evaluate the piles of script submissions. When the literary office receives a play, assistants catalog it and assign a number that indicates the year of its submission and the order in which it was received. If the play was written by a previous Humana Festival writer, an established playwright, or someone who has shown talent in the past but failed to make the cut, then the literary manager often reads the script herself. All other scripts are dispersed among the remaining full-time staff (the interns usually not making decisions about submissions).

After reading the play, a dramaturg writes on an index card all pertinent information about the playwright, including his or her name and address, the play's title, and the catalog number. On the reverse of the card, the reader briefly describes the plot in two or three sentences and offers critical analysis of its writing style, choice of language, character depiction, and so forth. Then the reader judges the play by means of a three-point rating system. Any script with a single positive element (i.e., well-drawn characters, good dialogue, interesting situation, unique concept, one funny moment, etc.) receives a rating of "two," meaning that another member of the literary department will read it. Any play designated with a "one" signifies at least two impressive elements and usually finds its way onto the literary manager's desk. A play designated with a "three" is not read again owing to its lack of merit. Because the process requires that any play containing a single redeeming component receive a score of "two," almost every play submitted to the literary department is read twice.

Since every play received by the literary department is represented on an index card, the literary office is filled with thousands of cards cataloged in alphabetical order by the playwright's last name. These cards come in handy when a disgruntled playwrights calls, complaining that his or her play was not thoroughly read or accusing the literary manager of not reading the play at all. Because of the opinions and criticisms written on each card, the filing system is guarded by the literary office and is considered to be off-limits to almost all of the Actors Theatre of Louisville staff.[39]

After the second round of readings, any play that has not received a "one" is eliminated from the competition, and the remaining plays either are dismissed (after another reading) or forwarded to Jon Jory for consideration. Depending on the literary manager's tastes and relationship with Jory, between twenty and sixty scripts were deemed worthwhile to be given to Jory each year. Furthermore, the quality of the submissions was never constant. According to playwright and former literary associate Valerie Smith, the challenge of finding six or seven good plays varied from year to year. She explained, "Some years it's easy. Some years it's just like pulling a tooth."[40] Crutcher described her function in the process: "I felt like I was the first sieve in the filter-down thing. My job was to find things that were in any way redeemable, producible, or interesting. . . . What's wonderful to one person isn't wonderful to another, and that became very clear early. I wasn't any better at finding good stuff than anybody else was, and my good stuff was somebody else's bad stuff. My bad stuff was somebody else's good stuff. So I wanted to make sure that I was objective as I could possibly be, because my job was to give him plays from which to pick, *not* to pick it. He picked it."[41] Crutcher's successor, Michael Bigelow Dixon, highlighted another challenge in selecting scripts: taking a pass on plays that later proved successful in other theatres. "I've found this career humbling when the plays I haven't responded to go on to great success elsewhere," Dixon admitted. "That's an ongoing reminder that dramaturgy is all about getting to what the other person is thinking, because when the play finds someone who does understand, it flourishes."[42]

Although the play-selection system ensures that every good script is read at least twice, the procedure does not rule out the possibility of bias. Personal preferences influence any play selection process, especially when a literary manager or artistic director dislikes a specific type of play (farce, melodrama, expressionism, etc.). Concerning the problem of bias, the issue was moot, since the final decision rested with Jon Jory, who admittedly allowed his preferences to influence his decisions. In one letter to a rejected playwright who attempted to adapt a popular comic strip into a theatrical piece, Jory bluntly admitted his bias by writing, "I think [the play] handles very candidly the problem of translating a comic strip to the stage, but it is a genre that does not appeal to me personally. Good luck with it in other markets."[43]

Another potential flaw of the process concerns the possibility of a lack of comprehension. Would a script be discarded because the reader failed to understand its style or intentions? This problem was solved with the policy that if a reader believes he or she did not understand the play or its intentions, the script would be passed to another staff member. Dixon described other difficulties with the judging of submitted scripts: "It doesn't take a genius to read a great play and recognize it. That's not the hard part of the job. The hard part of the job is finding the value in works-in-progress that can be developed into compelling new plays for the stage."[44] The task of evaluating scripts was not confined to the literary department, because Jory himself occasionally sought advice from others. Although he had the final say in determining all festival entries, he admitted that as the festival grew, he considered the opinions of others who shared an interest in new play development and had worked with him at Actors Theatre for a lengthy period.[45]

That Jory personally selected the plays for each festival proved an interesting challenge for both the literary staff and playwrights, as his preferences were hard to predict. By the time Jory retired, the style, tone, and thematic content of Humana Festival plays varied so greatly from year to year that it became impossible to identify a typical candidate for inclusion. In the earliest years, however, traditional plays dominated the festival's lineup, primarily because they were what the theatre received in the mail and what would satisfy the audience base. Despite their traditional form, however, several of the earliest festivals' plays enjoyed subsequent productions at other regional theatres, supporting Jory's claim that his priority was to locate quality scripts. As the festival grew and the lineup featured more daring works, collections exemplified trends in national playwriting rather than the producing director's personal tastes.

Given that the ultimate decisions about submitted plays rested with Jory, the hiring of Julie Crutcher as literary manager did not significantly alter the operations of the festival. Her organizational skills, however, ensured a smooth-running office that did not impede the growing legacy of the Humana Festival.[46] One of the most important roles of the literary manager at Actors Theatre of Louisville is to develop and nurture ongoing relationships with playwrights, as well as their agents. With Crutcher's administrative abilities, the literary office achieved a new level of professionalism and stability that helped Actors Theatre handle the growing demands of its play festival and allow its good fortune to continue. Playwrights, agents, and theatre professionals came to admire and emulate Crutcher's methods and her commitment to playwrights during her tenure as literary manager.[47]

The combination of four events during the 1980–82 period—the tour, the Tony Awards, the corporate sponsorship agreement, and the new stability and professionalism in the literary office—assured that the festival and Actors Theatre would remain in the national spotlight. The attention brought greater support from outside the city of Louisville.[48] Between 1975 and 1981, grant income (largely from the Humana Foundation) increased by 437 percent, from $159,484 to $856,000, while earned income increased 119 percent, from $702,006 to $1,537,000. The end of the Fifth Humana Festival of New American Plays in 1981 is a marker for the overall financial impact of the festival on the theatre. In 1975, the year before the first festival, the theatre's operating budget was $853,745; after receiving national and international acclaim for winning the Tony Award and for producing the *Getting Out* tour, as well as larger commitments from the Humana Foundation, the 1981 operating budget had nearly tripled to $2,349,000.[49]

With Actors Theatre's new security and its eyes on the future, critics asked less often whether the festival's days were numbered and more patrons and theatre artists recognized the annual event as an institution entrenched in American theatre. Despite continued criticism, confidence carried the festival through disappointing years and shielded it from competition with other new play festivals. Complaints that the plays presented during this phase were too safe, however, were still lodged by reviewers (primarily in the northeast) who failed to recognize the need for Jory to keep the festival relevant and well attended. Still, some criticism is valid; according to Mark Fearnow, "In the 1980s, the energy that built up a new and positive theatre came largely from formerly silenced groups—feminist, gay and lesbian, African American, Latina/o, and Asian American playwrights—and a renewed political drama arose in response to the conservative environment" of the early 1980s.[50] The Humana Festival presented no major works from any of these groups.[51] While some ten-minute plays (especially in *The America Project*) presented political or social themes, the most aggressive plays in this phase focused on religion (*Agnes of God*), materialism (*A Full Length Portrait of America*), the environment (*SWOP*), and violence (*Extremities*). Even though critics lamented the absence of these silenced groups in the earliest years of the festival (especially because contemporary theatre celebrates such diversity), it is unfair to expect that the festival in its foundational years would strive to satisfy every demographic while it struggled to secure audiences, respect, and financial support.

Still, there was a noticeable difference between the popular plays of the first two phases of the festival. The second period did not contain as many "fluff pieces" as the first three years of the festival, and all the popular works of the latter phase dealt with serious issues on some level; *Agnes of God*, *Extremities*, *My Sister in This House*, and *Talking With* each achieved commercial success while addressing weightier themes. Even though the Humana collections did not represent the groups listed in Fearnow's essay, Jory's 1980–82 festivals did exhibit his growing security in the future of the festival and his willingness to support edgier drama.

Regardless of critical reaction or awards, the true legacy of the festival was its contribution to the repertoire of American plays, and the two festivals of 1981 and 1982 marked the introduction of the notorious Jane Martin, as well as Lee Blessing and William Mastrosimone, into the canon of American playwriting. One local critic summarized the long-term affects of these playwriting discoveries: "There can no longer be any doubt that producing director Jon Jory and his Actors Theatre are making significant contributions to the dramatic history of the last quarter of the 20th century." By the end of the 1981–82 season, the Humana Festival had become an institution in the American theatre, thriving on its reputation and continuing to discover talented playwrights. The three years from 1980 to 1982 provided Actors Theatre with cherished opportunities, impressive accolades, financial stability, and a potential to expand its legacy and exert its influence on the American theatre.[52]

Having been established at the forefront of new play development in regional theatre, Actors Theatre of Louisville and the Humana Festival of New American Plays would be forced, over the next four years, to adapt its artistic, economic, and administrative endeavors to competition from other play festivals, as well as growing complaints from playwrights. After a short three years filled with expansions and opportunities, the festival struggled to meet high critical expectations and to respond to the changing demands and trends of professional theatre. Jory's decision to "institutionalize" his festival helped it weather the storms already on the horizon.

5   FROM PRODUCT TO PROCESS, 1983–86

As each festival approaches, Louisville theatergoers frequently gossip about the upcoming plays, prognosticating which ones might be the next to travel to Broadway. However, for the seventh festival, most talk centered on one play—a production about which most patrons knew little. As Jory became bolder with the number of productions (the 1983 festival having presented the largest offering to date of eight full-length productions and two bills of one-acts), he also exhibited his confidence and showmanship with the most enigmatic production in the annual event's history. This massive and problematic presentation was the impetus of a new phase during which the festival redefined its purpose.

Gary Leon Hill's *Food from Trash*, a cowinner of the Great American Play Contest, comments on "the critical issue of toxic waste disposal and its effects on the lives of people who must cope with it" as the poisonous material reduces garbage men to "snarling, soulless animals."[1] Actors Theatre offered such descriptions to the public through its massive mailing to subscribers in hopes of enticing Louisville patrons to see the production, but, surprisingly, few people were allowed to view a performance of Hill's play. As a result, *Food from Trash* would become the most mysterious play in the Humana Festival's history, but more important, the story behind the discovery, mounting, and critical reception of the play marked the beginning of the next phase in the festival's history.

While Jory certainly withheld information about *Food from Trash* to garner attention from the press, he also hesitated to provide specifics because he and his associates were debating how to mount the massive production. Hill's stage directions called for storage tanks, dump trucks, numerous sets, and multiple piles of garbage, and the play was deemed too demanding to stage at Actors Theatre during the festival, when plays were in repertory (three shows usually being performed in the larger Pamela Brown Auditorium). Because of their limited options, Jory and his staff agreed that the theatre would have to renovate a large space away from the theatre complex, and the local press followed their every move. Rumors swirled around Louisville and in the newspapers as to where and how *Food from Trash* would be performed; leading guesses included abandoned warehouses and airline hangars. A wild suggestion that the play would conclude with the spraying of garbage on the audience was also circulating. In the end, the designers settled on a Louisville Air Park warehouse, and carpenters quickly constructed bleachers for two hundred people, as well as a large stage, both of which had to be approved by fire inspectors. Hill's play also demanded large pathways for machines, as the play opened with the roar of dump trucks leaving the warehouse, and these vehicles returned occasionally throughout the production, leaving more work for the characters in the play.[2]

With construction deadlines, as well as constant worries about fire codes, the pressure to succeed and impress increased as a result of Jory's determination to produce Hill's play. In spite of the heightened anticipation from the Louisville community and press, Jory decided to limit the number of people who would be allowed to view the mysterious production by labeling *Food for Trash* a "workshop," meaning that tickets would not be available for the preview performances and that the production would be presented only to visiting critics, literary agents, newspeople, producers, and "friends" of the theatre. (The production was performed only five times for a total of one thousand patrons.) Jory defended his choice to mount the elaborate production for a limited audience by praising the merits of the play, proclaiming, "I'm proud we were the first theatre to produce [Hill's] work, and I would have done *Food from Trash* even if we had been forced to show it only to an audience of two hundred." Jory also claimed that the production was not ready for public viewing (hence the "workshop" label), and Jenan Dorman, a spokeswoman for Actors Theatre, said that a full run in the warehouse would have been too expensive owing to the limited seating capacity.[3]

In spite of his defensive justifications, Jory faced criticism not only from local theatergoers who were prohibited from viewing the production but also from the national press, many of whom were unimpressed with both Hill's text and the production. If Jory and Crutcher were enamored with Hill's writing, then they were in the minority, as critics condemned the dialogue for being too melodramatic. Although the play allowed Jory to adapt his festival to include unique performance spaces, the extravagant production and enormous warehouse forced the actors to play "larger than life."[4] Adding insult to injury, the dump trucks were so loud that audience members often could not hear the dialogue.[5]

It is not surprising that many critics questioned the grandeur of the production and dismissed the concept as a publicity gimmick. Critics labeled the show an overblown attempt to wow the out-of-town press and wondered what Jory hoped to accomplish. One critic surmised that Jory was getting restless and feared apathy from the public, but another critic dismissed

Hill's work and the production as "a dubious excuse for the expenditure of so much time and money."[6]

Nevertheless, *Food from Trash* represented a turning point in the festival's history: not only did the massive production expose the festival's reliance on productions to achieve (and define) success, but its critical drubbing instigated a series of alterations by Jory to improve the festival. After *Food from Trash*, the producing director decided to transform the festival's purpose from a celebration of hit productions to a process-oriented endeavor. No longer would Jory rely on productions to make a play successful; instead, he modified his theatre's priorities to emphasize the talents of the playwrights. Following the close of the 1983 festival, Jory began a series of four strategic alterations.

AN ALTERATION FOR PLAYWRIGHTS AND DRAMATURGS

Jory's 1983 collection of new plays received mostly negative responses from the national press—a first for the festival. Besides complaining about the poor quality of writing, critics bemoaned the number of veteran playwrights reappearing in Louisville, arguing that the seventh festival may have been a celebration of new plays but not one of new playwrights.[7] Linda Winer of *USA Today* sympathized with Jory and shared his concern over the discovery of new writers and scripts, lamenting, "I began to worry about this festival, which has become a supermarket for scripts-by-the-pound commodities. Faced with the same scarcity of 'product' as the rest of the USA's theatre, Jory must be worrying too."[8]

In his defense, Jory wisely rejected calls to include new playwrights in his festival if it meant accepting lesser-quality plays. However, because Jory refused to accept weaker scripts, he realized that he needed to institute changes to help the scripts that he did select reach their full potential. When plays from both external sources (like *Food from Trash* from the Great American Play Contest) and his own company (via commissions) failed, the results pointed to a need for change in the process of developing new plays. After enduring the critical dismissal of his seventh collection, Jory became more willing to explore change. In fact, in an interview with a critic from the *Washington Post*, Jory cited one of the problems that he wanted to address: the development of playwrights should be taken more seriously and that providing "some warmth and affection wouldn't hurt."[9] The solution that Jory was looking for came from one of his newest staff members and the one person whose sole purpose was to provide playwrights with affection.

Julie Crutcher pushed for the inclusion of *Food from Trash* in spite of its many production demands, but her influence with Jory extended beyond play selection. The process of adapting the festival's practices began after the seventh year, when Crutcher argued for a major change in Actors Theatre's methods of play production: the addition of the playwright into the entire rehearsal process. When the festival began, a playwright scarcely was involved in the development of his or her play, attending only a few rehearsals. In its infancy, the budget for the festival was so tight that the theatre funded playwrights on a limited basis, but once the festival began receiving substantial financial contributions, the playwrights questioned Actors Theatre's level of support. Crutcher explained that the writers thought it odd that they were invited and funded to attend only ten days of the rehearsal process, even if the rehearsals lasted for three or four weeks, and if they wanted to attend the remainder of the rehearsals, then they had to pay their own way. "They [the playwrights] really felt like that was unfair to them," she recalled, "and I agreed with them. But it kind of took me a while to understand why they felt that way."[10] In retrospect, Crutcher described the early years of the festival as a learning process for both the staff and the artists, and she credited the change (and the courage to adapt) to both the playwrights and to Jory.

In his essay in *Dramaturgy in American Theatre*, former Actors Theatre literary manager Michael Bigelow Dixon explained the significance of Jory's alteration: "That financial commitment to the playwright's presence was the most important expression of the theater's serious commitment to the process of new play development and production."[11] The decision to support playwrights financially throughout the entire rehearsal process not only reflected Jory's new agenda to adapt the festival to favor process over product but also illustrated how Jory began to change his methods to ensure the happiness of the playwrights. Crutcher explained, "He [Jory] became more adaptable. The initial response was always, 'Absolutely not. That's ridiculous. Why should we do that?' But, then, he would listen and then he would begin to understand why the playwrights needed to be there the whole time. Now a lot of them couldn't be there because they had other jobs, like this was not the way that they make money. . . . But, when they could, we really began to understand that it was important for them to be there through the whole process rather than hit-or-miss."[12]

With the increased presence of playwrights throughout the entire rehearsal process, the role of the dramaturg became more prominent.[13] The literary staff of Actors Theatre developed relationships with every Humana Festival playwright, bouncing from room to room to view simultaneous rehearsals and monitor the playwrights' progress and happiness. Actors Theatre's decision to augment its literary department's responsibilities to support the playwright represented the growing trend, in the early 1980s, of professional theatres enlarging and redefining the role of their literary managers and dramaturgs. Dixon justified the growing reliance on dramaturgs during this period: "These large institutions schedule five to ten productions a year. Nobody has that many productions a year in them for twenty years. So the theatres founded in the '60s and '70s started in the

'80s to look for ways to replenish, and the dramaturg was useful in changing the dynamic and enriching the work."[14] When many artistic directors attempted to include workshop productions or readings of new plays as a part of their theatre's activities, they expanded their literary departments to obtain managerial assistance.

The Circle Repertory Company illustrated this growth in the early 1980s as it expanded its new play workshops. The company formally created its literary department in 1977—the same year that founding artistic director Marshall Mason created a dramaturgy position to focus solely on play development. As opposed to the model of the Hamburg National Theatre, where a company's dramaturg selects the plays while a director controls the productions, the model for American dramaturgy usually stipulates that an artistic director controls the play selection, a literary manager (possibly an administrative position) monitors the handling of scripts, and the dramaturgs aid playwrights with writing projects.[15] Mason hired his first dramaturg in 1977, and as the theatre's many play development programs grew, the Circle Repertory Company found it necessary to expand its dramaturgical staff in 1982. The literary department operated and maintained the theatre's script evaluation service, its Friday Readings presentations, and its Projects-in-Projects series. Unfortunately, like so many other regional theatres later in the decade, the theatre struggled financially during economic recessions and the Reagan administration's assault on federal funding for the arts. Being the "new kids on the block" in American professional theatre, dramaturgs are often the first casualties of downsizing. Such was the case at the Circle Repertory Company as financial constraints forced it to eventually cut back its literary staff.[16]

As more and more nonprofit theatres attempted to create new play workshops, the expansion of literary departments often created confusion in the hierarchy of the institutions. Michael Donahue's *American Professional Regional Theatre Moving into the 21st Century* argues that because the role of dramaturgs in regional theatre is poorly defined, they continue "to struggle to find a place in the regional theatre setting."[17] For Actors Theatre, the roles of dramaturgs were defined by necessity: the Humana Festival provided enough dramaturgical work for the literary manager (who serves as a dramaturg as well), any literary associates, and the two literary interns. By choosing to support the playwright throughout the entire rehearsal process, Actors Theatre forced its literary department to serve its playwrights for weeks on end, in addition to processing and evaluating script submissions. Jory's decision to allow playwrights a greater role in rehearsals reflected the growing importance of dramaturgical support to the festival's success, eventually culminating in a major alteration of the literary department and an expansion of its responsibilities after the tenth festival.

Determined to take care of the playwright both in and out of the rehearsal process, Jory began to shift the focus of the festival away from the productions and toward the playwright, a transformation that would become more evident by the end of the ninth festival. This new policy, more than any other, helped Actors Theatre validate its reputation as a playwright's theatre, which, in turn, inspired playwrights to send their works to Actors Theatre in greater numbers. Furthermore, unlike the production of *Food from Trash*, which focused more on the product, the move to include the playwright in the entire rehearsal process helped increase chances for development of a successful script that, ideally, led to a better production. Still, this monumental alteration was only one of four important changes that forever impacted the festival, and as the demands on the staff increased, Jory realized that more changes were needed. After listening to complaints from the playwrights and hoping to avoid a re-peat of the unfortunate seventh festival, Jory began the play selection process for the next festival in hopes of maintaining the event's history of success while also adapting and responding to changing demands and pressures.

RELEASE AND RELEVANCE IN THE EIGHTH FESTIVAL

For each of the prior seven festivals, Jory's play selections were limited to either what the theatre commissioned or what it received in the mail, but Jory did have constant control over one aspect of every festival: himself. In a dedicated effort to expose any weakness in the festival, the producing director questioned his own actions and methodology. Jory realized that he could improve the festival by addressing two long-standing problems for which he alone was responsible: his overcontrolling producing methods and his penchant for popular works. Even though Jory's solution for the former problem was a culmination of years of growth for the festival, decisions made for the 1984 festival demonstrate his new intention to let playwrights be the focal point of the festival (instead of himself).

In support of his new agenda, Jory adapted his producing methods by altering his approach and his demeanor throughout the festival's long and stressful rehearsal process. Jory admitted that the hectic rehearsal schedule made fixing problems more difficult, and unlike the earliest festivals, he realized that recasting a role or assuming the job of director himself did not solve every problem.[18] This newer approach to management is not to infer that Jory was hands-off. On the contrary, he was known to attend rehearsals and give notes or even hold a few rehearsals of his own, with the director's permission (if the director had already left town), but he was also commit-ted to allowing the playwright freedom to develop his or her work as fully as possible in a supportive environment.

Jory was still protective of his festival, but he certainly loosened his grip on every aspect of production. Once known as a "benevolent dictator" who was willing to seize control of a production (e.g., *Circus Valentine*), he now seemed to have confidence in the future of the festival and a willingness to learn from his mistakes. Only Jory can explain the reason behind his change, but as the years went by, compliments about his production skills emphasized his hospitality, his mentoring, and his undying support of all of the artists involved in the festival.

Lee Blessing, whose *Independence* for the eighth festival would have benefited from a better director, sympathized with the challenges that Jory faced as a producer. "He's a very good director, as well as being a good producer," Blessing said, "so I think it can be hard for him to go in and watch a show that someone could be doing better." Blessing, however, argued that Jory never showed any indication of wanting to seize control of the faulty *Independence* production (as he might have in an earlier festival). Blessing perceived Jory more as a supporter than as a dictator: "He never came in and was an overbearing presence in rehearsal at all. He might check in and say, 'Hi,' but I thought he kept a lot of respectful distance."[19] In a published interview, Richard Dresser also praised Jory's supportive (and not overbearing) approach when developing a play. "When we talked about it [polishing a script], I never felt like anything was coming down from on high," Dresser recalled. "In fact, Jon is about as unpretentious as anyone I've every worked with. Everything is about, 'How do we make this work?'"[20]

In conjunction with his willingness to change his producing methods, Jory realized over time that he could also release some of the festival's administrative duties to his trusted staff. Jory's desire to lessen his administrative burden was one shared by artistic directors around the country. As more and more regional theatres instituted new play workshops and readings, artistic directors found themselves overwhelmed with administrative demands. According to Todd London, author of *The Artistic Home*, "The need for time away from the day-to-day demands of producing stems from a fundamental schizophrenia in the lives of American artistic directors, especially those who are primarily directors. The institution functions of their work as producers often directly contradict their needs as artists."[21]

Institutional demands isolated Jory and other artistic directors from artistic processes, making them feel cut off from other artists. For instance, Lloyd Richards bemoaned giving directors plays that he wanted to direct himself while serving as artistic director of the National Playwrights Conference at the Eugene O'Neill Memorial Theatre Center, and the Goodman Theatre's Robert Falls lamented the time-consuming expectations to raise money and meet with community members that compete with his many other administrative and artistic duties. Expressing their concerns at various conferences hosted by the Alliance Theatre, Berkeley Repertory Theatre, Center Stage, Eureka Theatre Company, Goodman Theatre, Mark Taper Forum, and Yale

Repertory Theatre, the artistic directors of these theatres called for "private" time away from their producing duties, greater involvement with their artists, and increased interaction with other disciplines. For Jory, the success of his festival, in conjunction with its shift from product to process, permitted him to delegate a portion of his administrative responsibilities to fulfill these desires and reconnect with artists.[22]

Jory's move to release certain responsibilities to his staff signified three important changes. First, while in step with the actions of other artistic directors around the country, Jory's cautious delegation of responsibility demonstrated that he was becoming more confident in the festival's continuation, allowing him to explore different performance opportunities (which he did with aplomb after the tenth festival). Second, by making the festival more of a collective effort, Actors Theatre continued to move toward being a playwright's theatre and away from status as a producer's theatre. This change garnered Jory further respect from festival playwrights, because he clearly understood and cared about issues and concerns confronting American playwrights. Finally, by not focusing on multiple rehearsal processes (although he did not entirely abandon this practice), Jory allowed himself greater freedom as a director to explore more interesting and challenging works—an opportunity that he seized for the eighth festival.

Jory addressed another problem for the eighth festival: his penchant for conventional comedies and dramas. When Actors Theatre appointed Jory as its producing director in 1969, he announced to the board that he loved to direct works that were comedic and entertaining. For his season selections, Jory kept his promise, but since the Humana Festival was a different beast, any desire that Jory may have had to select "popular" works was roundly criticized. After seven seasons, the press fiercely attacked Jory's selection of plays, arguing that the festival "doesn't take chances; that it doesn't experiment or do avant-garde works; that few of its plays tackle issues; that it sticks primarily with 'safe' plays that won't alienate or bore its audience."[23]

In step with his eagerness to ease his burdens as the festival's producer, Jory now exhibited a willingness to accept work deriving from a playwright's interest (as opposed to expecting plays to fit Jory's criteria). For the Eighth Annual Humana Festival of New American Plays, Jory presented two relevant and issue-oriented plays that featured adventurous forms of play structure. Playwright Emily Mann debuted in the Humana Festival with *Execution of Justice*, a provocative look at the assassinations of both San Francisco's mayor George Moscone and city supervisor Harvey Milk, as well as the trial of the confessed killer, Daniel James White. Although her script was repetitious at times in trying to provide a balanced view of the story, critics praised the structure of her play as "compelling" and "electrifyingly effective." Reviews of Mann's production also cited as crucial to the play's success the intense performance of the late John Spencer as Daniel White.[24] Jory's gamble in experimenting with new styles of playwriting paid off, since Mann was trumpeted as a wonderful new discovery and her play was transferred to New York, where it received numerous accolades.

The other issue-oriented play of the festival, however, did not fare as well. Ken Jenkins's *007 Crossfire* focuses on the 1983 shooting down of a Korean airliner that killed 289 people.[25] Jenkins's style for this play was described as "hyper-busy," meaning that the play unfolded as a series of one-line thoughts from the many characters (passengers, politicians, etc.) around the stage. This technique frustrated audiences and critics in that as soon as one thought was started, it was finished. Furthermore, when the tempo did change because a character delivered a monologue, critics often found the writing to be dull in comparison with the quick-moving one-line banter. Because director Jory kept the show moving, most critics praised him for accomplishing all that any director could with Jenkins's confusing script. Other reviewers, however, faulted Jory for the production, referring to his lack of confidence in the "adventurous" script and his reliance on "declamatory flamboyance" to move as quickly as possible through the text.[26]

In spite of the critics' complaints, Jenkins's drama reflected new directions in playwriting during the early 1980s. In his essay "Experimental Drama at the End of the Century," Ehren Fordyce argued that several established playwrights in the earliest years of the decade strove to challenge traditional dramatic conventions. These playwrights, including Maria Irene Fornes and Adrienne Kennedy, recognized that those who imitated the "sociological slice of life" often sacrificed "possibilities for transformation, and potentials for aesthetic and political changes."[27] Fordyce also listed several qualities of the experimental writings of Mac Wellman, Len Jenkin, and Jeffrey Jones, especially their "discarding of psychological subtext. Characters will simply declare or mis-declare their thoughts and feelings."[28] Regardless of the critics' dismissal of Jenkins's intentions with the script, *007 Crossfire* embodied both of these qualities, making the docudrama the most experimental script to date. While Fordyce's article exhibited the New York bias by primarily focusing on work mounted in Off and Off-Off Broadway theatres, Jory's selection of *007 Crossfire* not only proved his knowledge of current playwriting trends but also illustrated his confidence in the festival and in his ability to mount more experimental fare.

In addition to the premieres of several hit plays, including P. J. Barry's *The Octette Bridge Club*, John Patrick Shanley's *Danny and the Deep Blue Sea* (starring John Turturro), and Horton Foote's *Courtship*, Jory's willingness to expand the offerings of his festival by including relevant works prompted most reviewers to declare the Eighth Annual Humana Festival of New American Plays the best festival to date and that the annual event was "back on track."[29] With a dedicated staff, a producer who listened to and supported his artists and coworkers, and a wave of positive reviews from the previous year's presentations, Actors Theatre turned its attention toward the ninth collection, hoping to continue their extraordinary success. Unfortunately, the tide was about to turn, and the Humana Festival and Actors Theatre would never be the same.

UNDER ATTACK FOR THE NINTH FESTIVAL

In 1985, Jory found himself on the receiving end of harsh attacks from New York theatre critics, forcing him to defend his decisions and eventually announce a major change in his festival. Less than a month before the end of the ninth festival, the eighth festival's *The Octette Bridge Club* opened on March 5, 1985, at the Music Box Theatre in New York. John Simon, the infamously harsh critic for *New York Magazine*, was none too kind to both the play and the Louisville theatre from whence it came (even though Actors Theatre was not involved with the New York production). Not only did Simon trash the play "in entirely homophobic terms, but he also had tossed a stink bomb at Actors Theatre" by labeling Louisville the creator of the "latest trash" appearing on Broadway.[30] Simon's criticism that "Broadway might as well pack up and go rot in Louisville forever" became the talking point of the ninth festival, not only because everyone had read Simon's dismissive review but because Jory wore a button that displayed the quote.[31]

By wearing the button, Jory slyly acknowledged the criticism but also signaled his awareness of and response to a larger problem that had developed during the early 1980s. About a dozen Humana Festival plays had been produced in New York in the prior three years, and most failed to garner good reviews or audience support. One critic surmised, "This has engendered what Jory refers to as 'a certain crankiness among [theatre critics] with the Louisville product.'"[32] At a press conference during the ninth festival, Jory appeared "edgy and defensive" when several critics pressured him to respond to Simon's backhanded remarks. Instead of offering cheap retorts, Jory simply reiterated that Actors Theatre did not produce any of the shows in New York and that the Louisville theatre was satisfied if its festival plays traveled not only to Off Broadway but also to regional theatres around the country.

Regardless of Jory's dismissal of the criticism, many members of the national press focused on the Simon controversy and the negative reactions to festival plays in New York in their festival reviews. In his assessment for the ninth festival, *Los Angeles Times* critic Richard Stayton described the wave of negative reviews from New York critics as a backlash against Louisville, and numerous festival attendees agreed. New York producer Robert Pesola, who helped bring *Danny and the Deep Blue Sea* to Circle in the Square, concurred. "It does seem to be a trend for two years," Pesola explained, "that New York critics have begun holding a grudge against Louisville plays."[33] While some reviewers argued that these productions were simply "coasting on reputation, produced because they are 'Louisville plays' rather than works with individual merit," Julius Novick of the *Village Voice* offered a more practical perspective on the uproar: "Yes it's true that the last few plays to come in from ATL were badly received. Those who like those plays think there's a backlash. Those who don't like them think they were simply bad plays."[34] Jory's bold decision to wear the button signaled not only his ability to laugh it off but also his unwavering pride in his festival's plays being sent to New York.[35]

Needless to say, the annual press conference at the ninth festival was not fun for Jory. One attendee acutely perceived that "the constant pressures and critical carping were wearing him down. And one surmises that so much of his energy is expended on the *process* of the festival that the product is being neglected."[36] As much as Jory adapted his policies and actions to favor process over product, he knew that his play selections would face intense scrutiny from the national press after the successful eighth festival. Furthermore, he recognized that the best response to his critics would be to continue the achievements of the prior year. Unfortunately, the productions of the ninth festival did little to distract from the Simon controversy, as the critical responses only added to Jory's problems.

After answering the criticisms about "safe" plays by presenting both *Execution of Justice* and *007 Crossfire* during the eighth festival, the ninth one produced only one issue-oriented work and no play with an innovative structure or staging. The reason for this return to more traditional drama, however, was not intentional; each literary manager has stressed the inconstancy of the quality of scripts from year to year. Although Actors Theatre always received politically themed plays for consideration, the literary staff labeled most of them "topic" or "newspaper" plays because they simply recounted and reacted to the events of the previous year.[37] After producing two controversial plays in the eighth festival, Jory wisely resisted reactionary "headline" theatre simply to appease the critics; he knew that the resulting plays might be substandard scripts. Once again, Jory reaffirmed his priority for quality of product over popularity with the press.

The absence of topical scripts and the overwhelming dissatisfaction with the traditional plays in the 1985 collection, however, forced the theatre to travel into new territory.[38] Given Simon's criticisms and Jory's agenda to adapt the festival, the unequivocal failure of the ninth festival's productions provided further motivation for Jory to amend his play selection process, and his alterations had a long-lasting impact on the theatre and its reputation. Well aware of the questionable quality of productions that his ninth festival would be presenting, Jory announced a monumental change in the submission policy during the run of the Humana Festival, perhaps hoping to steal some of the focus away from the dreadful shows.[39] No longer allowing only unproduced scripts to be considered for the national play contest, Jory announced for the Tenth Humana Festival that "second production" scripts—plays that had already been produced once elsewhere and therefore would receive their second (yet first major) productions in Louisville—would be accepted and considered.

This minor adaptation of the submission guidelines may seem like a tedious detail but it in fact resulted in three noticeable changes within the festival and in the practices of producing new plays around the country. First of all, for the Louisville festival, the change in the submission requirements was a major decision, one that Crutcher overwhelmingly endorsed.[40] She said the decision to allow second-production scripts was long overdue and that the theatre needed to change its mentality. After initial good fortune with such critically lauded plays as *Extremities*, *My Sister in This House*, *Agnes of God*, *Getting Out*, *The Gin Game*, *Lone Star*, and *Crimes of the Heart* in its first five years, the festival entered a period when fewer plays traveled to New York, the most notable from the latter half of the first decade being Emily Mann's *Execution of Justice*. When New York stopped being the ultimate goal for Humana productions, the emphasis shifted to helping the playwright become established.[41]

Jory himself took the initiative to find out how best his festival could serve playwrights. Learning from playwrights that it was more difficult to get a second production of a new script than it was to find a willing producer for a premiere production, Jory decided to address their concerns. Crutcher credited Jory's decision with validating the theatre's reputation as a home for playwrights:

> I think that it became more of a writer's festival. As the years went by, it began to be more about process than product. In the beginning, it was very much about product, which is why we allowed the change, the change of allowing plays to have a second production. Jon always likes to be first—he's highly competitive. He wanted to be first, and he realized that he couldn't be. . . . [He realized] that a lot of plays got done once and then died. And by picking a play that had already been done once and then doing it again, he could not only give the play another life but he could also give the playwright another chance. And I always thought that that was pretty visionary for him to do that, because he had to give up being first. But for a while, it was "Well, we'll do it if it hasn't been done in any big theaters anybody would have heard of or seen." So you were still first, even though you weren't really first.[42]

The new goals of the festival helped Jory abandon the desire to find plays that could transfer to New York. Once Jory began pursuing his new agenda of adaptation and the festival became more process-oriented, the selection of plays began to change—no longer was Jory looking for ready-to-produce scripts. Instead, he was more willing to select plays that featured unique structures or daring writing and language and to allow the play to be developed further in the rehearsal process (as opposed to entering the process as a finished product).

Second, Jory's decision to allow second-production scripts not only helped the theatre's reputation but also fulfilled a need. This minor alteration in submission guidelines greatly increased the number of acceptable scripts and further promoted relationships with established playwrights and others who for the first time considered Louisville as a place to premiere their work.

Since most festival plays did not travel to New York or to other regional theatres, playwrights were familiar with the challenge of finding a second production. Gary Leon Hill's *Food from Trash* received only one other significant production after its run at the Humana Festival: a 1993 Chicago production by the American Theater Company. Several plays from each Humana Festival struggled to live beyond Louisville, and Jory's decision to support second-production plays mirrored a concern by artistic directors around the country. Jory even joked about second-production plays in a mock interview conducted with himself:

> Q: What is the primary need of the contemporary playwrights?
> A: A second production.
> Q: And the second most important need?
> A: A *good* second production.[43]

The decision to allow these scripts was also an act of necessity for American playwriting. Every year after a Humana Festival, many writers accepted offers to write for television or film, leaving the smaller paycheck of theatre commissions behind. Jory's minor alteration addressed a nationwide concern of how to keep playwrights committed to writing for the theatre and how best to support their work.

Jory was not alone in his efforts. Stressing the importance of developing long-term relationships with playwrights, the artistic director of Florida Studio Theatre, Richard Hopkins, argued that supporting multiple productions of a playwright's work allowed "the artist's whisper to become a voice," and artistic directors nationwide agreed.[44] In an interview with the *New York Times*, Ensemble Studio Theatre's founder and artistic director, Curt Dempster, articulated the importance of helping playwrights with a second production: "We've gone after people whose careers we feel should be salvaged. We say, 'We're going to produce this play for you, even though it has problems, because you're a gifted person.' It's like a logjam . . . [and] we do a lot of that logjam removing here."[45] Actors Theatre altered its submission policy in an effort to answer this national call to help playwrights hone their craft while working in an encouraging environment.

Finally, Jory's decision to allow second-production plays radically altered the perception of what makes a hit play. As Jory once suggested, plays may travel around the country from regional theatre to regional theatre yet never enjoy a production in New York City. That such a play received multiple productions made it a hit for the playwright and possibly led to other offers for work. This broadening of the definition of a hit not only let Actors Theatre share credit with other theatres in the development of new plays but also denied theatre critics such as Simon the opportunity to impact trends in playwriting, especially if a writer's work already had been produced successfully around the country. Several plays from the Humana Festival had been considered hits before ever playing New York, including *God's Man in Texas*, *Keely and Du*, *Anton in Show Business*, and *A Piece of My Heart*, to name a few. Proving that this new mentality benefited playwrights both in and out of the festival, Jerome Lawrence's hit drama *The Night Thoreau Spent in Jail* never played on Broadway yet has been performed in regional theatres across the country and has sold almost half a million copies.[46]

Now a hit would be based on whether it helped the playwright find an income and future work, as opposed to whether it had value for a producer.[47] By helping a playwright's work receive a second production, Actors Theatre aided in the development of a new mentality whereby playwrights no longer needed to travel to New York to gather supporters or financial security. Instead they could choose to develop a respectable career by presenting their works at a variety of theatres around the country. Artistic directors at other regional theatres approved of the changes made by Jory and his staff and followed suit.[48]

Jory's decision to allow second-production scripts was a logical and necessary maneuver, and he complemented this decision with another alteration in the theatre's play submission policy. Having received upwards of three thousand submissions each year for the festival and now being prepared to accept even more with the addition of second-production scripts, Jory needed to find a way to relieve the workload and time constraints on the literary department. After analyzing the history of the plays produced annually at the festival, Jory, Crutcher, and others discerned that almost every play included in the Humana Festival either had received a previous workshop or other nonprofessional production or had been submitted by a literary agent. Soon after this realization, Actors Theatre adopted a new restriction that all submissions come from either a literary agent or a playwright whose work has already received a production. Thus annual submissions dropped to between seven hundred and nine hundred scripts.

Obviously, this alteration angered many writers who had never broken into professional theatre; they argued that Jory no longer supported playwrights. But Jory's resourceful decision protected his festival and helped it further evolve into an event that favored its writers. Jory limited the number of submissions to ensure the happiness of his literary staff and the quality of support they afforded to the festival playwrights and their work. Since the Humana Festival remained the largest new play festival that promised productions, Actors Theatre continued to promote itself as the "playwright's theatre," even though it shunned many unproven playwrights with its new submission guidelines.

Actors Theatre, however, was not alone in its new policy—other regional theatres familiar with producing new work also amended their submission guidelines to reduce the number of unsolicited plays. In her history of the Circle Repertory Company, Mary S. Ryzuk explained, "It must be pointed out that statistically, the unsolicited manuscript process actually had limited success in terms of immediate result and product. During the five years of the Literary Department's heyday, only two unsolicited manuscripts ever made it all the way to mainstage production."[49] Manhattan Theatre Club, which previously devoted itself to the development of new plays, also stopped accepting unsolicited scripts in the mid-1980s.[50] Evolving into a national trend, similar restrictions on new play submissions became the standard policy of many regional theatres, including the La Jolla Playhouse, the Alliance Theatre, the Seattle Repertory Theatre, the Guthrie Theater, the Alley Theatre, and the Long Wharf Theatre. Regardless of criticism from disgruntled playwrights whose plays did not meet the new submission requirements, Jory and his staff completed their play-selection process and anxiously awaited the arrival of the anniversary edition of the festival, hoping to regain any critical support it might have lost from the previous year.

THE FOURTH ALTERATION AND THE TENTH FESTIVAL

After three major changes in three years—the inclusion of the playwright in the rehearsal process, Jory's allowance of artists and staff to take more responsibility and risks, and the acceptance of second-productions scripts, combined with the new submission restrictions—Jory had taken major steps in transforming his festival's emphasis from production to play development in hopes of decreasing the impact of any ridicule from New York theatre critics. Nevertheless, Simon's infamous criticism still affected Jory and his Louisville festival into the tenth festival, as other reviewers scrutinized the festival's efforts to discover another hit play. Critics anxiously awaited the new productions, yet some pessimists in the press prepared to pronounce the beginning of the end for the festival. In fact, Lee Blessing remarked that the critics from the *New York Times* lay in wait, eager to continue the

Louisville backlash by deriding the failures of the tenth festival. Blessing believed that editors and writers for the famed newspaper hoped to benefit from the festival's demise, adding, "I think they woke up to the fact that they didn't want a competing platform, a competing showcase. They want to take control of what is 'officially' good and what was done."[51]

After the abysmal ninth festival, Jory knew that he needed to discover a new talent or play. Unfortunately, the most memorable aspect of the 1986 festival could be how unremarkable it was. In fact, little is worth discussing, and this absence of achievement or impact was the tenth festival's greatest failing. With two questionable festivals in a row, Jory knew he needed to further adapt his play discovery process. Once again, Jory made a major announcement during the run of the festival, this time revealing his final alteration of the four-year phase: the end of the national playwriting contest.

The Great American Play Contest ended in 1986 for three reasons: first, Jory asserted that a contest for first-production plays was no longer necessary. As a result of his previous decision to allow the submissions of second-production scripts, Jory surprisingly announced that the top priority of the festival was no longer the discovery of new talent but the development of long-term relationships with playwrights. During the 1986 festival, Jory argued that Actors Theatre was sufficiently familiar with the talent pool of writers thanks to the Humana Festival, the National One-Act Contest, and other new play workshops around the country that had been created in the wake of Louisville's success. According to Jory, "I don't think there are as many violets blooming unseen. Instead, I see at least 1,000 authors concentrating on writing for the theatre. . . . We no longer need to identify talent in full-length plays."[52] The cancellation of the Great American Play Contest helped bolster the criticism of Jory as a prejudiced producer who favored certain established playwrights.

In response, Actors Theatre argued that the National Endowment for the Arts, as well as other corporations and foundations, provided sufficient funding for new works, but NEA funding decreased within a few years, lessening the competition that Actors Theatre faced from other new play development workshops. Nevertheless, with the decision to end the Great American Play Contest, Jory completely abandoned his initial desire to "be first." More important, this alteration signaled the extent to which the Humana Festival had become an institution in American theatre. Given its stature as the premiere new play festival in the country, Actors Theatre assigned the responsibility of discovering new talent to smaller theatres, expecting them to send their plays to Louisville for inclusion in a collection. By alleviating his theatre of this responsibility, Jory once again emphasized the importance of process over the discovery of a commercial product.

The second reason for the discontinuation of the contest reflected the Humana Festival's impact on the workings of Actors Theatre: Jory needed to adapt further the theatre's submission policy because he believed that the annual contest placed too great a strain on the literary department. Crutcher recalled, "We spent so much time reading through them, and I think Jon thought that our time could be better used."[53] Furthermore, the contest never directly translated into successful scripts, only an increase in submissions. Thanks to the acceptance of second-production scripts, the number of high-quality plays being sent to Actors Theatre increased, making the Great American Play Contest unnecessary. Even though prior festival plays such as *Food from Trash* resulted from the competition, the repeated mixed reception of these award-winning plays failed to prove that the contest ensured quality. Jory further relieved the burden on the literary department by allowing them to spend more time with festival playwrights in the rehearsal and development process and less time wading though the hundreds of submissions.

With less time spent wading through scripts, the literary department turned their attention toward another challenge, leading to the third and final reason for the elimination of the national play contest: the creation of a new festival and the hiring of Michael Bigelow Dixon as literary manager. First conceived in 1985, the Brown-Forman Classics in Context Festival was created "to revitalize dramatic literature's masterworks for today's audience by examining the social, political, and aesthetic contexts of their creation."[54] In conjunction with other Louisville arts organizations, Actors Theatre's Classics in Context Festival featured presentations on and productions of Italian comedy and tragedy, the Romantics, the Victorians, Moliere, Thornton Wilder, Pirandello, and even Anne Bogart.[55] Each festival provided several productions—full-lengths and one-acts—as well as lectures, films, and other exhibits to provide information and discussion about the impact of a particular period, artistic movement, or style.

The Classics in Context Festival may seem product-oriented, but like the Humana Festival, the new venture focused on process as well, one with which Actors Theatre was not quite familiar and that necessitated another change that affected the Humana Festival for many years to come. Because the literary department now engaged in academic research and writing for the Classics Festival, the new challenges of experimenting with a quasi-academic event, coupled with the responsibilities associated with the Humana Festival, signaled the need for a literary manager who could manage both festivals. Crutcher offered her perspective on the new demands on the literary manager, explaining, "I have a bachelor's degree in theatre . . . and I don't have a master's degree in dramaturgy. All of a sudden, we were doing this really esoteric, academic [work]. We really took this turn. I would have had to go back to school to [work on] the classics. . . . At that point, I couldn't take on a project like that."[56] With Dixon's dramaturgical background from the Alley Theatre and South Coast Repertory, he "came ready-made," according to Crutcher, and was "perfect" for handling the new Classics in Context Festival. "In an ideal situation," Crutcher lamented, "I could have stayed and done the new plays work, and he could have done the Classics [Festival]. And that would have been a perfect world, but it isn't a perfect world, and it was the Classics Festival which, frankly, Jon was interested in."[57]

With her dismissal, Crutcher offered a different explanation for the creation of the festival, boldly claiming that Jory was no longer as "invested" in the Humana Festival as he had once been. "I think frankly he got bored," she reported, "[and] I think he had felt like he had taken it as far as he could take it. He had done all the things that he wanted to do." Dixon, however, staunchly refuted Crutcher's claim that Jory lacked passion after the tenth festival, declaring, "Not only do [his concerns] remain the same, but they remain as intense as they ever did. . . . And I don't think that it's changed. Some of the expressions of it might have changed a little bit, but not much. He's still as smart and concerned a producer as he's always been."[58] Few people on the Actors Theatre staff doubted Jory's dedication to the new play festival.

Similar to Crutcher upon her arrival at Actors Theatre, Dixon retained King's criteria for judging new plays, but he also instituted major changes in the functions of the literary department. Dixon's vast experience as a dramaturg with both new and classic plays led to an expansion of the literary staff's influence beyond the Humana Festival, as they now performed additional dramaturgical services for the Classics in Context Festival, the ten-minute-play showcases, and the regular season. Before Dixon arrived in Louisville, the literary staff did not provide dramaturgical assistance for any of the regular-season productions except for program notes. If the director wanted to change something in the script, no literary staff members were consulted; the stage manager simply kept a record of the changes. With Dixon's arrival, dramaturgical support became an integral part of the rehearsal process for every Actors Theatre production: the literary staff conducted a fifteen-step process to determine how best to support a production and its artists through analysis, editing, and research.[59]

By reducing the burden on the literary department with the cancellation of the national playwriting contest and by creating the Classics in Context Festival, Jory again emphasized the importance of process. Even though the Classics Festival was separate from the Humana Festival, the decision to explore the contribution of dramaturgy to all aspects of the theatre's season directly derived from the new emphasis on process for the new play festival. Regardless of whether Jory maintained or lost interest in the Humana Festival, his fourth adaptation during this phase stressed the necessity of dramaturgical support and training. In terms of the Humana Festival, this emphasis translated into a more experienced staff and greater assistance for playwrights throughout the rehearsal process. In addition to his prior decisions to include playwrights in the lengthy rehearsal process and to accept second-production scripts, Jory's termination of the national playwriting competition confirmed that he and his staff followed a new agenda—choosing to help playwrights selected for the Humana Festival continue to hone their craft instead of expending considerable time and resources on locating new plays.

Most reviewers, however, disregarded Jory's new emphasis on process and continued to judge the festival solely by its productions; theatre critics from around the world complained about the current state of the festival. "Who knows if passion will come in the next decade of the [Louisville] theatre," lamented Lawrence Christon of the *Los Angeles Times*. "Right now, the thrill is gone."[60] Jory, however, was up to the challenge. Dixon's arrival in conjunction with the adjustments made by Jory throughout the product-to-process phase helped the producing director stop the growing perception that the festival was in decline. Emboldened by a new optimism concerning his festival's operations and his staff, Jory led his institution and its annual event into the next phase: an experimental period marked by decisions that challenged conventions and led to some of the most controversial productions in the festival's history.

6   THE EXPLORATORY YEARS, 1987–93

After four years of perfecting his festival's modus operandi, Jory took comfort that his efforts to improve the play development process resulted in a more efficient and experienced staff. Addressing playwrights' concerns was all well and good, but it did little to ensure audience support for the festival or critical acclaim for the productions. Heading into the second decade of the festival, Jory now had to address the perception that interest in the event was waning.

On the other hand, having spent the first six years of the festival securing its future and fine-tuning its operations, Jory could now enjoy the fruits of his labor. With the demise of the Great American Play Contest, the staff of Actors Theatre now relied on agents, veteran playwrights, and smaller theatres with play development workshops to filter good scripts to them. But if the literary department believed that the reduced number of submissions meant an easier workload for them, they were mistaken. With Michael Bigelow Dixon now on board, Jory asked him to help reinvigorate the new play festival. Knowing that good scripts would work their way up the ladder to Louisville, Jory set his sights on bolder creative endeavors for the festival, expecting his literary department staff to help him in following a new agenda of "exploration through experimentation."

Each new exploration would not only satisfy a personal interest of the producing director but also keep the festival relevant (and thus retain the interest of the national press). By no means did Jory succeed in all of his efforts during this phase—in fact, the various demands on him by critics, producers, and patrons cast Jory in a "damned if you do, damned if you don't" role. For instance, critics demanded more experimental work yet complained that the festival did not live up to its glory days of commercial success. In addition, the latest work of well-known playwrights attracted patrons to Louisville, yet the national press argued that Jory did not discover enough new talent. While Jory tried to appease several groups, he wisely understood that he could never satisfy everyone; therefore, he satisfied himself first by exploring his own artistic inclinations. Furthermore, he realized that he would be wasting his staff's talents if he did not explore new challenges in playwriting (a new endeavor of the reputed playwright's theatre).

For the next seven years (1987–93), Jory and his theatre engaged in numerous artistic and financial experiments that either benefited or burdened the theatre. Knowing that several of his explorations would meet with criticism, he persevered in his reinvigoration of the festival. Marked by explorations into new genres and other endeavors, the most notable and controversial experiments of the Humana Festival's latest phase began with an announcement from Jory, after the disastrous eleventh collection, about one of the most anticipated productions in the history of the festival.

EXPLORING PLAYWRIGHTS

If Broadway producers and *New York Times* critics felt threatened by the Humana Festival's ability to create lauded works outside their sphere of influence, the New York theatre establishment must have deplored the trends of the mid-to-late 1980s, when the Great White Way became less a home for the ingenuity and talents of America's best theatre artists and more an assemblage of lavish productions of questionable merit. The Tony Awards reflected this change: when the Humana Festival began in 1976, *A Chorus Line* and *Chicago* (both developed in New York) received nominations for best musical, but when the Louisville festival entered its eleventh year, imports *Les Misérables* and *Starlight Express* vied for the award as Broadway's best. This change symbolized a trend occurring throughout the American theatre as producers of both Broadway and regional theatre searched for new voices and talents to adorn their stages.

In 1985 *The New York Times* revealed the theatre establishment's insecurity when the article "On Broadway, the Accent Will Be Decidedly British" not only expressed amazement at the number of new faces on Broadway but also detailed the confusion about the failure of productions involving longtime Broadway personalities such as Harold Prince and Ben Vereen and the success of transfers such as *Big River*, which sold out nightly. According to another *New York Times* article, this one appearing in 1990, approximately one-third of Off Broadway's plays and musicals premiered in New Jersey alone before transferring to New York. Both of these articles listed import after import while also saying that many of the best American playwrights were no longer featured on Broadway.[1]

To remedy the dearth of new material originating in New York, producers around the country explored a wide variety of mediums to discover new voices in the American theatre, evidenced by folk musician Roger Miller's *Big River* and the increased presence of minority writers on Broadway.[2] Producers mined workshops and play festivals for potential projects, turning away from traditional drama and choosing instead to explore new writers, new genres, and new subject matter. For example, Joseph Papp's search for Asian American playwrights for his theatre resulted in the eventual prominence of David Henry Hwang, and Lloyd Richards consciously searched for black dramatists for his National Playwrights Conference. On the opposite side of the country, South Coast Repertory Theatre initiated a drive in 1986 to discover Hispanic playwrights with its Hispanic Playwrights Project, citing that few playwriting programs "recognized the Latino community as a source for unique and contemporary work."[3]

When Jory cancelled the Great American Play Contest after the tenth festival, he argued that his familiarity with the playwriting pool and the increased opportunities of playwriting workshops made the Actors Theatre competition unnecessary. The unfortunate eleventh festival, however, had no new playwriting discoveries or popular works, and critics questioned Jory's willingness to take risks on new talent. Without the contest, Jory mimicked the New York producers by scouring other regional theatres for quality scripts, but he also engaged in numerous controversial commissioning projects that promoted Actors Theatre's dedication to new playwrights while assuring the visibility of the festival.

At the end the eleventh festival, Jory proclaimed a new direction for the next annual event. He announced at a press conference that the theatre would undertake a new experiment by not only commissioning works from established playwrights such as Marsha Norman but also encouraging novelists to write plays, namely Susan Sontag and Jimmy Breslin. Besides the continuation of Jory's interest in the dramaturgical challenges of transitioning from prose to playwriting (e.g., Marsha Norman's evolution, Jory's own adaptations of literature for the stage, and the few Humana Festival productions of literary adaptations), the commissioning of famous novelists and journalists to write for the annual event helped maintain the visibility of the Humana Festival on a national level.[4]

Many playwrights, however, severely criticized Jory and Actors Theatre for paying nontheatre artists large sums to write plays while many talented playwrights struggled to be noticed. Even some of the playwrights who participated in the eleventh festival reported "guarded optimism" about Jory's new proposal. Grace McKeaney, author of the eleventh festival's mediocre *Deadfall*, quipped, "I hope it doesn't put a lot of playwrights out of business."[5] Even though Jory and company commissioned famous writers in part to attract attention to the festival, the new experiment elicited negative responses from the theatre's staff. Crutcher disapproved of the practice, arguing that it tarnished the theatre's reputation as a "playwright's theatre," sacrificing principle for popularity. "I think Jon was trying to find a way to make Humana still [marketable]," Crutcher claimed. "So I think . . . they thought that Humana would be big with name recognition—if you get the big names, then there's the Humana name, and the big names will recognize the big names."[6]

In spite of understanding the motives behind Jory's new commissioning experiment, Crutcher disagreed with his decision, characterizing it as "a big slap in the face to playwrights everywhere." While she understood Jory's desire to attract larger audiences with high-profile writers, she objected to the disproportionate commissions, explaining, "By saying, 'Look, we're gonna give these novelists $10,000, and we'll give you $500.' . . . I just thought that that money was just so misdirected, so misdirected. And I thought the reason it was done was wrong."[7] Many playwrights agreed with Crutcher, wondering why Jory chose to commission nonplaywrights. The detractors failed to consider that the new commissions also provided new challenges to the literary department. By working with professional writers who were novices as playwrights, Jory and Dixon explored the difficulties of playwriting, thus preparing the literary staff to assume larger roles in the play development process (a skill necessary for later commissioning projects).

Regardless of his multifaceted reasoning for the new creative endeavor, Jory battled the press and outraged playwrights while defending his experimentation with the commissioning of novelists and journalists. One year after Jory's announcement of the star-studded lineup, the critics anxiously awaited the results at the Twelfth Annual Humana Festival of New American Plays. Unfortunately, only one of the three commissions came through—Susan Sontag decided that this was "not the right year for her," and Marsha Norman's play was designated a workshop production.[8] Thanks to the most contentious decision made by Jory during his leadership of the festival, his wish to explore challenges in playwriting would not go unfulfilled: one play in the twelfth Humana Festival intensified the debate about his new agenda.

Due to the uproar over Jory's experimental commissions, the most anticipated production of the 1988 festival was Pulitzer Prize–winning columnist Jimmy Breslin's *Queen of the Leaky Roof Circuit*. Breslin's play details the struggle of Juliet Queen Booker, a single mother of two who is determined never to live in federal housing again, but she is in trouble with her landlord for refusing to pay rent, demanding that he fix the leaky roof in her apartment. Even with numerous rewrites, the script still needed work, according to reviewers, who argued that "nothing ever happens" in Breslin's play and that the characters existed simply as points of view rather than believable human beings. Labeled "a big disappointment" and "a social drama of the worst kind: all self-righteousness and no morality," Breslin's play was blasted by critics for its lack of craftsmanship.[9] Mootz humorously jibed, "As a playwright, Breslin is still a great columnist." Regardless of the critical dismissal of Breslin as a playwright, Jory's publicity ploy with popular writers worked—attendance at the festival, as well as during the regular season, jumped significantly.[10]

Jory took pride in the diverse collections of the twelfth festival, boasting about his experimentation: "We need to keep changing—messing around, if you will—to keep this process fresh to us artists."[11] Jory and his staff also relished the challenges inherent in exploring nonplaywright dramaturgy, as he and his staff learned a great deal from the 1988 festival. *Queen of the Leaky Roof Circuit* certainly was an educational experience for Michael Bigelow Dixon and his staff, who struggled to teach the fundamentals of playwriting to novice playwrights commissioned by Jory. A challenge cited by Dixon was teaching the established writers "what can't be done in the theatre. They have uncensored imaginations. They don't ask the producerial [*sic*] questions."[12]

Taking little notice of the other six productions in the 1988 festival, critics disparaged Breslin's flawed play and Jory's commissioning experiment. Throughout the festival weekends, the national press barraged Jory with questions about his determination to commission established writers, but he defended his decisions, asking one critic, "What's the difference between a new writer for the American theatre and Jimmy Breslin? No one's place is being taken by these commissions. We're still producing a festival with numerous scripts."[13] After weathering a storm of negative press, Jory was pleased that the overall critical reception of the twelfth festival was decidedly more positive than that of the previous offering, and he was determined to continue his artistic experiments with the thirteenth collection. At the close of the Twelfth Annual Humana Festival for New American Plays, Jory announced more commissions—from E. L. Doctorow, William F. Buckley Jr., Arthur Kopit, Erica Jong, and Harry Crews—to attract attention to the annual event. As in the previous year, only a few of the plays actually made it to the Louisville stage for the festival.[14]

The most anticipated production of the thirteenth festival, like the previous one, was a commissioned play by a famous novelist. Conservative pundit William F. Buckley Jr. adapted his own spy novel *Stained Glass* with hopes of receiving better reviews than Breslin's work. Unlike Breslin, Buckley was unable to attend every rehearsal, since he vacationed in the Swiss Alps during the beginning of the development process. Because of his absence, the director faxed notes to Buckley, and he responded between ski runs. Unfortunately, Buckley resembled Breslin in his playwriting talents. The national press blasted his play, arguing that Buckley failed to create interesting, viable characters. One critic complained that the central character was more like a postal worker than a James Bond spy.[15]

With the thrashing of *Stained Glass*, the chorus of criticism continued against Jory and his search for new voices. The controversy reached fever pitch with an article in the Sunday edition of the *New York Times* titled "Louisville Tries Noted Authors as Playwrights," which focused solely on the questionable motives behind Jory's commissions. Written by Hilary

DeVries, the article followed Buckley through the rehearsal process (when he was in town) and debated, with other playwrights and theatre professionals, the commissioning of authors. The article presented damning arguments against Jory's practice by numerous people, including Constance Congdon, the author of *Tales of the Lost Formicans*, a play included in the thirteenth festival along with Buckley's spy drama.[16] Congdon complained that Jory's commissioning of writers "doesn't send an encouraging message to a new playwright or someone like me, who's been writing for a decade but still not supporting herself."[17] The article said commissions were "known to run from $12,500 to $25,000—the highest among the nation's nonprofit theatres," and DeVries cited several writers and directors who argued that the theatre's recent commissions represented "a misuse of the theatre's limited resources and a thinly veiled pitch for publicity in the wake of several lackluster seasons."[18] Adding to the controversy, DeVries reported that many actors and directors participating in the Humana Festival—speaking on the condition of anonymity—believed that all playwrights should be paid the same fee for participating in the festival.[19]

Jory responded to the increasing criticism through word and action. First, in the *New York Times* article, Jory defended his experiment by "testily" arguing, "We can't make it nice for everybody. Our position is 'We're looking for work,' not 'We're supporting playwrights.'" Jory continued his defense by explaining his perception of the current state of American playwriting, declaring, "This is simply not a rich enough period in the history of the American playwright that we can afford not to try a lot [of different ways to find new writers]. It seems to me that if a writer has demonstrated a certain facility in one discipline, it would at least be interesting to try and translate that ability to the stage. . . . The name of the game is ultimately finding good work."[20]

Jory provided the best possible defense of his experimental commissions by directing one of the hits of the festival, a commissioned play by acclaimed novelist and professor Harry Crews. In *Blood Issue*, Crews presents Joe Boatwright's return to Georgia for his family reunion, hoping to free himself "from the ghosts of the past." A successful freelance writer and world traveler, Joe clashes with both southern culture and his family members as dark and dirty secrets are revealed. Crews's ability to capture the dialect impressed critics: "Crews' dialogue reflects a regionalism colored by casual profanity and rigid sociological stance. But one detects a sincerity that doubtlessly reflects the way many families have at it when only the members are present."[21] Critics questioned the production's length, but most reviewers praised Crews's "knife-blade wit," Jory's solid direction, and the talented ensemble cast, featuring Anne Pitoniak.[22]

With the success of Crews's play, Jory discovered the ammunition that he desperately needed to fend off critics and continue to support his experiment of commissioning novelists. The success was muted, however, by Crews having proclaimed to DeVries for the *New York Times* article that Jory should not have awarded him a commission. Crews admitted, "I'm not an established playwright, and if I can't get into a regional theater on my own, then I probably don't belong there."[23]

Undaunted, Jory enlisted novelists to write plays for the fourteenth festival, but each writer failed to deliver a play. After enduring two years of failed commissions, as well as disappointing reviews for a majority of the plays that were completed and produced, Jory's experiment ended, partially confirming the barrage of criticism by the national press (Jory would later say, "You would have thought I had hung my mother in public").[24] In fact, many of the endeavors inspired by the producing director's desire to pursue his own artistic inclinations—including his exploration for new playwrights—eventually ended because of negative critical responses or excessive funding demands. In spite of the substantial publicity about the controversial plays, Jory was forced to discontinue the commissioning of nonplaywrights, in part because of the increasing cost to the theatre (turning novelists into playwrights via full productions being an expensive method of teaching).[25] The extent to which the overwhelmingly negative critical responses to the productions influenced this decision is debatable. If the controversial productions were commercial and critical successes, then Jory might have found a way to continue producing them for the festival in spite of the cost.

Thankfully, not every attempt by Jory to discover new playwrights was controversial. In fact, after he abandoned his quest to elicit works from nonplaywrights, Jory's exploration for new writers continued in the 1992 festival with a proposal for the commissioning of high-profile playwrights, as well as the discovery of new talent. The sixteenth collection featured a new commissioning experiment, commonly called the "paired-playwright project"; Jory commissioned one established playwright to pen a one-act on a specific theme and then allowed that playwright to commission another writer of his or her choosing to compose a companion piece.

With great potential for publicity and for the discovery of new writers, Jory's first foray into the paired-playwright experiment succeeded on several levels. After the sensation of the Tony Award–winning play *M. Butterfly*, Jory commissioned the play's author, David Henry Hwang, to write a play about race and identity. The resulting play, *Bondage*, takes place in an S & M parlor, where two characters dressed head to toe in leather costumes play out their fantasies. Hwang raised racial issues in terms of erotic fantasies: Are they playing at being Asian or African American? Would assuming another race make the fantasy more erotic? Would their true racial identity make a difference in their relationship? In addition to these questions, "his play expands in emotional content, mocking racial attitudes and the easy racial clichés people invent to dignify their prejudices."[26]

Paired with Hwang's play under the title *Rites of Mating*, Suzan-Lori Parks's *Devotees in the Garden of Love* featured two women, a mother and her daughter, dressed in wedding attire, who wait on a mountain while men battle to the death on the plain below for the hand of the daughter in marriage. Although Parks's play suffered by comparison with Hwang's, *Rites of Mating* achieved the desired effect for Jory: the experiment of paired commissions successfully allowed Jory to attract established, popular playwrights who, by writing one-act plays, could be paid a smaller fee. Furthermore, the project supported the notion that Actors Theatre discovered new talent even though Jory himself did not choose several of the playwrights.[27] Unlike his short-lived decision to commission novelists and journalists, Jory's paired-playwright project continued outside the festival's exploratory phase and allowed Actors Theatre to premiere the latest works of Tony Kushner and John Patrick Shanley.

More important than bringing some of Jory's favorite writers to Louisville was satisfying a call by critics to present a larger number of minority playwrights in the festival. During the first three years of the paired-playwright project, Jory commissioned gay and lesbian, African American, and Latino playwrights in a concerted effort to diversify the festival. While critics wondered why he did not include such playwrights more often (a common misperception, because he often did), the fact is that Jory often commissioned playwrights whom he favored or had developed relationships with in prior festivals. Because of his festival's early struggles to find scripts, Jory desperately searched for *any* high-quality work, and the fact that the festival featured few minority writers at first was simply an unfortunate happenstance. Furthermore, many newly recognized playwrights had developed relationships with other theatres and their new playwriting programs (such as South Coast Repertory Theatre's Hispanic Playwrights Project), making Actors Theatre of Louisville less of a necessary stop for them.

While Dixon also recognized that the pressures of the festival forced Jory to select favored playwrights or writers with publicity potential, he argued that the commission projects proved worthwhile: "It got us plays. . . . Marsha Norman hadn't written a play in five years. . . . Novelists weren't the only part of it. It brought playwrights back to the theatre and made the theatre a home for writers of any genre, and I think that was valuable." In terms of the nonplaywrights, Dixon put a positive spin on Actors Theatre's commissions: "In retrospect, we know that Jimmy Breslin did not write a play afterwards without a commission, that Harry Crews didn't write a second play, that William F. Buckley didn't write a second play. So there are people in the world who are only going to write on commission, and we succeeded in getting them to write plays."[28]

Regardless of Dixon and Jory's reasoning, Breslin's play and others commissioned from novelists were by far the most harshly criticized experiment in the history of the Humana Festival. Usually so adept at knowing his audience and predicting trends in American playwriting, Jory was blindsided by the storm of criticism that followed the production of Breslin's play. For the critics who lay in wait, *Queen of the Leaky Roof Circuit* provided plenty of ammunition. In the end, Jory's experiment was simply that: an experiment. The commissioning of nonplaywrights failed to harm the festival in the long run, even though several critics still doubted the relevance of the event because of its diminishing impact on the yearly offerings in New York (about which Jory no longer cared).

Was it wise to have commissioned nonplaywrights when the money could have been used to commission struggling playwrights who already had a sense of the playwriting craft? Staff members avoided answering this question directly and instead described the commissioned plays as "experiments." While critics and disgruntled playwrights second-guessed Jory's commissions, the fact remained that the Humana Festival was *his* festival, and he had every right to guide the festival in a new direction. What these detractors failed to understand is that, in addition to securing an audience for his endeavors (via the appearance of high-profile writers in Louisville), Jory needed to provide his literary department with dramaturgical challenges to prepare them for his next series of experiments.

EXPLORING GENRES

With the festival still in the national limelight, Jory utilized his second exploration to appease critics who called for more nontraditional work. In keeping with his agenda of "exploration through experimentation," Jory diversified the festival's offerings by supporting work in two genres: docudramas and ensemble-created works. Actors Theatre's exploration of the docudrama began in earnest when the literary department assumed a vital role in the creation of several presentations. In his essay "The Dramaturgical Dialogue," Dixon writes that Jory initiated a series of docudramas focusing on the struggles of American farmers and the homeless. After the literary staff conducted research, including interviews, a commissioned playwright received the materials and created the dramatic text by adapting and editing the interviews, courtroom documents, transcripts, and other research materials. This process utilized the experienced dramaturg as a crucial participant in the creation of the piece, further increasing his or her importance in rehearsals but also blurring the line between dramaturg and playwright.

Dixon explained, "Because the research had been guided by the dramaturg's understanding of the passions, personalities, and issues, the dramaturg provided not only a critical perspective, but became a key contributor to the structure, metaphor, and themes of the dramatic event."[29]

Performed for only one night for selected guests of the eleventh festival in 1987, *Digging In: The Farm Crisis in Kentucky*, a commissioned docudrama cocreated by Julie Crutcher and Vaughn McBride with the support of a grant from the National Endowment for the Arts, resulted from two years of research and over seventy-five hours (fourteen hundred pages) of interviews. The duo staged an hourlong reading that featured six actors who described the hardships of farming in Kentucky, and at the end of the performance, Jory stood and asked for responses and suggestions about how to improve the script. While the piece impressed the Louisville critics, the national press was not as kind, believing the show would appeal only to local audiences.

In spite of its critical drubbing, *Digging In* was the initial offering in a long-term experiment undertaken by Jory and Actors Theatre.[30] Whereas *Execution of Justice* and *007 Crossfire* were the only docudramas in the festival's first ten years, *Digging In* initiated a five-year run of docudramas during the second decade.[31] Even though another commissioned piece for the twelfth collection (a musical exploring homelessness) failed, the next three years validated Jory's pursuit of the genre, as critics designated docudramas the hit plays of the festival, beginning with Steven Dietz's controversial *God's Country*, based on a true story about the violent white-supremacist group called the Order.[32] The fourteenth and fifteenth festivals presented a pair of critically acclaimed docudramas: 2 by Romulus Linney and *A Piece of My Heart* by Shirley Lauro, respectively.[33] These two plays fulfilled Jory's aim to present high-quality nontraditional work, with each receiving numerous awards, the most notable being an American Theatre Critics Association Award for Linney's work (the first for a Humana Festival play in nine years) and the Jefferson Award and the Barbara Demming Prize for Lauro's war drama.[34]

That Dietz's play and some later docudramas in the Humana Festival were not commissioned showed that Jory had accurately predicted a trend in American playwriting or that the work of previous Humana Festivals influenced many writers. For instance, Crutcher and McBride's *Digging In* was created long before Anna Deavere Smith presented her popular works *Fires in the Mirror* and *Twilight* in the early 1990s. The national attention paid to Actors Theatre's support for docudramas prompted further explorations of the form by playwrights in and outside the festival. Perhaps the greater number of docudrama submissions to the festival resulted from the belief by many playwrights that such work stood a better chance of being accepted.

It was no accident that as soon as the docudrama genre became widely accepted at the festival, Jory turned his attention elsewhere. (Commissioned docudramas rarely appeared in the Humana Festival after 1994.) Jory's new exploration, ensemble-created work, not only interested him personally but also challenged his literary staff. According to Dixon,

In 1991, Jory initiated a series of experiments in the ensemble creation of new work. To inaugurate that project for the Humana Festival, director and adaptor Paul Walker was commissioned to create a performance piece about the nineteenth-century antipornography crusader Anthony Comstock. With the aid of his cast and dramaturg Chiori Miyagawa, Walker deconstructed the published writings of Comstock and others. Their method imposed meanings on Comstock's text that differed radically from almost anything he might have intended. The result, ironically, was an entertaining performance that consciously distorted Comstock's words to show how he had purposefully twisted the words of his censorship victims.[35]

Receiving a response similar to that of Jory's earliest commissioned docudramas, the first ensemble-created piece in Humana Festival history, Paul Walker's *A Passenger Train of Sixty-One Coaches*, elicited mixed reviews from the press. Several critics denounced Walker's experimental production, claiming that the playwright never presented a believable character. In his review, Mootz claimed, "The work is more interested in calling attention to the theatrical chicanery of creator/director Walker than it is in giving dramatic credibility to a man who became a vivid symbol of American Puritanism run amok."[36] While a few critics described the production as avant-garde and engaging, most reviewers condemned Walker's handling of the material and questioned Jory's wisdom.[37]

Undeterred by the complaints from producers that his experiments had limited commercial appeal, Jory continued to explore ensemble-created work the following year. With this second attempt, he could have increased his chances for success by commissioning a playwright experienced with the genre. Instead, he commissioned a favorite scene designer to create "image theatre" in the mode of Robert Wilson.

For the sixteenth festival, in 1992, designer John Conklin explored ideas "inspired by issues inherent in Mt. Rushmore: public art and patriotic monuments on Native American lands, public funding of art, and the environmental impact of labor and tourism." Together with the cast and dramaturg, Conklin intercut poetry of William Carlos Williams into his play, *The Carving of Mount Rushmore*, in hopes of creating a choral effect. "The overall performance," Dixon explained, "flirted with hallmarks of Robert Wilson's work: a nonlinear construction, simultaneous action, and sense impression as a structural guide."[38] Again, critics were not receptive to the ensemble-created piece; most disapproved of Conklin's decision to isolate the actors from each other as they spoke randomly about the monument. One critic described the writing and performance thus: "The evening provides embarrassing testimony to his experience as a playwright and director. Actors wander around murmuring lines from poems, or declaiming excerpts from historical documents. . . . The result is dramatic bedlam."[39]

As with *007 Crossfire*, the critics failed to acknowledge that the conventions employed by Conklin were typical of experimental work written during the late 1980s and early 1990s. In his article "Experimental Drama at the End of the Century," Ehren Fordyce argued that the creation of such plays as *The Carving of Mount Rushmore* illustrated a new approach to playwriting at the end of the century. Anne Bogart and Charles L. Mee personified the growing trend of playwrights familiar with traditional dramatic forms and directorial approaches to such work. Fordyce labeled them members of "a generation of writers working after the rise of the director," those who created scripts in conjunction with a director or with a certain director in mind. Conklin's script also satisfied another of Fordyce's criteria for experimental work: "One effect of this trend is the writing of plays developed less with an eye to traditional considerations of dramatic structure (inciting action, narrative rise, tragic fall) and more attuned to the possibility of other structures; for instance, plays shaped by the architecture and history of a building."[40]

The critical dismissal of Conklin's work illustrated the difficulty Jory faced in finding approval for the experimental work of the festival. Although the national press called for edgier work, the experimental productions were often criticized for straying from conventional dramatic forms. Knowing that he could not appease every reviewer, Jory pursued his own agenda in reflecting a variety of playwriting modes on the festival stage, even if most critics failed to understand that these works were echoing trends in New York.

Hoping to finally strike gold with ensemble-created work, Jory increased the resources available for the next production, a multimedia extravaganza developed by director Brian Jucha. Described as "an exploration of virtue and sin" that blurred the delineation between the two, *Deadly Virtues* employed five actors who spouted references concerning sins and virtue from the Bible, Shakespeare, Shaw, Dante, opera, pop music, and contemporary newscasts. Mootz detailed the construction of the play, as well as the performance: "When *Deadly Virtues* deals only with jumbled texts, its skits run a narrow literary gamut between the solemnly pretentious and the portentously inarticulate. The evening exults in throwing up intellectual smoke screens, behind whose murky mists the performers strike extravagant poses."[41] Although several reviewers characterized the production as dull and "random"—*Variety*'s Jeremy Gerard called it "the longest ninety minutes in memory"—many critics appreciated Jucha's experimental effort but asked that the script be thoroughly edited and given a sharper focus.[42]

Much as the critically disappointing *Queen of the Leaky Roof Circuit* resulted from Jory's search for new playwrights, the plays by Walker, Jucha, and Conklin derived from Jory's desire to diversify the festival and to experiment with new genres even if they failed to please audiences. More important, Jory's exploration of dramaturgical challenges led the latest developments in American theatre, and these three productions opened the door for Anne Bogart, Naomi Iizuka, and JoAnne Akalaitis to present ensemble-created works for later Humana Festival collections. Bogart, who made her Humana Festival debut by directing Eduardo Machado's *In the Eye of the Hurricane* for the fifteenth festival, credited Jory's support of experimental playwriting—especially ensemble-created work—as a key to her development: "I am not a playwright, and yet Jon invited me to bring the kind of work I create with actors in my company and perform the result in a playwright's festival. This confidence in our idiosyncratic way of making plays gave me courage to move in exciting new directions."[43]

While theatre artists applauded Jory's exploration of ensemble-created work and nonlinear forms of writing, the press was often surprised and confused by his support of the genre. On the one hand, several critics blasted Jory for not presenting enough "daring" works, yet other reviewers criticized him for not producing Broadway-ready productions as he did in the early years. With this no-win situation, Jory wisely followed his own agenda.

FURTHER EXPLORATIONS

One of Jory's primary concerns when selecting plays at the beginning of this exploratory phase was that the "thrill" of the Humana Festival was gone. He hoped to reenergize the festival with a variety of artistic experiments. Valerie Smith said, "You have to be constantly aware that people are coming here year after year, and unless you find a way to jolt them a little bit to give them something to talk about, to write about, that it does become a habitual routine."[44] While Jory's high-profile commissions and explorations with new playwrights and new genres garnered national attention, he followed his personal preferences and catered to the public. These two minor experiments elicited vastly different responses and represented the extremes of success and failure.

In the publicity materials for the Eleventh Annual Festival of New American Plays, Jory proclaimed that the third production to premiere, Jonathan Bolt's *Glimmerglass*, would be the big-budget centerpiece. Perhaps inspired by the rash of novel adaptations on Broadway, including *The Adventures of Nicholas Nickleby* (in 1981 and 1986), *Foxfire* (1982), *Canterbury Tales* (1980), and *Wind in the Willows* (1985), Actors Theatre of Louisville explored the challenges of literary adaptation by commissioning a play based on James Fenimore Cooper's five Leatherstocking Tales, which followed the adventures of Natty Bumppo on the American frontier. Many critics wondered whether Jory would write the play himself, since he had expressed an interest in literary adaptations by utilizing two classic French comedies for his own *Tricks* and *In Fashion*.[45] When Jory announced that Jonathan Bolt, the author of the tenth festival's *To Culebra*, would adapt Cooper's tales, many critics wondered whether Bolt was capable of transferring Cooper's literary style and skill onto the stage.

To his credit, Bolt worked on adapting the five novels into one play for over a year, but he was forced to halt his writing when he was cast in two Actors Theatre productions in the winter. Although Bolt planned to revise the *Glimmerglass* script while Jory, as director, rehearsed the production, this hope proved impossible when Jory, because of a "conflicting personal time commitment," turned the directing reigns over to Bolt himself. Because of this last-minute change and the time-consuming responsibilities associated with directing, Bolt completed the rehearsal draft of the script only three days before rehearsals began.

While Bolt rehearsed the actors, crews constructed Paul Owen's elaborate set and the nearly two hundred costumes for the mammoth production, but in the midst of the rehearsal process, Bolt quickly realized that something was wrong: the theatrical style achieved in a bare rehearsal hall was completely at odds with the literal production elements, creating a "forced look of pageantry."[46] When the play opened for Louisville audiences in advance of the Theatre Professionals Weekend—the first of the two weekends specifically for out-of-town guests—local critics and audiences alike quickly dismissed the play, with one audience member declaring to *Courier-Journal* critic William Mootz, "If you find anything good to say about this [production], I'll never trust you again."[47] The Louisville critic denounced every aspect, including the set design by Owen, who usually received high marks. According to Mootz, Owen "created an ugly forest glade where treetops look like spinach leaves and forest trails seem made of AstroTurf."[48]

Mootz and other Louisville critics reserved their harshest criticism for Bolt, dismissing both his writing and his directing. Mootz described Bolt's play as "incoherent, lifeless and without a single character who enlivens the evening with the breath of human virtue" and Bolt's directing as "disastrously ineffective."[49] As for the performance, Mootz's blistering critique continued: "Actors paraded around in ill-fitting wigs. An Indian fell dead before one heard the rifle shot that supposedly killed him. Paths covered with artificial turf scuffed up and flopped about as settlers walked through forests. Rustic pioneer homes looked as if they had been constructed from a child's set of Lincoln Logs. Actors, searching in vain for a believable character to play, resorted to hammy theatrics."[50] Furthermore, Mootz railed against Jory's decision to commission the literary adaptation, complaining, "Armies on the march, Indians on the warpath, settlers on the rampage can be impressive when treated cinematically. But they almost invariably look foolish and under-populated on the stage."[51] One reviewer summarized opening night thus: "A fifty-year period is covered in three acts, but a patron may feel as if he has been in his theatre seat for the entire half-century."[52]

In spite of the horrific opening-night reviews, Bolt still believed he could salvage the show before the Theatre Professionals Weekend, but the constraints of the festival—most of the *Glimmerglass* cast was in rehearsals for other festival productions—prohibited any more rehearsal time. With no opportunity to fix the major problems, Bolt reluctantly agreed with Jory's decision to pull the big-budget show from the festival lineup after only five performances and before the national press arrived. Jory stated, "We didn't think it was useful to the play, to Jonathan or to the festival to put it on. . . . [*Glimmerglass* was] not living up to our expectations."[53] In a review for *USA Today*, Mootz agreed with Jory's decision to cancel the remaining performances, arguing, "Thankfully, visitors were spared *Glimmerglass* . . . [which] had all the dramatic intensity of a Boy Scout troop playing cowboys and Indians."[54] To this day, *Glimmerglass* remains a dark moment in Humana's history, and several staff members have treated the subject as taboo, refusing to talk about the abysmal failure.

Glimmerglass not only signified the start of a brief exploration into literary adaptations (soon ended with 1989's *Stained Glass*) but also revealed a limitation of the festival and of professional theatre at large.[55] According to Todd London's *The Artistic Home*, regional theatre directors and "independent artists alike are frustrated with a system that makes working on a production after it has opened almost impossible. . . . This rigidity reinforces the 'product' mentality artistic directors are determined to break out of."[56] Faced with the restrictive rehearsal schedule of the play development process, playwrights have taken their work to several theatres in hopes of revising the script. For instance, after receiving a workshopped reading at the O'Neill Center, August Wilson's *Fences* was produced at Yale Repertory Theatre, the Goodman Theatre, and the Seattle Repertory Theatre before premiering on Broadway. Unlike Broadway, where producers pushed back the opening date if a show needed additional work, the rehearsal and production schedule for the Humana Festival provided limited opportunities for exploration or correction, regardless of Jory's determination to support process over product. The modern production calendar does not allow for major alterations once a show opens, forcing many artistic directors to shy away from experimental work that might demand more time than usually allotted to a rehearsal process.[57]

If Jory's experiment with literary adaptation limited the festival, then his consistent support for Jane Martin's work during this phase expanded it: he allowed the playwright to explore new genres and new themes, redefining herself as a playwright in the process. Martin's first appearance in the festival after eight years (since the sixth festival in 1982) could not have been timelier. Given the questions about her identity, Martin reignited the authorship debate by participating in the Fourteenth Humana Festival, which celebrated female playwrights (six of the seven being women). With female domination of the festival (and the awarding of the Pulitzer Prize to Wendy Wasserstein for *The Heidi Chronicles*), questions about Martin's true gender and her ability to present an assertive female voice immediately made *Vital Signs* the most highly anticipated play that year.

To create a collection of monologues, Martin reportedly delivered approximately one hundred different pieces to Jon Jory, who selected the resulting thirty-four texts. While not every monologue was praised as a solid piece of writing, patrons expressed their favorites, and all reviewers praised not only Martin's mastery of the monologue form (though some questioned whether she could write full-length plays) but also Jory's direction and pacing of the show.[58] Regardless of the praise or criticism, most reviewers focused on the mysterious identity of Martin and continued to suspect the producing director.

In addition to her inclusion in a year dominated by female playwrights, the timing of the Louisville native's return was peculiar for a second reason. Todd London reported that artistic directors yearned to explore new artistic endeavors, and if the prior success of the festival gave Jory the freedom to explore (or revisit) artistic challenges through experiments, then playwriting easily would have satisfied those desires. After the success of Martin's *Talking With* in the sixth festival, little was heard from the playwright, yet once Jory felt secure in the festival's success and began to delegate more responsibility, he might have found time to experiment with writing plays under a pseudonym. In fact, he had already exhibited his desire and ability to write plays: in addition to numerous one-acts that Jory penned for apprentice showcases throughout the 1980s, Jory and his wife, Marcia Dixcy, adapted Charles Dickens's *A Christmas Carol* for Actors Theatre's annual holiday moneymaker, premiering in the 1989–90 regular season.[59] Furthermore, Jory would have learned early enough during play selection for the fourteenth festival about the numerous failed commissions. Even if Jory had been writing sporadically for numerous years, it would have been easy to assemble a collection of monologues. Regardless of whether Jory is or is not Jane Martin, it was wise for the mysterious playwright to rediscover playwriting through the familiar format of monologues.

Jory's support for Martin continued with the fifteenth festival in 1991, when she experimented with a full-length script for the first time. *Cementville* is the story of three professional female wrestlers stranded in a small

Tennessee town. Reviewers praised Martin's writing and unique characters (as they did for her previous work), as well as her daring theatricality. As with previous Martin presentations, however, the production was accompanied by further questions concerning the true identity of the playwright.[60] Critics quietly pondered the content of *Cementville*—featuring women in underwear—and asked what would inspire a female playwright to focus on such matters.[61] Several reviewers and staff members found the content to be too "masturbatory" to be written by a woman, saying that it evoked more a male middle-aged crisis than an honest exploration of women's issues.[62] One former Actors Theatre employee remarked, "There's no way that a woman could have written those plays . . . the wrestling one in particular where all the girls were out on stage in their skimpy little outfits. I mean, that was just one big masturbatory exercise was all I could figure. You would never ask a woman to be on a stage in her underwear. No fucking way. You would never do it. . . . [No woman] would."[63]

Regardless of the debate over authorship, Jory continued to support Martin's maturation as a playwright, as she turned away from monologues and quirky humor and began to explore social issues with resounding success. When Martin reappeared the following year, any questions about her identity were overshadowed by the phenomenal reception of her latest play. In April 1992, Operation Rescue had begun a series of protests outside Buffalo abortion clinics, eventually resulting in 597 arrests.[64] Almost a year later, the Seventeenth Humana Festival featured Jane Martin's best (and most controversial) play, *Keely and Du*.[65] While most reviewers predicted that the abortion drama would be the hit of the festival and would be produced around the country within the next year, critics wondered whether Martin's anonymity would hurt her chances of winning the Pulitzer Prize.[66] In the end, although the voting for the Pulitzer Prize is secret, members of Actors Theatre learned that Martin's play was initially designated the winner of the 1993 competition, but after a second round of voting, *Keely and Du* lost by only a couple of votes to Edward Albee's *Three Tall Women*.[67]

Both Jonathan Bolt and Jane Martin explored new territory with their respective literary adaptations and social dramas, but their drastically different experiences at the Humana Festival symbolized the uncertainty of the rehearsal process. Even though *Glimmerglass* was pulled to protect Bolt from the critics, he never again appeared in a Humana Festival (though even Breslin appeared in a later festival). On the other hand, Jane Martin represented success, and her exploration of new forms and themes in three works during this phase illustrated the festival's dedication to an individual playwright's career. As opposed to Breslin, who needed to be taught several fundamentals of playwriting, Martin needed only consistent support to hone her craft and to explore her potential as a dramatist. Her reemergence marked not only her growth as a playwright but also the beginning of her transition into a symbol for the festival. With her critically lauded plays and her mysterious identity, she came to embody the formula for the festival's success: part substance, part showmanship.

While the mixed results of Jory's numerous playwriting explorations might have hindered the growth of the festival, its traditional offerings helped the annual event remain the preeminent new play festival in the country. During this seven-year phase of exploration, the festival featured numerous lauded debuts, such as *T Bone N Weasel* by Jon Klein, *Alone at the Beach* by Richard Dresser, *Autumn Elegy* by Charles Redick, *Zara Spook and Other Lures* by Joan Ackermann-Blount, and *Marisol* by José Rivera. In addition to these hits, the latest work by Lee Blessing, Jane Anderson, John Olive, Kevin Kling, Regina Taylor, Lynn Nottage, Joyce Carol Oates, Marsha Norman, Lanford Wilson, Arthur Kopit, Constance Congdon, and Suzan-Lori Parks, among others, helped the Humana Festival retain national relevance. Thanks to the popularity of these playwrights, the continued success of the festival during this phase allowed Jory and his theatre to explore a product-oriented project in the form of new performance spaces. In addition to satisfying his playwriting curiosities through the Humana Festival commissions and play selections, Jory looked to please other artistic impulses while also expanding the Louisville theatre's production capabilities.

EXPLORING EXPANSION

The largest exploration (and risk) undertaken during the 1987–93 phase was a physical one that greatly influenced the future offerings of the Humana Festival. Even though Actors Theatre had played to near-capacity houses for many years, Jory eschewed expansion plans until he was assured of his theatre's and festival's continued success. By the end of the 1980s, Jory believed that the time was right to tout his theatre's success with the addition of a new theatre. In May 1990, Actors Theatre launched a $9.5 million building campaign titled "Casting the Future." The new construction would include a 420-space multilevel parking facility, additional backstage space, and a new arena theatre. Executive director Alexander Speer spearheaded the operation, overseeing the $12.5 million project and collecting most of the money through gifts and pledges: "In addition, a portion of the theatre construction was financed by a tax-free municipal bond issue ($4.275 million) to be repaid from pledges and garage revenues."[68]

Speer justified the decision to expand, stating that the theatre was financially sound in the mid-to-late eighties and was "doing well" in terms of its income and reputation. Actors Theatre's desire to expand because of its success was not a rarity, as financial security allowed several nonprofit theatres to expand their operations in the early 1990s. For example, with its growing success due to its Broadway transfers, the Roundabout Theatre opened its new space in the Criterion Center in October 1991, the Steppenwolf Theatre Company celebrated its growing popularity with the grand opening of its new theatre complex in April 1991, and after creating an experimental theatre known as the Guthrie Laboratory, the Guthrie Theater completed a $3.5 renovation project in February 1993.[69]

When the board of directors asked Speer and Jory to identify some needs of the theatre, they expressed concerns about the space limitations of the Victor Jory Theatre and their desire to "enlarge it and make it a more reasonable theatre to operate in." At the same time, the board of directors wanted to capitalize on an adjacent piece of property that functioned as a parking lot, debating which courses of action might result in the greatest income. "We decided to take a look at a fairly major development of the block that we were in, and we even acquired some additional property adjacent that we didn't own at that point . . ." Speer recalled, "and there were some conversations at that point [in time] whether should we remain in a downtown location [or] should we consider moving and selling the property."[70]

The numerous possibilities resulted in much "soul searching," that is, addressing current problems facing the theatre, as well as predicting the theatre's needs for the future. Speer explained, "[The] whole process began by taking a look at the Victor Jory Theatre within the supposed new development, and trying to see how we can make it work and enlarge it and make it a more reasonable theatre to operate in. And the more we worked on it, the more we felt that changing it would be almost as expensive as it would be to build a new space . . . and so then the idea of a third theatre came up. Jon was very interested in a different style of theatre—the possibility of working in the round appealed to him, just as a visual difference from what we already had. And so that was really how that came about."[71]

While the expansion project called for a remodeling of the backstage spaces of both the Pamela Brown Auditorium and the Victor Jory Theatre, construction efforts extended outside the theatre as well. The multilevel parking facility provided easy access for patrons, as well as needed income from daily users. The most notable change, however, was the addition of the Bingham Theatre, a large arena theatre that seated more than three hundred patrons. The new space allowed Jory to expand the festival's offerings and to explore artistic challenges by directing in a new space. He stated, "I happen to like the arena stage because as I get older, the less stuff there is on stage, the better I like it. So it makes me happy to see things basically done on a bare stage and a floor. I think there is some movement aesthetically within any artist toward a kind of austerity as you get older."[72]

When Actors Theatre announced the expansion project, Jory justified the move thus: "In 1972, we were a young company and our theatres were more than adequate for the skills we then possessed. But we have grown and matured in eighteen years. We are now stymied by our physical limitations."[73] Even though many staff members credited the building of the new theatre to the success of the Humana Festival, a few of them questioned the decision to build a third theatre. According to several staff members, the financial risk of expansion failed to pay off, because the company has never been able to fill the seats of the new theatre. In fact, several inside sources claimed that Actors Theatre went into debt due to overhead costs from the Bingham Theatre and led some to criticize Jory's judgment and to question Actors Theatre's financial standing.

One former employee, speaking on the condition of anonymity, stressed that the addition of the third theatre typified a larger problem within the theatre: Jory's incredible success with the festival gave him extraordinary freedom to run the theatre. According to the former staff member, "I don't think that there is anybody that will disagree with him. No one will say, 'This is the most stupid-ass idea I've ever heard in my life.' Nobody says that. . . . There's no disagreement." Although Jory consulted Michael Dixon and Sandy Speer on literary and financial matters, he reportedly enjoyed far-reaching control over all operations of and decisions about the theatre, as well as great sway over the board of directors. However, he may deserve such influence, given that he salvaged the theatre and directed the institution to its national and international acclaim. Nevertheless, according to former staff members, the theatre lost money "hand over fist" because of the expansion, though the financial burden was lightened by income from its new parking garage. In hindsight, argued one employee, the theatre should not have built the Bingham Theatre, claiming, "They can't keep the audience. It's too much. They should have two and not three theatres."[74] In other words, these critics believed that any benefits derived from Jory's exploration of a new performing space did not outweigh the long-term financial burden to Actors Theatre.

Regardless of whether the deficit was a major concern, the expansion of Actors Theatre gave Jory the ability to experiment with a new space while also allowing the theatre to solve practical problems and better manage the repertory offerings of the festival. After seventeen years of producing the Humana Festival, Jory discovered new ways to experiment with the festival though commissioning new authors and exploring new genres, but—in terms of directing and design—Jory and his staff exhausted all the possibilities provided by the Pamela Brown Auditorium and the Victor Jory Theatre. While any $9.5 million campaign involves risk, Jory's desire to expand the festival and the theatre's offerings through a new performance space was a logical step in the growth of the theatre.

More than any other time in the history of the festival, this unique phase of exploration is marked by a change in the critical perception of Jory's leadership of the festival. Whereas skeptics greeted his prior decisions to cancel the Great American Play Contest and to allow second productions with a wait-and-see attitude, they were aggressively unwilling to let the producing director alter the festival's offerings and challenge the critics' expectations. Because the early success of the festival led critics (especially those in the New York establishment) to an initial and faulty assumption that Jory created the festival to send production-ready scripts to Broadway, the national press questioned the relevance of the Humana Festival and denounced many of the experiments undertaken by Actors Theatre. Certainly critics needed to evaluate the offerings of the festival, but their staunch resistance to Jory's explorations exposed a bias held by a majority of them who refused to accept Jory's changes or attempted to dictate the content of the Louisville festival. On the other hand, the heated responses perhaps revealed a feeling of ownership of the festival by the national media, which would further the perception of the festival as a national event and suggest that Jory failed to meet his responsibilities as a producer by exploring his own artistic projects.

Regardless of the critics' motivations, Jory and his staff took advantage of their resources and pushed the limits of the festival (and, in turn, the critics). Even though the national press complained about Jory's new direction for the festival, every decision he made during this phase derived from his sincere efforts to improve the festival while also satisfying his artistic curiosities. Critics pointed out, however, that Jory's record of accomplishment with experimental fare was mixed at best. His support of the paired-playwright project and ensemble-created work continued for many years, but several of his explorations were critical disappointments. His interest in exploring literary adaptations in the Humana Festival ended with *Glimmerglass* and *Stained Glass*, and his concerted effort to commission novelists and journalists for the festival also failed.

In Jory's defense, Breslin's *Queen of the Leaky Roof Circuit* was by no means the worst production in the history of the festival. The controversy surrounding the play, however, created an intense response, and even though it may never be produced again, it symbolizes Jory's explorations, as well as the difficulty he encountered in expanding the artistic aesthetics of his festival. Nevertheless, these seven years of exploration represent Jory at his freest, secure in the continued success of the festival through his commissions of established playwrights but also able to explore new genres and unproven playwrights. On the other hand, the 1987–93 festivals also found Jory at his most defensive, perhaps surprised by the level of resistance from theatre critics and professionals to his explorations.

That Jory refused to rest on his laurels by producing one traditional play after another but instead opted to challenge his staff and playwrights deserves commendation. The producing director maintained the visibility of the festival by appeasing interests of both critics and audiences, but his greatest assets were his own artistic passion and curiosity that motivated him to pursue his own agenda. While some experiments failed and others succeeded, Jory remained determined to continue a few of his experimental commissioning projects. Yet as he guided the festival into the next phase, Jory seemed to have lost some of his drive. After seven bold yet difficult years, the Humana Festival of New American Plays had survived unscathed and headed into its eighteenth year and a period marked by a lack of innovation.

7   FALLING INTO A RUT, 1994–98

After Jory's exploratory phase, critics again complained that the festival lacked the novelty and energy of its early years. Even though some harshly attacked Jory for his experiments, many soon called for him to return to his exploratory agenda. Jory ignored them. This is not to say that subsequent festivals received less than their fair share of critical praise; in fact, the next five festivals produced several Susan Smith Blackburn nominees and winners, American Theatre Critics Association winners, an Obie Award winner, and the festival's first Pulitzer Prize–winning play since *Crimes of the Heart*. Still, many critics considered the output from Actors Theatre routine in comparison with the experimentation of the previous phase.

For his part, Jory spent the seven years of the prior phase pushing writers and challenging theatrical conventions, only to find his efforts chastised and unappreciated by the national press, who often concerned themselves with what would be commercial or with work that was playing at the regional theatre close to home. Jory understandably lost interest in exploring genres and playwrights after numerous years of harsh criticism, and the continued success of the festival allowed him simply to follow national trends.

Jory's decision not to push the envelope ushered in a new phase of reluctance and redundancy—the only period in the festival's history when Jory and his staff apparently were content to rest on their laurels. This conservatism gave credence to the "shopping mall" criticism. The dismissive label derives not from the critical reception to the annual offerings but from the festival's intentions with the plays. In the earliest years of the festival, reviewers often bandied about the term "shopping mall for plays" when Jory focused on producing more commercial and New York–ready scripts. When the festival became more experimental, the perception of the event as a shopping mall waned, but after Jory's extraordinary exploratory period and before his last two years at Actors Theatre, when the festival was filled with controversy and buoyed by national attention, the relatively tame 1994–98 collections offered little ingenuity or variation. Three factors explain why the festival fell into a rut: the predictability of the plays Jory selected, the limited quality of the plays available to him, and his susceptibility to other events in his theatre. Although Jory certainly was responsible for all of the festival decisions, events outside the Humana Festival influenced (and limited) his options.

DISTRACTIONS AWAY FROM THE HUMANA FESTIVAL

The festival fell into a rut largely because of Jory's activities outside the Humana Festival. Former literary manager Julie Crutcher once claimed that Jory lost interest in the Humana Festival, but another former literary manager, Michael Bigelow Dixon, staunchly disagreed with that statement. Even if Jory was not uninterested in the Humana Festival, as Crutcher proposed, he was distracted by other events at Actors Theatre. After the press criticized Jory for his experiments with the Humana Festival, the producing director continued his exploratory inclinations through the creation of a third festival. Out from under the microscope of the national press, this new venture allowed Jory to explore different forms of playwriting and performance while building Actors Theatre's audience base.

In the months following the close of the Seventeenth Annual Humana Festival of New American Plays, Jory and his theatre inaugurated the Flying Solo and Friends Festival, a collection of solo performers and performance artists presenting their work in the Victor Jory Theatre. Seizing on the increasing popularity of the solo-performer genre in the 1990s and again proving Jory's ability to predict national trends, the festival annually received as many as three hundred submissions (which would eventually plateau at 150 to 200). According to former literary associate Valerie Smith, who served as the "main filter" for the submissions to the festival, "The solo performer genre was very big for a while. . . . We got some truly fine work that I don't think we would have seen otherwise. So I think that for in-house and for a certain percentage of the Louisville community, it really meant something."[1] Similar to the Humana Festival, the immediate success of the new festival prompted other organizations to follow Actors Theatre's lead, evidenced by the Kentucky Center for the Arts' decision to invite solo performers throughout the year (but not in the context of a festival).[2]

Given that the Classics in Context Festival attracted academics and that the Humana Festival, with its national reputation, brought critics and theatre professionals to Louisville, Jory hoped that this new festival would entice younger audiences to the theatre, and he selected performers, including Danny Hoch, Lisa Kron, Tim Miller (three times), Roger Guenveur Smith, Kevin Kling, and Jane Comfort, who might best attract new patrons. Dixon expected the work to appeal to particular "subcultures in Louisville" and said youth audiences were a main target (especially with the selection of Hoch's critically acclaimed *Some People* in 1995), along with "multicultural-specific, sexual-orientation-specific, age-specific [senior citizens], or experience-specific [World War II]" or politically inclined audiences.[3]

Rejecting the "Danny Newman hard-sell" philosophy of marketing to the white, middle-class demographic, Jory and his staff presented work that would bring diverse crowds to the theatre. But the Flying Solo and Friends experiment lasted only five years owing to disappointing audience support.[4] Smith said that because of the solo performers, Actors Theatre "found the gay audience" but struggled to attract African American audience members. Although Jory and his staff were encouraged by initial support, audience attendance plateaued, suggesting that the Flying Solo Festival had discovered all the local patrons that it would attract. Smith expressed her disappointment in the theatre's inability to entice new patrons to the theatre. "We never really found the audience," she admitted, "and I'm not quite sure why we didn't. Maybe it just wasn't possible."[5]

Unlike the steady progress Jory achieved when building his audience to support his new play festival, the challenge of enticing new audiences to the theatre through the solo performer festival proved more difficult than Jory anticipated. The demise of the event represented a rare misstep by Jory in building trust with local patrons, as he misjudged the level of support the Louisville community would deliver. For the Humana Festival, Jory spent years preparing and educating local audiences to support new work; for the solo performance festival, however, his commitment of time and energy was less, and the idea of a solo performer in a small theatre apparently appealed to only limited numbers of patrons. To employ a metaphor from an earlier discussion, the Flying Solo and Friends Festival marked a rare occurrence when Louisville theatergoers simply opted not to go on a "walk down a forbidding path" with Jory.

The second distraction from the Humana Festival, the Classics in Context Festival, also met its demise in 1998 but for different reasons. Since its inception, the Classics in Context Festival blossomed into a citywide celebration of the arts. All of the major arts institutions in Louisville (the J. B. Speed Museum, the opera company, the symphony, etc.) participated in the year's theme, and each provided an educational dimension to their presentation, allowing Louisville patrons a unique opportunity to understand the political and social construct that inspired the works of art. Even though Actors Theatre received some funding from Brown-Forman Corporation, the expiration of a grant from the National Endowment for the Humanities made the festival too expensive to continue.[6]

Given his theatre's explorations of the solo-performer genre and his continued support for the Classics in Context Festival, Jory did not need the Humana Festival to satisfy his artistic inclinations. The timing is too coincidental to be dismissed: the creation of the Flying Solo and Friends Festival in 1994 and the demise of both festivals in 1998 encapsulate the same period when the Humana Festival suffered from an absence of vision and a decrease in experimentation. With the closing of both the Flying Solo and the Classics in Context festivals, Jory faced no further distractions within his own institution, allowing (or forcing) him to refocus his creative energy on fixing a major problem of his new play festival—its banal plays.

JORY'S PREDICTABLE AND CONVENTIONAL PLAY SELECTIONS

During this 1994–98 phase, Actors Theatre presented fifty-one plays in its Humana Festivals, but only two of these scripts have become contenders for admittance into the American canon of playwriting: Tony Kushner's *Slavs!* and Donald Margulies's *Dinner with Friends* (the first Pulitzer Prize–winning festival play since *Crimes of the Heart*). While many of the remaining plays presented between 1994 and 1998 received high praise, all of Jory's selections contributed to a period when the festival presented similar types of plays year after year. This characterless approach to the festival was inconsistent with Jory's reason for creating the event—to further the development of American playwriting—yet Actors Theatre seemed content to absolve itself of that responsibility and to become a follower (and not an instigator) of trends. With the predictability of these collections, the festival became less of an event and therefore less important. For example, each collection featured a variety of conventional dramas and comedies, including a surprise hit (e.g., Naomi Wallace's *One Flea Spare* and Joan Ackermann's *The Batting Cage*), a failed debut (Guillermo Reyes's *Chilean Holiday* and a trio of plays in the 1997 festival), a triumphant return of a Jory-favored writer (Jane Martin's *Middle-Aged White Guys* and Wallace's *The Trestle at Pope Lick Creek*), a name-recognition commission, a disappointing homecoming for a veteran playwright (Marsha Norman's *Trudy Blue* and Jane Martin's *Mr. Bundy*), a one-hit wonder (Susan Miller's *My Left Breast* and Wendy Hammond's *Julie Johnson*), and a token experiment.[7]

These categories were not intentional, yet the fact that each year offered the same type of work reinforced the notion that Jory and his staff were content to maintain the status quo. The festival's lack of an aggressive agenda for this five-year period, however, did not mean that the event did not enjoy great success. On the contrary, the yearly number of hits kept the festival well attended by patrons and critics. This phase featured stunning debuts by Wallace, Naomi Iizuka, and Anne Bogart, as well as several hits that appeared around the country, most notable among them being Jane Martin's *Jack and Jill*, Stephen Dietz's *Private Eyes*, Richard Dresser's *Below the Belt* and *Gun-Shy*, and Ackermann's *The Batting Cage*. Success, however, often comes at a price, and for the Humana Festival, the cost of Jory's play selection was that the festival stopped serving as a signpost for the direction of American playwriting.

Whereas prior phases altered the festival's purpose to suit Jory's artistic inclinations, the perception of the festival during this phase changed because playwrights now viewed the festival as simply another opportunity for them to be seen and heard. Granted, many playwrights relished the opportunity to have their work performed in front of hundreds of critics, but without Jory's vision, the Louisville festival now operated like any other new play development opportunity (only larger in scale). In other words, the Humana Festival became a place of business rather than a home for ingenuity.

No evidence bears this out more completely than the high number of name-recognition commissions Jory utilized during this phase and that these commissions often resulted in traditional plays as opposed to experimental forms. Given the reduction in innovative work during this five-year period, these high-profile commissions became the focus of the festival, even though they often were only ten-minutes long. Ten-minute plays by Craig Lucas, David Henry Hwang, Romulus Linney, and Tony Kushner enticed patrons and critics to attend the festival in droves, yet each of these works seemed an obvious attempt to remain in the national spotlight. Not all high-profile playwrights enjoyed success, however, as exhibited by the "disappointing homecomings" of Marsha Norman (*Trudy Blue*), Jane Martin (*Mr. Bundy*), and John Patrick Shanley (*Strange Encounters*, later renamed *Missing/Kissing*).

With its commercial commissions and its reliance on traditional fare, the Humana Festival was perceived to have gone stale. By ignoring new artistic endeavors and refusing to explore challenges that faced playwrights, Jory let his festival slip from a position of leadership to one of passivity. No longer setting the future direction of American playwriting, the formulaic play selections during this period revealed how much the festival depended on Jory for its creativity and innovation. Liz Engelman, former literary manager of the McCarter Theatre and Seattle's A Contemporary Theatre, agreed with this perception. "I think [the focus now] is much more on the playwrights," Engelman explained. "It is 'Look who is coming out of Humana this year' versus 'Look at what Jon Jory is bringing to the world.'"[8] While the purpose of the festival might have changed temporarily, its reputation and popularity did not wane during this phase, in part because of happenstance events that helped the Humana Festival remain the nation's premier new play festival.

LIMITATIONS IN THE TALENT POOL

A former literary manager once lamented that the quality of the scripts presented in each year's Humana Festival depended on the scripts that came in the mail. If such was the case (Jory's decision not to commission more experimental fare notwithstanding), then Jory's predictable play selections resulted from a lack of inventive or progressive plays during the mid-1990s. Actors Theatre of Louisville was not the only regional theatre to be criticized for its uninspired presentations. The growing influence of the Theatre Communications Group during the 1980s and early 1990s led to the homogenization of regional theatres. Because numerous theatres utilized TCG's casting service, the same actors often were employed in productions around the country, and because institutions often sought counsel from the same advisors recommended by TCG through its visitation program, artistic directors followed similar philosophies.

Furthermore, the popularity of Danny Newman's hard-sell marketing approach resulted in many regional theatres not only employing the same marketing tactics and playing to similar audience demographics but also using the same slogans to advertise their organizations.[9] Not only did these theatres share marketing strategies, but institutions interested in new work often shared writers as well. With plays traveling from theatre to theatre to undergo further development, many works became conventional in an effort to appeal to a wider audience. Jory easily could have remedied this problem by commissioning writers to experiment with new genres and forms (as he had in the past), but he opted to avoid controversy by withdrawing from his endowed leadership position and relying more heavily on other play development programs.

The growing homogeneity of product limited Jory's ability to discover inspired new work, but the predictability of the festival productions mirrored a national trend. Just as the Humana Festival plays received great acclaim yet failed to inspire new developments in American playwriting, the Great White Way underwent a similar transformation which, in turn, affected development opportunities in regional theatres. Broadway no longer was a home for accomplished new playwrights; legitimate theatre suffered from "Disneyfication," the predominance of predictable yet financially successful presentations produced by corporations without regard for advancements in the musical form.[10] Exploring the relationship between major corporations and Broadway, James Traub's *The Devil's Playground: A Century of Pleasure and Profit in Times Square* argues that because many corporations, including Disney, utilized the advertising and investment opportunities provided by Times Square to "confirm their status as world players," they also began to support Broadway productions and the development of works in regional theatres.[11]

Citing the influence of Disney and Clear Channel, critics, including Frank Rich, complained of the corporatization of Broadway, that is, the predictability of its product and big businesses' primary desire for profits rather than artistic merit. In his book *On Broadway*, Steven Adler writes that corporations' desire to discover and develop works affected not only the artistic offerings on Broadway but also those in the nonprofit market. Given regional theatre's never-ending pursuit of funding, corporations utilized the power of their purse by selectively supporting productions with an expectation for commercial success. Corporate sponsors often discouraged experimentation, as they focused on product, not process. Artistic directors, well aware that unpopular results might eliminate further support from their corporate donors, favored projects with greater commercial appeal. Even though businesses supported individual productions, Rich argued that these newly formed partnerships proved detrimental for the theatre at large. He cautioned that "a not-for-profit's mission is compromised when it collaborates with commercial producers, for whom the institution's long-term health may not be a primary consideration during the production process."[12]

Unfortunately, playwrights whose work was not attractive to Broadway producers also found dwindling opportunities in the regional theatre landscape, further limiting the number of high-quality, innovative scripts available to Jory and his new play festival.[13] Cuts in funding from the National Endowment for the Arts affected theatres across the country, and some institutions were forced to close.[14] Because a decrease in the number of regional theatres limited new play development opportunities, many theatres looked to replace the NEA monies with ticket sales by producing more commercial work. For those theatres that did receive NEA funding, the organization's tendency to withdraw support from "obscene" art reinforced the mentality that only works with commercial appeal or artists with a popular following would win various grants. Todd London once wrote of this change, "The impetus to break away, found, and pioneer has been replaced by the need to maintain, hold on, secure."[15] Once again, the economic realities of American theatre in the 1990s failed to encourage ingenuity in its writers.

As funding dwindled, so did the talent pool of writers that Jory claimed to have known when he cancelled the Great American Play Contest; successful playwrights left the theatre profession and moved to Los Angeles for larger paychecks. For Actors Theatre, the Humana Festival's success had become a double-edged sword. Just as Louisville theatre enjoyed the publicity that the discovery of a new writer or a film adaptation of one of its plays brought, attendance at the festival by Hollywood producers hoping to spy and steal new talent also hindered Jory's ability to retain the best playwrights and encourage them to write for the stage.[16] Knowing that Hollywood representatives flocked to the festival, many playwrights now simply perceived the event as a stepping-stone to greater fortune, not just an opportunity to hone their craft in hopes of securing future commission from other theatres.[17]

The culmination of these various limitations—the homogeneity of product, corporate-driven development agendas, and the shrinking talent pool of playwrights—hindered Jory and his literary staff from finding quality scripts.

Not only did this absence of originality result in predictable offerings, but the growing importance of commercial-driven productions outside the Humana Festival limited the practicality of Jory's experimental phase. Theatre critics who bemoaned Jory's decision not to pursue an aggressive, exploratory agenda failed to realize that his support of traditional plays during this phase was consistent with his desire to aid playwrights, to help build their careers by moving their work to other regional theatres and obtaining future commissions. If artistic directors were succumbing to the financial pressure to present more traditional works that would compete with touring shows and other forms of accessible entertainment, then Jory's experimental fare might have been critically acclaimed but not have received a second production in another theatre. The work of Anne Bogart during this phase demonstrates this problem: her plays routinely received rave reviews, but given the complexity of her productions, few regional theatres produced it after its premiere at the Humana Festival. As a result, Jory selected (often by commissioning) only one experimental work per festival to demonstrate the variety of theatre presentations and to satisfy critics; however, during this five-year phase, such innovative work took a backseat to more traditional forms that allowed Actors Theatre simply to follow national playwriting trends.

PREMIER BY DEFAULT

Throughout the seven years of the exploratory phase, Jory utilized his experiments to maintain a place in the national spotlight for the festival. Furthermore, competition from a groundswell of new play development opportunities motivated Jory to appease critics and remain relevant by commissioning and supporting more daring and experimental work. After sixteen years, however, the festival was in a privileged position. The final reason for the festival's falling into a rut is decreasing competition from other new play development programs. That factor contributed not only to Jory's decision to follow national playwriting trends but also to the freedom that he felt to create other festivals.

Attempting to mimic Actors Theatre's early success, numerous other theatres explored new play development. Julie Crutcher recalled how quickly other play competitions arose around the country: "For a while, it was first-production frenzy. Everybody wanted to find that [one hit]. They wanted to find the play that would be the breakthrough play that would go to New York and would make you money. But there were only so many of those [plays] around."[18] It is not surprising that several of these theatres miscalculated the time it took to build an audience, find financial support, and locate staff qualified to work on new plays, and many of these development opportunities quickly folded. Valerie Smith discussed the emergence of new play programs, recalling, "There were a whole bunch of festivals cropping up all over the country. It went through that phase, and now once it didn't pan [out], a lot of those festivals have been dropped. So the fact that we're continuing to do this, that we're continuing to get corporate support for it, is really incredible."[19]

Michael Bigelow Dixon concurred with Smith's assessment of the demise of many new play programs, saying that several of the new play festivals created during the mid- to late-1980s folded, including ones in New Haven (Winterfest), Denver, and Seattle, as well as the California Play Festival through South Coast Repertory Theatre. The trend continued in the 1990s, when Theatre Communications Group reported that "the output of workshops and new play development programs had dropped sixty percent" within the first three years of the decade.[20] Although these and other festivals closed, Dixon explained that other opportunities still existed for playwrights. "In their place have cropped up a number of play-development circumstances," Dixon argued, "so the opportunities for getting plays read and workshopped have probably expanded, [but] the opportunity for getting plays produced has probably decreased."[21]

Thanks in part to the declining number of new play productions in regional theatres, the intense pressure to succeed abated during this phase. The Humana Festival remained the preeminent new play festival by default, and its offer of fully realized productions, as opposed to workshopped readings, remained a rarity in American theatre. For instance, the Alabama Shakespeare Festival initiated in 1991 a play development workshop devoted to discovering and supporting southern playwrights. Considered one of the Humana Festival's leading competitors, the Southern Writers Project and its Festival of New Plays offered only a few fully produced plays in addition to its staged readings and workshops. Two other major and well-respected competitors, PlayLabs at the Playwrights' Center in Minneapolis and the National Playwright's Conference at the Eugene O'Neill Theatre Center, have contributed plays to the Humana Festival, but these two events presented only workshops and readings.

Given the lack of competition from other new play development programs, Jory used the guaranteed national spotlight on his festival to further promote Actors Theatre as a "playwright's theatre." While the Louisville theatre's devotion to its writers never wavered, it was apparent to many theatre professionals and critics that the so-called home for playwrights was not as important a breeding ground for ingenuity and creative exploration as it once had been. Although Actors Theatre presented a few experimental plays during the 1994–98 festivals, the perception of the festival having fallen into a rut applies to these five years. The predictable selection of plays, the commercial and critical success rate for each festival, and the "event" feeling created for each festival were indistinguishable from year to year. By not pursuing experiments through commissions, Jory removed himself not only from any controversy but also from the festival itself. More than at any other time in its history, the Humana Festival simply followed playwriting trends, as opposed to serving as a leader of American playwriting by challenging conventional writing and performance practices. Without a bold agenda to criticize, the national press turned their attention away from Jory and toward the festival playwrights, allowing the writers to become the true focus of the event and allowing Jory to focus his time and energy on other projects.

At the close of the Twenty-Second Annual Humana Festival of New American Plays in 1998, Jory had no other festivals to distract him. Knowing that his departure from Louisville would occur sooner rather than later, he turned his attention back to the Humana Festival, which was in a rut. While Broadway increasingly offered uninspired, Disneyfied shows such as *Aida*, *Hairspray*, and *Mamma Mia!*, and regional theatres continued to curtail their play development programs, Jory was about to emerge like a phoenix from the ashes, once again becoming a force to be recognized and respected. No longer resting on his laurels, Jory began planning for the final festival of the millennium, determined to provide a fresh and exciting experience unlike that of any prior festival. The astonishing results would re-create the enthusiasm of the early days of the festival and relegate the "predictable" years to the past, while breaking new ground in playwriting.

8   THE LAST HURRAH, 1999–2000

Shortly after the twenty-second Humana Festival in 1998, visitors to the literary office would have been distracted by a large flip chart featuring scribbled drawings of coffee cups, sleeping heads, pieces of cake, bottles of liquor, and a few other doodles. Placed in four rows, this assortment of doodles was Michael Bigelow Dixon's attempt to explain the predictable and boring routine of the visitor's experience at the Humana Festival. As Dixon pointed to each figure, he traced a spectator's journey, from her arrival, through a series of repeatable events—eating food, watching a show, getting a drink, watching another show, getting some sleep, eating more food, and so on—until her eventual departure (represented by a plane). Facing growing criticism that the festival was no longer an "event" after two years of mediocre collections, Dixon utilized the flip chart as a motivational tool. He used it to prod his literary staff to think of ways to enliven the festival, part of a theatrewide effort to revitalize the organization's signature event. After years of routines and the formulaic offerings of the last five festivals, Jory was ready for a change, and his staff followed suit.

The last years of Jory's reign as producing director of Actors Theatre of Louisville were a wonderful period of creative freedom, experimentation, and sweeping changes, best exemplified by his final two Humana Festival collections leading up to and including the twenty-fourth anniversary. For this phase, Jory decided to celebrate the potential of theatre by not only recognizing the art form's ability to engage audiences through a variety of performance mediums but also commemorating theatre's past achievements, as well as its bright future. As part of his celebration, these two years presented a different "last hurrah" for Jory—a last burst of experimentation and a final salute to his festival. This final phase under Jory's leadership found the festival unintentionally retreading history when it again became more about Jory than about the productions. The difference between this phase and the "lucky" years was that Jory did not need to garner attention as he did twenty years earlier. For his last hurrah, Jory reacted to the lackluster festivals of the "shopping mall" phase by experimenting, advising, and bidding farewell.

Always concerned with the national reputation of the festival, Jory regained his position at the center of the limelight in both years, and when he bowed out as the longtime producing director of Actors Theatre, he showed that he knew how to leave in a blaze of glory.

CONTROVERSY OVER THE FINAL EXPERIMENTS

Dixon's flip charts worked. In fact, the rejuvenation of the twenty-third Humana Festival—or the attempt to "unstodgy" the event, as Jory put it—worked so successfully that it overshadowed the varied success of the six major presentations.[1] Mirroring the motivation behind Dixon's flip charts, Jory discussed the need for innovation at the annual event in an interview with journalist Rich Copley:

> I sort of said to important people who work here, "You know, I went to the festival last year, and it sort of felt like the festival the year before that and the festival the year before that." So I think we consciously decided to change the atmosphere a little bit. In a certain sense, we keep trying stuff. It's sort of like evolution. Some of it grows up to be a humanoid and some doesn't. What it has given us is an idea that dramatic form doesn't have to be constricted by the endless idea that people come buy their tickets and sit in the theatre for two-and-a-half hours to see a play.[2]

The reputation of the festival and the national press's constant clamoring for more experimental work were reason enough for Jory to revitalize the event. To challenge conventional theatrical practices, Jory and Dixon explored actor-audience relationships through a variety of new formats; their effort resulted in the most sensational audience response in years, as well as frequent dismissals by critics.

For the prior festivals, the beautiful Sara Shallenberger Lobby served as a functional space for the festival and its patrons; the voluminous hall provided guests with easy access to all three theatres and was the site of the Saturday night postshow festivities during the two big festival weekends. The large lobby—with its off-white walls, high, arched ceilings, and collection of paintings—was a holding pen where patrons quickly grabbed a drink from the cash bar or small-talked other guests while they waited for Actors Theatre volunteers to open the doors for a performance. For the 1999 festival, however, Jory transformed this lobby into a venue, meaning that presentations of the Humana Festival were no longer confined to the stage but were everywhere, all the time. This space became the center of activity for the twenty-third festival's VIP Weekend, as the three playwriting and performance experiments were all within easy reach of patrons passing through the lobby.

The most controversial presentations were on display (and for sale) at the Actors Theatre Bookstore, a temporary structure in the lobby that allowed theatergoers to purchase books by Humana Festival playwrights, both past and present. High on the wall behind the shelves of books rested the T(ext) Shirt Plays, a series of short plays printed on the backs of T-shirts, in theory allowing the wearer of a shirt to become a performer. Dixon conceived the idea for the T(ext) Shirt while reading scripts during his business trips and vacations: "I just kept looking up on the back of the person in front of me, and I thought, 'It would sure be easier if the play was just written on his back.'" Fascinated by the relationship of the text to the new "performer," Dixon argued, "It's the flipside of the normal relationship to the actor, to dramatic text, to audiences. Normally, the actor speaks the text to the audiences. This way, the text is externalized."[3]

The decision to celebrate theatre's potential to engage audiences by presenting plays as T-shirts received mixed and confused responses by many national critics. Michael Grossberg of the *Columbus Dispatch* assailed the T(ext) Shirts as a gimmick and a shallow marketing ploy in his review of the festival weekend, arguing, "I would urge Actors Theatre to be more clear: A 'T-shirt play' is *not* a play; it is merely an upscale T-shirt. . . . What a waste of talent and cotton."[4] While several reviewers blasted Jory and Dixon for their claims that the shirts signified a new mode of performance, almost every critic enjoyed reading the plays by the popular playwrights, and the playwrights enjoyed the challenge of writing a T(ext) Shirt as well. Dixon claimed that many playwrights, especially Wendy Wasserstein, jumped at the chance to explore a new mode of drama. Making her only Humana Festival appearance through the T(ext) Shirt, Wasserstein recalled her willingness to accept the odd challenge, stating, "I have twenty (other) deadlines, but it was a lot of fun putting everything aside to write a T-shirt."[5] An unofficial competition developed as the V.I.P. Weekend guests watched the bookstore shelves to see which playwright's shirts sold the fastest. By the close of the festival, the unofficial winners were Wasserstein's *To T or Not to T* and Tony Kushner's *And the Torso Even More So*, beating out T(ext) Shirts from David Henry Hwang, Mac Wellman, Jane Martin, and Naomi Wallace.

Overall, critics viewed the T(ext) Shirts as an amusing gimmick rather than a serious attempt at creating a new form of drama, with one critic asking, "When does a play cease to be a play and become a merchandising tool?"[6] However, Jory's second gimmick—the phone plays—exhibited its staying power by reappearing in three festivals. Considered the least popular of the three gimmicks offered in the 1999 festival, five graffiti-scrawled phones booths, each offering a different phone play, were erected in the mezzanine lobby. Donated by Bell South, each phone was connected to a computer-activated recording of the play every time the receiver was lifted.

Dixon articulated the challenge of writing a phone play: "When we're on the telephone, we only use one of our five senses—we listen. We listen for content, we listen for inflection, we listen for silence and any other clues that might help us piece together the unseen picture at the other end of the line. And how perfect that is for playwrights—a medium that relies on language, listening and the active engagement of an audience member's imagination to piece together a play."[7]

Proving that the idea of a phone play required an explanation and encouragement, Dixon commissioned playwright Rebecca Reynolds to pen a phone play, but at first she was confused because she had never heard of such a play. Dixon explained that it would be "like eavesdropping on a party line," and he dictated some limitations: nothing X-rated (or phone sex), a maximum of three minutes, and a recommendation of three characters or fewer.[8] Critics never seriously considered the phone plays, written by Reynolds, Neal Bell, Diana Son, David Greenspan, and Rebecca Gilman, as a new form of theatre. Instead, most reviewers saw them as a diversion or a way to pass the time between shows. While the T(ext) Shirts received a higher profile because of the popularity of the writers involved in the project (which perhaps added some credibility to the endeavor), the phone plays were often likened to radio dramas (as opposed to theatre pieces)—they might be an interesting challenge for the writers, but as theatre pieces they failed to impress the critics.

Ironically, Jory's final gimmick—a car play—elicited rave reviews from critics who considered it a legitimate exploration of actor-audience relationships, as well as an unconventional yet successful attempt at "stretching the boundaries" of performance. But it never appeared in another festival. Actors Theatre enlisted the talents of Humana Festival alum Richard Dresser to pen a short play to be performed in the front seat of a car while the audience sat in the back. Initially, Jory suggested that the actors drive the car around the block while performing the play, but Actors Theatre's insurance company quickly forbid that possibility. Dresser humorously recalled his reaction to the proposal, joking, "I told Jon that I wasn't sure that [being commissioned] was a compliment. Didn't he think that my work could draw an audience of more than three?" Dresser admitted that he enjoyed the challenge of writing for a new performance space, one that required him "to strip away everything that is not essential. Not an extra word, not an extra syllable. The limitations turned out to give the play its shape."[9]

The resulting play, *What Are You Afraid Of?*, quickly became the hottest ticket of the festival weekends, as three passengers at a time exited the lobby doors and filed into the backseat of a parked 1986 Lincoln Town Car to watch actors Trip Hope and Ginna Hoben perform in the front seat. To give the illusion of travel, the car was wired for aural effects, including radio signals, traffic, and a running engine. The short performance began with the male driver picking up a hitchhiker, and a romance quickly ensued. At one point, the actors began to make love and fell over in the front seat, out of view of the backseat passengers. While the young couple kissed, the actors threw a bra and a pair of boxers into the rear of the car, provoking laughter from the patrons. Soon after, the couple appeared again, yet time had quickly shifted to many years later as the couple imagined married life with kids—and, in a stroke of genius by Dresser, the theatergoers became the children. The father figure at one point angrily turned around to yell directly at the children/passengers, "Would you kids shut up!"[10] Critics and audiences alike were impressed by Dresser's witty writing, the actors' devotion to the task, and Jory's willingness to explore new performance spaces. After watching a performance while seated between two critics, Dresser declared, "I love the fact that theater can exist in different forms and different ways."[11]

More than a gimmick, the car play represented a growing trend in regional theatres—that of expansion. In prior festivals, Jory experimented within the festival through commissions. With these gimmicks, Jory experimented with the festival itself by expanding its number of offerings and performance spaces, enlarging the festival both artistically and physically. Unlike prior Humana Festival works *Food from Trash* and *Doctors and Diseases*, which utilized different locations but transformed them into conventional theatrical spaces, the car play celebrated the creative potential for theatre by discovering a new venue for performance that gave Jory the freedom to challenge conventions while also altering the traditional actor-audience relationship.[12]

While the car play itself did not expand past the façade of the Actors Theatre building, Jory's motivation to establish and discover new performance spaces typified the actions of many regional theatres around the country. Many institutions sought to expand their facilities to attract larger audiences and new talent. Ben Cameron, executive director of Theatre Communications Group, argued that the fiscal conservatism of the early 1990s need not dictate artistic conservatism. Nonprofit theatres across the country benefited from a strong economy and expanded their facilities to include new performance spaces, the most notable companies being the Goodspeed Opera House, the Goodman Theatre, and the Guthrie Theater, with its $100 million construction project that included a new 150-seat theater devoted to the development of new work.[13] According to Emily Mann, artistic director of the McCarter Theater, these new performance opportunities provided new benefits, and "a variety of spaces expands the potential for repertory and offers a different kind of experience for audiences."[14]

With its three theatres, Actors Theatre did not need to add another performance space, yet the spirit of expansion sweeping across many regional theatres exhibited itself in the form of unconventional venues for the festival's new plays, namely a phone booth, a car, and a T-shirt. Judith Newmark, critic for the *St. Louis Post-Dispatch*, approved of Actors Theatre's endeavors, writing, "Humana makes a key point: Theater isn't as much about money as it is about imagination. The challenge lies in discovering new ways to stretch its boundaries. And that exploration could lead to theater that is less expensive to produce and attend, more exciting to established customers and more appealing to new ones."[15]

Jory's explorations of actor-audience relationships existed not only in the lobby but also on the stage of the Pamela Brown Auditorium in one of the greatest Humana Festival productions of Jory's final phase. For the twenty-fourth festival in 2000, Jory continued to celebrate the capability of theatre to engage audiences by commissioning Anne Bogart to spearhead a joint project with the Louisville theatre. As part of her research into actor-audience relationships, Bogart interviewed Louisville test audiences about their theatrical experiences and opinions and asked them to keep journals of their personal reactions to performances. Her play *Cabin Pressure*—developed with an ensemble of actors from her Saratoga International Theatre Institute (SITI)—pokes fun at academics, critics, theatre history, and audience responses while exploring the unique and hard-to-define relationship between the performers and the audience. Even though most critics assumed that Bogart's latest play had limited appeal outside the festival (they were wrong), reviewers praised her bold and inventive work, commending Jory for his continued willingness to provide experimental work.[16]

The success of *Cabin Pressure* was not limited to Louisville, however. Thanks to the interest and acclaim that accompanies a hit of the festival, SITI toured their production around the country. A small tour of an experimental show is a rare occurrence, yet the success of *Cabin Pressure* at the festival allowed other audiences around the country to see the provocative work, and helped establish Bogart's reputation as a premier director. Although other Humana Festival plays may have enjoyed larger audiences in numerous regional theatre productions around the country, Jory's commitment to exploring actor-audience relationships and his belief in Bogart's vision helped maintain Actors Theatre's reputation as a home for innovative playwriting and as a leader of artistic movements in American theatre.

Overshadowing the success of David Rambo's *God's Man in Texas* (easily the favorite of audiences and critics at the twenty-third festival), the talk of the town was Jory's spirit of experimentation. Thanks to the innovative gimmicks, the excitement of the festival as an event returned to Louisville, and as in the earliest years, the attention was on Jory. If his agenda of celebration derived from his resolve to "unstodgy" the event, then his experiments certainly worked, perhaps to a fault by overshadowing the main-stage productions. The overall reaction to the gimmicks, however, was mixed: while many critics appreciated Jory's attempt to revitalize the festival and to explore new performance opportunities, an equal number dismissed the gimmicks, saying the most experimental work should have been presented on the main stage. Nevertheless, many reviewers put the gimmicks in perspective and asked in their reviews, "What is theatre?" To this end, Jory achieved the goals on his agenda for celebrating the potential of theatre with the phone plays, T(ext) Shirts, and car play: to revitalize the festival, to make it relevant to the development of new drama, to remain at the center of debate in American Theatre, to continue the festival's popularity and reputation, and to support new playwrights while continuing relationships with established writers.[17]

The detractors—many of the same critics who had complained that Jory spent too much time on experimental work instead of discovering commercial scripts—failed to realize Jory's wisdom in limiting the experimentation to the gimmicks in the lobby. Jory needed to keep commercial works on the main stage as much as possible to appeal to local patrons, who viewed these shows for weeks before the VIP Weekend. Proof of this need can be seen in subscriptions not having been affected by the success of the festival. From the beginning of the new play festival in 1976 to the peak year of subscriptions for the 1989–90 season, subscriptions increased by only 20 percent, or a little more than three thousand, but by the twentieth anniversary of the Humana Festival, the increase dropped to a mere 6.3 percent over the initial level of subscriptions in 1976.

The limited impact of the festival on subscription levels meant that Jory needed to provide low-risk productions to subscribers to ensure continued local support. Furthermore, by allowing the public access to the gimmicks in the lobby, Jory created an "event" atmosphere for Louisville patrons as well, making them a part of the festival.[18] Jory defended his decision to employ the gimmicks by stating, "Frankly, this is all just a way to involve more writers in the festival than we normally can."[19] And Jory wanted festival patrons—especially the many producers, directors, and literary agents who attend the annual event—to "get a look at the next generation of writers." Since, Jory argued, "It's harder for young people to break in," the variety of presentations at the festival provided these writers a rare chance to appear before the national press.[20] To Jory's credit, the twenty-third festival presented the largest number of works by the largest number of writers (twenty-five) to date. Furthermore, Dixon said that the experiments proved rewarding for the writers as well: "There wasn't an experiment we undertook that didn't yield more than enough success to merit the undertaking. . . . We never had a playwright refuse one of these offers. There's a hunger on both sides of the artist/audience equation for doing it a little differently."[21]

Much as in the early years of the festival, when Jory picked commercial works to garner critical attention, his high-profile commissions for the 1999 festival's gimmicks attracted the attention of the national press and theatre professionals around the country. By their asking "What will Jory do next?" the Louisville producer seized the limelight again with a bold and intelligent campaign to revitalize the festival. As in the first festivals when Jory's own tastes and talents guided the festival to success, he again relied on his keen sense of showmanship and resourcefulness to cost-effectively garner press for the festival after several lackluster years. Just as Jory found success in the first two phases of the festival, he now faced the question of how best to utilize the critical attention to further celebrate the potential of theatre.

JORY'S CELEBRATION OF THE FESTIVAL

Jory was retreading festival history without knowing it. For the early phases, the national press converged in Louisville to see whether Jory's perceived luck would again provide Broadway's next big play. With the 1999 festival, he wowed critics and had them excited to return to Louisville to see what new experiments he would present. The press arrived for the millennium festival not only to see what Jory's festival would offer but, more important, to see Jory himself. A major announcement from Jory before the festival enticed numerous critics to Louisville. This time, however, instead of celebrating the potential of theatre through gimmicks, Jory presented a conventional comedy to revel in the festival's past achievements while also offering advice for the future. As in his product-to-process phase, when he altered the practices of the theatre to benefit future festival playwrights, Jory used the spotlight to initiate a discussion about the future of regional theatre.

After three years of mediocre responses to the Humana Festival offerings, the twenty-fourth edition delivered one of the strongest collections in the annual event's history.[22] Overshadowing the ballyhooed return of big-name playwrights (Anne Bogart, Tina Howe, Naomi Wallace, and Naomi Iizuka) and the successful debuts of the work by new festival play-wrights (Charles L Mee's *Big Love*, Stephen Belber's *Tape* and Toni Press-Coffman's *Touch*) was one show that dominated conversations for the entire weekend. The commotion had begun with a press release two months prior, on January 18, 2000, when Jory announced his resignation from Actors Theatre to take a teaching position at the University of Washington School of Drama. Jory justified the timing of his decision, explaining, "It seemed a good time for me to move on. You know, nothing lasts forever. The company is in first-rate financial shape. New leadership for a new millennium makes sense to me. I did one century. Now it's time for somebody else to take on the next."[23]

Jory had good reason to feel confident about the condition of the theatre and festival when he departed, thanks in part to his continued good fortune. A parallel can be made between the arrivals of Jory and his successor in that the Bingham family played an instrumental role in allowing for a new leader to take control of the theatre. Just as the Bingham family's newspaper foundation helped erase the theatre's deficit when Richard Block departed, the Binghams again saved the theatre after the 1994 expansion left Actors Theatre with a growing deficit. Charitable donations of nearly $4 million from Barry Bingham Jr. and his wife, Edith, and others helped erase the remaining debt in 1999. Without the generous gift from the Bingham family, Jory might have stayed longer at Actors Theatre so as not to burden any new artistic director with massive debt. Ironically, the actions of the Bingham family helped Jory both in accepting the position in 1969 and in resigning from the theatre in 2000.[24]

During the VIP Weekend, Jory provided further justification for his departure while being interviewed by the many critics in attendance: "I have a lot of practical knowledge of the craft of directing to pass along, and I want to do it in the classroom and in a book or two."[25] In one honest exchange with Christine Dolen of the *Miami Herald*, Jory admitted, "There are parts of the job I just plain wasn't liking anymore. I knew someone else would think it was a kick."[26] Frequently mentioned in interviews was the fact that Jory's daughter would be attending the University of Washington the following fall, and the teaching position provided an opportunity to remain close to her. Rumors abounded that Alexander Speer would leave as well, but he quashed such suspicions quickly, declaring, "I'm here to stay, at least for the foreseeable future. This is Jon's baby, and he wants it to stay healthy. I can help see that it does."[27]

Easily one of the most anticipated moments in Humana Festival history occurred before the Saturday evening performance on April 1, 2000, when Jon Jory addressed the large gathering of festival guests from the stage of the Pamela Brown Auditorium. In addition to the usual festival patrons, the American Theatre Critics Association held its annual meeting in conjunction with the Twenty-Fourth Annual Humana Festival, resulting in attendance by a reported two hundred critics from around the globe. With the large number of critics at the festival, the number at the VIP Weekend jumped from its usual 175–200 visitors to more than four hundred attendees.[28] When Jory ascended the steps of the stage to give his traditional (and last) welcome to the weekend guests, he was greeted with a long, overwhelming standing ovation. During the long applause, one can only imagine how much pride and accomplishment Jory must have felt as he scanned the audience, recognizing old friends and critics who had been attending the festival from its inception. If the moment was moving toward sentimentality, Jory quickly ended it as the applause died down and he humorously quipped, "Is that all?"

Jory's short speech to the throngs of critics might have been perceived as his official good-bye, but it was an unofficial farewell that took the Humana

Festival by storm. With *Anton in Show Business*, Jane Martin again achieved another hit at the festival, but this production was different; with its references and in-jokes about the challenges of running a nonprofit regional theatre, the text and performance seemed tailor-made for its presentation at the Twenty-Fourth Humana Festival.[29] Considered a valedictory by Jory to national critics and Louisville audiences, *Anton* follows three actresses as they struggle to mount a production of Chekhov's *The Three Sisters* in San Antonio. Throughout the play, a critic planted in the audience stands and objects to the play, often engaging the actresses in theoretical disputes about the current state of American theatre. In the context of Jory's departure, *Anton* was more than mere entertainment; it provided Jory with a forum to express his love and concern for the future of the festival that he would soon be leaving. Furthermore, with Martin's criticisms of regional theatre, the metatheatrical comedy also provides an opportunity to evaluate the accuracy of her assertions concerning the state of nonprofit theatres at the end of the millennium.

Martin's references suggested an intimate knowledge of the challenges and frustrations of a producer of nonprofit theatre. Of course, Martin is a playwright, but many of the criticisms within *Anton* exhibited a comprehensive understanding of production difficulties with which Jory was extraordinarily familiar. As Charles Isherwood of *Variety* wrote, "Perhaps only a theater producer with Jory's particular experience could have penned such a keenly observed dissection of the trials of life on the regional theatre circuit."[30] A case in point occurs in the opening moments of the play, when stage manager T-Anne offers a point of view concerning the financial health of American theatre to the audience: "The American theatre's in a shitload of trouble. That's why the stage is bare, and it's a cast of six, one non-union. . . . Like lots of plays you've seen at the end of the twentieth century, we all have to play a lot of parts to make the whole thing economically viable."[31] These opening lines reflected experience with which Jory was familiar—to cut expenses, the festival format forced Jory to cast actors in multiple roles in multiple shows. Furthermore, T-Anne's comment about the one nonunion actor could easily refer to the many Acting Apprentices who fill roles for the Humana Festival productions and save the theatre money in production costs.

Contrary to Martin's assertion that regional theatres struggle to remain economically viable, financial statistics published in Theatre Communications Group's *Theatre Facts* showed improvement in the fiscal health of nonprofit institutions, considered to be a reflection of the strong national economy. "The economy of 2000 was a boost to most theatres' bottom lines," claimed the TCG report. "The strength of the economy over the past four years has had a positive overall impact on the industry. Theatre's average balance of all unrestricted net assets has doubled from $2 million at the start of 1997 to \$4 million at the end of 2000."[32] Other figures demonstrated the growing fiscal health of regional theatres: 7 percent fewer theatres operated with deficits than in the prior year, and contributions to regional theatres grew substantially in 2000, outpacing inflation by 36 percent over the prior four years.[33] Martin's concerns, however, were not unfounded, because when the economy faltered during the following year, endowment earnings hit a five-year low and almost half the theatres that participated in the TCG study operated with a deficit. Nevertheless, analysis of long-term trends shows that regional theatre enjoyed fiscal growth, providing more optimism for the new millennium than what Martin foresaw in her play.[34]

Also in *Anton*, Martin complains that a majority of the audience is "three months away from the nursing home" and stresses that the San Antonio theatre struggles to attract patrons, especially young audiences. According to the 2000 TCG survey of regional theatres across the country, however, total attendance reached its highest level in six years, with a 4.7 percent increase since 1995. Not all of the news from *Theatre Facts* was positive: instead of audience members buying subscriptions, single-ticket income exceeded subscription income for the first time in 2000, signifying a change in patrons' purchasing habits. Dean Gladden, managing director of the Cleveland Play House, explained the shift, "People are unwilling to commit to packages and prefer to pick and choose."[35] Jacques Lamarre, the director of marketing and public relations for the Hartford Stage Company, concurred and elaborated on the reason behind the declining subscription rate: "Subscribers' expectations have changed. . . . The level of service has had to increase for people to feel okay about making the investment. There are so many people out there clamoring for their money, you have to be careful. If they have *one* bad experience, they'll say, 'Fine. I'll go somewhere else.'"[36] Partially blamed for contributing to the decrease in subscriptions were Broadway tours that encouraged patrons to support a single, lavish production instead of their local institution. In spite of the increase in attendance, the steady decline in subscriptions proved troubling for regional theatres, not allowing them to rely on projected income. Finding themselves more dependent on single-ticket sales, artistic directors might have been more likely to cater to public tastes to ensure well-attended productions.[37]

While larger institutions have an easier time of fund-raising due to their heightened reputations, the fictitious theatre company in *Anton in Show Business*, Actors Express, signifies how small theatres struggle to produce quality work on a tight budget. In Louisville the annual budget of Actors Theatre certainly dwarfs those of its local competitors, but Martin's play gives voice to the concerns of these smaller organizations, including the Louisville children's theatre Stage One, the Actors Guild of Lexington, Horse Cave Theatre (south of Louisville), and the University of Louisville's

African American Theatre Program. According to TCG's *Theatre Facts*, smaller nonprofit theatres such as those in Louisville are more vulnerable to economic fluctuations because their subscription base is small and they usually do not receive support from wealthy donors or local corporations. Theatres in smaller towns, like the Bloomsburg Theatre Ensemble, which operates in a Pennsylvania town of twelve thousand, struggle in their audience development efforts owing to their limited outreach and advertising budgets (not to mention that their productions are rarely reviewed in local newspapers). Jeffrey Herrmann, the producing director of Alaska's Perseverance Theatre, described the pressures on his theatre as a double standard: "We're expected to perform at a certain level, but we can't charge high ticket prices because we also have to compete for customers with amateur theatres in our market."[38]

When asked whether these smaller theatres can survive under Actors Theatre's shadow, Dixon asserted, "We don't think of the other local theatres as living under our shadow. . . . Each Louisville theatre casts its own light."[39] Given the extensive resources for and high quality of Actors Theatre's productions, Juergen Tossmann, the founding director of Louisville's Bunbury Theatre, discussed the pressure that Actors Theatre creates, stating, "We have *got* to be good. . . . Our lives depend on it."[40] In spite of Actors Theatre's dominance in fund-raising, other artistic directors did not begrudge the famous theatre. "Actors Theatre is like a big tree spreading seeds all over," Stage One's founding director Moses Goldberg claimed. "That's how smaller theatres grow."[41] Even though Martin's play made light of the struggles endured by these companies, *Anton in Show Business* celebrated the potential of these smaller organizations by not only sympathizing with the difficulties they encountered but also praising their perseverance and their determination to connect with their respective communities by providing quality theatre to willing audiences.[42]

In a demonstration of the cyclical nature of the festival, Jory once again used his stature and showmanship to aid in the development of professional theatre. Earlier in the history of the festival, he felt free to shift the festival's focus from production to process in an effort to better assist playwrights and define how best to perform new play dramaturgy. For the twenty-fourth festival, his legacy and his approaching farewell gave him the opportunity to unashamedly lecture theatre professionals and critics about the power and challenges of regional theatre. Knowing that critics from around the country would be sitting in his theatre during their annual conference, he boldly selected (and perhaps wrote) a play that took them to task, once again risking negative critical reaction to pursue an agenda. Jory's great care and concern for the health of regional theatre motivated him to take the opportunity of his last festival to declare his opinions about the art and business of theatre.

Anton in Show Business was his valedictory speech before his impending departure to academe.

Indeed, these two years deserve the label "last hurrah": a final period of great accomplishment, inspired creativity, and bold decisions. While the gimmicks of this phase certainly garnered much attention, it was the presentation of *Anton in Show Business* and its many inferences and in-jokes that became the talk of Jory's final festival. While some theatre critics questioned the authorship of Martin's plays (as they do to this day), most reviewers wrote about the uncertainty of the playwright's future (Would she be leaving Actors Theatre?), as well as her bold arguments concerning the problems facing professional regional theatres. One critic summarized, "If Jory is Martin, he takes full advantage of his impending departure to put regional theater through an affectionate spanking machine."[43] As he had done numerous times, Jory refused to discuss the identity of the playwright or whether her works would now debut in Seattle. Instead, Jory focused on the merits of the work: "It's a great play. It's about the pain of living and how to go on living in difficult circumstances, and as such, it's also a great metaphor for the theatre."[44] This quote could not be more apt as Jory's renaissance came to a close and as Actors Theatre was about to face its greatest challenge: the departure of Jon Jory and the introduction of a new producing director.

9   THE EDUCATION OF MARC MASTERSON, 2001–6

On the evening of August 8, 2000, the Actors Theatre board of directors concluded its seven-month search and confirmed its choice for a new artistic director. Having attended the festival as a guest for ten years, Marc Masterson was already a familiar face to several staff members when Actors Theatre of Louisville formally invited him to fill the position vacated by Jon Jory. As for his credentials, Masterson served as the producing director of Pittsburgh's City Theatre for nineteen years, receiving great acclaim for his devotion to the development of new plays. In fact, the City Theatre's mission to produce only new plays made him an attractive candidate for managing the Humana Festival.[1] In an article published the following day in the *Courier-Journal*, board members lavished praise on Masterson, as did others who influenced the search, including Jory and director Anne Bogart. Board president Amanda Foard Tyler boasted that Masterson's ability to engage the community and to energize the staff and city with his adventuresome spirit and sense of vision made him the clear choice for the position. Masterson, of course, humbly accepted the position, praising Jory and his staff for their work and leadership in the American theatre while also expressing his excitement to begin working toward the 2001 Humana Festival.

Even though Jory's departure left unanswered many questions about the future of the Humana Festival, the transition into the Masterson era was relatively painless; a large number of staff remained throughout the changeover period and into Masterson's tenure. Trish Pugh Jones—who arrived with Jory at Actors Theatre, left to work for several arts organizations in Louisville, and then returned to the theatre as the manager of patron services—described the difference between the management styles of Jon and Marc: "Jon always called himself a benevolent dictator, and Marc is more open to consensus. Both are valid. . . . I admire Marc, and I love Jon."[2] When he first accepted the position, Masterson stressed that he anticipated no immediate changes in the Actors Theatre staff, as he looked forward to working with Speer and Dixon. Some changes, however, were not of Masterson's choosing.

Considered a candidate for the artistic director position, Michael Bigelow Dixon resigned, after nearly fifteen years with Actors Theatre, to become the literary director of the Guthrie Theater.[3] Only six months before he resigned, on September 25, 2000, Dixon had assumed the title of associate artistic director, and his rise in the theatre's hierarchy reflected a common occurrence in many regional theatres as literary managers assumed more responsibilities. Todd London, author of *The Artistic Home*, explained the motivation behind the trend: "Many artistic directors are enthusiastic about the creation of associate artistic positions in their theatres. This title often applies to a full-time colleague . . . who works with the artistic director on season planning, scouting, finding and developing projects, and who functions as a resident artist, doing his or her work (e.g., directing plays) for the theatre."[4] In his study of regional theatres in the northeast, Michael Donahue wrote that several dramaturgs accepted these newly created positions for purposes of advancement: "Dramaturgs have, in numerous instances, assumed increasingly important roles in the artistic process. Initially this partnership with the artistic director lead [*sic*] to the assumption that the dramaturgy was the quickest route to artistic leadership. It is not generally agreed, however, that the dramaturg best serves the artistic leader by assuming a similarly subordinate role as that of the management leader—that of a vice-president to the artistic leader."[5]

Only forty-seven days after Actors Theatre named Masterson its new artistic director, Dixon accepted his promotion to associate artistic director as well, suggesting that the new leadership did not influence Dixon's announcement of his impending departure. Explaining the timing of his decision, Dixon said he had grown tired of reading the hundreds of scripts a year required for the Humana Festival, admitting, "Maybe this Humana job is for younger people. . . . It was time for me to do something else."[6]

Regardless of the low turnover in staff, Masterson's arrival at Actors Theatre provoked several valid questions concerning his ability to manage the large institution, as well as the impact he would have on the festival. After seven years on the job, Masterson has succeeded in part because he learned some of the same lessons that Jory discovered in his earliest years. Although Masterson's festivals have yet to produce a Pulitzer Prize–winning play, his tireless efforts in audience building and his creative vision helped maintain the success of the festival through his earliest and most difficult years in Louisville. First and foremost, the education of Marc Masterson provides an answer to the most prevalent question about the festival since he arrived in Louisville: Can Masterson succeed at Actors Theatre?

Long before Jory announced his retirement, theatre professionals—including a few staff members at Actors Theatre of Louisville—predicted difficulty, if not doom, for whoever followed in Jory's footsteps. Perceived as too big a pair of shoes to fill, many of these fortunetellers proposed that any successor to Jory would crash and burn, giving the next leader a clean slate and a fair opportunity to succeed. If theatre professionals and critics anticipated that Masterson would repeat the substantial achievements of Jory, then these expectations were foolish and impossible to satisfy. What Jory accomplished in his thirty-one years in Louisville cannot be repeated because of drastic changes in the economic realities that dictate arts funding, entertainment accessibility, audience attendance trends, and production costs. What Masterson could achieve was keeping the festival and the theatre successful and relevant while making the festival his own.

To appease critics and alleviate concerns, Masterson proclaimed in almost every interview that he planned to maintain the successful format of the festival. "To me, the festival is very, very successful doing things the way it does," he explained. "The fundamental idea of the festival is extremely sound—the best way to develop new plays is to fully produce them and do many at the same time and to commit to the relationship with the playwrights as completely as possible. That won't change."[7] Although Masterson may have asked for few changes upon his arrival, Dixon's decision to accept the Guthrie Theater's offer was not the only challenge Masterson faced as he headed into his first Humana Festival. The national press' eagerness to use the 2001 collection as a gauge for Masterson's leadership proved daunting to the new artistic director, because two factors—the timing of his arrival in Louisville and his decision to direct—hindered his ability to impress critics and calm fears about his handling of future festivals.

Masterson did not begin working at Actors Theatre until the new year, allowing him to conclude business with the City Theatre while also finding a home and settling his wife and two children in Louisville. Because of his late arrival, Jory and Dixon had already chosen the Twenty-Fifth Annual Humana Festival of New American Plays lineup with some additional input by Masterson. Reports differ as to how much influence Masterson actually had in the play-selection process. Masterson stated that "Jon picked about half the shows, and I picked the other half," while another report said that Masterson had a say in only one selection from a list of possibilities provided by Dixon and Jory.[8]

Regardless of which leader picked the most plays, Masterson's preferences for the 2001 collection were evident. Masterson selected the creators of the phone plays, turning away from commissioning name-recognition playwrights and, instead, selecting five alternative theatres to produce the work (most notably Chicago's NeoFuturists, Washington's African Continuum Theater Company, and San Antonio's Jump Start Performance Company). The majority of the main-stage shows in the twenty-fifth festival, however, were selected by Jory and Dixon, and most of them were written by veteran Humana Festival playwrights. In fact, of the six major productions of the 2001 festival, only one was penned by a festival newcomer. The decision by Jory to fill the festival with established writers signified his effort to ensure quality during a time of transition. Unfortunately for Masterson, the one production that he reportedly selected for the festival elicited a mixed response: critics and patrons questioned whether his tastes were compatible with those of Louisville audiences (or even the national press).

Obie-Award winner Mac Wellman officially made his Humana Festival debut with *The Fez*, one of the T(ext) Shirts from 1999, but his play for the twenty-fifth festival marked the first appearance of his work on the Louisville stage. Masterson's selection of Wellman's *Description Beggared; or the Allegory of WHITENESS* proved problematic for the national press. While several critics appreciated the complex structure and language in Wellman's text, most reviewers remained both fascinated and befuddled by the play.[9] Easily the most confusing play in the Humana Festival's history, it left many critics puzzled at the meaning of both the production and the text. Wellman's love of word play resulted in some critics inanely dismissing the work out of frustration and others simply discussing the production values.[10] Wellman's play, however, represented the new direction in which Masterson would take the Humana Festival, eventually featuring less mainstream productions and more experimental works (a concern for the critics who favored the festival's commercial output). This contrast—between Wellman's dazzling and dense play and some of the more traditional fare usually presented at the Humana Festival—illuminated the differences between Jory and Masterson, but a true comparison would be made during the VIP festival weekend, as each director would be judged in an unofficial competition that became the talk of the twenty-fifth festival.

The second factor that hindered Masterson's ability to instill confidence in critics and patrons—his decision to direct in the twenty-fifth festival—led to an intense (and perhaps unfair) level of scrutiny, as Masterson faced challenges from a variety of sources. Unlike other Humana Festival directors who simply hoped to mount a good production or make connections to obtain future work, Masterson needed to debut with a winning production because theatre professionals and the Louisville community looked for assurances that he would be able to continue the success established by Jory.

With anticipation and expectations high for his premiere, an article by Chris Jones in the *New York Times* increased the pressure on the new artistic director to succeed and angered several staff members at Actors Theatre. In "Will a New Broom at Humana Sweep the Old Era Away?" Jones discussed the uncertainty among playwrights over Masterson's penchant for experimental fare, stating that his prior work with Anne Bogart and Maria Irene Fornes suggested that his festivals will contradict Jory's selections of "mainstream commercial plays based in realism." Furthermore, Jones criticized Jory and Dixon for their unwillingness to find new writers (citing 2001's lineup as proof) and for their poor track record in producing works by African American playwrights. Playwrights Charles Smith and Tazewell Thompson remarked on the few opportunities for writers of color, one point of contention being that Actors Theatre had to hire actors who could perform in more than one production, which might have forced the festival to select plays that fit a specific casting pool. While this assertion was absurd because Jory and Actors Theatre selected casts in New York, Jory answered the charge in the article by explaining, "We have never got [sic] a lot of plays by African-Americans in the mail. Of the good ones, we have turned down very few."[11] In addition to limited submissions, Jory acknowledged that the festival reflected (as it always has) his and Dixon's tastes, and for that Jory was unapologetic.

Expectations for the new artistic director to sweep away the tastes and trends of his predecessor were not isolated to Louisville; Masterson was not alone in his struggle to assume the helm of an institution. In fact, the challenges that Masterson faced mirrored the pressures that many newly instituted artistic directors faced around the country. The 1999–2001 period was one of substantial turnover in the management of America's regional theatres, including many new artistic directors assuming leadership from the founding directors of institutions. Whether through retirement or through demise, new artistic directors replaced lauded leaders such as Zelda Fichandler at Washington's Arena Stage, Adrian Hall at Trinity Square Rep, Doug Hughes at the Long Wharf Theatre, Sharon Ott at the Berkeley Repertory Theatre, Joseph Papp at the New York Shakespeare Festival, and Kenny Leon at the Alliance Theatre. Unfortunately, during the 1990s, decreased funding from the National Endowment for the Arts caused many smaller nonprofit theatres to fold, reducing the number of skilled directors and leaders as potential candidates for a position at a larger theatre.

These developments caused great concern among critics and the artistic directors themselves. Dan Hulbert, critic for the *Atlanta Journal-Constitution*, expressed his worries about how these new leaders would guide their institutions into the future, writing, "With the departure of younger top artistic directors to the bigger paydays of commercial theater and movies, the resident nonprofits are drifting to the margins of American life. Slipping beneath the radar. Championing women, gays, and minorities but failing to engage the political middle."[12] In addition to finding the balance between satisfying their artistic impulses and appeasing their subscribers, many artistic directors battled financial deficits, as well as homogenization of product through the growing trend of coproductions (which Masterson pursued during his tenure).[13]

Even if Masterson's employment represented a national trend, few artistic directors needed to read about the variety of challenges facing them in the *New York Times*. In addition to play selection concerns, another subject in Jones's article also added pressure to Masterson's first Humana Festival experience. When asked whether the Humana Foundation would continue its support of the festival under Masterson's watch, David A. Jones, the foundation's chairman, sounded a cautionary affirmation: "We are willing to continue our support through at least 2003. That gives Marc Masterson at least three years to put his stamp on things."[14] Whether intended as an ultimatum or not, Jones's statement of support only added to the anticipation on VIP Weekend, when national critics got their first look at Masterson's directorial work in the Humana Festival.

Because of his decision to direct, Masterson endured constant comparisons with a man not even in attendance. When scheduling conflicts left Jory unable to travel to the VIP Weekend, Masterson was thrust into the spotlight alone during his first festival as artistic director. That Jory did not attend the festival that weekend was seen as a generous move on his part, giving Masterson the opportunity to emerge from Jory's long shadow. Without the presence of Jory, however, the national press perceived the latest festival to be Masterson's alone, even though he participated little in its composition. Critics quickly looked to two productions—one directed by Jory and the other by Masterson—to evaluate the new artistic director and compare him with his predecessor.

Jory's presence loomed large, as the audience favorite of the festival was Jane Martin's raucous comedy *Flaming Guns of the Purple Sage*, directed (of course) by Jory. Subtitled "A B-Western Horror Flick for the Stage," Martin's play resurrected Big 8, the tough-talking rodeo star from *Talking With*, yet the new play finds her taking in the wayward Shedevil, a pregnant, pierced, and pink-haired girl running from a Ukrainian biker, Black Dog. The play, far from Martin's best and without social merit, descended into moments (albeit humorous ones) of gunshots, blood, crude humor, and violent spectacle. Many critics appreciated the play for what it was and predicted that it would become a popular selection on the regional theatre circuit, yet most reviewers spent as much newspaper space as always in discussing the play as they did in hypothesizing the fate of Martin now that Jory was no longer in Louisville.

With Jory's *Flaming Guns* a crowd-pleaser, an unofficial competition arose between the old guard and the new regime. Ironically, Masterson had not planned to direct in the 2001 festival—he hoped to watch the festival's workings as a spectator—but when he read Richard Dresser's dark comedy *Wonderful World*, he changed his mind. Opening on March 17, 2001, *Wonderful World* initially received rave reviews from the local press. Judith Egerton offered her opinions on Masterson's debut: "Last night's audience got its first look at the directing hand of A.T.L.'s new leader, Marc Masterson. . . . Anyone who wondered about the skill of A.T.L.'s new artistic director surely came away from *Wonderful World* impressed and reassured."[15] During the Saturday evening performance of the VIP Weekend, however, the production did not run as smoothly and failed to receive similar reviews. Paul Owen's set of sliding panels and pocket doors appeared to falter during the performance, causing extended transitions, misplaced panels, and gaps in the walls that allowed spectators to see backstage. Critics also assailed Dresser's writing, claiming that the play stretched fifteen minutes of material into a two-hour play, leaving the audience to suffer through many dull moments.[16]

By the end of the VIP Weekend for the Twenty-Fifth Annual Humana Festival of New American Plays, the competition resulted in a draw: critics found greater fault with Dresser's writing than with Masterson's directing abilities, and Jory silenced any unofficial competition by praising Masterson's work as an artistic director. Trish Pugh Jones blamed the tension on the media, claiming, "I do think that it was really, really hard for Marc to come into the new play festival. I think critics coming in the first year were very, very hard and shouldn't have been. They were unfair because Marc wasn't Jon, and Marc was incredibly courageous, I think, in inviting Jon to direct at his first festival and to direct the other main-stage production in the Pamela Brown. People would inevitably compare [the two productions], and Jon got the better play to direct."[17]

Even though Masterson assured many critics and theatre professionals that he would not tamper with the Humana Festival formula, much about the annual event was left in a state of uncertainty by the end of 2001 festival. The day after the close of the VIP Weekend, Michael Bigelow Dixon departed Louisville for Minneapolis, leaving the literary department in the hands of two of his protégées, Tanya Palmer and Amy Wegener, and prompting many questions: How would Masterson work with these new literary managers? How would the untested relationship between Masterson and his new literary managers help or hinder the choices and productions of the next festival? Could Marc Masterson prove to the Humana Foundation that his choices and productions would be worthy of its continued support? How would Masterson alter the festival to accentuate his tastes and interests while still maintaining its national recognition? How long would Masterson have to endure comparisons with Jory and his formula for success? Would Masterson simply rely on the prior achievements of the festival, or would he find success by exploring his own personal artistic interests? With the Louisville institution firmly under his direction, Masterson would have to articulate his own agenda and discover his own success as he guided Actors Theatre though its next phase, leaving the sometimes tense, somewhat controversial, and highly publicized celebratory years of the Humana Festival in the past.

Coming from a much smaller theatre, Masterson knew he would be facing an extraordinary challenge, but during his first five years (2002–6), he found success by eventually utilizing the same formula Jory had employed to launch the new play festival: establishing and then exploiting a local foundation with an eye toward national visibility. By following these three principles—developing an audience, building trust, and remaining relevant—Masterson wisely learned the tastes and preferences of his theatergoing public, in addition to the challenges of producing a critically and commercially successful festival. Proof of this education was shown in his early decisions about management of the theatre and, like Jory, his willingness to adapt. Masterson's alterations, in conjunction with his determination to succeed, helped transform the Louisville theatre into a reflection of his own artistic tastes, successfully proving the doomsday prophets wrong.

When Jory first arrived in Louisville in 1969, he was determined to demonstrate his leadership abilities, but unlike his predecessors, he possessed an artistic vision that benefited both the entire community and himself. Jory's first action was to introduce himself to the Louisville community so that he could personally publicize his new vision for the theatre. By the time Masterson arrived in Louisville, Actors Theatre already enjoyed substantial community support in the form of subscriptions and corporate donations. His challenge, therefore, was to follow in Jory's footsteps: introduce himself to the community to retain their support or, in the worst-case scenario, find new audiences to replace those who might not like the new direction of the theatre (i.e., regular-season play selections). Wisely, Masterson placed great importance on establishing a new audience (and himself within the community), but his methods and goals differed from those of his predecessor. Masterson is certainly personable but not a showman like Jory. Keeping true to his personality and to his interests of expanding and diversifying his audiences, Masterson reached out to the community by creating the theater's first education department, resulting in the doubling of the number of performances for young audiences. Furthermore, under Masterson's leadership, Actors Theatre presented August Wilson plays for the first time. Masterson justified his decision to produce three Wilson plays in four years, stating, "It's important for Louisville audiences to see what others are seeing."

The selection of *The Piano Lesson, Jitney,* and *Fences* represented not only Masterson's preference for the late Wilson's work but also his attempt to connect with the Louisville African American community.[18] Naturally, questions arose as to why Jory never selected an August Wilson play during his thirty-one years as producing director. While several theories are possible, it is irresponsible to imply that Jory simply ignored the African American community in his play selections. Actors Theatre did mount, in addition to work in the Flying Solo and Friends Festival, many productions intended to attract African American audiences; during Jory's final five years, he presented *Having Our Say, Once on This Island, Ali, Blues in the Night,* and *Home.*

Actors Theatre, however, received criticism for these productions—not for its decision to offer presentations intended to entice new audiences to the theatre but for the type of work it offered. A perception was created that Actors Theatre would produce work about African Americans only if it was either a local story (*Ali*) or a musical that might also appeal to all audiences. The exception to this perception was the last presentation, *Home,* but critics erroneously interpreted the other selections as slights to the African American community. Having established and maintained his audience through Danny Newman's philosophy and given his cautious approach as a producer, Jory simply picked plays or musicals that satisfied two objectives: catering to the African American community and ensuring large audiences. Given the dire state of Actors Theatre finances before the Binghams' generous gift, Jory's selections might have been timid but they were wise. Masterson, however, benefited from financial security on his arrival because of the Binghams' donation, providing him with the opportunity to intensively target new audiences through educational outreach and relevant productions.

While Actors Theatre enjoys resources that allow it to engage in numerous activities, Masterson utilized the theatre's financial stability to pursue an agenda that applies to every nonprofit theatre, especially in times of struggling economies when patrons tighten their wallets: the theatre must provide the community with a reason for attending and supporting the theatre. Throughout the history of the Humana Festival, Jory believed that theatres had to pay attention to the needs and desires of the community and that it would be folly to consider an institution "essential" to a community (as Martin's character does in *Anton*). Furthermore, an institution should never believe that its play selections will appeal to audiences simply because the artistic director favors the scripts or because the playwright is an up-and-coming talent. Even though some patrons and professionals criticized Jory for his early, more popular selections, his growing audience base allowed him to produce works catering to audiences outside Danny Newman's target group. Masterson understood the need to secure audience support and followed Jory's example by establishing an audience, through his education department, who helped justify why members of every community should support the famed Louisville institution.

During his first years as artistic director, Masterson faced difficulty in establishing (or maintaining) his audiences thanks to conditions that were not entirely of his own making, but he quickly learned from his mistakes. Even though the Bingham family helped erase Actors Theatre's debts from the 1994 expansion, the theatre still operated under a budget shortfall. Shortly after Jory's departure to Washington, an article by Judith Egerton angered Actors Theatre by exposing the dire state of its finances. According to the piece in the *Courier-Journal*, the theatre reported a loss of $419,295 for Jory's last season (not including building depreciation and endowment income) and predicted a budget shortfall of almost six hundred thousand dollars for Masterson's first full year. Egerton stated that one reason for the deficit was a summertime musical, *Jouét*, chosen by Masterson that failed to meet earning expectations. Even though the theatre had produced summertime fare that attracted large audiences (e.g., *Forever Plaid* and *Always, Patsy Cline*), Masterson's choice of the unknown musical failed to entice either younger audiences or Actors Theatre regulars—proof of his difficulty in gaining the trust of Louisville theatergoers. In retrospect, Masterson admitted, "The play had no name recognition. I think there is an audience for a play like that in Louisville, but . . . in that particular slot, it was a hard sell."[19] Masterson quickly learned his lesson and, the following year, like Jory in his earliest years in Louisville, presented less adventuresome (and more popular) fare in the form of *My Way: A Musical Tribute to Frank Sinatra*.

Once Masterson began tailoring the presentations to the tastes of the Louisville community, he began to build a trust with his patrons, and support for him was exhibited through a remarkable achievement. Upon his arrival in Louisville, Masterson inherited the daunting problem of decreasing subscriptions. According to Egerton, subscriptions to Actors Theatre dropped by nearly fifteen hundred during the two years encompassing both Jory's final year and Masterson's arrival. Even though most regional theatres suffered from declining subscriptions rates, Masterson's success in establishing new audiences and building a trust with his patrons helped Actors Theatre buck the trend, reporting in May 2004 that their subscriptions rose by 8 percent. "We are selling more tickets than we have in the last few years, and that's terrific," Masterson boasted in an interview. "The fact that subscriptions are up by that number, particularly when the economy has been down, is a sign we're on track."[20] Similar to Jory's determination, on his arrival, to engage the public and reverse the trend of declining subscriptions, Masterson's efforts at outreach and education succeeded in bringing new audiences to Actors Theatre. The community's growing approval of his leadership and his play selections finally allowed him to emerge from his predecessor's shadow.[21]

The rise in subscriptions in 2004 is impressive, given that Masterson stumbled during his first years with several questionable play selections. For the summer productions, *Jouét* proved that he needed to build trust before local audiences would attend productions with which they were not familiar. The same lack of trust hindered the success of the first two years of the Humana Festival under Masterson's control, as several of his choices for the 2002 and 2003 collections failed to find support from the national press or local audiences. Although his alterations for the festival were minor and his decisions illustrated a lack of salesmanship, by his fifth collection in 2006, Masterson proved that he had in fact mastered Jory's formula.

Masterson's format for the Humana Festival remained similar to Jory's, but the new artistic director made two changes to make the festival his own. First and foremost, the major play selections became much more experimental in nature, featuring many writers who before had never been a part of the Humana Festival. In an interview, Masterson detailed his own vision for the festival: "I want to open up the question of what constitutes an American playwright. There's a vital scene to our north and just to our south. I am also interested in including translations of plays from other cultures."[22] While Jory certainly had not focused on the development of southern drama in the last fifteen years of his tenure, Masterson's statement was interpreted by some to be a declaration of a new direction—away from writers familiar to Louisville audiences and toward the discovery of new playwrights (who might not supply the commercial fare that often appeased local patrons).

Indeed, Masterson risked the relevance and the popularity of the festival, as such audience favorites as Arthur Kopit, Jane Martin, Naomi Wallace, and Marsha Norman were nowhere to be found. Instead of commissioning or selecting past staples of the festival, Masterson invited several up-and-coming playwrights to the Louisville stage for the twenty-sixth festival. Of the newcomers, Adam Rapp's East Village drama *Finer Noble Gases* received the best, though mixed, reviews. Writing for the *Boston Phoenix*, critic Scott T. Cummings best summarized the reaction to Rapp's play: "For some, *Finer Noble Gases* was self-indulgent silliness; for me, it provided a troubling thrill."[23] While two remaining newcomers, Jerome Hairston and Marlane Meyer, stumbled in their first Louisville festival, several veteran playwrights also presented harshly criticized work. Tina Howe's *Rembrandt's Gift* was unanimously labeled the disappointment of the festival, and Anne Bogart's "pretentious snooze" *Score* received approval from a few critics who admired her attempt to explore the challenges of creativity through the work of Leonard Bernstein; many reviewers, unfortunately, found the material overblown and difficult to comprehend.[24]

Masterson's first foray into the festival as its sole producer received mixed to negative reviews, and his second collection in 2003 fared no better. Critic Michael Phillips of the *Chicago Tribune* expressed his disappointment with the selection of plays and what it implied about the future of the annual event: "Two years into the Masterson tenure, one senses a 27-year-old tradition unsure of its future."[25] Numerous critics echoed Phillips's concern and dissatisfaction with the new artistic director's selections, not to mention the faulty writing exhibited in the productions. Much like the prior collection, the Humana Festival presented a few successes (Theresa Rebeck and

Alexandra Gersten-Vassilaros's *Omnium-Gatherum* and Russell Davis's *The Second Death of Priscilla*), a unanimous failure (Bridget Carpenter's *The Faculty Room*, an uneven drama about teachers), and numerous productions on which critics could not agree. As a whole, however, Masterson continued to suffer from the exceptionally high (and perhaps unfair) expectations of the national press, as reviewers wondered whether Masterson knew how to make the Humana Festival an "event" again.[26]

The most common criticism of the 2002 and 2003 festivals was the timidity of the playwriting; the national press frequently questioned Masterson's tastes and his ability to select quality scripts. Masterson once commented, "I believe that it's possible to do things that are artistically advanced and popular at the same time," but his earliest festivals achieved only the former attribute.[27] With his commissions and play selections, Masterson answered the long-standing critical call for the festival to present more daring work by lesser-known playwrights, but the popularity of the festival suffered. Even though several critics called for the return of former Humana Festival playwrights so that the event could rediscover the popularity it enjoyed in its first years (a futile request), Masterson consistently commissioned younger and less-established playwrights. As a result, even though the 2002 and 2003 collections featured faulty productions, the festivals were a learning period for the press and festival patrons, who had to familiarize themselves with Masterson's new priorities and his tastes.

Even though Masterson might not have been as interested as Jory in national relevance or publicity when deciding his commissions and selections, many of the plays featured in the twenty-sixth and twenty-seventh festivals did move on to other regional theatres, and almost every playwright from these two years found support for their new work at other theatres as a result of their appearance in the Louisville festival. For instance, even though critics fiercely attacked Bridget Carpenter's *The Faculty Room*, her play won the 2003 Kesserling Prize. Furthermore, several works transferred to New York, including *Omnium-Gatherum*, *The Mystery of Attraction*, and *Finer Noble Gases*, while other works such as *The Faculty Room*, Charles L. Mee's *Limonade Tous les Jours*, Kia Corthron's *Slide Glide the Slippery Slope,* and *Rembrandt's Gift* toured regional and university theatres. Though critics consistently dismissed the efforts of the Humana Festival in 2002 and 2003, Masterson, much like Jory, continued to present hit plays, but the visibility of the annual event was one issue the new artistic director still needed to address.

Masterson's second alteration in the festival concerned the phone plays: he replaced them with more experimental fare. On his arrival at Actors Theatre in 2001, Masterson said, "I am interested in the way that technology and the Internet are impacting our art. Maybe that's worth exploring at the festival."[28] Masterson fulfilled his wish a year later in the Twenty-Sixth Humana

Festival with the Technology Project, a collection of three diverse works that emphasized the use of electronics as a means of exploring the boundaries of live performance. According to former literary manager Tanya Palmer, "In order to explore this increasingly complex territory, Actors Theatre—in partnership with the EST/Sloan Foundation Science and Technology Project and Carnegie Mellon University's Entertainment Technology Center—asked three playwrights to interface with technologies that ranged from the mundane to the mind-boggling."[29] Of the three works, Alice Tuan's *F.E.T.C.H.* garnered the most attention. The play employed actors, attached to a tall pole, who maneuvered up and down the post, interacting with the audience and creating a "virtual hypertext" performance.

Having attempted to attract younger audiences in 2002 with the Technology Project, Masterson hoped to entice local African American patrons to the theatre with *Rhythmicity: A Convergence of Poetry, Theatre, and Hip-Hop*, a collective of New York's finest poets and slam artists, including reg e. gaines (the writer of *Bring in 'da Noise, Bring in 'da Funk*) and Regie Cabico, a former National Slam champion. While some critics questioned the value of the *Rhythmicity* collection because of its likelihood never to be performed anywhere else again, most reviewers considered the performance a refreshing change. Nevertheless, they also noted the limited appeal of these artists to mainstream theatergoers, some labeling *Rhythmicity* a gimmick to diversify the festival.

In total, the first two years were not kind to Masterson and the Humana Festival, and the national press pondered the demise of the annual event. After the twenty-sixth festival, Hedy Weiss of the *Chicago Sun Times* stated, "The Humana Festival, which has always been uneven at best, seemed for the most part to be a warehouse for new scripts that had nowhere to go."[30] The following year, Dag Ryen, who had been covering the festival for many years from nearby Lexington, sounded grave cautions concerning the 2003 festival: "Judging from the 'special visitors' festivities last weekend, the Humana Festival seems to have hit a snag. Attendance was down, with fewer critics and foreign visitors on hand. . . . It showcased a couple of intriguing experimental plays. It offered a few good laughs. But did it offer enough to keep the theater elite coming back for more? Is that a fair expectation to begin with? Can Louisville hope to keep its renowned festival franchise forever? These are questions to which Masterson must find answers."[31]

Unlike the strong local support for Actors Theatre's regular season, the declining patronage of the 2002 and 2003 Humana Festivals revealed problems about trust and relevance (or national interest in Jory's formula). Instead of beginning cautiously and commissioning high-profile playwrights, the new artistic director favored his own writers and emphasized his own tastes, but this disregard for audience preferences and critical expectations alienated both the international press and local audiences. Not knowing what to expect from his play selections (or from the playwrights in each of the first two festivals), some patrons had insufficient trust in Masterson and decided to stay away from the festival.

Critics were confused about and frustrated over Masterson's new direction for the festival, but the artistic director received a vote of confidence from a crucial supporter. Silencing those who predicted the immediate demise of the festival, Actors Theatre received another three-year commitment from the Humana Foundation in the form of $1.95 million, a strong sign of support for Masterson and his new direction. Having obtained financial support and having learned from his first two festival outings, Masterson made a slight change in the next festival. If the first two years under new leadership was a learning period for festival attendees, then the overwhelmingly successful Twenty-Eighth Annual Humana Festival proved that festival guests understood and appreciated his new direction. On the other hand, while the 2004 festival was not as lauded as the fourteenth (1990) or the twenty-fourth (2000), its success also demonstrated that Masterson understood the value of returning playwrights (favoring several writers from his prior festivals): only three of the ten playwrights made their Humana Festival debut in 2003.[32]

Even though several plays elicited positive notices from critics (especially Gina Gionfriddo's *After Ashley*), a closer look at one production in the 2004 festival illustrated how Masterson began to build trust with local audiences and with critics. As if taking a page from Jory's playbook (or, in this case, formula), the twenty-eighth festival featured a play that focused on Louisville (similar to *The Louisville Zoo* and Jory's selecting a local playwright) and was staged in an off-site location (much like *Food from Trash*). To ensure local support, Actors Theatre commissioned Naomi Iizuka to write a play about the Louisville neighborhood Butchertown and its residents.[33] Certainly this play helped entice local patrons to the theatre, since it sold out most of its performances. More important, the return of Iizuka to the festival with a full-length work marked a change in Masterson's play selections. In his first two festivals, the most high-profile playwright to appear in Louisville was Lee Blessing, with his ten-minute play *The Roads That Lead Here* in 2003, but the commissioning of Iizuka for a main-stage show (even though it was performed in an abandoned auto body repair shop in Butchertown) signaled Masterson's realization that he needed to present more established writers to appease local audiences and entice the national press to travel to the Kentucky city.[34]

To celebrate its latest successful collection, Actors Theatre listed its accomplishments from the twenty-eighth festival on its Web site, heralding an increase in ticket sales of 14 percent, an attendance of nearly thirty thousand, a tourist-package increase of over 60 percent, sold-out performances, and a large contingent of international press. This blatant public-relations maneuver not only illustrated that Masterson recognized the lackluster performance of the twenty-sixth and twenty-seventh festivals but also represented an attempt to quell the premature rumors of the festival's demise.[35]

Masterson built on his success with the Twenty-Ninth Annual Humana Festival of New American Plays in 2005, offering a strong collection and a balance of new and returning playwrights. Unlike prior Humana Festival plays that appealed to local audiences yet lacked merit (*Digging In*, *Lighting Up the Two-Year Old*, and *Indulgences in a Louisville Harem*, to name a few), *Pure Confidence*, Carlyle Brown's drama about African American jockeys, wowed critics and audiences alike and easily became the hit of the festival. John Belluso's stunning *A Nervous Smile* impressed attendees, as well, with its discomforting tale of a couple's inability to care for (and their eventual abandonment of) their special-needs child. Easily the most disappointing play belonged to Kia Corthron and her political tirade *Moot the Messenger*. While some critics enjoyed her 2003 play *Slide Glide the Slippery Slope*, almost every critic dismissed her latest effort as a rant in dialogue form, belaboring the same point over and over again while a flimsy plot line simply prolonged the audience's suffering.

Masterson further transformed the festival into his own event by replacing another of his predecessor's experiments with a popular and accessible production. The *Back Story* experiment appeared in several festivals since its inception in 1999, but with each passing year, the collection of monologues and short scenes became less and less valid, with critics dismissing the work as a showcase for the Acting Apprentices. For the 2004 festival, Masterson commissioned the Neo-Futurists's Greg Allen, Richard Dresser, and a few other writers to create *Uncle Sam's Satiric Spectacular: On Democracy and Other Fictions Featuring Patriotism Acts and Blue Songs from a Red State*. In this "Brechtian vaudeville" production, Uncle Sam, dressed in a flashy red, white, and blue suit made of sequins, served as the emcee and announced his intention to present wholesome family entertainment. The various acts included a magician, a knife thrower, and an escape artist, but much to Uncle Sam's dismay, the performers commented on political and social issues ranging from abortion and bad parenting to the country's inept foreign policy. Even though the show frequently featured a barbershop quartet who sang about the misinterpretation and abuse of the Geneva Conventions, a few critics believed that the musical collection suffered from a lack of focus. These critics failed to realize that the writers kept true to the eclectic nature of vaudeville, striking a balance between dazzling entertainment and commentary and providing a rare festival experience not seen since *Doctors and Diseases* in the fourth festival.[36]

This biting and hysterical collection quickly became an audience favorite and was transferred to New York for the 2005 New York International Fringe

Festival, where it "won rave reviews and [has] been touted as a 'must see' from the *New York Times, Oprah Magazine*, NYTheatre.com and more."[37] It was no mistake that Masterson abandoned the tired format of the *Back Story* collection, and *Uncle Sam's Satiric Spectacular* mirrored a move made by Jory in his earliest festivals—selecting (or, in this case, commissioning) a work because of its popular entertainment value. In many ways, this show found Masterson reverting to Jory's older mentality, stressing product over process, but more important, Masterson's decision to present this simpler, lighter fare reflected his learning to strive for the balance that Jory pursued: a mix between popular and experimental plays. This production further proved Masterson's mastery of the festival, that he understood his local audiences as well as the demands of the critics while also rebuilding the reputation of the festival after his first two efforts.

Given the positive reception of the 2004 and 2005 festivals, critics anxiously awaited the next year's anniversary collection, curious to see whether Masterson could enjoy continuous good fortune as Jory did in his first years with the festival. For the thirtieth festival in 2006, the national press once again lavished praise on Masterson and his latest collection. Lexington critic Ryen reported, "Maybe it was a little short on experimentation, but it was surely long on entertainment," and the *New York Times* raved, "The three stages at the Actors Theatre of Louisville are awash in bold ideas wrapped in colorful theatrical packaging."[38] Although the festival was replete with lauded works, two productions in particular symbolized Masterson's achievements with the festival in five years and showed that he had learned Jory's formulas for success (balance and visibility).

Following the VIP weekend, the standout of the festival was easy to determine. Serving as the headline for his review, *Chicago Tribune* critic Chris Jones declared, "*The Scene* steals the show at Humana," and most critics agreed.[39] Theresa Rebeck's simple yet accomplished parody of celebrity culture and the singles' scene in New York left critics wondering when this small but affecting play would transfer to New York or appear in their local regional theatres. The discovery of this overwhelmingly lauded play not only helped the festival retain its "event" status (several attendees having heard positive press about the play in advance of the festival weekend) but also showed how Masterson had successfully transformed the festival into *his* festival. Besides having her play *Bad Dates* presented in Actors Theatre's regular season in 2006, Rebeck made her second appearance in the festival with *The Scene*, becoming one of Masterson's favorites and leading a few critics to bemoan (again) that the festival supported established playwrights instead of discovering new talent. In his first five years, Masterson developed his own festival veterans, and even though these writers were not well known or cherished by local audiences in their first appearances, their return provided familiarity for local patrons and the national press. In this sense, even though he faced the same criticism as Jory for some of his selections, he established an aesthetic difference from Jory that was distinctly his own. In a few short years, Masterson made Actors Theatre a home for Jordan Harrison (a three-time festival participant), Kia Corthron, the late John Belluso, Adam Bock, and Allison Moore, among others.

The second production of note at the thirtieth festival came from the most-produced playwright in festival history, Jane Martin. Jon Jory returned to Louisville to direct the ten-minute play *Listeners*, a "dark and jarringly comic imagining of the Bush Administration's domestic spying program taken to its limits as two government agents in suits and ties invade the home of Eleanor Leftwich after technology has identified her as 'a valued citizen who just might be a little cranky.'"[40] The play, however, marked more than the return of Martin to the festival after a four-year absence. While Masterson's dreadful production of *Wonderful World* during the 2001 festival instigated a competition between himself and Jory, the inclusion of Martin in the 2006 event signaled that the artistic director now felt confident enough in his accomplishments with the festival to invite immediate comparisons with Jory. Furthermore, *Listeners* proved that Masterson understood that the festival had to be visible—a key component of Jory's formula for success. With the addition of Martin to the balanced lineup of high-profile playwrights, including Charles L. Mee, Anne Bogart, and Masterson's favored writers, the festival continued to surge in popularity, and the public relations department of Actors Theatre again detailed its achievements on its Web page, reporting that more than twenty-six thousand patrons (representing thirty-seven states and sixteen countries) attended shows during the five weeks of the festival.[41]

With the many lauded works in the 2006 collection, the festival once again provided its attendees with a feeling of excitement, that indescribable energy that makes the festival a special event. Even though Masterson's Humana Festivals have not been as popular or as relevant as some of Jory's collections (in terms of plays becoming a part of the American canon or traveling to Broadway), the festival again regained its prominence in the landscape of American playwriting with its consistent devotion to the development of playwrights through discovery and through continued support. More important, Masterson accomplished what few theatre professionals or critics predicted that he could—he transformed the festival into his own event, giving him the freedom to present annual collections with little comparison between him and his predecessor. Even though the first two years of the festival were difficult, Masterson successfully educated his audiences about his tastes and agenda with the festival while, at the same time, he learned how to entice patrons to the Louisville theatre and maintain the visibility of the festival.

Masterson still has work to do, however, to make the festival as successful as possible. For future Humana Festivals, Masterson needs to continue to follow Jory's example and prove the festival's relevance through the commissioning of more popular playwrights, in addition to up-and-coming talents. During the past five years of Masterson's Humana Festival, he certainly exhibited his willingness to experiment with new writers, but he needs to remember that these achievements and discoveries will not mean anything if a large contingent of the national press fails to attend the festival; in other words, without good fortune, he cannot enjoy the freedom to support his favorite writers. The commissioning of well-known playwrights attracts more theatre professionals (who may want to add the play to their next season), West Coast executives (who look for new vehicles or projects), as well as members of the national press (who like to view the latest work of established playwrights). The most successful festivals during Jory's tenure provided a balance of new and proven writers, and recently Masterson implemented the proven formula in the 2006 collection. After Masterson wisely pursued an extensive publicity effort, the thirtieth festival did attract more attendees, but he should continue to recognize that the reputation of the festival is also determined by the success of the plays after the Humana Festival. If festival audiences decrease again, he will feel pressure to sacrifice his artistic inclinations and include more popular (i.e., less experimental) fare, providing a greater likelihood that other theatres will produce Humana Festival plays in the future.

Conclusion: Looking Back and Looking Forward

Among the many great figures in the development of regional theatre in America, the most notable include Zelda Fichandler, Margo Jones, Nina Vance, Tyrone Guthrie, and Joseph Papp. Given his astounding achievements in Louisville, Jon Jory deserves equal commendation. While the likes of Fichandler and Jones were certainly pioneers and the work of Guthrie and Papp won wide acclaim, Jory and his festival perhaps have had the greatest overall affect on regional theatre for the last three decades of the century.

It is remarkable, then, that few analyses of the theatrical work of the twentieth century recognize Jory and his massive contribution to playwriting. Instead they focus on smaller enclaves or movements. But the far-reaching achievements that shape Jory's legacy affect playwrights around the country. Jory's work helped reestablish the prominence of the playwright in the rehearsal process in theatres nationally and promoted the inclusion of dramaturgs on the staffs of professional theatres. Thanks to the success of his festival, new opportunities for playwriting development sprang up across the country as other artistic directors attempted to mimic his good fortune. Even though some of these festivals are now defunct, Jory's support of new American playwrights instilled in the minds of many theatre professionals that new play development must be a priority if regional theatre is to survive.

The most recognizable aspect of Jory's legacy is the discovery of hundreds of playwrights and the support, through productions, of their careers, regardless of critical responses. Because of his decisions for and artistry within the Humana Festival, his contribution to the landscape of American playwriting cannot be denied. It is primarily his discovery of and support for southern female playwrights that led to an increased presence of such writers on Broadway, Off Broadway, and eventually around the country. Furthermore, his willingness to take risks helped expose national critics to experimental playwrights, whose work might otherwise have been relegated to major cities or theatres on either coast. Also, his controversial commissioning of projects initiated passionate discussions about the nature of playwriting and the challenges that face undiscovered writers (debates that Jory was happy to instigate, even at the expense of attacks from the national press and other playwrights).

More important, Jory increased the perceived value of playwriting on two fronts. First, his festival and its dedication to the needs and concerns of the playwright demonstrated the importance of process (and art) over product (and commercialism). Second, his dogged determination to maintain the visibility of his festival helped playwrights by altering the perception of success. By no longer needing to go to New York for validation as a writer, the festival changed the perception of what a successful playwright could be. Because of current economic demands, few plays ever make it to Broadway, and even those works that do premiere on the Great White Way are most likely the product of development processes in regional theatre. Knowing that Broadway often is an unrealistic expectation for a writer, the producers of the Humana Festival and the numerous new play development programs that it inspired provide playwrights with opportunities to have their work seen all around the country and, over time, build a reputation without the benefit (or burden) of playing in New York. Without the Humana Festival and its impact on play development opportunities, writers who once perceived New York as the only goal might have given up hope of finding supporters of their work and American playwriting would decline further. Because of the many festivals and workshops around the country, a gentler, more inclusive network of playwriting opportunities allows the best work in the country to be seen and to travel to numerous regional theatres.

Given his festival's unchallenged position as the premier new play festival in the country, Jory's risky pursuit of artistic challenges in new forms of playwriting and production is extraordinarily admirable. If other theatres had been so fortunate as to enjoy a success comparable to that of the Humana Festival, many artistic directors would have been content to play it safe and not risk criticism by experimenting with the festival. However, Jory's resolve to investigate the multifaceted question "What is theatre?" is exactly what made his festival thrive and remain relevant. His willingness to take on critics, endure personal attacks, and celebrate forms and writers that riled other theatre professionals, all in the name of exploration, were challenges from which Jory never shied away. It would have been easy for him to simply search for production-ready scripts and turn his festival into a shopping mall for plays from its inception, but Jory was unwavering in his agenda of discovery and experimentation. In other words, he relished the artistic freedom that his festival's success provided to him, and he made sure to use it.

Jory's legacy is not limited to the Humana Festival; his work as the producing director of a thriving regional theatre also deserves recognition. Of course, not every regional theatre developed a festival of the size and scope of the Humana Festival, and the reason for it is simple: Jon Jory. Here is a man who worked tirelessly to secure an audience base, catered to its needs to gain its trust, and then slowly but methodically introduced new work to his conservative audience with great success. Thanks to Jory's willingness to sacrifice his personal artistic preferences to ensure his institution's financial health, Actors Theatre established records for attendance and subscriptions, making the Louisville theatre a model for audience building. While there is proof that Jory benefited from a community eager to support the arts, it should not be construed that funding and support for Actors Theatre were permanent conditions; on the contrary, Block's failed leadership drove down subscriptions and reflected the community's rejection of his agenda.[1] Both Block and Jory came to a city where the citizens supported the idea of a thriving regional theatre, but Jory knew how to mobilize this support with charisma to cultivate his own projects. In short, Jory created his own opportunities.

Jory's showmanship was crucial in establishing his festival. Like Papp, Jory needed to strike a perfect balance between catering to public preferences and educating and challenging audiences. Unlike the New York producer, who scheduled work for a larger audience base, Jory adroitly balanced the preferences of two vastly different yet demanding audiences: conservative local patrons and national critics. Few producers would be able to sell a collection of plays to two such divergent groups, yet Jory did it while producing a long-running annual festival (by enticing critics to travel to Louisville) and maintaining his local subscription base (by persuading patrons to support new plays). Jory understood the need for publicity and promotion to keep his theatre and its festival successful, and his selfless nature—to work for the betterment of his institution as opposed to personal glory—allowed the festival to evolve from a small event of Jory's favorite plays to a crucial participant in the landscape of new play development.

More important than his surprising ability to build a nationally recognized theatre in a small Kentucky city is Jory's concern for and promotion of the regional theatre movement. In addition to his numerous writings about the state of regional theatre in America and his willingness to offer advice and share the secrets of his theatre's success, Jory's dedication to Actors Theatre and its festival spoke volumes about the potential and value of regional theatre. Instead of finding immediate success and then leaving for greater fame or more lucrative opportunities, Jory chose to shun the theatre establishment and remain in Louisville, thus emphasizing his belief in the quality and importance of the work of regional theatres. By dedicating himself to a life in regional theatre and by exploring how such an institution can become a pivotal part of its community, Jory transformed Actors Theatre from an entertainment venue to a vital part of the Louisville community and a leader in the development of American playwriting.

Thanks to his leadership, Jory left behind a theatre that had come to symbolize creative freedom. At the close of the twentieth century, the creative endeavors of Jory and his staff were the most ambitious and wide-reaching pursuits of any regional theatre in the country. In addition to exploring new play development, Jory supported solo performances, academic explorations through classic plays, national and international touring, and short-form play competitions, not to mention endeavors not discussed in this study, such as the Free Theatre Project, Apprentice Winter and Summer productions, playwrights-in-residence, and Free Children's Theatre. All of this in a small city not previously known for its support of the arts.

Jory has exerted immense influence over the development and practices of American theatre, and the professional theatre community will be reminded of his visionary talents every spring, when a new batch of writers make its debut in Louisville, further enforcing Jory's legacy. Often perceived as a mysterious person who made history by creating a landmark festival in a random city while never utilizing its fame for his own self-promotion, Jory has become a colossal figure in contemporary American theatre, primarily because an analysis of his accomplishments and methodology has never been provided. As much as he accomplished in Louisville, Jory's tenure at Actors Theatre was not free of missteps, nor were his decisions easy, obvious choices. Jory labored for thirty-one years to discover and maintain his success, and even if the national press and other theatre professionals did not understand how he achieved it, the Louisville patrons who had seen their local institution develop into an internationally acclaimed theatre greatly respected Jory and are reminded of his remarkable accomplishments every time they drive down Main Street or attend one of the hundreds of performances each year. Jory was a local celebrity when he lived in Louisville; now that he has moved to Washington state, Jory has become a legend to the Louisville community.

Even though other artistic directors may strive to cast their new play workshops in the mold of the Humana Festival, Jory's accomplishments came from opportunities that he created, along with his willingness to accept the additional responsibilities that accompany success. These opportunities arose not only because of his hard work but because he followed a formula of establishing a local base while also pursuing national visibility. Once he had built his audience, the success that Jory enjoyed resulted from his keen sense of what would appeal to local audiences and what would also interest New York producers. In addition to his extraordinary skills as a director, his calculated and savvy decisions as a producer helped create the conditions that delivered quality scripts to his doorstep, making his perceived luck the result of determination, skill, and awareness—three qualities that cannot easily be copied.

Jory enjoyed artistic freedom within the festival, but he also learned that with success came responsibility—not to explore works that are so far out of the mainstream as to discourage patrons from attending and not to force his audience to accept experimental work without methodically educating them as to the value of theatrical exploration. Even though some of his experimental selections failed to appease critics or audiences, his commissions always featured a recognizable component: an author, topic, or performance style that intrigued and enticed theatergoers to witness the result. Jory consistently monitored the visibility of the festival and tempered his artistic inclinations when necessary to maintain the reputation of the event, an action best exemplified by his abandoning of the commissioning of nonplaywrights to pen plays.

After following the same methods and philosophies as his predecessor, Marc Masterson had quick success with the Humana Festival. Jory's proven methodologies thus are valuable to others, yet, at the same time, reliance on them does not guarantee success. Jory possessed a phenomenal gift for recognizing the needs of the American theatre (especially among its playwrights, audiences, and dramaturgs) and for creating solutions through his own showmanship and management decisions. In the short history of regional theatre, few artistic directors have matched Jory's keen sense of purpose or his ability to predict trends.

Appropriately, Jory has moved into a teaching position at the University of Washington, where the best performers are those who possess talents that are not taught but are innate. Although he may have become a professor late in life, his work at Actors Theatre has taught not only countless audience members to appreciate new work but also artistic directors around the world to mount a successful new play program. Long after Jory retires from his professorship, he will continue to teach through the Humana Festival, which serves as a model for ingenuity, encouraging the future practitioners of theatre to seek good fortune through planning and passion and to pursue an agenda of artistic freedom that continuously challenges and progresses the current state of theatre. Masterson may have made his stamp on the festival, but whether he will provide new lessons through the Humana Festival remains to be seen.

APPENDIX
NOTES
WORKS CITED
INDEX

Appendix: Humana Festival Production History

First Festival of New American Plays (1976–77)

The Gin Game by D. L. Coburn
Indulgences in a Louisville Harem by John Orlock

Second Annual Festival of New American Plays (1977–78)

The Bridgehead by Frederick Bailey
Daddies by Douglas Gower
Does Anybody Here Do the Peabody? by Enid Rudd
Getting Out by Marsha Norman
An Independent Woman by Daniel Stein
The Louisville Zoo by anonymous authors

Third Annual Festival of New American Plays (1978–79)

Circus Valentine by Marsha Norman
Crimes of the Heart by Beth Henley
Find Me by Owlen Wymark
Holidays: A Compendium of Short Plays
  Bar Play by Lanford Wilson
  Fireworks by Megan Terry
  The Great Labor Day Classic by Israel Horovitz
  I Can't Find It Anywhere by Oliver Hailey
  Independence Day by Tom Eyen
  In the Fireworks Lie Secret Codes by John Guare
  Juneteenth by Preston Jones
  Merry Christmas by Marsha Norman
  New Year's by Ray Aranha
  Redeemer by Douglas Turner Ward
Lone Star by James McLure
Matrimonium by Peter Ekstrom

BECOMING AN INSTITUTION, 1980–82

Fourth Annual Festival of New American Plays (1979–80)

Agnes of God by John Pielmeier

The America Project: A Compendium of Short Plays
  American Welcome by Brian Friel
  The Drummer by Athol Fugard
  The Golden Accord by Wole Soyinka
  Hooray for Hollywood by John Byrne
  San Salvador by Keith Dewhurst
  The Side of the Road by Gordon Dryland
  Star Quality by Carol Bolt
  Switching by Brian Clark
  Tall Girls Have Everything by Stewart Parker
  Vicki Madison Clocks Out by Alexander Buzo
Doctors and Diseases by Peter Ekstrom
Power Plays by Shirley Lauro: Two One-Acts
  The Coal Diamond
  Nothing Immediate
Remington by Ray Aranha
Sunset/Sunrise by Adele Edling Shank
They're Coming to Make It Brighter by Kent Broadhurst
Today a Little Extra by Michael Kassin
Weekends Like Other People by David Blomquist

Fifth Annual Festival of New American Plays (1980–81)

The Autobiography of a Pearl Diver by Martin Epstein
Early Times: A Compendium of Short Plays
  The A**hole Murder Case by Stuart Hample
  Chapter Twelve—The Frog by John Pielmeier
  Propinquity by Claudia Johnson
  Quadrangle by Jon Jory
  Spades by Jim Beaver
  Twirler by Jane Martin
  Watermelon Boats by Wendy MacLaughlin
Extremities by William Mastrosimone
A Full Length Portrait of America by Paul D'Andrea
Future Tense by David Kranes: Two One-Acts
  After Commencement
  Park City: Midnight
My Sister in This House by Wendy Kesselman
Shorts: Three One-Act Plays
  Chocolate Cake by Mary Gallagher
  Chug by Ken Jenkins
  Final Placement by Ara Watson
SWOP by Ken Jenkins

Sixth Annual Humana Festival of New American Plays (1981–82)

Clara's Play by John Olive
A Different Moon by Ara Watson
Full Hookup by Conrad Bishop and Elizabeth Fuller
The Grapes of Wrath by Terrence Shank
The Informer by Thomas Murphy
Oldtimers Game by Lee Blessing
Shorts: Three One-Act Plays
    The Eye of the Beholder by Kent Broadhurst
    The New Girl by Vaughn McBride
    The Groves of Academe by Mark Stein
Solo: A Compendium of Short Plays
    Butterfly, Marguerite, Norma . . . & Irma Jean by Trish Johnson
    Cemetery Man by Ken Jenkins
    Rupert's Birthday by Ken Jenkins
    Sidekick by Jim Beaver
    Slow Drag, Mama by Dare Clubb and Isabell Monk
    The Subject Animal by Larry Atlas
    The Survivalist by Robert Schenkkan
Talking With by Jane Martin

FROM PRODUCT TO PROCESS, 1983–86

Seventh Annual Humana Festival of New American Plays (1982–83)

Chapter and Verse by Ken Jenkins
Courage by John Pielmeier
Eden Court by Murphy Guyer
Fathers and Daughters: Two One-Acts
    A Tantalizing by William Mastrosimone
    The Value of Names by Jeffrey Sweet
Food from Trash by Gary Leon Hill
In a Northern Landscape by Timothy Mason
Neutral Countries by Barbara Field
Sand Castles by Adele Edling Shank
Shorts: Three One-Act Plays
    Bartok as Dog by Patrick Tovatt
    The Habitual Acceptance of the Near Enough by Kent Broadhurst
    Partners by Dave Higgins
Thanksgiving by James McLure
A Weekend near Madison by Kathleen Tolan

Eighth Annual Humana Festival of New American Plays (1983–84)

007 Crossfire by Ken Jenkins

Courtship by Horton Foote
Danny and the Deep Blue Sea by John Patrick Shanley
Execution of Justice by Emily Mann
Husbandry by Patrick Tovatt
Independence by Lee Blessing
Lemons by Kent Broadhurst
The Octette Bridge Club by P. J. Barry
The Undoing by William Mastrosimone

Ninth Annual Humana Festival of New American Plays (1984–85)

Available Light by Heather McDonald
Days and Nights Within by Ellen McLaughlin
Ride the Dark Horse by J. F. O'Keefe
Shorts: Two Bills of One-Act Plays
    Advice to the Players by Bruce Bonafede
    The American Century by Murphy Guyer
    The Black Branch by Gary Leon Hill with Jo Hill
    The Root of Chaos by Douglas Soderberg
Tent Meeting by Larry Larson, Levi Lee, and Rebecca Wackler
Two Masters by Frank Manley
The Very Last Lover of the River Cane by James McLure
War of the Roses by Lee Blessing

Tenth Annual Humana Festival of New American Plays (1985–86)

Astronauts by Claudia Reilly
How to Say Goodbye by Mary Gallagher
No Mercy by Constance Congdon
The Sharper by John Steppling
Smitty's News by Conrad Bishop and Elizabeth Fuller
*Some Things You Need to Know before the World Ends: A Final
    Evening with the Illuminati* by Larry Larson and Levi Lee
To Culebra by Jonathan Bolt
Transports: Two One-Act Plays
    21A by Kevin Kling
    How Gertrude Stormed the Philosopher's Club by Martin Epstein

THE EXPLORATORY YEARS, 1987–93

Eleventh Annual Humana Festival of New American Plays (1986–87)

Deadfall by Grace McKeaney
Digging In: The Farm Crisis in Kentucky by Julie Crutcher and
    Vaughn McBride
Elaine's Daughter by Mayo Simon

Glimmerglass by Jonathan Bolt
Gringo Planet by Frederick Bailey
Shorts: Three One-Act Plays
    Chemical Reactions by Andy Foster
    Fun by Howard Korder
    The Love Talker by Deborah Pryor
T Bone N Weasel by Jon Klein
Water Hole by Kendrew Lascelles

Twelfth Annual Humana Festival of New American Plays (1987–88)

Alone at the Beach by Richard Dresser
Channels by Judith Fein
Lloyd's Prayer by Kevin Kling
The Metaphor by Murphy Guyer
The Queen of the Leaky Roof Circuit by Jimmy Breslin
Sarah and Abraham by Marsha Norman
Whereabouts Unknown by Barbara Damashek

Thirteenth Annual Humana Festival of New American Plays (1988–89)

Autumn Elegy by Charles Redick
Blood Issue by Harry Crews
Bone the Fish by Arthur Kopit (later retitled *Road to Nirvana*)
The Bug by Richard Strand
God's Country by Steven Dietz
Incident at San Bajo by Brad Korbesmeyer
Stained Glass by William F. Buckley Jr.
Tales of the Lost Formicans by Constance Congdon

Fourteenth Annual Humana Festival of New American Plays (1989–90)

2 by Romulus Linney
In Darkest America by Joyce Carol Oates: Two One-Acts
    The Eclipse
    Tone Clusters
Infinity's House by Ellen McLaughlin
The Pink Studio by Jane Anderson
The Swan by Elizabeth Egloff
Vital Signs by Jane Martin
Zara Spook and Other Lures by Joan Ackermann-Blount

Fifteenth Annual Humana Festival of New America Plays (1990–91)

Cementville by Jane Martin
The Death of Zukasky by Richard Strand

Down the Road by Lee Blessing
In the Eye of the Hurricane by Eduardo Machado
Night-side by Shem Bitterman
Out the Window by Neal Bell
A Passenger Train of Sixty-One Coaches by Paul Walker
A Piece of My Heart by Shirley Lauro
What She Found There by John Glore

Sixteenth Annual Humana Festival of New American Plays (1991–92)

Bondage by David Henry Hwang
The Carving of Mount Rushmore by John Conklin
D. Boone by Marsha Norman
Devotees in the Garden of Love by Suzan-Lori Parks
Eukiah by Lanford Wilson
Evelyn and the Polka King by John Olive
Hyaena by Ross MacLean
Lynette at 3AM by Jane Anderson
Marisol by José Rivera
Old Lady's Guide to Survival by Mayo Simon
Procedure by Joyce Carol Oates

Seventeenth Annual Humana Festival of New American Plays (1992–93)

Deadly Virtues by Brian Jucha
The Ice Fishing Play by Kevin Kling
Keely and Du by Jane Martin
Poof! by Lynn Nottage
Shooting Simone by Lynne Kaufman
Stanton's Garage by Joan Ackermann
Tape by José Rivera
Various Small Fires by Regina Taylor: Two One-Acts
   Jennine's Diary
   Watermelon Rinds
What We Do with It by Bruce MacDonald

FALLING INTO A RUT, 1994–98

Eighteenth Annual Humana Festival of New American Plays (1993–94)

1969 by Tina Landau
Betty the Yeti by Jon Klein
Julie Johnson by Wendy Hammond
The Last Time We Saw Her by Jane Anderson
My Left Breast by Susan Miller

Slavs! (Thinking about the Longstanding Problems of Virtue and Happiness) by Tony Kushner
Shotgun by Romulus Linney
Stones and Bones by Marion McClinton
The Survivor: A Cambodian Odyssey by Jon Lipsky
Trip's Cinch by Phyllis Nagy

Nineteenth Annual Humana Festival of New American Plays (1994–95)

Below the Belt by Richard Dresser
Beast on the Moon by Richard Kalinoski
Between the Lines by Regina Taylor
Cloud Tectonics by José Rivera
Head On by Elizabeth Dewberry
Helen at Risk by Dana Yeaton
July 7, 1994 by Donald Margulies
Middle-Aged White Guys by Jane Martin
Tough Choices for the New Century: A Seminar for Responsible Living by Jane Anderson
Trudy Blue by Marsha Norman
Your Obituary Is a Dance by Bernard Cummings

Twentieth Annual Humana Festival of New American Plays (1995–96)

The Batting Cage by Joan Ackermann
Chilean Holiday by Guillermo Reyes
Contract with Jackie by Jimmy Breslin
Flesh and Bone by Elizabeth Dewberry
Going, Going, Gone by Anne Bogart and The Saratoga International Theatre Institute (SITI)
Jack and Jill by Jane Martin
Missing/Kissing by John Patrick Shanley
One Flea Spare by Naomi Wallace
Reverse Transcription by Tony Kushner
Trying to Find Chinatown by David Henry Hwang
What I Meant Was by Craig Lucas

Twenty-first Annual Humana Festival of New American Plays (1996–97)

Gun-Shy by Richard Dresser
Icarus by Edwin Sanchez
In Her Sight by Carol K. Mack
Lighting Up the Two-Year Old by Benjie Aerenson
Misreadings by Neena Beber
Polaroid Stories by Naomi Iizuka

Private Eyes by Steven Dietz
Stars by Romulus Linney
Waterbabies by Adam LeFevre

Twenty-second Annual Humana Festival of New American Plays (1997–98)

Acorn by David Graziano
Dinner with Friends by Donald Margulies
Let the Big Dog Eat by Elizabeth Wong
Like Totally Weird by William Mastrosimone
Meow by Val Smith
Mr. Bundy by Jane Martin
Resident Alien by Stuart Spencer
Ti Jean Blues adapted from the works of Jack Kerouac by
    JoAnne Akalaitis
The Trestle at Pope Lick Creek by Naomi Wallace

THE LAST HURRAH, 1999–2000

Twenty-third Annual Humana Festival of New American Plays (1998–99)

Aloha, Say the Pretty Girls by Naomi Iizuka
Cabin Pressure by Anne Bogart and the SITI Company
The Cockfighter by Frank Manley and adapted by Vincent Murphy
God's Man in Texas by David Rambo
Y2K (later retitled *BecauseHeCan*) by Arthur Kopit
Life under 30: A Bill of 10-Minute Plays
    The Blue Room by Courtney Baron
    Dancing with the Devil by Brooke Berman
    Drive Angry by Matt Pelfrey
    Forty Minute Finish by Jerome Hairston
    Just Be Frank by Caroline Williams
    Labor Day by Sheri Wilner
    MPLS., St. Paul by Julia Jordan
    Slop-Culture by Robb Badlam
T(ext) Shirt Plays
    And the Torso Even More So by Tony Kushner
    The Fez by Mac Wellman
    Manifesto by Naomi Wallace
    Merchandising by David Henry Hwang
    Stuffed Shirts by Jane Martin
    To T or Not to T by Wendy Wasserstein
Phone Plays
    Happy Birthday Jack by Diana Son
    Speech Therapy by Rebecca Gilman

Them by David Greenspan
Visitation by Rebecca Reynolds
Will You Accept the Charges? by Neal Bell
Car Play
What Are You Afraid Of? by Richard Dresser

Twenty-fourth Annual Humana Festival of New American Plays (1999–2000)

Anton in Show Business by Jane Martin
Arabian Nights by David Ives
Big Love by Charles L. Mee
The Divine Fallacy by Tina Howe
No. 11 (Blue and White) by Alexandra Cunningham
Standard Time by Naomi Wallace
Tape by Stephen Belber
Touch by Toni Press-Coffman
War of the Worlds conceived by Anne Bogart, created by the SITI
  Company, and written by Naomi Iizuka
Back Story: A Dramatic Anthology by Joan Ackermann, Courtney
  Baron, Neena Beber, Constance Congdon, Jon Klein, Shirley Lauro,
  Craig Lucas, Eduardo Machado, Donald Margulies, Jane Martin,
  Susan Miller, John Olive, Tanya Palmer, David Rambo, Edwin
  Sanchez, Adele Edling Shank, Mayo Simon, Val Smith
Phone Plays
  Beside Every Good Man by Regina Taylor
  Lovers of Long Red Hair by José Rivera
  The Reprimand by Jane Anderson
  Show Business by Jeffrey Hatcher
  Trespassion by Mark O'Donnell

THE EDUCATION OF MARC MASTERSON, 2001–6

Twenty-fifth Annual Humana Festival of New American Plays (2000–2001)

bobrauschenbergamerica by Charles L. Mee
Chad Curtiss, Lost Again by Arthur Kopit
Description Beggared; or The Allegory of WHITENESS by Mac Wellman
Flaming Guns of the Purple Sage by Jane Martin
Quake by Melanie Marnich
When the Sea Drowns in Sand by Eduardo Machado
Wonderful World by Richard Dresser
Heaven and Hell (on Earth): A Divine Comedy by Robert Alexander,
  Jenny Lyn Bader, Elizabeth Dewberry, Deborah Lynn Frockt,

Rebecca Gilman, Keith Glover, Hilly Hicks, Jr., Karen Hines, Michael Kassin, Jane Martin, William Mastrosimone, Guillermo Reyes, Sarah Schulman, Richard Strand, Alice Tuan, Elizabeth Wong

Phone Plays

Call Waiting by Rachel Claff

Click by Brighde Mullins from Thick Description

Hype-R-Connectivity by Andy Bayiates from The Neo-Futurists

Message Sent by Sterling Houston from Jump-Start Performance
  Company

Owls by Erin Courtney from Clubbed Thumb

Somebody Call 911 by Jennifer L. Nelson from African Continuum
  Theatre Company

Subliminable by Greg Allen

Twenty-sixth Annual Humana Festival of New American Plays (2001–2)

a.m. Sunday by Jerome Hairston

Bake Off by Sheri Wilner

Classyass by Caleen Sinnette Jennings

Finer Noble Gases by Adam Rapp

Limonade Tous Les Jours by Charles L. Mee

The Mystery of Attraction by Marlane Meyer

Nightswim by Julia Jordan

Rembrandt's Gift by Tina Howe

Score conceived and directed by Anne Bogart, created by the SITI
  Company, adapted by Jocelyn Clarke

Snapshot: A Dramatic Anthology by Tanya Barfield, Lee Blessing,
  Michael Bigelow Dixon, Julie Jensen, Honour Kane, Sunil Kuruvilla,
  David Lindsay-Abaire, Victor Lodato, Quincy Long, Deb Margolin,
  Allison Moore, Lynn Nottage, Dan O'Brien, Val Smith, Annie
  Weisman, Craig Wright, and Chay Yew

The Technology Project

F.E.T.C.H. by Alice Tuan

Virtual Meditation # 1 by Sarah Ruhl in collaboration with students
  and faculty at Carnegie Mellon University's Entertainment
  Technology Center

Voice Properties (On a First Date after a Full Year of Februarys) by
  John Belluso

Twenty-seventh Annual Humana Festival of New American Plays (2002–3)

The Faculty Room by Bridget Carpenter

Fit for Feet by Jordan Harrison

The Lively Lad: A Play with Songs by Quincy Long, music by Michael Silversher

Omnium-Gatherum by Alexandra Gersten-Vassilaros and Theresa Rebeck

Orange Lemon Egg Canary: A Trick in Four Acts by Rinne Groff

The Roads that Lead Here by Lee Blessing

Rhythmicity: A Convergence of Poetry, Theatre, and Hip-Hop curated by Mildred Ruiz and Steven Sapp; featuring Regie Cabico, Gamal Abdel Chasten, reg e. gaines, Willie Perdomo, Rah Goddess, Mildred Ruiz and Steven Sapp

The Second Death of Priscilla by Russell Davis

Slide Glide the Slippery Slope by Kia Corthron

Trash Anthem by Dan Dietz

Trepidation Nation—A Phobic Anthology by Keith Josef Adkins, Stephen Belber, Hilary Bell, Glen Berger, Sheila Callaghan, Bridget Carpenter, Cusi Craml, Richard Dresser, Erik Ehn, Gina Gionfraddo, Kireten Greenidge, Michael Hollinger, Warren Leight, Julie Marie Myatt, Victoria Stewart and James Still

Twenty-eighth Annual Humana Festival of New American Plays (2003–4)

After Ashley by Gina Gionfriddo

At the Vanishing Point by Naomi Iizuka

A Bone Close to My Brain by Dan Dietz

Fast and Loose: An Ethical Collaboration by Jose Cruz Gonzalez, Kirsten Greenidge, Julie Marie Myatt, and John Walch

Foul Territory by Craig Wright

Kid-Simple by Jordan Harrison

Kuwait by Vincent Delaney

The Ruby Sunrise by Rinne Groff

Sans-Culottes in the Promised Land by Kirsten Greenidge

The Spot by Steven Dietz

Tallgrass Gothic by Melanie Marnich

Twenty-ninth Annual Humana Festival of New American Plays (2004–5)

Hazard County by Allison Moore

Memory House by Kathleen Tolan

Moot the Messenger by Kia Corthron

A Nervous Smile by John Belluso

Pure Confidence by Carlyle Brown

The Shaker Chair by Adam Bock

Uncle Sam's Satiric Spectacular: On Democracy and Other
Fictions Featuring Patriotism Acts and Blue Songs from a Red
State, a satiric anthology by Greg Allen, Sheila Callaghan, Bridget
Carpenter, Eric Coble, Richard Dresser, Michael Friedman, and
Hilly Hicks

Thirtieth Annual Humana Festival of New American Plays (2005–6)

Act a Lady by Jordan Harrison
Hotel Cassiopoeia by Charles L. Mee
Listeners by Jane Martin
Low by Rha Goddess
Natural Selection by Eric Coble
Neon Mirage by Liz Duffy Adams, Dan Dietz, Rick Hip-Flores, Julie
Jensen, Lisa Kron, Tracey Scott Wilson and Chay Yew
The Scene by Theresa Rebeck
Six Years by Sharr White
Sovereignty by Rolin Jones
Three Guys and a Brenda by Adam Bock

Thirty-first Annual Humana Festival of New American Plays (2006-7)

The As If Body Loop by Ken Weitzman
Batch: An American Bachelor/Ette Party Spectacle conceived by Whit
MacLaughlin and Alice Tuan, with text by Alice Tuan, created by
New Paradise Laboratories
Clarisse & Larmon by Deb Margolin
dark play or stories for boys by Carlos Murillo
I Am Not Batman by Marco Ramirez
Mr. & Mrs. by Julie Marie Myatt
The Open Road Anthology by Constance Congdon, Kia Corthron,
Michael John Garcés, Rolin Jones, A. Rey Pamatmat, and Kathryn
Walat, with music by GrooveLily
Strike-Slip by Naomi Iizuka
The Unseen by Craig Wright
When Something Wonderful Ends by Sherry Kramer
365 Days/365 Plays by Suzan-Lori Parks
November 14, Father Comes Home from the Wars (Part 1)
December 18, The Great Army in Disgrace
January 3, 2 Marys
December 18, The Birth of Tragedy
January 31, If I Had to Murder Me Somebody
February 13, (Again), The Butchers Daughter (For Bonnie)

March 21, A Play for the First Day of Spring Entitled "How Do You Like the War?"
April 1, George Bush Visits the Cheese & Olive

Thirty-second Annual Humana Festival of New American Plays (2007–8)

All Hail Hurricane Gordo by Carly Mensch
Becky Shaw by Gina Gionfriddo
the break/s by Marc Bamuthi Joseph
Game On by Zakiyyah Alexander, Rolin Jones, Alice Tuan, Daryl Watson, Marisa Wegrzyn, and Ken Weitzman, music and lyrics by Jon Spurney
Great Falls by Lee Blessing
Neighborhood 3: Requisition of Doom by Jennifer Haley
Ten-Minute Plays
    Dead Right by Elaine Jarvik
    In Paris You Will Find Many Baguettes but Only One True Love by Michael Lew
    One Short Sleepe by Naomi Wallace
    Tongue, Tied by M. Thomas Cooper
This Beautiful City by Steven Cosson and Jim Lewis, music and lyrics by Michael Friedman; from interviews by The Civilians

NOTES

INTRODUCTION

1. Greg Evans, "Truces and Deuces Mark Twentieth Play Fest," *Variety*, April 8, 1996.

2. Bob Bahr and James Nold Jr., *The Insider's Guide to Louisville* (Manteo, NC: Insiders' Publishing, 1997), 4.

3. Stephen M. Archer, "Actors Theatre of Louisville," in *Cambridge Guide to American Theatre*, ed. Don B. Wilmeth (New York: Cambridge University Press, 1996), 26.

4. Ethan Mordden, *One More Kiss: The Broadway Musical of the 1970s* (New York: Palgrave Macmillan, 2003), 115–16.

5. Actors Theatre of Louisville, "Actors Theatre of Louisville—Humana Festival Fun Facts," http:// www.actorstheatre.org/humana_facts.htm (accessed July 31, 2005).

1. THE FOUNDING OF A DIVIDED THEATRE

1. Joseph Wesley Zeigler, *Regional Theatre: The Revolutionary Stage* (New York: Da Capo Press, 1977), 4.

2. Margo Jones, *Theatre-in-the-Round* (New York: Rinehart, 1951), 55–56.

3. Most notable are George Toutliatos's Front Street Theatre in Memphis, the Charles Playhouse in Boston, and the Mummer's Theatre in Oklahoma City. Zeigler, *Regional Theatre*, 17–19, 60–61.

4. Zeigler, *Regional Theatre*, 17–19, 60–61.

5. Zeigler, *Regional Theatre*, 55–56, 60–61.

6. Daniel Mufson, "Interactive Archive: The Actor's Workshop," 2001–2, http://www.alternativetheater.com/cgi-bin/int_archive/entry_index.cgi?ARC_ID= 00019 (accessed August 1, 2005).

7. Gerald M. Berkowitz, *New Broadways: Theatre across America—Approaching a New Millennium* (New York: Applause Books, 1997), 73.

8. Berkowitz, *New Broadways*, 70.

9. Zeigler, *Regional Theatre*, 26.

10. Berkowitz, *New Broadways*, 71; Zeigler, *Regional Theatre*, 27.

11. Other theatres, such as the Repertory Theatre New Orleans, the Inner City Repertory Company of Los Angeles, and the Trinity Square Repertory Company, were established by the federal Office of Education and by grants from the National Endowment for the Arts, as actors performed for students during the day and paying adults in the evening. Berkowitz, *New Broadways*, 77–79; Zeigler, *Regional Theatre*, 136–40.

12. W. McNeil Lowry, "The University and the Creative Arts," *Educational Theatre Journal*, 14, no. 2 (May 1962): 106.

13. Berkowitz, *New Broadways*, 75–77.

14. Both men chose New Haven because no major theatre was in the vicinity and both men already were living there. Berkowitz, *New Broadways*, 75–77.

15. Zeigler, *Regional Theatre*, 90; Julius Novick, *Beyond Broadway: The Quest for Permanent Theatres* (New York: Hill and Wang, 1968), 168–69.

16. Zeigler, *Regional Theatre*, 90–91; Novick, *Beyond Broadway*, 168–69.

17. Richard Block, interviewed by Teka Ward, Notes on History of Actors Theatre Collection, 1964–1989, University Archives and Records Center, University of Louisville, Louisville. All subsequent references to interviews conducted by Teka Ward and other documents taken from the same collection will be cited as Notes on History of Actors Theatre Collection.

18. Lucretia (Teka) Baldwin Ward, "Actors Theatre of Louisville: An Oral History of the Early Years, 1964–1969" (master's thesis, University of Louisville, 1993), 2–5; Block, Notes on History of Actors Theatre Collection.

19. Bingham even supplied Block with money to travel to Louisville from New York.

20. William Mootz, interviewed by Teka Ward, Notes on History of Actors Theatre Collection.

21. Ward, "Actors Theatre of Louisville," 6–8; Block, Notes on History of Actors Theatre Collection; Barry Bingham Jr., interviewed by Teka Ward, Notes on History of Actors Theatre Collection.

22. Ward, "Actors Theatre of Louisville," 10.

23. Ewel Cornett, interviewed by Teka Ward, Notes on History of Actors Theatre Collection.

24. According to Karl Victor, "The actors came in and out the back on a fire escape." Karl Victor, interviewed by Teka Ward, Notes on History of Actors Theatre Collection; Ward, "Actors Theatre of Louisville," 11–2; Cornett, Notes on History of Actors Theatre Collection.

25. Ward, "Actors Theatre of Louisville," 14; Roanne H. Victor, interviewed by Teka Ward, Notes on History of Actors Theatre Collection.

26. Block, Notes on History of Actors Theatre Collection; Ward, "Actors Theatre of Louisville," 16–17; Karl Victor, Notes on History of Actors Theatre Collection.

27. Dann C. Byck, interviewed by Teka Ward, Notes on History of Actors Theatre Collection.

28. Jack Johnson, interviewed by Teka Ward, Notes on History of Actors Theatre Collection.

29. Block, Notes on History of Actors Theatre Collection; Bingham, Notes on History of Actors Theatre Collection.

30. Ward, "Actors Theatre of Louisville," 19; Mootz, Notes on History of Actors Theatre Collection; Dudley Saunders, interviewed by Teka Ward, Notes on History of Actors Theatre Collection.

31. The issue of the press in Louisville is interesting, since both critics—Mootz and Saunders—wrote for the same publisher yet supported different theatres. Saunders wrote several articles about the founding and goals of his Actors Inc. company, while Mootz consistently published stories about Block's endeavors, as well as some negative responses to Cornett's activities. Saunders said, "I believe . . . that there was a bit of hostility on the part of the *Courier-Journal* toward Actors Inc. at that time. I don't know whether it was because the people at that time felt that Cornett was undercutting something that got a head start or what. . . . I sensed that there was some hostility at the *Courier-Journal* toward it." Mootz, aware of allegations of bias, has consistently denied favoritism or bias in any of his reviews. Saunders, Notes on History of Actors Theatre Collection; Mootz, Notes on History of Actors Theatre Collection.

32. Ward, "Actors Theatre of Louisville," 23, 58.

33. Karl Victor, Notes on History of Actors Theatre Collection.

34. Cornett, Notes on History of Actors Theatre Collection; Roanne H. Victor, Notes on History of Actors Theatre Collection; Ward, "Actors Theatre of Louisville," 25.

35. Block, Notes on History of Actors Theatre Collection; Cornett, Notes on History of Actors Theatre Collection.

36. Block, Notes on History of Actors Theatre Collection.

37. Saunders, Notes on History of Actors Theatre Collection; Ward, "Actors Theatre of Louisville," 27–31.

38. Roanne H. Victor, Notes on History of Actors Theatre Collection.

39. Yandell Smith, interviewed by Teka Ward, Notes on History of Actors Theatre Collection.

40. Cornett, Notes on History of Actors Theatre Collection; Saunders, Notes on History of Actors Theatre Collection; Johnson, Notes on History of Actors Theatre Collection.

41. Johnson, Notes on History of Actors Theatre Collection; Cornett, Notes on History of Actors Theatre Collection.

42. Saunders, Notes on History of Actors Theatre Collection.

43. William Mootz, "Actors Theatre's First Ten Years: From Rags to Riches," *Courier-Journal* (Louisville), May 26, 1974.

44. Mootz, Notes on History of Actors Theatre Collection.

45. Cornett, Notes on History of Actors Theatre Collection.

46. Block, Notes on History of Actors Theatre Collection; Johnson, Notes on History of Actors Theatre Collection; Ward, "Actors Theatre of Louisville," 32–34.

47. Mootz, Notes on History of Actors Theatre Collection.

48. Karl Victor, Notes on History of Actors Theatre Collection.

49. Saunders, Notes on History of Actors Theatre Collection; Mootz, Notes on History of Actors Theatre Collection.

50. Johnson, Notes on History of Actors Theatre Collection.

51. Cornett, Notes on History of Actors Theatre Collection; Billy Edd Wheeler, "Billy Edd Wheeler: Fiction," 2005, http://www.billyeddwheeler.

com/books.htm (accessed November 2, 2005); Ward, "Actors Theatre of Louisville," 38–39.

52. Saunders, Notes on History of Actors Theatre Collection.

53. Zeigler, *Regional Theatre*, 103; Ward, "Actors Theatre of Louisville," 40–42; Bingham, Notes on History of Actors Theatre Collection; Novick, *Beyond Broadway*, 76.

54. Lynne Conner, "On the Arts: Pittsburgh Audiences Are Way More Sophisticated Than You'd Guess from City's Image," *Pittsburgh Post-Gazette*, November 9, 2003; "Highlights: Twenty-five Years in the American Theatre," *Theatre Profiles 7* (New York: Theatre Communications Group, 1986), xi; Ward, "Actors Theatre of Louisville," 55; Roanne H. Victor, telephone interview by the author, June 14, 2005.

55. Novick, *Beyond Broadway*, 76–77; Ward, "Actors Theatre of Louisville,"47–52; Karl Victor, Notes on History of Actors Theatre Collection.

56. Ward, "Actors Theatre of Louisville,"52, 58.

57. Advertisers were also confused by the fact that Block's name was listed among the board of directors (of which he was not a member), giving the impression that the notes were written with the board's approval. "Actors Theatre of Louisville Board of Directors' Minutes—October 6, 1966," Notes on History of Actors Theater Collection.

58. Block, Notes on History of Actors Theatre Collection; "Actors Theatre of Louisville Board of Directors—October 6, 1966," Notes on History of Actors Theatre Collection.

59. Gene Roberts, "Integration in South: Erratic Pattern," *New York Times*, May 29, 1967; Tom Dent, "Black Theatre in the South: Report and Reflections," *The Theatre of Black Americans*, ed. Errol Hill (New York: Applause Theatre Books, 1987), 261–64; Holly Hill, "Black Theatre into the Mainstream," in *Contemporary American Theatre*, ed. Bruce King (New York: St. Martin's Press, 1991), 81–82.

60. Plays for the 1967–68 season also included *All the King's Men, Long Day's Journey into Night, Misalliance, Night of the Dunce*, and *Thieves' Carnival*. Ward, "Actors Theatre of Louisville," 75, 77, 79, 112; "Actors Theatre of Louisville Board of Directors' Minutes—April 25, 1968," Notes on History of Actors Theatre Collection; Block, Notes on History of Actors Theatre Collection.

61. Block, Notes on History of Actors Theatre Collection; Roanne Victor, Notes on History of Actors Theatre Collection; Bernard Dahlem, interviewed by Teka Ward, Notes on History of Actors Theatre Collection.

62. Saunders, Notes on History of Actors Theatre Collection; Smith, Notes on History of Actors Theatre Collection; Mootz, Notes on History of Actors Theatre Collection; Brian Clark, interviewed by Teka Ward, Notes on History of Actors Theatre Collection; "Highlights," xi.

63. Ian Henderson, interviewed by Teka Ward, Notes on History of Actors Theatre Collection.

64. Block, Notes on History of Actors Theatre Collection; Dahlem, Notes on History of Actors Theatre Collection.

65. Bingham, Notes on History of Actors Theatre Collection; Mootz, Notes on History of Actors Theatre Collection; Zeigler, *Regional Theatre*, 240; Saunders, Notes on History of Actors Theatre Collection.

66. Ward, "Actors Theatre of Louisville," 87–89.

67. Henderson, Notes on History of Actors Theatre Collection.

2. THE EDUCATION OF JON JORY

1. Zelda Fichandler, quoted in Joseph Wesley Zeigler, *Regional Theatre: The Revolutionary Stage* (New York: Da Capo Press 1977), 1.

2. Zeigler, *Regional Theatre*, 104.

3. Bernard Dahlem, interviewed by Teka Ward, Notes on History of Actors Theatre Collection, 1964–1989, University Archives and Records Center, University of Louisville, Louisville. All subsequent references to interviews conducted by Teka Ward and other documents from this collection will be cited as Notes on History of Actors Theatre Collection.

4. Barry Bingham Jr., interviewed by Teka Ward, Notes on History of Actors Theatre Collection.

5. "Actors Theatre Promotes Speer to Manager," *Courier-Journal* (Louisville), February 20, 1969.

6. The run of each show, however, was extended from two and a half weeks to three and a half weeks. Jory also argued for the hiring of a smaller resident company that, in turn, allowed the theatre to pay better salaries and import actors for specific roles. Zeigler, *Regional Theatre*, 103

7. "Actors Theatre of Louisville Board of Directors' Minutes—March 9, 1969," Notes on History of Actors Theatre Collection.

8. Yahoo.com, "Victor Jory Biography," http://movies.yahoo.com/movie/contributor/1800013598/bio (accessed March 2, 2007).

9. Nancy Wick, "Making It Work," *Columns Magazine*, March 2002, http://www.washington.edu/alumni/columns/march02/jory1.html (accessed March 2, 2007).

10. Joe Adcock, "Lifetime of Theatre Hefty Credentials for Jon Jory at UW," *Seattle Post-Intelligencer*, February 3, 2000.

11. Jon Jory, quoted in Wick, "Making It Work."

12. Jory, quoted in Wick, "Making It Work."

13. Dudley Saunders, Notes on History of Actors Theatre Collection; William Mootz, Notes on History of Actors Theatre Collection; Lucretia (Teka) Baldwin Ward, "Actors Theatre of Louisville: An Oral History of the Early Years, 1964–1969" (masters thesis, University of Louisville, 1993), 94.

14. Zeigler, *Regional Theatre*, 91; Julius Novick, *Beyond Broadway: The Quest for Permanent Theatres*, New York: Hill and Wang, 1968, 175–76.

15. Zeigler, *Regional Theatre*, 105.

16. Jon Jory, quoted in "New Director Wants to Help A.T.L. to 'Run'" by Joan Riehm, *Courier-Journal* (Louisville), March 11, 1969.

17. Zeigler, *Regional Theatre*, 3.

18. Joe Adcock, "Director Finds Lessons for Modern Souls in Shaw's 90-Year-Old *Heartbreak House*," *Seattle Post-Intelligencer*, July 28, 2006.

19. A former assistant administrative director for Actors Theatre, Jim Hayzen, described this approach as a wise and necessary tactic for attracting and educating the Louisville audiences, stating, "Jon did a lot of *Life with Father* before he could do *Getting Out*." Hayzen, quoted in "Blueprint for Actors Theatre Not Easily Copied," by Sean Mitchell, *Dallas Times Herald*, February 20, 1979.

20. Bingham, Notes on History of Actors Theatre Collection; Zeigler, *Regional Theatre*, 104–5.

21. Richard Block, Notes on History of Actors Theatre Collection.

22. Alexander Speer, Notes on History of Actors Theatre Collection; William Mootz, "A Great Experiment," *Courier-Journal* (Louisville), September 19, 1993; "Actors Theatre Opens $38,000 Fund Campaign," *Courier-Journal* (Louisville), March 26, 1969; Yandell Smith, Notes on History of Actors Theatre Collection; Bingham, Notes on History of Actors Theatre Collection.

23. Zeigler, *Regional Theatre*, 177–78.

24. H. V. Savitch and Ronald K. Vogel, "Louisville: Compacts and Antagonistic Cooperation," in *Regional Politics: America in a Post-City Age*, ed. H. V. Savitch and Ronald K. Vogel (Thousand Oaks, CA: Sage Publications, 1996), 136–37.

25. Gerald M. Berkowitz, *New Broadways. Theatre across America: Approaching a New Millennium* (New York: Applause Books, 1997), 220.

26. Trish Pugh Jones, telephone interview by the author, May 12, 2004.

27. Trish Pugh Jones (known as Trish Pugh at the time of her employment at A.T.L.) met Jory at the Pittsburgh Playhouse when he was directing there. She had resigned from her position with the Playhouse and moved back to her native England when Jory contacted her, asking her to return to the United States and work for him in Louisville. "Jory Promises Quality from Actors Theatre," *Courier-Journal* (Louisville), September 5, 1989; Jones, interview by author; Roanne H. Victor, telephone interview by the author, June 14, 2005.

28. "A.T.L.'s Jory Pleased as Sales Top 5,000," *Courier-Journal* (Louisville), November 30, 1969; "A.T.L. Sets U.S. Record," *Courier-Journal* (Louisville), October 4, 1970.

29. Roanne H. Victor, Notes on History of Actors Theatre Collection.

30. Helen Epstein, *Joe Papp: An American Life* (Boston: Little, Brown, 1994), 184–86; David Crespy, *The Off-Off-Broadway Explosion* (New York: Back Stage Books, 2003), 148, 186–91.

31. Epstein, *Joe Papp*, 275–79.

32. Edith Bingham, "Notes on Preservation History in Louisville," in *Louisville Guide*, ed. Gregory A. Luhan, Dennis Domer, and David Mohney (New York: Princeton Architectural Press, 2004), 37–39; Robert L. Miller, "Chattanooga, Other Cities, Use the Arts and Culture to Restore Aging Riverfront Areas," in *Cities and the Arts: A Handbook for Renewal*, ed. Roger L. Kemp (Jefferson, NC: McFarland, 2004), 46, 60–61, 71, 116.

33. The theatre hoped to raise $1,080,000 from local donors, which would result in a grant of $360,000 from the Ford Foundation. "Ford Foundation Agrees to Pay for a Fourth of Actors Theatre's Building Campaign," *Courier-Journal* (Louisville), August 3, 1971; "Actors Theatre of Louisville Given $13,000 Federal Grant," *Courier-Journal* (Louisville), December 17, 1969; "Bach Group and A.T.L. Get Grants," *Courier Journal* (Louisville), March 8, 1970; William Mootz, "Thirty Seasons in the Spotlight" *Courier-Journal* (Louisville). August 30, 1998; Trish Pugh Jones, interview by author, May 12, 2004.

34. Trish Pugh Jones, "History," *An ATL Portfolio* (Louisville: Studio Gallery, 1972), iii.

35. Zeigler, *Regional Theatre*, 240.

36. Arts Council of Oklahoma City, "Stage Center History," 2002, http://www.stagecenter.com/history.html (accessed August 9, 2005); William Mootz, "Jon Jory Frets: 'Will Success Spoil Actors Theatre?'" *Courier-Journal* (Louisville), September 10, 1972.

37. Bingham, Notes on History of Actors Theatre Collection; Trish Pugh Jones, telephone interview by the author, June 22, 2005.

38. Even before the move to the West Main Street building, Jory would stage avant-garde productions and contemporary plays for a smaller audience on Monday nights, commonly referred to as Adventure Theatre.

39. Zeigler, *Regional Theatre*, 191–92; "Nonprofit Theaters to Get Ford Aid for New Plays," *New York Times*, July 15, 1976.

40. Trish Pugh Jones, interview, May 12, 2004.

41. Trish Pugh Jones, interview, May 12, 2004.

42. Mootz recalled that Jory waited until subscriptions reached approximately twelve to thirteen thousand before he decided to do new plays. Mootz, Notes on History of Actors Theatre Collection.

43. Richard L. Coe, "A Comedy Tonight (All Summer)," *Washington Post, Times Herald*, June, 4 1972.

44. Jon Jory, quoted in "Jon Jory Gives His Regards to Broadway," by John Christensen, *Louisville Times*, January 8, 1972.

45. Jory quoted in Christensen, "Jon Jory."

46. Epstein, *Joe Papp*, 215–16.

47. Epstein, *Joe Papp*, 262–63.

48. Jon Jory quoted in "'Everybody Gained except the Investors,'" by Dudley Saunders, *Louisville Times*, January 13, 1973.

49. Ethan Mordden, *One More Kiss: The Broadway Musical in the 1970s* (New York: Palgrave Macmillian, 2003), 115–16; Clive Barnes, "Stage: 'Tricks,' Musical Based on Moliere, Arrives," *New York Times*, January 9, 1973; Jory quoted in Saunders, "'Everybody Gained.'"

50. Mordden, *One More Kiss*, 115–16.

51. Jon Jory quoted in Saunders, "'Everybody Gained.'"

52. Trish Pugh Jones, interview, May 12, 2004; Jon Jory quoted in Adcock, "Lifetime of Theatre."

53. Epstein, *Joe Papp*, 217.

54. Jory also collaborated on two more works: the 1974 musical *Chips 'N' Ale* and a space-age musical adaptation of *Titus Andronicus* in 1977. Betteontheboards.com, "Bette Midler: Playbill Biographies," http://www.betteontheboards.com/boards/link-06–01.htm (accessed August 10, 2005).

55. Jon Jory, interview by the author, Louisville, June 18, 1999.

56. Jon Jory quoted in "A.T.L. Rated One of the Healthiest Theaters," by William Mootz, *Courier-Journal* (Louisville), May 16, 1976.

57. William Mootz, "The Art of Beginning," *Courier-Journal* (Louisville), November 20, 1976.

3. THE LUCKY YEARS, 1976–79

1. James Leverett, "After the Revolution," *Program for the Tenth Annual Humana Festival of New American Plays* (Louisville: Actors Theatre of Louisville, 1986), 9–10.

2. Jory quoted in "A Festival of New U.S. Plays," *Theatre Communications Group Newsletter*, 5, no. 10 (October 1977).

3. *American Buffalo* premiered at Chicago's Goodman Theatre in 1975, *Streamers* premiered at Long Wharf Theatre in 1976, and *Annie* opened at Connecticut's Goodspeed Opera House in 1976. "Highlights: Twenty-five Years in the American Theatre," *Theatre Profiles 7* (New York: Theatre Communications Group, 1986), xii.

4. James M. Nederlander, quoted in Stephen Langley, ed., *Producers on Producing*, (New York: Drama, 1974), 301–2.

5. Tanya Palmer, "Risky Business," *Theatre Topics* 13, no. 1 (2003): 66

6. Jon Jory, interview by the author, Louisville, June 18, 1999.

7. ElizaBeth Mahan King, "Actors Theatre of Louisville's New Play Program History," October 1979, p. 1, Actors Theatre of Louisville Literary Office manuscript collection, Louisville; William Mootz, "Astonishing New Plays," *Courier-Journal* (Louisville), October 20, 1976.

8. William Mootz, "A Brilliant Season at Actors Theatre," *Courier-Journal* (Louisville), May 22, 1977.

9. Jon Jory, quoted in Ira J. Bilowit, ed. and moderator, "Regional Theatres and Their Relationship to New York," *New York Theatre Review*, January 1979.

10. Jon Jory, "We Love Writers," in *Humana Festival of New American Plays: 25 Years at Actors Theatre of Louisville*, ed. Michael Bigelow Dixon and Andrew Carter Crocker (Louisville: Actors Theatre of Louisville, 2000), 11.

11. William Glover, "The Stage of the Stage," *Courier-Journal* (Louisville), April 17, 1977; William Glover, "Regional Theatres Trying Own Thing," *Columbus Dispatch*, April 17, 1977.

12. Jon Jory, quoted in William Glover, "Regional Theaters Doing New Plays," *Atlanta Journal-Constitution*, April 10, 1977; William Mootz, "*Medal of Honor Rag* Probes Guilt of Survival with Spellbinding Drama," *Courier-Journal* (Louisville), October 12, 1976; Dudley Saunders, "*Medal of Honor*

Rag Is Haunting Exploration of 'Survivor Guilt,'" *Louisville Times*, October 12, 1976.

13. Jean Dietrich, "A.T.L.'s *Vanities* Is Nearly Flawless as It Follows the Lives of Three People," *Courier-Journal* (Louisville), October 18, 1976; Dudley Saunders, "*Vanities* Is Likable, Somewhat Unbelievable," *Louisville Times*, October 18, 1976.

14. Dudley Saunders, "*Sexual Perversity* Is Good Comedy, but the Language May Disturb Some," *Courier-Journal* (Louisville), October 12, 1976; William Mootz, "*Sex* Is Clever Cartoon; *Reunion* Oddly Affecting," *Louisville Times*, October 13, 1976.

15. William Mootz, "How Should New Playwrights Be Nurtured?," *Courier-Journal* (Louisville), November 20, 1976.

16. Mootz, "How Should."

17. Jory Johnson, quoted in Mootz, "How Should."

18. Johnson, quoted in Mootz, "How Should."

19. Jon Jory quoted in Mootz, "How Should."

20. Jory, quoted in Michael Billington, untitled article, *Guardian* (London), March 2, 1979.

21. David Savran, "New Realism: Mamet, Mann and Nelson," *Contemporary American Theatre*, ed. Bruce King (New York: St. Martin's Press, 1991), 64; Billington, untitled article, *Guardian* (London), March 2, 1979.

22. Jon Jory, quoted in Lucretia (Teka) Baldwin Ward, "Actors Theatre of Louisville: An Oral History of the Early Years, 1964–1969" (masters thesis, University of Louisville, 1993), 95.

23. William Mootz, "Stretching the Sensibilities," *Courier-Journal* (Louisville), November 13, 1977.

24. Jory quoted in Edwin Wilson, "Playwrights: Three Full Days of Fresh Talent," *Wall Street Journal*, February 23, 1979.

25. Although the plays featured at Playfaire 76/77 had been workshopped or staged at other theaters, A.T.L. promoted them as world premieres owing to the scale of the productions and the press attending the festival. "What the Critics Said . . ." 1978, Actors Theatre of Louisville Literary Office, Louisville.

26. Jory, interview by author. John Orlock, quoted in "Louisville Is Play Setting by Luck Only," by Jean Dietrich, *Courier-Journal* (Louisville), March 2, 1977.

27. Before becoming a playwright, Coburn was the advertising man responsible for creating the "Pepsi Challenge" campaign. Gregg Hunter, "A Fine First Play," *New-Press Daily Review Star* (Los Angeles), October 14, 1976; Joseph S. Caruso, "Los Angeles After Dark: *The Gin Game*," *NewsWest* (Los Angeles), October 1–15, 1976), Richard Bernard, "*Gin* Has the Cards," *Casting News Entertainment Guide* (Los Angeles), October 21, 1976; William Mootz, "*Gin Game* Endearing, Funny," *Courier-Journal* (Louisville), March 8, 1977; Dale Sandusky, "Review: *The Gin Game*," *New Albany Tribune*, March 10, 1977; Clifford A. Ridley, "Elusive Possibilities in Two New Fables," *National Observer* (Washington, D.C.), March 19, 1977.

28. D. L. Coburn quoted in Richard L. Coe, "Best Acting West of Broadway," *Washington Post*, November 27, 1977; "Author Credits Actors Theatre in Pulitzer Win; *New York Times* Collects Record Three Awards," *Louisville Times*, April 18, 1978.

29. Jory, "We Love Writers," 11.

30. Frazier Marsh, "Humana Festival Production Manager," in Dixon and Carter, *Humana Festival*, 48.

31. Reginald Stuart, "Louisville Backing Home-Based Arts," *New York Times*, March 6, 1977; William Glover, "Regional Theaters Doing New Plays," *Atlanta Journal-Constitution*, April 10, 1977; Richard Christiansen, "Lively Actors Theater Puts Drama to Work," *Chicago Daily News*, March 11, 1977.

32. Jon Jory, quoted in William Mootz, "ATL's November Play Festival Boasts Six Never-Staged Works," *Courier-Journal* (Louisville), September 4, 1977; Jory, interview by author.

33. "Actors Theatre Is Looking for Plays," *Courier-Journal* (Louisville), February 11, 1977. (The one-thousand- and five-hundred-dollar prizes in 1977 are equal to thirty-four hundred and seventeen hundred dollars, respectively, in 2006 values, according to www.westegg.com/inflation/.)

34. ElizaBeth Mahan King, "The New Play Program," September 1980, Actors Theatre of Louisville Literary Office manuscript collection, Louisville; Mootz, "ATL's November Play Festival."

35. Jory quoted in Mootz, "ATL's November Play Festival."

36. The cowinners were Marsha Norman's *Getting Out* and Frederick Bailey's *The Bridgehead*. ElizaBeth Mahan King, "Actors Theatre of Louisville's New Play Program History," October 1979, Actors Theatre of Louisville Literary Office manuscript collection, 3; King, "Actors Theatre of Louisville: A Brief History," May 1979, Actors Theatre of Louisville Literary Office manuscript collection, Louisville, 3.

37. Mootz, "A.T.L.'s November Play Festival."

38. Jory quoted in William Mootz, "Jory Pleased Louisvillian's Play Is Chosen," *Courier-Journal* (Louisville), September 4, 1977.

39. Mootz, "Jory Pleased"; Matthew C. Roudané, *American Drama since 1960: A Critical History* (New York: Twayne Publishers, 1996), 124–25.

40. William Mootz, "*Getting Out* Is a Stunning Achievement," *Courier-Journal* (Louisville), November 4, 1977; Dudley Saunders, "Exciting *Getting Out* Wrenches Emotions," *Louisville Times*, November 4, 1977.

41. William Mootz, "Personal Favorites," in Dixon and Carter, *Humana Festival*, 32.

42. Founded in 1974, the American Theatre Critics Association is composed of hundreds of theatre critics from around the country. At their annual meeting at the Humana Festival, the organization recognizes three stellar new plays presented during the prior year. Dan Sullivan, "Louisville Picks a Winner," *Los Angeles Times*, November 20, 1977; Richard Eder, "Louisville Festival Offers Six New Plays," *New York Times*, November 15, 1977; Clifford A. Ridley, "Don't Call It 'Regional' Stage," *Detroit Sunday News*, December 11, 1977; King, "Actors Theatre of Louisville: A Brief History," 3.

43. "Awards, Prizes, Honors and Recognition," in Dixon and Crocker, *Humana Festival*, 96; Coe, "Best Acting West of Broadway."

44. Eder, "Louisville Festival."

45. Eder, "Louisville Festival"; Tom McElfresh, "Louisville Theatre's Thirty-four Hour Play Fest Earns Unabashed," *Cincinnati Enquirer*, November 20, 1977.

46. Jon Jory, foreword, in *Ten-Minute Plays, Volume Four from Actors Theatre of Louisville*, ed. Michael Bigelow Dixon and Liz Engelman (New York: Samuel French, 1998), iv.

47. William Mootz, "Jon Jory Not Only Survived His Festival, He Thrived on It," *Courier-Journal* (Louisville), February 25, 1979.

48. William Glover, "Regional Theaters Doing New Plays," *Atlanta Journal-Constitution*, April 10, 1977.

49. Most critics credited the success of the production to the three actresses who played the sisters. In fact, many critics specifically cited Kathy Bates's portrayal of the eldest sister as the best of festival. T. E. Kalem, "Third Running of the Derby," *Time*, March 5, 1979; Edwin Wilson, "Playwrights: Three Full Days of Fresh Talent," *Wall Street Journal*, February 23, 1979.

50. Charles S. Watson, *The History of Southern Drama* (Lexington: University of Kentucky Press, 1997), 2–5.

51. Sally Burke, "Lillian Hellman and Marsha Norman," in *Southern Women Playwrights*, ed. Robert L. McDonald and Linda Rohrer Paige (Tuscaloosa: University of Alabama Press, 2002), 108; Richard Poirier, Introduction, in *Three*, by Lillian Hellman (Boston: Little, Brown, 1979), vii–xxv.

52. Elizabeth S. Bell, "Role-ing on the River: Actors Theatre and the Southern Woman Playwright," in *Southern Women Playwrights*, ed. Robert L. McDonald and Linda Rohrer Paige (Tuscaloosa: University of Alabama Press, 2002), 93; Actors Theatre of Louisville, "Actors Theatre of Louisville History: Production History," http://www.actorstheatre.org/about_production_2.htm (accessed August 28, 2005).

53. Andrew B. Harris, *Broadway Theatre* (New York: Routledge, 1994), 131.

54. Mel Gussow, "Louisville Again Mines Rich Ore of Stage Talent," *New York Times*, February 20, 1979.

55. King, "Actors Theatre of Louisville: A Brief History," 3; Julius Novick, "Too Much, Too Small," *Village Voice*, March 12, 1979; Jeffrey Borak, "Actors Theatre of Louisville: Proving Ground for New York," *Poughkeepsie Journal*, April 15, 1979; Thomas Lask, "James McLure Can Write Plays He Can Act in Now," *New York Times*, June 16, 1979; Mel Gussow, "Theater: Country Plays Make the Big City Laugh," *New York Times*, June 8, 1979.

56. Mark Fearnow, "1970–1990: Disillusionment, Identity, and Discovery," *A Companion to Twentieth-Century American Theatre*, ed. David Krasner (Malden, MA: Blackwell, 2005), 423.

57. Fearnow, "1970–1990," 423.

58. Dudley Saunders, "*Circus Valentine* Too Often Strained, Artificial," *Louisville Times*, February 2, 1979; William Mootz, "*Valentine*: Powerful,

but Not Yet in Focus," *Courier-Journal* (Louisville), February 2, 1979; Debbi Wasserman, "Louisville Round-Up: The Third Annual Festival of New American Plays at the Actors Theatre of Louisville," *New York Theatre Review*, April 1979.

59. Mootz, "Jon Jory Not Only Survived"; Gussow, "Theater: Country Plays."

60. These staff members spoke on the condition of anonymity; interviews in Louisville, 1999.

61. Julie Crutcher, telephone interview by the author, July 2, 1999; Valerie Smith, telephone interview by the author, July 2, 1999.

62. Dominque Paul Noth, "The Louisville Idea Grows," *Milwaukee Journal*, March 11, 1979.

63. While Jory is an intimidating figure, he also is praised as loyal to his staff, among whom the turnover rate is low. Concerning his job as a producer, Jory said watching a Humana production fail was frustrating for the entire staff. Jon Jory, interview by author.

64. Crutcher's speculation that Norman would never forgive Jory is questionable, given that she has returned to the festival on numerous occasions. Crutcher, interview by author.

65. Jory, interview by author.

66. Noth, "Louisville Idea Grows."

67. Kalem, "Third Running of the Derby."

68. Mel Gussow, "Actors Theatre of Louisville Is Flourishing under Jon Jory," *New York Times*, September 1, 1979.

69. Sean Mitchell, "Louisville Actors Theatre: A Regional Success Story," *Los Angeles Herald Examiner*, February 1979.

70. In an interview for *New York Theatre Review*, Jory boasted, "What I really enjoy most of all is literally producing new playwrights. An enormous amount of the work we've done in the last three years are *first* plays. And that is an area that a lot of other theatres are not doing." Perhaps this quote is most fascinating because only three years earlier, Jory defended his theatre's decision to produce "second-stage" scripts as a necessity for exposing playwrights to a larger audience. Although Jory was not discrediting the merits of his first festival, he now emphasized the latter portion of the festival's formula—attracting national interests—by comparing the new work presented at Actors Theatre with the work of other regional theatres. Jon Jory quoted in "An End, Not a Means: Developing Local Playwrights," *New York Theatre Review*, April 1979.

71. Michael Ward, "Jory: Eye of a Dramatic Storm," *Cleveland Plain-Dealer*, April 23, 1979.

72. Emily Gnadinger, former director of corporate and foundation relations for the theatre, claimed that the fame of the annual new play festival helped Actors Theatre raise funds from new sources, including the National Endowment for the Arts. Emily Gnadinger, interview by the author, Louisville, August 19, 1999.

73. M. Ward, "Jory: Eye"; Jory, "We Love Writers," 11.

74. Liz Engelman, interview by the author, Louisville, November 3, 1998.

4. BECOMING AN INSTITUTION, 1980–82

1. Jon Jory, quoted in William Mootz, "Actors Theatre's First Ten Years: From Rags to Riches," *Courier-Journal* (Louisville), May 26, 1974.

2. Gerald Schoenfeld, quoted in Gregg Swem, "ATL Wins Vaughan Award for Contribution to Theatre," *Courier-Journal* (Louisville), May 31, 1979; William Mootz, "Jory and ATL Win Margo Jones Award," *Courier-Journal* (Louisville), March 23, 1979; Swem, "ATL Wins Vaughan Award."

3. Isabelle Stevenson, ed., *The Tony Award* (Portsmouth, NH: Heinemann, 1994), 84, 87, 90.

4. The Louisville community celebrated the theatre's accomplishments in New York and exhibited their support through ticket sales. In 1980, annual attendance at Actors Theatre was 169,366, but after the reception of the Tony Award, that number increased by 45 percent within three years, to 246,432. "Actors Theatre of Louisville," *Theatre Profiles 5*, ed. Laura Ross (New York: Theatre Communications Group, 1982), 5; "Actors Theatre of Louisville," *Theatre Profiles 6*, ed. Laura Ross (New York: Theatre Communications Group, 1984), 6.

5. These sources wished to remain anonymous; notes from interviews at Actors Theatre of Louisville. Actors Theatre of Louisville, "Press Release: Nine Premieres Highlight Actors Theatre's Festival of New American Plays," November 25, 1979, 3, Actors Theatre of Louisville Literary Office, Louisville; William Mootz, "Foreign Playwrights Take Jabs at America, but It's All in Fun," *Courier-Journal* (Louisville), February 28, 1980.

6. Owen Hardy, "A.T.L. Makes Its Mark in Europe," *Courier-Journal* (Louisville), October 12, 1980; William Mootz, "Drama: The Season's Most Important Event Won't Even Happen in Louisville," *Courier-Journal* (Louisville), September 14, 1980.

7. Mootz, "Drama: The Season's Most Important Event."

8. Owen Hardy, "A.T.L. Makes Its Mark in Europe."

9. Muharem Pervic, "Fourteenth B.I.T.E.F. Bitter, Sharp-Tasting, and Documentary," *Politika* (Belgrade), September 22, 1980.

10. Tim Harding and Emmanuel Kehoe, "A Bird Never Flew on One Wing," *Sunday Press* (Dublin), October 6, 1980.

11. Hava Novak, "The Guests from Louisville—Professionals of the First Order," *Davar* (Haifa), October 9, 1980. While the company reveled in its expanded creative efforts and newfound international recognition, the artistic and administrative leaders realized the relationship between the *Getting Out* tour and the new play festival. Jeffrey Rodgers, assistant general manager for the theatre, said, "I think that [our tour] again heightened our reputation. And I think that all the things that heighten our reputation make people want to work here." Jory believed that the tour helped further the theatre's reputation by highlighting the quality of the company's productions. Jeffrey

Rodgers, interview by the author, Louisville, August 20, 1999; Jon Jory, quoted in Hardy, "A.T.L. Makes Its Mark in Europe."

12. Jon Jory, quoted in Hardy, "A.T.L. Makes Its Mark in Europe."

13. Jon Jory, interview by Gerald M. Berkowitz, transcript, December 19, 1995; Dudley Saunders, "A.T.L. Festival Revisited," *Louisville Times*, February 13, 1979; Jack Kroll, "New Blood in Louisville," *Newsweek*, March 19, 1979; T. E. Kalem, "Third Running of the Derby," *Time*, March 5, 1979; Edwin Wilson, "Playwrights: Three Full Days of Fresh Talent," *Wall Street Journal*, February 23, 1979; William Mootz, "Thirty Seasons in the Spotlight," *Courier-Journal* (Louisville). August 30, 1998.

14. The Humana Corporation eventually shifted its arts-funding responsibilities to its philanthropic arm, the Humana Foundation. The foundation raised its profile in the community by supporting, besides Actors Theatre, numerous Louisville arts institutions, including the Greater Louisville Fund for the Arts, the Kentucky Opera Association, and the J. B. Speed Art Museum. "Humana Inc.," *Humana Festival '98: The Complete Plays*, ed. Michael Bigelow Dixon and Amy Wegener (Lyme, NH: Smith and Kraus, 1998), i.

15. Jon Jory, interview by the author, Louisville, June 18, 1999.

16. David A. Jones, interview by the author, correspondence, June 22, 1999; "A Standing Ovation from Humana," *Humana Festival of New American Plays: 25 Years at Actors Theatre of Louisville*, ed. Michael Bigelow Dixon and Andrew Carter Crocker (Louisville: Actors Theatre of Louisville, 2000), 13.

17. David A. Jones, quoted in Mootz, "Thirty Seasons in the Spotlight."

18. The yearly donation increased according to the requests of Actors Theatre. Mootz, "Thirty Seasons in the Spotlight"; Jory, interview by the author.

19. Jon Jory, quoted in Alan Judd, "Humana Takes Lead in Helping Keep the Arts in Business," *Courier-Journal* (Louisville), May 10, 1985; Jeffrey Rodgers, interview by the author, Louisville, August 20, 1999; Christen McDonough Boone, telephone interview by the author, May 4, 2005.

20. Alexander Speer, interview by the author, Louisville, August 20, 1999.

21. In addition to the prior Festivals of New American Plays, the Playfaire 76/77 would be designated as the First Humana Festival of New American Plays. Former director of development Emily Gnadinger, however, provided a slightly different version of the decision to rename the festival, claiming that the leaders of Humana proposed the name change after funding the festival for several years. Gnadinger suggested that the theatre erred in not proposing it first. Emily Gnadinger, interview by the author, Louisville, August 19, 1999.

22. Speer, interview by author.

23. Speer, interview by author; Boone, interview by author.

24. Robert Holley, "Theatre Facts 84," *American Theatre* 1, no. 11 (1985), 10.

25. Barbara Janowitz Ehrlich, "Theatre Facts 88," *American Theatre* 6, no. 1 (1989): 10.

26. Gerald M. Berkowitz, *New Broadways: Theatre across America—Approaching a New Millennium* (New York: Applause Theatre Books, 1997), 117; Jon Jory, interview by Berkowitz.

27. Steven Adler, *On Broadway* (Carbondale: Southern Illinois University Press, 2004), 76; Boone, interview by author.

28. Jones, interview by author.

29. Jory, interview by author.

30. ElizaBeth Mahan King, general solicitation letter to critics, May 1979, Actors Theatre of Louisville Literary Office, Louisville.

31. ElizaBeth Mahan King, university contact inquiry, 1978–79, Actors Theatre of Louisville Literary Office, Louisville; King, general solicitation letter, 1978; King, general solicitation letter to workshops, 1976, Actors Theatre of Louisville Literary Office, Louisville.

32. Also commended were Paul Owen, for his sparse set design of stairs and platforms, and the three actresses: Anne Pitoniak as Mother Miriam Ruth, company member Adale O'Brien as Dr. Martha Livingstone, and Mia Dillon as Agnes. William Mootz, "*Agnes of God*: Another Brilliant Play in a Drama Festival that Fairly Shines," *Courier-Journal* (Louisville), March 8, 1980; Actors Theatre of Louisville, "Press Release: Nine Premieres Highlight Actors Theatre's Festival of New American Plays," November 25, 1979, Actors Theatre of Louisville Literary Office, Louisville, 1.

33. Jory, interview by author.

34. William Mootz, "*Early Times* Presents Seven Plays by Beginners Bursting with Talent," *Courier-Journal* (Louisville), February 21, 1981; Dudley Saunders, "Lively *Early Times* Captures Youth at A.T.L.," *Louisville Times*, February 21, 1981; Dale Sandusky, "Youth Theme in *Early Times*," *New Albany Tribune*, February 23, 1981; Dudley Saunders, "At A.T.L., More from the Mysterious Jane Martin," *Louisville Times*, March 22, 1982; William Mootz, "Monologues by 'Martin' Are Bizarre, Fascinating," *Courier-Journal*, (Louisville), March 21, 1982.

35. Julie Crutcher, telephone interview by the author, Louisville, July 2, 1999.

36. Crutcher, interview by author.

37. All attempts to locate ElizaBeth Mahan King have proved futile. Jory, interview by author; Crutcher, interview by author.

38. Crutcher recalled, "When Beth [King] decided that she was going to leave, Jon said 'You can do this job.' I said, 'How do you know I can read plays?' 'That I know you can do,' he said, 'but I worry more that there's someone in there who can not administrate.'" Crutcher, interview by author; Michael Bigelow Dixon, telephone interview by the author, Louisville, April 18, 1999.

39. These files of cards still exist and are available to only the artistic director and the literary staff. Not even other staff members, including the executive director and board members, are allowed to read them.

40. Valerie Smith, interview by the author, Louisville, June 18, 1999.

41. Crutcher, interview by author.

42. Michael Bigelow Dixon, quoted in Lynn M. Thomson, "Michael Bigelow Dixon," *Between the Lines* (Toronto: Playwrights Canada Press, 2002), 185.

43. Jon Jory, letter to playwright, February 25, 1976, Actors Theatre of Louisville Literary Office, Louisville.

44. Dixon, interview by author.

45. Jory, interview by author.

46. Dixon, interview by author.

47. According to Dixon, the literary manager's role in the process is clear: "We have always offered advice and counsel to Jon Jory, and Jon makes the final decision." Crutcher concurred: "I wanted to make sure that I was objective as I could possibly be, because my job was to give him plays from which to pick, *not* to pick it. He [Jory] picked it." Dixon, interview by author; Crutcher, interview by author.

48. Speer cited the growing support of the Shubert Foundation, the Mellon Foundation, and other charitable trusts. According to Speer, "Although none of those monies are related directly to the Humana Festival, we receive them in good part because of the reputation that has been created by the festival itself." Speer, interview by author.

49. "Actors Theatre of Louisville," *Theatre Profiles 2*, ed. Lindy Zesch (New York: Theatre Communications Group, 1975), 11; "Actors Theatre of Louisville," *Theatre Profiles 5*, 5.

50. Mark Fearnow, "1970–1990: Disillusionment, Identity, and Discovery," in *A Companion to Twentieth-Century American Theatre*, ed. David Krasner (Malden, MA: Blackwell Publishing, 2005), 423.

51. *Talking With* is negated from consideration owing to Jory's likely authorship.

52. William Mootz, "Drama: The Season's Most Important Event Won't Even Happen in Louisville," *Courier-Journal* (Louisville), 14 September 1980; "Actors Theatre of Louisville," *Theatre Profiles 5*, 5.

5. FROM PRODUCT TO PROCESS, 1983–86

1. Dudley Saunders, "Rumors Fly over 'Secret' Production," *Louisville Times*, February 18, 1983; William Mootz, "Society's Waste Viewed in *Food from Trash*," *Courier-Journal* (Louisville), March 27, 1983.

2. William Mootz, "A.T.L. Festival Produced Challenging New Works," *Courier-Journal* (Louisville), May 29, 1983.

3. Jon Jory, quoted in William Mootz, "A.T.L. Festival Reflected Unparalleled Creativity," *Courier-Journal* (Louisville), April 3, 1983; Saunders, "Rumors."

4. Mootz, "A.T.L. Festival Reflected Unparalleled Creativity"; Jean Howerton Coady, "A Play That Even Its Author Calls Trash," *Courier-Journal* (Louisville), March 20, 1983; Owen Hardy, "Award-Winning Writer Gary Leon Hill Once Had a Job Hauling Garbage," *Courier-Journal* (Louisville), March 20 1983; Saunders, "Rumors"; Mootz, "Society's Waste"; Dudley Saunders, "Warehouse Is Theatre for A.T.L.'s Mystery Play," *Louisville Times*, March 18, 1983; Dudley Saunders, "A.T.L.'s *Trash* Stuns the Senses," *Louisville Times*, March 28, 1983; Jean Howerton Coady, "Visitors to Actors Get to Experience *Food from Trash*," *Courier-Journal* (Louisville), March 27, 1983.

5. Saunders, "A.T.L.'s *Trash*."

6. Mootz, "A.T.L. Festival Produced Challenging New Works;" Mel Gussow, "Theatre: Louisville Humana Festival," *New York Times*, March 31, 1983.

7. Actors Theatre welcomed back several writers to the seventh festival: John Pielmeier, who wrote an engaging one-man show, *Courage*; James McLure, whose story of three couples who gather on a holiday was titled *Thanksgiving*; Adele Edling Shank, with *Sand Castles*; and William Mastrosimone, whose one-act, *A Tantalizing*, was dismissed by critics as ridiculous, unpleasant, and irritating. Owen Hardy, "John Pielmeier Takes His Theme from Barrie's Life," *Courier-Journal* (Louisville), February 27, 1983; Dudley Saunders, "Paul Collins Riveting in One-Man *Courage*," *Louisville Times*, March 2, 1983; William Mootz, "A.T.L.'s *Courage* Bares a Curious Bloodless Soul," *Courier-Journal* (Louisville), March 2, 1983; Owen Hardy, "*Thanksgiving* and *Courage* at A.T.L.," *Courier-Journal* (Louisville), February 27, 1983; William Mootz, "*Thanksgiving* Offers a Feast Fueled by Funny Friendships," *Courier-Journal* (Louisville), March 7, 1983; Dudley Saunders, "*Thanksgiving* Doesn't Live up to Expectations," *Louisville Times*, March 7, 1983; Dianne Aprile, "*Sand* Set Better than the Play," *Louisville Times*, March 4, 1983.

8. Jon Jory, interview by the author, Louisville, June 18, 1999; Linda Winer, "More Is Less at Louisville Theatre Festival," *USA Today*, April 4, 1983.

9. Hap Erstein, "Q&A: New American Plays Encouraging: Jory," *Washington Post*, April 27, 1983.

10. Julie Crutcher, telephone interview by the author, July 2, 1999.

11. Michael Bigelow Dixon, "The Dramaturgical Dialogue: New Play Dramaturgy at Actors Theatre of Louisville," in *Dramaturgy in American Theatre: A Source Book* (Fort Worth: Harcourt Brace College Publishers, 1997), 417.

12. Crutcher, interview by author.

13. Hosting and housing a playwright for a monthlong rehearsal process also helped develop personal and professional relationships that enticed many writers to return to the festival. Many playwrights complimented the literary department and the Actors Theatre staff for their dedication to supporting the playwright in and out of rehearsals. Lee Blessing concurred, stating "They [the literary staff] treated me extremely well—a lot of respect, a lot of empathy." Crutcher, interview by author; John Pielmeier, "Hospitality," *Program for the Tenth Annual Humana Festival of New American Plays* (Louisville: Actors Theatre of Louisville, 1986), 21; Lee Blessing, telephone interview by the author, May 3, 2004.

14. Michael Bigelow Dixon, quoted in "Michael Bigelow Dixon" by Lynn M. Thomson, *Between the Lines* (Toronto: Playwrights Canada Press, 2002), 176.

15. In the preface to their book, Susan Jonas and Geoff Proehl cited advancements, as several dramaturgs now ran theatres, including the Magic Theatre, Portland Stage, Trinity Rep, and Playwrights Horizons. Susan Jonas and Geoff Proehl, Preface, *Dramaturgy in American Theatre: A Source Book* (Fort Worth: Harcourt Brace College Publishers, 1997), x.

16. Mary S. Ryzuk, *The Circle Repertory Company: The First Fifteen Years* (Ames: Iowa State University Press, 1989), 158, 162–66.

17. Michael Donahue, *American Professional Regional Theatre Moving into the 21st Century* (Freeport, ME: Theatre Matters Research, 1999), 79; Ryzuk, *Circle Repertory Company*, 162–66. This topic is discussed further later on in this book.

18. Jory, interview by author.

19. Lee Blessing, interview by author.

20. Richard Dresser, quoted in Nancy Wick, "Making It Work," *Columns Magazine*, March 2002, <http://www.washington.edu/alumni/columns/march02/jory02.html> (accessed 6 June 2006).

21. Todd London, *The Artistic Home* (New York: Theatre Communications Group, 1988), 2–4, 81.

22. London, *Artistic Home*, 2–4, 81; Lloyd Richards, "Lloyd Richards: Reflections from the Playwrights' Champion—An Interview," *TDR: The Drama Review* 47 (Summer 2003): 21; Gerald M. Berkowitz, *New Broadways: Theatre across America—Approaching a New Millennium* (New York: Applause Theatre Books, 1997), 122.

23. As Jory stated himself, "I can't imagine doing family plays set in rooms for the rest of my life." Jon Jory, quoted in Bernard Weiner, "Louisville Showcases Some Political Scripts," *San-Francisco Examiner-Chronicle*, April 1, 1984; Dudley Saunders, "Confusing Clutter Downs *007 Crossfire*," *Louisville Times*, March 14, 1984.

24. Saunders, "Confusing Clutter"; Dudley Saunders, "Despite Flaws, *Execution* Is Compelling," *Louisville Times*, March 9, 1984; William Mootz, "High Drama in the Courtroom: Mann's *Execution of Justice* Places All of America on Trial," *Courier-Journal* (Louisville), March 9, 1984; Mel Gussow, "Stage: In Washington, *Execution of Justice*," *New York Times*, May 29, 1985.

25. Portraying the airline disaster as a pawn in the Cold War game played by the two superpowers, Jenkins used *007 Crossfire* to criticize the White House's handling of the tragic event. As arguments between the east and west nuclear powers continue in Jenkins's play, life-sized puppets represent the passengers on the downed airliner and one of the flight attendants reads names from the passenger list throughout the production.

26. This criticism of Jory's directing is similar to an early one at Long Wharf that his plays are filled with bits of "business." Mel Gussow, "Nine New Plays at Louisville Festival," *New York Times*, March 29, 1984; William Mootz, "*007 Crossfire* Produces More Noise than Poise," *Courier-Journal* (Louisville), March 14, 1984; Saunders, "Confusing Clutter."

27. Ehren Fordyce, "Experimental Drama at the End of the Century," in *A Companion to Twentieth-Century American Theatre*, ed. David Krasner (Malden, MA: Blackwell Publishing, 2005), 537.

28. Fordyce, "Experimental Drama," 539.

29. Both *Danny and the Deep Blue Sea* and *The Octette Bridge Club* transferred to Off Broadway. William Mootz, "Humana Festival's First Play

a Bowl of Cherries," *Courier-Journal* (Louisville), February 27, 1984; Dudley Saunders, "Vivid, Amusing *The Octette Bridge Club* Opens New Play Festival at Actors," *Louisville Times*, February 27, 1984; Dudley Saunders, "*Danny* Is Amusing One Minute, Revolting the Next," *Louisville Times*, February 25, 1984; Gussow, "Nine New Plays at Louisville Festival"; William Mootz, "A.T.L.'s *Danny* Is a Wild Voyage through Rage to Love, Salvation," *Courier-Journal* (Louisville), February 25, 1984; Holly Hill, "This Year's Festival of New Plays in Louisville Deemed Best Yet," *Houston Chronicle*, April 6, 1984; Hilary DeVries, "Fresh Air for American Theater," *Christian Science Monitor* (Boston), April 11, 1984; David R. Goetz, "Works by Mastrosimone, Mann Top Louisville Play Festival," *Variety* (Los Angeles), April 4, 1984; Lawrence DeVine, "Quirky Productions are Some of Louisville's Pleasures," *Detroit Free Press*, April 1, 1984.

30. William B. Collins, "A Growing Rift between N.Y., Local Theaters," *Philadelphia Inquirer,* April 1, 1985; John Simon, quoted in Alan Stern, "Highly Regarded Louisville Is Slipping," *Denver Post*, March 31, 1985; Alan Stern, "New York Critics Assail *Octette* in Inexplicable Ways," *Denver Post*, March 28, 1985.

31. John Simon, quoted in Stern, "Highly Regarded Louisville."

32. Jory, quoted in Stern, "Highly Regarded Louisville."

33. Robert Pesola, quoted in Richard Slayton, "Louisville Festival Is a Hothouse for the American Theater," *Los Angeles Herald Examiner*, March, 31 1985.

34. Julius Novick, quoted in Slayton, "Louisville Festival Is a Hothouse."

35. The New York backlash, however, was not the only topic of conversation during the ninth festival. Only three days after the opening, Peter Sellars debuted his American National Theatre in Washington, D.C., with a production of Shakespeare's *Henry IV, Part One*. A new controversy was derived from Sellars's comments about "single-handedly rejuvenating and redefining the American theatre," a claim that offended several artistic directors and theatre critics. Hap Erstein, "Louisville's Play Festival Points toward New Direction," *Washington Times Magazine*, April 12, 1985.

36. Stern, "Highly Regarded Louisville."

37. In fact, Crutcher kidded about the large quantity of newspaper-themed plays that the literary department received: "We used to always joke in the office every time there was a big national crisis, 'Oh shit! Oh God, that's what's going to be in the mailbag next year! Oh God, Son of Sam plays!' We could just make stacks of them. We could chart the social history of America by what was in the mailbag." Crutcher, interview by author; Hill, "This Year's Festival of New Plays"; Dennis Fiely, "Actors Theatre of Louisville Offers Hits of Tomorrow at Yearly Festival," *Columbus Dispatch*, March 26, 1984; Bob Hicks, "Festival Turns Louisville into Center of Contemporary Theater," *Oregonian* (Portland), April 2, 1984.

38. Strong acting overshadowed the playwrights' works in the ninth festival. Kathy Bates's compelling performance in Frank Manley's *Two Masters*

and Delroy Lindo and Tom Wright in Bruce Bonafede's *Advice to the Players* impressed critics. Along with Murphy Guyer's one-act play *The American Century* and Larry Larson, Levi Lee, and Rebecca Wackler's *Tent Meeting*, they were the only positives to be taken from the ninth festival. The remaining shows received some of the most negative criticisms of any Humana production. For example, critics jokingly referred to Heather McDonald's *Available Light* as "Available Seats" due to the number of patrons who left during intermission. Kevin Kelly, "New Playwright Rescues Festival," *Boston Globe*, March 26, 1985; William Mootz, "*Two Masters* Has Local Premiere at Actors," *Courier-Journal* (Louisville), February 25, 1985; Dudley Saunders, "Frank Manley's *Two Masters* Visits Southern Gothic Territory," *Louisville Times*, February 25, 1985; Tom Carter, "Humana Festival Weaker Than Usual," *Lexington Herald-Leader*, March 31, 1985; William B. Collins, "Down Home: Drama Continues to Spring from the South," *Philadelphia Inquirer*, March 31, 1985; William T. Liston, "Humana Festival of Plays Is Theatre Lover's Dream," *Muncie Star*, March 31, 1985; Michael Billington, "The Sixty Minute Theatre," *Guardian* (London), March 27, 1985; Mel Gussow, "In New Plays, Mystical Visions and Broken Glass," *New York Times*, March 28, 1985; Hal Lipper, "Human Relationships Mark '85 Productions," *Dayton Daily News*, March 31, 1985; P. Gregory Springer, "The Excitement of Discovering New Plays," *Champaign-Urbana News-Gazette*, March 29, 1985; Julius Novick, "What Is This Thing Called A.T.L.?," *Village Voice*, April 23, 1985; Linda Winer, "Drama Festival Strays from Innovative Path," *USA Today*, March 28, 1985; Stayton, "Louisville Festival Is a Hothouse."

39. The most interesting failure of the ninth festival was a production that provided one of the most intense moments in Humana Festival history. James McLure returned to Louisville with another Texas comedy, *The Very Last Lover of the River Cane*, hoping to repeat the success of his *Lone Star*. The production featured a lengthy fight that received comments such as "a masterpiece of timing and acrobatics" and "the most sickeningly brutal fight I've ever seen on stage." Dale Sandusky, "Texas Barroom Play Is Best of the Lot at A.T.L.," *New Albany Tribune*, March 11, 1985; William Mootz, "*Very Last Lover of River Cane* at Actors Theatre of Louisville," *Courier-Journal* (Louisville), March 6, 1985; Dudley Saunders, "Comic Lightning Strikes Unevenly," *Louisville Times*, March 6, 1985; Bill O'Connor, "Here Are Brief Sketches of Louisville Productions," *Akron Beacon Journal*, March 31, 1985; Edward Hayman, "Fine Acting, Slick Sets, but . . . at New Play Festival, a Shortage of Ideas," *Detroit News*, March 31, 1985"; Dan Hulbert, "*Cane*: Life of the Louisville Fest," *Dallas Times Herald*, March 27, 1985; Lawrence DeVine, "Slapstick, Sob Story: Anything Plays," *Detroit Free Press*, April 1, 1985.

40. Crutcher, interview by author.

41. Crutcher, interview by author.

42. Crutcher, interview by author.

43. Jon Jory, "Quo Vadis?" *Humana Festival of New American Plays* (10th Anniversary Program; Actors Theatre of Louisville, 1986), 3; American

Theater Company, "Welcome to the American Theater Company—History," http://www.atcweb.org/ home/history/ (accessed September 8, 2005).

44. Richard Hopkins, quoted in London, *Artistic Home*, 21–22.

45. Curt Dempster, quoted in Mel Gussow, "Dempster's Ensemble Studio Invests in Plays and People," *New York Times*, May 14, 1976.

46. Mark Fearnow, "1970–1990: Disillusionment, Identity, and Discovery," in Krasner, *Companion*, 425.

47. Jory, interview by author.

48. Curt Dempster, quoted in Jeremy Gerard, "Where the Accent Is on New Plays and Playwrights," *New York Times*, April 25, 1982; Berkowitz, *New Broadways*, 162; London, *Artistic Home*, 21, 25, 32, 34.

49. Ryzuk, *Circle Repertory Company*, 165; Michael Bigelow Dixon, telephone interview by the author, April 18, 1999.

50. Berkowitz, *New Broadway*, 173.

51. Blessing, interview with author.

52. Jon Jory, quoted in Richard Christiansen, "Louisville Festival's Decade-Long Hunt for Playwrights Finds Lifetime of Talent," *Chicago Tribune*, March 27, 1986.

53. Crutcher, interview by author.

54. "Commedia Dell'Arte and the Comic Spirit" ed. Michael Dixon, Actors Theatre of Louisville Literary Office, Louisville, 56.

55. The Classics in Context Festival usually featured two plays, a collection of relevant films, workshops, other performances, several lectures, lobby exhibits, and a panel discussion led by academics. "Commedia Dell'Arte."

56. Crutcher, interview by author.

57. Crutcher had a negative perspective on the festival, stating, "The thing about academic theatre that so scares me is that they think they [academics] are so right." Crutcher, interview by author.

58. Crutcher, interview by author; Dixon, interview by author.

59. In his interview with Thomson, Dixon elaborated on the many efforts of the dramaturgical staff: "I think directors were pleased about the variety of support offered by the literary department: not only image murals, but also extensive actor research packets, videos, field trips, expert consultations, and our psych squad—a group of local psychologists and psychiatrists who would talk with playwrights and directors about characters and complexes." Dixon, quoted in Thomson, "Michael Bigelow Dixon," 184; Dixon, interview by author.

60. Lawrence Christon, "A Parade of New Plays in Louisville," *Los Angeles Times*, March 30, 1986.

6. THE EXPLORATORY YEARS, 1987–93

1. Samuel G. Freedman, "On Broadway, the Accent Will Be Decidedly British," *New York Times*, September 8, 1985; Alvin Klein, "New York Welcomes New Jersey Plays," *New York Times*, October 7, 1990.

2. Steven Adler, *On Broadway: Art and Commerce on the Great White Way.* (Carbondale: Southern Illinois University Press, 2004), 112.

3. Jeremy Gerard, "David Hwang: Riding on the Hyphen," *New York Times*, March 13, 1988; Mel Gussow, "O'Neill Center Thriving in 10th Season," *New York Times*, July 31, 1974; José Cruz González and Juliette Carillo, Foreword, in *Latino Plays from South Coast Repertory* (New York: Broadway Play Publishing, 2000), viii.

4. Jory's decision to commission writers from other fields had precedent in the form of Wynn Handman's American Place Theatre (founded in 1964), which produced new plays by up-and-coming playwrights, as well as established poets and novelists, including Robert Penn Warren, Philip Roth, and Robert Lowell. Julie Crutcher, interview by the author, Louisville, July 2, 1999; Mel Gussow, "Louisville New-Play Festival as Dumping Ground," *New York Times*, March 26, 1987; David Crespy, *The Off-Off-Broadway Explosion* (New York: Backstage Books, 2003), 149–50.

5. John Harding, "Noting New Play in Louisville," *Columbia Observer*, April 9, 1987.

6. Crutcher, interview by author.

7. Crutcher, interview by author.

8. Although Norman's play was listed as a Humana play and was labeled "the most accomplished piece of writing" in the festival, her play was not "subject for review or literary criticism at this point." As a result, discussion of her play, *Sarah and Abraham*—an improvised drama about the Biblical figures—is not possible for the purposes of this chapter. P. Gregory Springer, "Some Promise, No Major Plays at Refocused Louisville Festival," *Variety*, April 6, 1988.

9. Tom Carter, "Plays Get First Try at Louisville Festival," *Knight-Ridder* (Albuquerque), March 27, 1988; Mike Pearson, "Play Havoc: Works Don't Equal Prestige of Festival," *El Paso Herald-Post*, March 28, 1988.

10. William Mootz, "Theatre Review: *The Queen of the Leaky Roof Circuit*," *Courier-Journal* (Louisville), February 26, 1988; Springer, "Some Promise, No Major Plays"; Dale Sandusky, "A.T.L.'s *Queen* Proves Mostly a Royal Mess," *New Albany Tribune*, February 26, 1988; "Financial Comparisons," Actors Theatre of Louisville Literary Office, Louisville, 1981–99.

11. Dan Hulbert, "Back to Drawing Board for Many Humana Plays," *Atlanta Journal and Constitution*, March 27, 1988.

12. Don Corathers, "Baby Gets a New Pair of Plays," *Dramatics*, May 1988.

13. Hilary DeVries, "Louisville Tries Using Cash to Get New Plays," *Christian Science Monitor*, March 31, 1988.

14. Bob Hicks, "Louisville Plays to the Future," *Oregonian* (Portland), March 27, 1988.

15. *Stained Glass* is one of Buckley's Blackford Oakes thriller novels in which the aforementioned hero is sent on a CIA assignment in Germany in the fall of 1952. Tom Carter, "*Stained Glass* Least Impressive of Louisville Plays," *Lexington Herald-Leader*, April 2, 1989; William Mootz, "Theatre Review: *Stained Glass*," *Courier-Journal* (Louisville), March 25, 1989; Dale Sandusky, "*Stained Glass* Fails to Deliver at Actors Theatre," *New Albany*

Tribune, March 27, 1989; Fred Allen, "*Stained Glass* Is a Cold War Morality Production," *Kentucky Standard* (Bardstown), March 31, 1989; Roger Grooms, "*Stained Glass* Needs Polishing," *Cincinnati Enquirer*, March 28, 1989.

16. Congdon's play received the George Oppenheimer/Newsday Award, as well as a prize in the L. Arnold Weissberger Playwriting Competition.

17. Constance Congdon, quoted in Hilary DeVries, "Louisville Tries Noted Authors as Playwrights," *New York Times*, March 26, 1989.

18. Hilary DeVries, "Louisville Tries Noted Authors as Playwrights," *New York Times*, March 26, 1989.

19. DeVries, "Louisville Tries."

20. Jon Jory, quoted in DeVries, "Louisville Tries."

21. Dale Sandusky, "Though Long, Familiar, *Blood Issue* Debuts Well," *New Albany Tribune*, March 8, 1989.

22. David Nowlan, "*Blood Issue* Steals the Show at Louisville," *Irish Times*, April 19, 1989; William Mootz, "Theatre Review: *Blood Issue*," *Courier-Journal* (Louisville), March 5, 1989; Thomas B. Harrison, "Humana Festival: The Plays," *St. Petersburg Times*, April 9, 1989; Fred Allen, "Alcoholism, Racism Boil in *Blood Issue*," *Kentucky Standard* (Bardstown), March 8, 1989; Sandusky, "Though Long, Familiar"; Mootz, "Theatre Review: *Blood Issue*."

23. Harry Crews, quoted in DeVries, "Louisville Tries."

24. William Mootz, "Thirty Seasons in the Spotlight," *Courier-Journal* (Louisville), August 30, 1998.

25. Jon Jory, interview by the author, Louisville, June 18, 1999; Mootz, "Thirty Seasons in the Spotlight."

26. William Mootz, "Theatre Review: *Rites of Mating*," *Courier-Journal* (Louisville), March 2, 1992.

27. Marianne Evett, "New-Play Festival Provides Uneven Outing," *Plain Dealer* (Cleveland), March 29, 1992; Dag Ryen, "Pair of Plays Takes Creative Look at Rituals of Love," *Lexington Herald-Leader*, March 15, 1992; Mootz, "Theatre Review: *Rites of Mating*"; Dale Sandusky, "Two Plays Differ in Entertainment Value," *New Albany Tribune*, March 2, 1992; Fred Allen, "Two Plays Explore the Language of Love," *Kentucky Standard* (Bardstown), March 2, 1992.

28. Michael Bigelow Dixon, telephone interview by the author, April 18, 1999.

29. Michael Bigelow Dixon, "The Dramaturgical Dialogue: New Play Dramaturgy at Actors Theatre of Louisville," in *Dramaturgy in American Theatre: A Sourcebook*, ed. Susan Jonas and Geoffrey S. Proehl (Fort Worth: Harcourt Brace College Publishers, 1997), 417–18.

30. Gussow, "Louisville New-Play Festival as Dumping Ground"; Roger McBain, "Reality Puts Drama in *Digging In*," *Courier-Journal* (Louisville), March 29, 1987; William Mootz, "Danger Signs Evident at A.T.L.'s New-Play Festival," *Courier-Journal* (Louisville), March 29, 1987.

31. When Susan Sontag failed to follow through with her commission for the twelfth festival, Actors Theatre filled her slot with Barbara Damashek's

Whereabouts Unknown. One attendee astonishingly admitted his prejudice and criticized Damashek for forcing the audience to attend to issues of homelessness for more than two hours when the audience felt more comfortable ignoring the problem. William Albright, "Verbal Wizardry a Delight at Louisville Play Fest," *Houston Post,* March 27, 1988; Springer, "Some Promise, No Major Plays"; William Mootz, "Theatre Review: *Whereabouts Unknown,*" *Courier-Journal* (Louisville), March 6, 1988; Dale Sandusky, "*Whereabouts* Speaks for Homeless People," *New Albany Tribune,* March 6, 1988.

32. Mel Gussow of the *New York Times* summarized the play as "a seemingly unprocessed collage of data about neo-Nazism in America." Gussow, "A Three-Day Immersion in New Plays," *New York Times,* April 5, 1989; William Mootz, "Theatre Review: *God's Country,*" *Courier-Journal* (Louisville), March 10, 1989; Dale Sandusky, "*God's Country* Brings Hate to A.T.L. Stage," *New Albany Tribune,* March 10, 1989; Fred Allen, "In the Humana Festival, *God's Country* Presents Machinations of The Order," *Kentucky Standard* (Bardstown), March 17, 1989.

33. Linney presented the Nazi Hermann Göring as an intelligent, charming, and proud man who saw his guilt only through the eyes of his captors. One critic summarized, "[Linney] draws an engrossing portrait of a charismatic antihero whose warped morality is shielded by a sleek wit and strong code of duty." Richard Christiansen, "Louisville Festival," *Chicago Tribune,* April 5, 1990; Angela Wibking, "New Plays Recycle Other, Better Ideas," *Nashville Business Journal,* April 9–13, 1990; William Mootz, "Theatre Review: *2,*" *Courier-Journal* (Louisville), March 25, 1990; Fred Allen, "With *2,* A.T.L. Saves the Best until Last," *Kentucky Standard* (Bardstown), March 28, 1990; Dale Sandusky, "Excellent Performances Make *2* the Best in Festival," *New Albany Tribune,* March 26, 1990.

34. Presenting a unique perspective on the horrors and effects of the Vietnam War as experienced by six women, *A Piece of My Heart* quickly became the favorite of the 1991 festival. Critics praised Allen R. Belknap's directing and the ensemble cast. The six women who had been interviewed for Walker's book attended the opening-night performance. Deborah Yetter, "The Emotional War: Women Are Moved by Play They Inspired," *Courier-Journal* (Louisville), April 8, 1991; Mootz, "Theatre Review: *A Piece of My Heart,*" *Courier-Journal* (Louisville), March 24, 1991; Edwin Wilson, "Humana Festival Returns to Its Roots," *Wall Street Journal,* April 15, 1991; Mel Gussow, "A Catharsis in Louisville for the Women of Vietnam," *New York Times,* April 10, 1991.

35. Dixon, "Dramaturgical Dialogue," 418.

36. William Mootz, "Theatre Review: *A Passenger Train of Sixty-One Coaches,*" *Courier-Journal* (Louisville), March 7, 1991.

37. Joe Adcock, "Humana Plays Take a Sobering Look at Social Issues," *Seattle Post-Intelligencer,* April 10, 1991; Mootz, "Theatre Review: *A Passenger Train of Sixty-One Coaches*"; Anita-Carol Money, "Comstock Portrayal Is Strange in *Passenger,*" *Louisville Cardinal,* March 14, 1991; Dale Sandusky,

"*Train* Only Scratches the Surface," *New Albany Tribune*, March 7, 1991; Tom Carter, "Actors Theatre's *Passenger Train* a Runaway Hit," *Lexington Herald-Leader*, March 8, 1991; Fred Allen, "Play Focuses on Anti-Smut Crusader," *Kentucky Standard* (Bardstown), March 20, 1991.

38. Dixon, "Dramaturgical Dialogue," 418.

39. William Mootz, "Theatre Review: *The Carving of Mount Rushmore*," *Courier-Journal* (Louisville), March 13, 1992; Dale Sandusky, "*Carving of Mount* Addresses Issues Not Often Tackled," *New Albany Tribune*, March 13, 1992; Fred Allen, "Festival of New American Plays Continues at Actors Theatre," *Kentucky Standard* (Bardstown), March 15, 1992.

40. Ehren Fordyce, "Experimental Drama at the End of the Century," in *A Companion to Twentieth-Century American Theatre*, ed. David Krasner (Malden, MA: Blackwell Publishing, 2005), 541.

41. William Mootz, "Theatre Review: *Deadly Virtues*," *Courier-Journal* (Louisville), March 13, 1993.

42. Jeremy Gerard, "Sluggers Hit Louisville," *Variety*, March 29, 1993; Michael Grossberg, "Some Playlets Shine; Others Come Up Short," *Columbus Dispatch*, March 28, 1993; Alec Harvey, "In Louisville, the Play's the Thing," *Birmingham News*, March 28, 1993; Mootz, "Theatre Review: *Deadly Virtues*"; Fred Allen, "*Deadly Virtues* Dulls the Senses at Actors Theatre," *Kentucky Standard* (Bardstown), March 24, 1993; Dale Sandusky, "*Deadly Virtues* is Unusual Enough to Keep You Interested," *New Albany Tribune*, March 13 1993.

43. Anne Bogart, "An Artistic Home," in *Humana Festival of New American Plays: 25 Years at Actors Theatre of Louisville*, ed. Michael Bigelow Dixon and Andrew Carter Crocker (Louisville: Actors Theatre of Louisville, 2000), 52; William Mootz, "That's Entertainment," *Courier-Journal* (Louisville), April 11, 1991.

44. Valerie Smith, interview by the author, Louisville, August 20, 1999; Lawrence Christon, "A Parade of New Plays in Louisville," *Los Angeles Times*, March 30, 1986.

45. Further evidence of Jory's interest in literary adaptations can be seen through his 2006 adaptation of *Pride and Prejudice* for the Arizona Theatre Company.

46. Jill Charles, "Report from Louisville: New Play Festival Enters Second Decade," *Backstage*, March 20, 1987.

47. Mootz, "Danger Signs Evident."

48. William Mootz, "Theatre Review: *Glimmerglass*," *Courier-Journal* (Louisville), February 27, 1987.

49. Mootz, "Theatre Review: *Glimmerglass*."

50. Mootz, "Danger Signs Evident."

51. Mootz, "Danger Signs Evident"; Mootz, "Theatre Review: *Glimmerglass*."

52. Dale Sandusky, "There's No Bolting through ATL's Epic *Glimmerglass*," *New Albany Tribune*, February 27, 1987.

53. Jon Jory, quoted in Bob Hicks, "Offstage Happenings Most Notable Part of Humana Festival," *Oregonian* (Portland), March 29, 1987; Mootz, "Danger Signs Evident"; Sandusky, "There's No Bolting."

54. William Mootz, "Louisville's Theatre Fest: An Unimpressive Marathon," *USA Today*, March, 31 1987.

55. Even though an adaptation of *The Grapes of Wrath* appeared in the sixth festival to dismal reviews, the relative absence of literary adaptations in the festival until their frequent appearance in this phase justifies the perception that Jory made a concerted effort to explore this genre.

56. Todd London, *The Artistic Home* (New York: Theatre Communications Group, 1988), 25.

57. Andrew B. Harris, *Broadway Theatre* (New York: Routledge, 1994), 127.

58. William Mootz, "Theatre Review: *Vital Signs*," *Courier-Journal* (Louisville), March 22, 1990; Tom Carter, "Actors Theatre's *Vital Signs* an Uneven Mix of Monologues," *Lexington Herald-Leader*, March 30, 1990; Dale Sandusky, "*Vital Signs* Pumps Life into Festival," *New Albany Tribune*, March 22, 1990.

59. In addition to his work on musicals, Jory cowrote *Gold Dust* in 1979 and presented several one-act plays in Apprentice showcases, beginning in 1980 with *Camping*.

60. William Mootz, "Theatre Review: *Cementville*," *Courier-Journal* (Louisville), March 15, 1991; Dale Sandusky, "*Cementville* has Raunchy Opening at A.T.L.," *New Albany Tribune*, March 15, 1991; Mootz, "Theatre Review: *Cementville*"; Fred Allen, "*Cementville* Explores the Rigors of Women Wrestling," *Kentucky Standard* (Bardstown), March 22, 1991; Tom Carter, "*Cementville* Is a Rowdy View of Heroines Down for the Count," *Lexington Herald-Leader*, March 22, 1991.

61. Crutcher, interview by author.

62. The staff members wished to remain anonymous. Notes from interviews, Actors Theatre of Louisville, Louisville, 1999.

63. Notes from interviews, Actors Theatre of Louisville, Louisville, 1999.

64. Arthur M. Schlesinger, Jr., ed. *The Almanac of American History* (New York: Barnes and Noble Books, 1993), 642.

65. Anne Pitoniak returned to the Louisville stage in the role of the motherly Du, and both she and Julie Boyd (performing the role of Keely) received rave reviews for their emotion-charged performances. Lawrence DeVine, "Louisville Fest Wakes Up American Theatre," *Detroit Free Press*, March 28, 1993.

66. William Mootz, "Theatre Review: *Keely and Du*," *Courier-Journal* (Louisville), March 18, 1993; Dale Sandusky, "*Keely and Du* Fuels Abortion Debate, Offers No New Insight to Issue," *New Albany Tribune*, March 19, 1993; Fred Allen, "Powerful *Keely and Du* Raises Questions about Rights," *Kentucky Standard* (Bardstown), March 31, 1993; DeVine, "Louisville Fest Wakes Up American Theatre."

67. Besides being nominated for the Pulitzer, *Keely and Du* also received an American Critics Association Award in 1994.

68. William Mootz, "Much Ado about Something," *Courier-Journal* (Louisville), September 24, 1994; Sheldon Shafer, "Actors Theatre of Louisville Casts Its Eye on Expansion," *Courier-Journal* (Louisville), May 19, 1990.

69. Roundabout Theatre Company, "Roundabout Theatre Company—A Short History of Roundabout," September 8, 2004, http://www.roundabout-theatre.org/history2.htm (accessed September 30, 2005); Guthrie Theater, "Guthrie Theater—Timeline," <http:// www.guthrietheater.org/act_II/history.htm> (accessed September, 30 2005).

70. Alexander Speer, interview by the author, Louisville, August 20 1999.

71. Speer, interview by author.

72. Jon Jory, telephone interview by Gerald M. Berkowitz, transcript, December 19, 1995.

73. Jon Jory, quoted in William Mootz, "A.T.L. Endowment Campaign Is Aimed at Letting Theater Build for Tomorrow," *Courier-Journal* (Louisville), June 3, 1990.

74. These sources wished to remain anonymous, and financial reports that might confirm their claims were not made public. Note from interviews, Actors Theatre of Louisville, Louisville, 1999. Adding speculation to the theatre's financial woes was the noticeable inclusion of popular musicals (*Peter Pan* and *The Wizard of Oz*) among the selections for the regular season, which some say was meant to help eliminate the debt. However, these claims fail to acknowledge that Jory had a long history of directing (and even writing) musicals, so his decision to produce musicals did not represent a completely random choice. Nevertheless, when Jory first assumed the role of producing director, he often selected musicals for the regular season to increase patronage for the then-struggling theatre, but once it enjoyed financial stability, musical productions became less frequent. Mootz, "Thirty Seasons."

7. FALLING INTO A RUT, 1994–98

1. Valerie Smith, interview by the author, Louisville, June 18, 1999.

2. The Kentucky Center for the Arts' complex is on Main Street, only a few blocks away from Actors Theatre.

3. Michael Bigelow Dixon, telephone interview by the author, Louisville, July 13, 1999.

4. Dixon, interview by author.

5. Smith, interview by author; Jon Jory, interview by the author, Louisville, June 18, 1999.

6. Ibid.

7. These plays are only a few examples of the works that would qualify for the various categories.

8. Liz Engelman, interview by the author, Louisville, November 3, 1998.

9. Gerald M. Berkowitz, *New Broadways: Theatre across America—Approaching a New Millennium* (New York: Applause Theatre Books, 1997, 190–91; Trish Pugh Jones, telephone interview by the author, Louisville, May 12, 2004.

10. Independent producers subsidized productions themselves less and less often, as these wealthy individuals elicited support from corporations to provide the increasingly large sums necessary to produce Broadway shows. During the 1994–98 period, Disney Theatrical Productions opened three family-oriented productions on Broadway—*Beauty and the Beast*, *The Lion King*, and a limited engagement for Alan Menken and Tim Rice's *King David*—while also purchasing and renovating the New Amsterdam Theatre. Of course, many critics of this Disneyfication point to *Beauty and the Beast*, *Tarzan*, *Mary Poppins*, and *Aida* as examples, excluding Julie Taymor's critically acclaimed *The Lion King*.

11. James Traub, *The Devil's Playground: A Century of Pleasure and Profit in Times Square* (New York: Random House, 2004), 171, 230. *IBDB–Internet Broadway Database*, "Big," http://www.ibdb.com/ production.asp?ID=4790 (accessed September 30, 2005).

12. Steven Adler, *On Broadway: Art and Commerce on the Great White Way* (Carbondale: Southern Illinois University Press, 2004), 116.

13. Unwilling to take new risks on unknown playwrights, most theatrical producers turned to established writers such as Arthur Miller, Edward Albee, Sam Shepard, John Guare, and Christopher Durang, in addition to such icons as Tennessee Williams and Eugene O'Neill, to guarantee an audience. This heralding of the "classic" American repertoire and its writers reinforced perceptions of what legitimate theatre should be, making it difficult (if not impossible) for more experimental writers to ever hope of seeing their work on Broadway or even Off Broadway.

14. Berkowitz, *New Broadways*, 218–21; June Schlueter, "American Drama of the 1990s On and Off-Broadway," in *A Companion to Twentieth-Century American Theatre*, ed. David Krasner (Malden, MA: Blackwell Publishing, 2005), 504–15.

15. Todd London, quoted in Berkowitz, *New Broadways*, 123.

16. Todd London explained the challenges facing nonprofit theatres: "[Artistic directors] argue that new play production has become common enough to cut its risks and continue to take no share [in royalties], preserving instead all future earnings for the playwright. Many others still see new work as a risky business which draws on the theatre's resources in a way that earns for the theatre a stake in or share of future profits." London, *The Artistic Home* (New York: Theatre Communications Group, 1988), 33.

17. Two "one-hit wonders" of the formulaic phase—Neena Beber's *Misreadings* and David Graziano's *Acorn*—illustrate how two unknown playwrights used the festival's national spotlight to find work outside theatre. Graziano never returned to the Louisville stage; his Louisville success led him to Hollywood, where he served on the writing staff of NBC's prime-

time drama *Las Vegas* and produced ABC's *What about Brian*. Beber provided a short monologue in 2000, but high-profile playwrights such as Jane Martin, Craig Lucas, and Donald Margulies overshadowed her work. Like Graziano, Beber also found work in Hollywood, penning the screenplay for 2003's Mandy Moore vehicle *How to Deal*. Christine Dolen, "Work of Florida Playwrights among Best at Festival," *Miami Herald*, April 13, 1997; Christine Dolen, "New Voices Take the Stage," *Miami Herald*, April 13, 1997; Greg Evans, "Louisville Sluggers: Actors Score in Fest," *Variety*, April 14, 1997; Richard Christiansen, "Play's the Thing at Humana Fest," *Chicago Tribune*, April 9, 1997.

18. Julie Crutcher, telephone interview by the author, Louisville, July 2, 1999.

19. Smith, interview by author.

20. Berkowitz, *New Broadways*, 219–20.

21. Michael Bigelow Dixon, telephone interview by the author, Louisville, July 13, 1999.

8. THE LAST HURRAH, 1999–2000

1. Mark de la Vina, "New Plays Enjoy the Humana Touch," *San Jose Mercury News*, March 28, 1999.

2. Jon Jory quoted in Rich Copley, "Innovation the Real Star at Humana," *Lexington Herald-Leader*, February 21, 1999.

3. Dixon, quoted in Copley, "Innovation the Real Star at Humana."

4. Michael Grossberg, "Best of the Fest," *Columbus Dispatch*, March 25, 1999.

5. Wendy Wasserstein, quoted in Copley, "Innovation the Real Star at Humana."

6. Julie Beckett, "T-shirts, Telephones, and ATL," *Louisville Magazine*, March 1999. Beckett also provided this humorous thought in her article: "The discerning critic would have liked to have been a fly on the wall at the Dramatists Guild when *that* contract negotiation came up."

7. Michael Bigelow Dixon and Amy Wegener, "The Phone Plays," in *Humana Festival '99* (Lyme, NH: Smith and Kraus, 1999), 335.

8. Martin F. Kohn, "The Play's the Ring for Northern Michigan Writer," *Detroit Free Press*, March 7, 1999.

9. Richard Dresser, quoted in Judith Newmark, "So Many Plays, So Little Time; But Humana Festival Is Worth It," *St. Louis Post-Dispatch*, March 28, 1999.

10. Richard Dresser, *What Are You Afraid Of?* In *Humana Festival '99*, 330.

11. Richard Dresser, quoted in Martin F. Kohn, "Short Play's Two Acts Take Place on Four Wheels," *Detroit Free Press*, April 4, 1999; Sara Skolnick, "Introduction," *Humana Festival '99*, 324; Newmark, "So Many Plays"; Roger McBain, "Humana Plays Show the Car's the Thing," *Evansville Courier & Press*, March 25, 1999; Judith Egerton, "This Is Theater?" *Courier-Journal*

(Louisville), March 5, 1999; Michael Grossberg, "Humana Event Loads Up," *Columbus Dispatch*, January 9, 1999.

12. For the fourth festival, Peter Ekstom wrote and performed a cabaret-style satire called *Doctors and Diseases* in the Starving Artists Bar (in the basement of the Actors Theatre complex) to the enjoyment of both critics and patrons. This production marked the first official presentation outside the two theatres. Actors Theatre of Louisville, "Press Release: Nine Premieres Highlight Actors Theatre's Festival of New American Plays," Actors Theatre of Louisville Literary Office, Louisville, 3; Dudley Saunders, "*Doctors* Bubbles with Wit," *Louisville Times*, March 13, 1980.

13. Bruce Weber, "A Burst of Energy in the Regional Theater," *New York Times*, December 5, 2000; Theatre Communications Group, "Theatre Facts 1999," http://www.tcg.org/programs/theatrefacts/tf99_page15.html (accessed June 7, 2005); Guthrie Theater, "Guthrie Theater—Moving Toward the Future," http://www.guthrietheater.org/act_II/ moving.htm (accessed September 30, 2005).

14. Emily Mann, quoted in Alvin Klein, "The Theater Is Not Dead: It's into the Second Stage," *New York Times*, November 29, 1999.

15. Newmark, "So Many Plays."

16. Judith Egerton, "New Bogart Play Explores Audience-Actor Relationship," *Courier-Journal* (Louisville), March 20, 1999; Rich Copley, "Humana Festival's *Cabin* Faces Deadline Pressure," *Lexington Herald-Leader*, March 14, 1999; Kevin Nance, "Bogart's *Cabin Pressure* a Valentine to the Theater," *Tennessean* (Nashville), March 28, 1999; Misha Berson, "Humana Hopes Its Novelty Plays Fit Theater Fans Like a T-shirt," *Seattle Times*, March 28, 1999.

17. Two critics best summarized the responses to the gimmicks: the *Chicago Tribune*'s Richard Christiansen represented the appreciative yet dismissive faction of the national press, stating, "None of these novelties was substantial, but none was an embarrassment either." *The St. Louis Post-Dispatch* critic, however, provided a "wait and see" approach similar to that of many critics by concluding, "Now that the ten-minute format almost feels familiar, it's worth remembering that just a few years ago, it was considered a gimmick." Richard Christiansen, "Louisville Festival Puts a Spin on Itself," *Chicago Tribune*, April 1, 1999; Newmark, "So Many Plays."

18. Marilee Hebert Miller, interview by the author, Louisville, August 24, 1999; Actors Theatre of Louisville, "Subscription Comparison 1981–1999," Actors Theatre of Louisville Literary Office, Louisville, 1999.

19. Jon Jory, quoted in Berson, "Humana Hopes."

20. One production in the twenty-third festival helped achieve this goal. *Life under 30* was a collection of eight ten-minute plays by writers under the age of thirty. Jory and Dixon reportedly had trouble finding young writers to commission, signifying the struggles that young playwrights faced in getting their plays produced or workshopped. Jon Jory, quoted in Judith Egerton, "It's Playtime," *Courier-Journal* (Louisville), December 20, 1998; Julie York, "GenX Playwrights Turn Slop Culture into High Culture in Louisville," *South Bend*

Tribune, April 4, 1999; Martin F. Kohn, "Young Playwrights Get 10 Minutes to Tell a Tale," *Detroit Free Press*, April 4, 1999.

21. Michael Bigelow Dixon, quoted in Lynn M. Thomson, "Michael Bigelow Dixon," in *Between the Lines* (Toronto: Playwrights Canada Press, 2002), 192.

22. The only failed main-stage production was Alexandra Cunningham's *No 11. (Blue and White)*. David Ives's ten-minute play *Arabian Nights* was disappointing as well.

23. Jon Jory, quoted in Judith Egerton, "Jon Jory to Leave ATL," *Courier-Journal*, January 19, 2000; Kenneth Jones, "Jon Jory, Champion of New Plays, to Leave Actors Theatre of Louisville in Fall," *Playbill Online*, http://www.playbill.com/cgi-bin/pbl/news?cmd=show&code=92902 (accessed January 19, 2000).

24. Christen McDonough Boone, telephone interview by the author, May 4, 2005.

25. Dan Hulbert, "Humana's Jory Steps Down, Looks Ahead," *Atlanta Journal-Constitution*, April 9, 2000.

26. Christine Dolen, "Festival Director Says Goodbye to His American Theater Legacy," *Miami Herald*, April 9, 2000.

27. Alexander Speer, quoted in Egerton, "Jon Jory to Leave ATL."

28. Julie Kistler, "Humana Still a Festival Fantastic," *Champaign News-Gazette*, April 7, 2000; Michael Barnes, "Five Plays and Fifteen Plays at Louisville's Humana Festival," *Austin American-Statesman*, April 6, 2000; Marion Garmel, "New-Play Festival Draws a Crowd," *Indianapolis Star*, April 12, 2000; Rick Pender, "Splendid Variety," *CityBeat* (Cincinnati), April 6, 2000.

29. Bruce Weber, "When the Theater Sends Up Itself in Order to Save Itself," *New York Times*, April 4, 2000.

30. Charles Isherwood, "Humana Festival Bids Farewell to Founder Jory," *Variety*, April 10, 2000.

31. Jane Martin, *Anton in Show Business*, in *Humana Festival 2000: The Complete Plays*, ed. Michael Bigelow Dixon and Amy Wegener (Hanover, NH: Smith and Kraus, 2000), 173.

32. Zannie Giraud Voss and Glenn B. Voss, with Christopher Shuff and Dan Melia, *Theatre Facts 2000* (New York: Theatre Communications Group, 2001), 19.

33. Linda Geeson, "Millennium Approaches," http://www.tcg.org/am_theatre/at_articles/AT_Volume_18/September01/at_web0901_thtrfacts.html (accessed June 7, 2005).

34. Stephen Nunns, "Shifting Currents," http://www.tcg.org/am_theatre/at_articles/AT_Volume_19/September02/at_web0902_thtrfacts.html (accessed June 7, 2005).

35. Dean Gladden, quoted in Stephen Nunns, "The Rest of the Story," http://www.tcg.org/am_theatre/at_articles/AT_Volume_19/September02/at_web0902_thtrfact.html (accessed June 7, 2005); Cleveland Play House,

"CPH—The Managing Director," http://www.clevelandplayhouse.com/about/mandir.htm (accessed September 30, 2005).

36. Jacques Lamarre, quoted in Nunns, "Rest of the Story"; "Hartford Stage Staff List," http://www.hartfordstage.org/2005–2006/infopages/aboutus/staff.htm (accessed September 30, 2005).

37. Nunns, "Rest of the Story."

38. Jeffrey Herrmann, quoted in Geeson, "Millennium Approaches."

39. Michael Bigelow Dixon, quoted in David Leftowitz, "More to Louisville than ATL? Little Theatres Speak Up," May 9, 2000, http://www.playbill.com/news/article/ 51878.html (accessed September 30, 2005).

40. Juergen Tossmann, quoted in Leftowitz, "More to Louisville than ATL?"

41. Moses Goldberg, quoted in Leftowitz, "More to Louisville than ATL?"

42. Jane Martin, *Anton in Show Business*, 218.

43. Dominic P. Papatola, "Stage Craft," *St. Paul Pioneer Press*, April 9, 2000.

44. Rich Copley, "*Anton* Sends Sisters down the Rabbit Hole of American Theatre," *Lexington Herald Leader*, March 10, 2000.

9. THE EDUCATION OF MARC MASTERSON, 2001–6

1. Judith Egerton, "Actors Theatre of Louisville Picks New Leader," *Courier-Journal* (Louisville), August 9, 2000.

2. Trish Pugh Jones, telephone interview by the author, May 12, 2004.

3. Dixon resigned from the Guthrie Theater in May 2007, even though he still serves as a consultant for the theatre and performs freelance work for them.

4. Todd London, *The Artistic Home* (New York: Theatre Communications Group, 1988), 39.

5. Michael Donahue, *American Professional Regional Theatre Moving into the 21st Century* (Freeport, ME: Theatre Matters Research, 1999), 79.

6. Michael Bigelow Dixon, quoted in Chris Jones, "Will a New Broom at Humana Sweep the Old Era Away?" *New York Times*, March 11, 2001.

7. Marc Masterson, quoted in Judith Egerton, "ATL's Marc Masterson Is at the Center of Attention," *Courier-Journal* (Louisville), March 25, 2001.

8. Rick Pender, "Taking a Risk," *CityBeat* (Cincinnati), February 22, 2001; Leslie (Hoban) Blake, "Louisville Sluggers," *Theatre Mania.com*, April 13, 2001, http://www.TheatreMania.com/news/features/index.cfm?story=1322&cid=1 (accessed September 13, 2004).

9. David Wohl, "Lots of Legs to Break," *Gazette-Mail* (Charleston), February 25, 2001; Elizabeth Maupin, "At Humana Festival, There Is Life after Jory, "*Orlando Sentinel*, April 8, 2001.

10. Judith Egerton, "Play Fascinates and Confuses," *Courier-Journal* (Louisville), March 14, 2001; Claudia Harris, "The Next Wave," *Salt Lake Tribune*, April 22, 2001; Michael Grossberg, "Humana Festival Is Latest Lab

for Experimental Playwright," *Columbus Dispatch*, March 21, 2001; Rich Copley, "*Bob* Saves the Day for Humana Festival," *Herald-Leader* (Lexington), April 1, 2001.

11. Jon Jory, quoted in Jones, "Will a New Broom."

12. Dan Hulbert, "Humana's Jory Steps Down, Looks Ahead," *Atlanta Journal-Constitution*, April 9, 2000.

13. Bruce Weber, "Managers with a Mission to Avoid the Status Quo," *New York Times*, February 22, 1998; Robin Pogrebin, "Offstage Drama at Long Wharf," *New York Times*, June 25, 2001.

14. David A. Jones, quoted in Jones, "Will a New Broom"; Jan Sjostrom, "Festival of Plays a Gold Mine for Regional Theater," *Palm Beach Daily News*, March 30, 2001.

15. Judith Egerton, "Masterson's Direction Proves Masterful," *Courier-Journal* (Louisville), March 18, 2001.

16. Michael Kuchwara, "Curtain Goes Up for Act Two at Humana Festival," *Post-Star* (Glens Falls), April 5, 2001; Michael Phillips, "America, the Bountiful," *Los Angeles Times*, April 3, 2001; Tony Brown, "Festival Plays Range from Politics to Comedy," *Birmingham News*, April 8, 2001.

17. Pugh, interview with author.

18. Marc Masterson, quoted in Judith Egerton, "Actors on Track for 41st Season," *Courier-Journal* (Louisville), May 16, 2004.

19. Marc Masterson, quoted in Judith Egerton, "Louisville's Award-Winning A.T.L. Finds Itself in the Red," *Courier-Journal* (Louisville), October 21, 2001.

20. Masterson, quoted in Egerton, "Actors on Track for 41st Season."

21. Egerton, "Louisville's Award-Winning A.T.L."

22. Marc Masterson, quoted in Chris Jones, "The Most Interesting New Play in Town," *Courier-Journal* (Louisville), March 18, 2001.

23. Scott T. Cummings, "Louisville Slugger," *Boston Phoenix*, http://www.bostonphoenix.com/boston/arts/theater/documents/02243169.htm (accessed June 6, 2006).

24. Cummings, "Louisville Slugger"; Charles Whaley, "The Humana Festival: 2002," http://www.curtainup.com/humana2002.html (accessed June 6, 2006); Scott T. Cummings, "26th Annual Humana Festival of New American Plays," *Theatre Journal*, 54:4 (2002); Toby Zinman, "Louisville Slugger," *City Paper*, http://citypaper.net/ articles/2002–04–25/theater.shtml (accessed June 6, 2006); Michael Phillips, "Irrelevant Fest," *Chicago Tribune*, April 10, 2002.

25. Michael Phillips, "Report from Louisville," *Chicago Tribune*, April 10, 2003.

26. Phillips, "Report from Louisville"; Joseph Bowen, "The 27th Annual Humana Festival of New American Plays," http://centerstage.net/theatre/articles/humana2003.html (accessed June 6, 2006); Charles Whaley, "The Humana Festival: 2003," http://www.curtainup.com/humana2003.html (accessed June 6, 2006); Judith Egerton, "Risk Pays Off," *Courier-Journal*

(Louisville), April 13, 2003; Bruce Weber, "Critic's Notebook," *New York Times*, April 11, 2003.

27. Marc Masterson, quoted in Alice T. Carter, "Former City Theatre Exec Masterson Enjoying New Role," *Pittsburgh Tribune-Review*, April 10, 2001.

28. Marc Masterson, quoted in Jones, "Most Interesting New Play in Town."

29. Tanya Palmer, "The Technology Project," in *Humana Festival 2002: The Complete Plays*, ed. Tanya Palmer and Amy Wegener (Hanover, NH: Smith and Kraus, 2002), 366.

30. Hedy Weiss, "Bernstein, Paris, and a Big Mess," *Chicago Sun Times*, April 9, 2002.

31. Dag Ryen, "Maintaining Relevance Is Humana's Challenge," *Monterey Herald.com*, http://www.montereyherald.com/mld/kentucky/living/5608313. htm (accessed April 13, 2003).

32. Egerton, "Actors on Track for 41st Season."

33. The commission was funded, in part, by the NEA and TCG.

34. Bruce Weber, "Where Plays Escape the Curse of the Unseen," *New York Times*, April 6, 2004; Rick Pender, "Humana Treatment," *City Beat*, http:// www.citybeat.com/2004–04–07/onstage2.shtml (accessed June 6, 2006); Joseph Bowen, "The 28th Annual Humana Festival of New American Plays," http:// www.centerstage.net/theatre/articles/humana2004.html (accessed June 6, 2006); Judith Egerton, "Space Solutions," *Courier-Journal* (Louisville), March 21, 2004; Judith Egerton, "A New Stage," *Courier-Journal* (Louisville), March 17, 2004; Judith Egerton, "Theatre Review: *Vanishing* Captures the Heart of Butchertown," *Courier-Journal* (Louisville), March 16, 2004.

35. Egerton, "Actors on Track for 41st Season"; Actors Theatre of Louisville, "28th Humana Festival Hails Artistic and Financial Triumphs—2004 Festival Most Lauded and Best Attended in Years," http://www.actorstheatre. org/humana_ festival.htm (accessed November 30, 2004).

36. Anne Marie Welsh, "At Humana Festival, Plenty of Themes, but Not Enough Drama," *San Diego Union-Tribune*, April 10, 2005; Judith Egerton, "2005 Humana Festival of New American Plays: Three Hits and Three Misses," April 10, 2005; Charles Whaley, "The 29th Humana Festival: 2005," http://www.curtainup.com/humana2005.html (accessed June 6, 2006).

37. Actors Theatre of Louisville, "Actors Theatre of Louisville—News Flash!" http://www.actorstheatre.org/ newsflash.htm (accessed October 15, 2005).

38. Dag Ryen, "At Actors Theatre, a Great Crop of Drama," *Lexington Herald-Leader*, April 9, 2006; Charles Isherwood, "Louisville's Humana Festival Offers New Plays by the Fest-Full," *New York Times*, April 5, 2006.

39. Jones has a long history of not being kind to the Louisville festival, beginning with his controversial article asking about Jory's support of minority writers. His praise for the festival in 2006 is another sign of Masterson's

accomplishment. Chris Jones, "The Scene Steals the Show at Humana," *Chicago Tribune*, April 5, 2006.

40. Charles Whaley, "The 30th Humana Festival of New American Plays Celebrates Its 30th Anniversary," http://www.curtainup.com/ humana2006. html (accessed June 6, 2006).

41. Actors Theatre of Louisville, "America Loves the Humana Festival," Actors Theatre of Louisville, http://www.actorstheatre.org/humana_recap. htm (accessed June 13, 2006).

CONCLUSION: LOOKING BACK AND LOOKING FORWARD

1. In comparison with other united arts groups, Louisville's Fund for the Arts has always performed exceedingly well, better than cities of comparable size, including Cincinnati, Orlando, Charlotte, and Memphis. Corporations, foundations, and individuals in the Louisville community give to its Fund for the Arts, exhibiting the community's eagerness to help support artistic endeavors. Nord Thoman, "Arts Are Good Business, Leaders Say," *Courier-Journal* (Louisville), October 21, 2001; Fund for the Arts, "Fund for the Arts: Our History," http://www.fundforthearts.com/history.php (accessed June 27, 2005); Mary Ellen Hutton, "United Arts Groups Set $10.75 Million Goal," *Cincinnati Post*, February 14, 2005, http://www.cincypost.com/2005/ 02/14/finearts021405.html (accessed July 27, 2005); Thoman, "Arts are Good Business"; Dick Kaukas, "Louisville Fund Reaches Out for Community Involvement," *Courier-Journal* (Louisville), March 14, 1977; Fund for the Arts, "Fund for the Arts: Frequently Asked Questions," http://www.fundforthearts. com/faq.php (accessed June 27, 2005); Hutton, "United Arts Groups Set $10.75 Million Goal"; CincinnatiUSA.com, "Cincinnati USA—Frequently Asked Questions," http://www.cincinnatiusa.org/faq.asp (accessed July 30, 2005); Fund for the Arts, *State of the Arts* (Fund for the Arts, Louisville, July 28 1998), 55; Memphis Chamber, "Memphis Regional Chamber," June 2004, http://www. memphischamber.com/ default.asp? content Type = static & browse Path = MemphisFacts,Demographics (accessed July 30, 2005); Memphis Arts Council, "Memphis Arts Council—Arts Funding," July 1, 2005, http://www. memphisartscouncil.org/AboutUs/News/AllNews/Arts-Funding.cfm (accessed July 30, 2005). Figures were compiled with data from 2004 fund-raising supplied by the respective councils and from 2000 census figures.

WORKS CITED

"Actors Theatre Is Looking for Plays." *Courier-Journal* (Louisville), February 11, 1977.

Actors Theatre of Louisville. "Actors Theatre of Louisville History: Production History." http://www.actorstheatre.org/about_production_2.htm (accessed August 28, 2005).

———. "Actors Theatre of Louisville: Humana Festival Fun Facts." http://www.actorstheatre.org/humana_facts.htm (accessed July 31, 2005).

———. "Actors Theatre of Louisville: News Flash!" http://www.actorstheatre.org/newsflash.htm (accessed October 15, 2005).

———. "America Loves the Humana Festival." http://www.actorstheatre.org/humana_recap.htm (accessed June 13, 2006).

———. "Press Release: Nine Premieres Highlight Actors Theatre's Festival of New American Plays." Actors Theatre of Louisville Literary Office. November 25, 1979.

———. "Subscription Comparison 1981–1999." Actors Theatre of Louisville Literary Office, Louisville, 1999.

———. "28th Humana Festival Hails Artistic and Financial Triumphs: 2004 Festival Most Lauded and Best Attended in Years." http://www.actorstheatre.org/humana_festival.htm (accessed November 30, 2004).

"Actors Theatre of Louisville." *Theatre Profiles 2*. Edited by Lindy Zesch. New York: Theatre Communications Group, 1975.

"Actors Theatre of Louisville." *Theatre Profiles 5*. Edited by Laura Ross. New York: Theatre Communications Group, 1982.

"Actors Theatre of Louisville." *Theatre Profiles 6*. Edited by Laura Ross. New York: Theatre Communications Group, 1984.

"Actors Theatre of Louisville Board of Directors' Minutes: April 25, 1968." In Ward, Notes on History.

"Actors Theatre of Louisville Board of Directors' Minutes: March 9, 1969." In Ward, Notes on History.

"Actors Theatre of Louisville Board of Directors' Minutes: October 6, 1966." In Ward, Notes on History.

"Actors Theatre of Louisville Given $13,000 Federal Grant." *Courier-Journal* (Louisville), December 17, 1969.

"Actors Theatre Opens $38,000 Fund Campaign." *Courier-Journal* (Louisville), March 26, 1969.

"Actors Theatre Promotes Speer to Manager." *Courier-Journal* (Louisville), February 20, 1969.

Adcock, Joe. "Director Finds Lessons for Modern Souls in Shaw's 90-Year-Old *Heartbreak House*," *Seattle Post-Intelligencer*, July 28, 2006.

———. "Humana Plays Take a Sobering Look at Social Issues." *Seattle Post-Intelligencer*, April 10, 1991.

———. "Lifetime of Theatre Hefty Credentials for Jon Jory at UW." *Seattle Post-Intelligencer*, February 3, 2000.

Adler, Steven. *On Broadway: Art and Commerce on the Great White Way.* Carbondale: Southern Illinois University Press, 2004.

Albright, William. "Verbal Wizardry a Delight at Louisville Play Fest." *Houston Post*, March 27, 1988.

Allen, Fred. "Alcoholism, Racism Boil in *Blood Issue*." *Kentucky Standard* (Bardstown), March 8, 1989.

———. "*Cementville* Explores the Rigors of Women Wrestling." *Kentucky Standard* (Bardstown), March 22, 1991.

———. "*Deadly Virtues* Dulls the Senses at Actors Theatre." *Kentucky Standard* (Bardstown), March 24, 1993.

———. "Festival of New American Plays Continues at Actors Theatre." *Kentucky Standard* (Bardstown), March 15, 1992.

———. "In the Humana Festival, *God's Country* Presents Machinations of The Order." *Kentucky Standard* (Bardstown), March 17, 1989.

———. "Play Focuses on Anti-Smut Crusader." *Kentucky Standard* (Bardstown), March 20, 1991.

———. "Powerful *Keely and Du* Raises Questions about Rights." *Kentucky Standard* (Bardstown), March 31, 1993.

———. "*Stained Glass* Is a Cold War Morality Production." *Kentucky Standard* (Bardstown), March 31, 1989.

———. "Two Plays Explore the Language of Love." *Kentucky Standard* (Bardstown), March 2, 1992.

———. "With 2, A.T.L. Saves the Best until Last." *Kentucky Standard* (Bardstown), March 28, 1990.

American Theater Company. "Welcome to the American Theater Company—History." http://www.atcweb.org/ home/history/ (accessed September 8, 2005).

Aprile, Dianne. "*Sand* Set Better than the Play." *Louisville Times*, March 4, 1983.

Archer, Stephen M. "Actors Theatre of Louisville." *Cambridge Guide to American Theatre*. Edited by Don B. Wilmeth. New York: Cambridge University Press, 1996.

Arts Council of Oklahoma City. "Stage Center History." 2002. http://www.stagecenter.com/history.html (accessed August 9, 2005).

"A.T.L. Sets U.S. Record." *Courier-Journal* (Louisville), October 4, 1970.

"A.T.L.'s Jory Pleased as Sales Top 5,000." *Courier-Journal* (Louisville), November 30, 1969.

"Author Credits Actors Theatre in Pulitzer Win; *New York Times* Collects Record Three Awards." *Louisville Times*, April 18, 1978.

"Awards, Prizes, Honors and Recognition." In Dixon and Crocker, *Humana Festival of New American Plays*, 96–97.

"Bach Group and A.T.L. Get Grants." *Courier Journal* (Louisville), March 8, 1970.

Bahr, Bob, and James Nold Jr. *The Insider's Guide to Louisville*. Manteo, NC: Insiders' Publishing, 1997.

Barnes, Clive. "Stage: 'Tricks,' Musical Based on Moliere, Arrives." *New York Times*, January 9, 1973.

Barnes, Michael. "Five Plays and Fifteen Plays at Louisville's Humana Festival." *Austin American-Statesman*, April 6, 2000.

Beckett, Julie. "T-Shirts, Telephones, and ATL." *Louisville Magazine*, March 1999.

Bell, Elizabeth S. "Role-ing on the River: Actors Theatre and the Southern Woman Playwright." In *Southern Women Playwrights*. Edited by Robert L. McDonald and Linda Rohrer Paige. Tuscaloosa: University of Alabama Press, 2002.

Berkowitz, Gerald M. *New Broadways: Theatre across America—Approaching a New Millennium*. New York: Applause Theatre Books, 1997.

Bernard, Richard. "*Gin* Has the Cards." *Casting News Entertainment Guide* (Los Angeles), October 21, 1976.

Berson, Misha. "Humana Hopes Its Novelty Plays Fit Theater Fans Like a T-shirt." *Seattle Times*, March 28, 1999.

Bette on the Boards Web Site. "Bette Midler: Playbill Biographies." http://www.betteontheboards.com/boards/link-06–01.htm (accessed August 10, 2005).

Billington, Michael. Untitled article. *Guardian* (London), March 2, 1979.

———. "The Sixty Minute Theatre." *Guardian* (London), March 27, 1985.

Bilowit, Ira J., ed. "Regional Theatres and Their Relationship to New York." *New York Theatre Review*, January 1979, 16–23.

Bingham, Barry, Jr. Interview by Lucretia (Teka) Baldwin Ward. In Ward, *Notes on History*.

Bingham, Edith. "Notes on Preservation History in Louisville." In *Louisville Guide*. Edited by Gregory A. Luhan, Dennis Domer, and David Mohney. New York: Princeton Architectural Press, 2004.

Blake, Leslie (Hoban). "Louisville Sluggers." *Theatre Mania.com*. April 13, 2001. http://www.Theatremania.com/news/features/index.cfm?story=1322&cid=1 (accessed September 13, 2004).

Blanchard, Jayne M. "Play Grounds." *St. Paul Pioneer Press*, April 20, 1996.

Blessing, Lee. Telephone interview by the author, May 3, 2004.

Block, Richard. Interview by Lucretia (Teka) Baldwin Ward. In Ward, *Notes on History*.

Bogart, Anne. "An Artistic Home." In Dixon and Crocker, *Humana Festival of New American Plays*, 50–53.

Boone, Christen McDonough. Telephone interview by the author, May 4, 2005.

Borak, Jeffrey. "Actors Theatre of Louisville: Proving Ground for New York." *Poughkeepsie Journal*, April 15, 1979.

Bowen, Joseph. "The 27th Annual Humana Festival of New American Plays." http://centerstage.net/theatre/articles/humana2003.html (accessed June 6, 2006).

———. "The 28th Annual Humana Festival of New American Plays." http://www.centerstage.net/theatre/articles/humana2004.html (accessed June 6, 2006).

Brown, Tony. "Festival Plays Range from Politics to Comedy." *Birmingham News*, April 8, 2001.

Burke, Sally. "Lillian Hellman and Marsha Norman." *Southern Women Playwrights*. Edited by Robert L. McDonald and Linda Rohrer Paige. Tuscaloosa: University of Alabama Press, 2002.

Byck, Dann C. Interview by Lucretia (Teka) Baldwin Ward. In Ward, Notes on History.

Carter, Alice T. "Former City Theatre Exec Masterson Enjoying New Role." *Pittsburgh Tribune-Review*, April 10, 2001.

Carter, Tom. "Actors Theatre's *Passenger Train* a Runaway Hit." *Lexington Herald-Leader*, March 8, 1991.

———. "Actors Theatre's *Vital Signs* an Uneven Mix of Monologues." *Lexington Herald-Leader*, March 30, 1990.

———. "*Cementville* Is a Rowdy View of Heroines Down for the Count." *Lexington Herald-Leader*, March 22, 1991.

———. "Humana Festival Weaker Than Usual." *Lexington Herald-Leader*, March 31, 1985.

———. "Plays Get First Try at Louisville Festival." *Knight-Ridder* (Albuquerque), March 27, 1988.

———. "*Stained Glass* Least Impressive of Louisville Plays." *Lexington Herald-Leader*, April 2, 1989.

Caruso, Joseph S. "Los Angeles After Dark: *The Gin Game*." *NewsWest* (Los Angeles), October 1–15, 1976.

Charles, Jill. "Report from Louisville: New Play Festival Enters Second Decade." *Backstage*, March 20, 1987.

Christiansen, Richard. "Lively Actors Theater Puts Drama to Work." *Chicago Daily News*, March 11, 1977.

———. "Louisville Festival." *Chicago Tribune*, April 5, 1990.

———. "Louisville Festival Puts a Spin on Itself." *Chicago Tribune*, April 1, 1999.

———. "Louisville Festival's Decade-Long Hunt for Playwrights Finds Lifetime of Talent." *Chicago Tribune*, March 27, 1986.

———. "Play's the Thing at Humana Fest." *Chicago Tribune*, April 9, 1997.

Christon, Lawrence. "A Parade of New Plays in Louisville." *Los Angeles Times*, March 30, 1986.

CincinnatiUSA.com. "Cincinnati USA—Frequently Asked Questions." http://www.cincinnatiusa.org/ faq.asp (accessed July 30, 2005).

Cleveland Play House. "CPH—The Managing Director." http://www.clevelandplayhouse.com/about/mandir.htm (accessed September 30, 2005).

Clark, Bryan. Telephone interview by Lucretia (Teka) Baldwin Ward. In Ward, Notes on History.

Coady, Jean Howerton. "A Play That Even Its Author Calls Trash." *Courier-Journal* (Louisville), March 20, 1983.

———. "Visitors to Actors Get to Experience *Food from Trash.*" *Courier-Journal* (Louisville), March 27, 1983.

Coe, Richard L. "Best Acting West of Broadway." *Washington Post*, November 27, 1977.

———. "A Comedy Tonight (All Summer)." *Washington Post, Times Herald*, June 4, 1972.

Coe, Robert. "The Evolution of John Patrick Shanley." *American Theatre* 21, no. 9 (November 2004): 23–26, 97–99.

Collins, William B. "Down Home: Drama Continues to Spring from the South." *Philadelphia Inquirer*, March 31, 1985.

———. "A Growing Rift between N.Y., Local Theaters." *Philadelphia Inquirer*, April 1, 1985.

"Commedia Dell'Arte and the Comic Spirit." Edited by Michael Dixon. Actors Theatre of Louisville Literary Office, Louisville.

Copley, Rich. "*Anton* Sends Sisters down the Rabbit Hole of American Theatre." *Lexington Herald Leader*, March 10, 2000.

———. "*Bob* Saves the Day for Humana Festival." *Herald-Leader* (Lexington), April 1, 2001.

———. "Humana Festival's *Cabin* Faces Deadline Pressure." *Lexington Herald-Leader*, March 14, 1999.

———. "Innovation the Real Star at Humana." *Lexington Herald-Leader*, February 21, 1999.

Conner, Lynne. "On the Arts: Pittsburgh Audiences Are Way More Sophisticated Than You'd Guess from City's Image." *Pittsburgh Post-Gazette*, November 9, 2003.

Corathers, Don. "Baby Gets a New Pair of Plays." *Dramatics*, May 1988.

Cornett, Ewel. Interview by Lucretia (Teka) Baldwin Ward. In Ward, Notes on History.

Crespy, David. *The Off-Off-Broadway Explosion*. New York: Back Stage Books, 2003.

Cristensen, John. "Jon Jory Gives His Regards to Broadway." *Louisville Times*, January 8, 1972.

Crutcher, Julie. Telephone interview by the author, July 2, 1999.

Cummings, Scott T. "26th Annual Humana Festival of New American Plays." *Theatre Journal* 54, no. 4 (2002).

———. "Louisville Slugger." *Boston Phoenix*. http://www.bostonphoenix.com/boston/arts/theater/documents/02243169.htm (accessed June 6, 2006).

Dahlem, Bernard. Interview by Lucretia (Teka) Baldwin Ward. In Ward, Notes on History.

de la Vina, Mark. "New Plays Enjoy the Humana Touch." *San Jose Mercury News*, March 28, 1999.

Demaline, Jackie. "Not Much Ado about Nothing." *Cincinnati Enquirer*, April 7, 1996.

Dent, Tom. "Black Theatre in the South: Report and Reflections." In *The Theatre of Black Americans*. Edited by Errol Hill. New York: Applause Theatre Books, 1987.

DeVine, Lawrence. "Louisville Fest Wakes Up American Theatre." *Detroit Free Press*, March 28, 1993.

———. "Quirky Productions are Some of Louisville's Pleasures." *Detroit Free Press*, April 1, 1984.

———. "Slapstick, Sob Story: Anything Plays." *Detroit Free Press*, April 1, 1985.

DeVries, Hilary. "Fresh Air for American Theater." *Christian Science Monitor* (Boston), April 11, 1984.

———. "Louisville Tries Using Cash to Get New Plays." *Christian Science Monitor*, March 31, 1988.

———. "Louisville Tries Noted Authors as Playwrights." *New York Times*, March 26, 1989.

Dietrich, Jean. "A.T.L.'s *Vanities* Is Nearly Flawless as It Follows the Lives of Three People." *Courier-Journal* (Louisville), October 18, 1976.

———. "Louisville Is Play Setting by Luck Only." *Courier-Journal* (Louisville), March 2, 1977.

Dixon, Michael Bigelow. "The Dramaturgical Dialogue: New Play Dramaturgy at Actors Theatre of Louisville." In Jonas and Proehl, *Dramaturgy in American Theatre*.

———. Telephone interviews by the author, April 18 and July 13, 1999.

Dixon, Michael Bigelow, and Andrew Carter Crocker, eds. *Humana Festival of New American Plays: 25 Years at Actors Theatre of Louisville*. Louisville: Actors Theatre of Louisville, 2000.

Dixon, Michael Bigelow, and Amy Wegener, eds. *Humana Festival '99*. Lyme, NH: Smith and Kraus, 1999.

Dixon, Michael Bigelow, and Amy Wegener. "The Phone Plays." In Dixon and Wegener, *Humana Festival '99*, 334–35.

Dolen, Christine. "Festival Director Says Goodbye to His American Theater Legacy." *Miami Herald*, April 9, 2000.

———. "New Voices Take the Stage." *Miami Herald*, April 13, 1997.

———. "Work of Florida Playwrights among Best at Festival." *Miami Herald*, April 13, 1997.

Donahue, Michael. *American Professional Regional Theatre Moving into the 21st Century*. Freeport, ME: Theatre Matters Research, 1999.

Dresser, Richard. *What Are You Afraid Of?* In Dixon and Wegener, *Humana Festival '99*.

Eder, Richard. "Louisville Festival Offers Six New Plays." *New York Times*, November 15, 1977.

Egerton, Judith. "2005 Humana Festival of New American Plays: Three Hits and Three Misses." April 10, 2005.

———. "Actors on Track for 41st Season." *Courier-Journal* (Louisville), May 16, 2004.

———. "Actors Theatre of Louisville Picks New Leader." *Courier-Journal* (Louisville), August 9, 2000.

———. "ATL's Marc Masterson Is at the Center of Attention." *Courier-Journal* (Louisville), March 25, 2001.

———. "It's Playtime." *Courier-Journal* (Louisville), December 20, 1998.

———. "Jon Jory to Leave ATL." *Courier-Journal*, January 19, 2000.

———. "Louisville's Award-Winning A.T.L. Finds Itself in the Red." *Courier-Journal* (Louisville), October 21, 2001.

———. "Masterson's Direction Proves Masterful." *Courier-Journal* (Louisville), March 18, 2001.

———. "New Bogart Play Explores Audience-Actor Relationship." *Courier-Journal* (Louisville), March 20, 1999.

———. "A New Stage." *Courier-Journal* (Louisville), March 17, 2004.

———. "Play Fascinates and Confuses." *Courier-Journal* (Louisville), March 14, 2001.

———. "Risk Pays Off." *Courier-Journal* (Louisville), April 13, 2003.

———. "Space Solutions." *Courier-Journal* (Louisville), March 21, 2004.

———. "Theatre Review: *Strange Encounters*." *Courier-Journal* (Louisville), March 4, 1996.

———. "This Is Theater?" *Courier-Journal* (Louisville), March 5, 1999.

———. "Theatre Review: *Vanishing* Captures the Heart of Butchertown." *Courier-Journal* (Louisville), March 16, 2004.

Ehrlich, Barbara Janowitz. "Theatre Facts 88." *American Theatre* 6, no. 1 (April 1989)..

"An End, Not a Means: Developing Local Playwrights." *New York Theatre Review*, April 1979.

Engelman, Liz. Interview by the author, Louisville, November 3, 1998.

Epstein, Helen. *Joe Papp: An American Life*. Boston: Little, Brown, 1994.

Erstein, Hap. "Q&A: New American Plays Encouraging—Jory." *Washington Post*, April 27, 1983.

———. "Louisville's Play Festival Points toward New Direction." *Washington Times Magazine*, April 12, 1985.

Evans, Greg. "Louisville Sluggers: Actors Score in Fest." *Variety*, April 14, 1997.

———. "Truces and Deuces Mark Twentieth Play Fest." *Variety*, April 8, 1996.

Evett, Marianne. "New-Play Festival Provides Uneven Outing." *Plain Dealer* (Cleveland), March 29, 1992.

Fearnow, Mark. "1970–1990: Disillusionment, Identity, and Discovery." In Krasner, *Companion to Twentieth-Century American Theatre*.

Fiely, Dennis. "Actors Theatre of Louisville Offers Hits of Tomorrow at Yearly Festival." *Columbus Dispatch*, March 26, 1984.

"Financial Comparisons." Actors Theatre of Louisville, 1981–99. Actors Theatre of Louisville Literary Office, Louisville.

"Ford Foundation Agrees to Pay for a Fourth of Actors Theatre's Building Campaign." *Courier-Journal* (Louisville), August 3, 1971.

Fordyce, Ehren. "Experimental Drama at the End of the Century." In Krasner, *Companion to Twentieth-Century American Theatre.*

Freedman, Samuel G. "On Broadway, the Accent Will Be Decidedly British." *New York Times*, September 8, 1985.

Fund for the Arts. *State of the Arts.* Louisville, July 28, 1998.

———. "Fund for the Arts: Frequently Asked Questions." http://www.fundforthearts.com/faq.php (accessed June 27, 2005).

———. "Fund for the Arts: Our History." http:// www.fundforthearts.com/history.php (accessed June 27, 2005).

Garmel, Marion. "New-Play Festival Draws a Crowd." *Indianapolis Star*, April 12, 2000.

Gerard, Jeremy. "David Hwang: Riding on the Hyphen." *New York Times*, March 13, 1988.

———. "Sluggers Hit Louisville." *Variety*, March 29, 1993.

———. "Where the Accent Is on New Plays and Playwrights." *New York Times*, April 25, 1982.

Geeson, Linda. "Millennium Approaches." http://www.tcg.org/am_theatre/at_articles/AT_Volume_18/September01/at_web0901_thtrfacts.html (accessed. June 7, 2005).

Glover, William. "Regional Theatres Trying Own Thing." *Columbus Dispatch*, April 17, 1977.

———. "Regional Theaters Doing New Plays." *Atlanta Journal-Constitution*, April 10, 1977.

———. "The Stage of the Stage." *Courier-Journal* (Louisville), April 17, 1977.

Gnadinger, Emily. Interview by the author. Louisville, August 19, 1999.

Goetz, David R. "Works by Mastrosimone, Mann Top Louisville Play Festival." *Variety* (Los Angeles), April 4, 1984.

González, José Cruz, and Juliette Carillo. Foreword. In *Latino Plays from South Coast Repertory.* New York: Broadway Play Publishing, 2000.

Grooms, Roger. "*Stained Glass* Needs Polishing." *Cincinnati Enquirer*, March 28, 1989.

Grossberg, Michael. "Best of the Fest." *Columbus Dispatch*, March 25, 1999.

———. "Humana Event Loads Up." *Columbus Dispatch*, January 9, 2000.

———. "Humana Festival Is Latest Lab for Experimental Playwright." *Columbus Dispatch*, March 21, 2001.

———. "Some Playlets Shine; Others Come Up Short." *Columbus Dispatch*, March 28, 1993.

Gussow, Mel. "Actors Theatre of Louisville Is Flourishing under Jon Jory." *New York Times*, September 1, 1979.

———. "A Catharsis in Louisville for the Women of Vietnam." *New York Times*, April 10, 1991.

———. "Dempster's Ensemble Studio Invests in Plays and People." *New York Times*, May 14, 1976.

———. "Louisville Again Mines Rich Ore of Stage Talent." *New York Times*, February 20, 1979.

———. "Louisville New-Play Festival as Dumping Ground." *New York Times*, March 26, 1987.

———. "In New Plays, Mystical Visions and Broken Glass." *New York Times*, March 28, 1985.

———. "Nine New Plays at Louisville Festival." *New York Times*, March 29, 1984.

———. "O'Neill Center Thriving in 10th Season." *New York Times*, July 31, 1974.

———. "Stage: In Washington, *Execution of Justice*." *New York Times*, May 29, 1985.

———. "Theater: Country Plays Make the Big City Laugh." *New York Times*, June 8, 1979.

———. "Theatre: Louisville Humana Festival." *New York Times*, March 31, 1983.

———. "A Three-Day Immersion in New Plays." *New York Times*, April 5, 1989.

Guthrie Theater. "Guthrie Theater: Moving toward the Future." http://www.guthrietheater.org/act_II/moving.htm (accessed September 30, 2005).

———. Guthrie Theater: Timeline." http://www.guthrietheater.org/act_II/history.htm (accessed September 30, 2005).

Harding, John. "Noting New Play in Louisville." *Columbia Observer*, April 9, 1987.

Harding, Tim, and Emmanuel Kehoe. "A Bird Never Flew on One Wing." *Sunday Press* (Dublin), October 6, 1980.

Hardy, Owen. "A.T.L. Makes Its Mark in Europe." *Courier-Journal* (Louisville), October 12, 1980.

———. "Award-Winning Writer Gary Leon Hill Once Had a Job Hauling Garbage." *Courier-Journal* (Louisville), March 20, 1983.

———. "John Pielmeier Takes His Theme from Barrie's Life." *Courier-Journal* (Louisville), February 27, 1983.

———. "*Thanksgiving* and *Courage* at A.T.L." *Courier-Journal* (Louisville), February 27, 1983.

Harris, Andrew B. *Broadway Theatre*. New York: Routledge, 1994.

Harris, Claudia. "The Next Wave." *Salt Lake Tribune*. April 22, 2001.

Harrison, Thomas B. "Humana Festival: The Plays." *St. Petersburg Times*, April 9, 1989.

Hartford Stage. "Hartford Stage Staff List." http://www.hartfordstage.org/20052006/infopages/aboutus/staff.htm (accessed September 30, 2005).

Harvey, Alec. "Of Friends and Family." *Birmingham News*, April 7, 1996.

———. "In Louisville, the Play's the Thing." *Birmingham News*, March 28, 1993.

Hayman, Edward. "Fine Acting, Slick Sets, but . . . at New Play Festival, a Shortage of Ideas." *Detroit News*, March 31, 1985.

Henderson, Ian. Interview by Lucretia (Teka) Baldwin Ward. In Ward, Notes on History.

Hicks, Bob. "Festival Turns Louisville into Center of Contemporary Theater." *Oregonian* (Portland), April 2, 1984.

———. "Louisville Plays to the Future." *Oregonian* (Portland), March 27, 1988.

———. "Offstage Happenings Most Notable Part of Humana Festival." *Oregonian* (Portland), March 29, 1987.

"Highlights: Twenty-five Years in the American Theatre." In *Theatre Profiles 7*. New York: Theatre Communications Group, 1986.

Hill, Holly. "Black Theatre into the Mainstream." In B. King, *Contemporary American Theatre*.

———. "This Year's Festival of New Plays in Louisville Deemed Best Yet." *Houston Chronicle*, April 6, 1984.

Holley, Robert. "Theatre Facts 84." *American Theatre* 1, no. 11 (March 1985).

Hulbert, Dan. "Back to Drawing Board for Many Humana Plays." *Atlanta Journal and Constitution*, March 27, 1988.

———. "*Cane*: Life of the Louisville Fest." *Dallas Times Herald*, March 27, 1985.

———. "Humana's Jory Steps Down, Looks Ahead." *Atlanta Journal-Constitution*, April 9, 2000.

"Humana Inc." In *Humana Festival '98: The Complete Plays*. Edited by Michael Bigelow Dixon and Amy Wegener. Lyme, NH: Smith and Kraus, 1998.

Hunter, Gregg. "A Fine First Play." *New-Press Daily Review Star* (Los Angeles), October 14, 1976.

Hutton, Mary Ellen. "United Arts Groups Set $10.75 Million Goal." *Cincinnati Post*, February 14, 2005. http://www.cincypost.com/2005/02/14/finearts021405.html (accessed June 27, 2005).

Internet Broadway Database. "IBDB: Internet Broadway Database—*Big*." http://www.ibdb.com/production.asp?ID =4790 (accessed September 30, 2005).

Isherwood, Charles. "Humana Festival Bids Farewell to Founder Jory." *Variety*, April 10, 2000.

———. "Louisville's Humana Festival Offers New Plays by the Fest-Full." *New York Times*, April 5, 2006.

Johnson, Jack. Interview by Lucretia (Teka) Baldwin Ward. In Ward, Notes on History.

Jonas, Susan, and Geoffrey S. Proehl, eds. *Dramaturgy in American Theatre: A Source Book*. Fort Worth: Harcourt Brace College Publishers, 1997.

———. Preface. In Jonas and Proehl, *Dramaturgy in American Theatre*.

Jones, Chris. "The Most Interesting New Play in Town." *Courier-Journal* (Louisville), March 18, 2001.

———. "*The Scene* Steals the Show at Humana." *Chicago Tribune*, April 5, 2006.

———. "Will a New Broom at Humana Sweep the Old Era Away?" *New York Times*, March 11, 2001.

Jones, David. Interview by the author. Correspondence. June 22, 1999.

Jones, Kenneth. "Jon Jory, Champion of New Plays, to Leave Actors Theatre of Louisville in Fall." *Playbill Online*. www.playbill.com/cgi-bin/pbl/news?cmd=show&code=92902 (accessed January 19, 2000).

Jones, Margo. *Theatre-in-the-Round*. New York: Rinehart, 1951.

Jones, Trish Pugh. "History." In *An ATL Portfolio*. Louisville: Studio Gallery, 1972.

———. Telephone interview by the author. May 12, 2004.

Jory, Jon. Letter, February 25, 1976. Actors Theatre of Louisville Literary Office, Louisville.

———. Foreword. In *Ten-Minute Plays, Volume Four from Actors Theatre of Louisville*. Edited by Michael Bigelow Dixon and Liz Engelman. New York: Samuel French, 1998.

———. Interview by the author. Louisville, June 18, 1999.

———. "Quo Vadis?" In *Humana Festival of New American Plays* (tenth-anniversary program). Louisville: Actors Theatre of Louisville, 1986.

———. Telephone interview by Gerald M. Berkowitz. Transcript. December 19, 1995.

———. "We Love Writers." In Dixon and Crocker, *Humana Festival of New American Plays*, 8–11.

"Jory Promises Quality from Actors Theatre." *Courier-Journal* (Louisville). September 5, 1989.

Judd, Alan. "Humana Takes Lead in Helping Keep the Arts in Business." *Courier-Journal* (Louisville), May 10, 1985.

Kalem, T. E. "Third Running of the Derby." *Time*, March 5, 1979.

Kaukas, Dick. "Louisville Fund Reaches Out for Community Involvement." *Courier-Journal* (Louisville), March 14, 1977.

Kelly, Kevin. "New Playwright Rescues Festival." *Boston Globe*, March 26, 1985.

King, Bruce, ed. *Contemporary American Theatre*. New York: St. Martin's Press, 1991.

King, ElizaBeth Mahan. "Actors Theatre of Louisville: A Brief History." May 1979. Actors Theatre of Louisville Literary Office, Louisville.

———. "Actors Theatre of Louisville's New Play Program History." October 1979. Actors Theatre of Louisville Literary Office, Louisville.

———. General solicitation letter to critics, May 1979. Actors Theatre of Louisville Literary Office, Louisville.

———. General solicitation letter to stage managers, 1978. Actors Theatre of Louisville Literary Office, Louisville.

———. General solicitation letter to workshops, 1976. Actors Theatre of Louisville Literary Office, Louisville.

———. "The New Play Program." September 1980. Actors Theatre of Louisville Literary Office, Louisville.

————. University contact inquiry, 1978–79. Actors Theatre of Louisville Literary Office, Louisville.

Kistler, Julie. "Humana Still a Festival Fantastic." *Champaign News-Gazette,* April 7, 2000.

Klein, Alvin. "New York Welcomes New Jersey Plays." *New York Times,* October 7, 1990.

————. "The Theater Is Not Dead. It's into the Second Stage." *New York Times,* November 29, 1999.

Kohn, Martin F. "The Play's the Ring for Northern Michigan Writer." *Detroit Free Press,* March 7, 1999.

————. "Short Play's Two Acts Take Place on Four Wheels." *Detroit Free Press,* April 4, 1999.

————. "Young Playwrights Get 10 Minutes to Tell a Tale." *Detroit Free Press,* April 4, 1999.

Krasner, David, ed. *A Companion to Twentieth-Century American Theatre.* Malden, MA: Blackwell, 2005.

Kroll, Jack. "New Blood in Louisville." *Newsweek,* March 19, 1979.

Kuchwara, Michael. "Curtain Goes Up for Act Two at Humana Festival." *Post-Star* (Glens Falls, NY), April 5, 2001.

Langley, Stephen, ed. *Producers on Producing.* New York: Drama, 1974.

Lask, Thomas. "James McLure Can Write Plays He Can Act in Now." *New York Times,* June 16, 1979.

Leftowitz, David. "More to Louisville than ATL? Little Theatres Speak Up." May 9, 2000. http://www.playbill.com/news/article/ 51878.html (accessed September 30, 2005).

Leverett, James. "After the Revolution." *Program for the Tenth Annual Humana Festival of New American Plays.* Louisville: Actors Theatre of Louisville, 1986.

Lipper, Hal. "Human Relationships Mark '85 Productions." *Dayton Daily News,* March 31, 1985.

Liston, William T. "Humana Festival of Plays Is Theatre Lover's Dream." *Muncie Star,* March 31, 1985.

London, Todd. *The Artistic Home.* New York: Theatre Communications Group, 1988.

Lowry, W. McNeil. "The University and the Creative Arts," *Educational Theatre Journal,* 14, no. 2 (May 1962).

Marsh, Frazier. "Humana Festival Production Manager." In Dixon and Crocker, *Humana Festival of New American Plays,* 48.

Martin, Jane. *Anton in Show Business.* In *Humana Festival 2000: The Complete Plays.* Edited by Michael Bigelow Dixon and Amy Wegener. Hanover, NH: Smith and Kraus, 2000.

Maupin, Elizabeth. "At Humana Festival, There Is Life after Jory." *Orlando Sentinel,* April 8, 2001.

McBain, Roger. "Humana Plays Show the Car's the Thing." *Evansville Courier & Press,* March 25, 1999.

———. "Reality Puts Drama in *Digging In*." *Courier-Journal* (Louisville), March 29, 1987.

McElfresh, Tom. "Louisville Theatre's Thirty-four Hour Play Fest Earns Unabashed." *Cincinnati Enquirer*, November 20, 1977.

Memphis Arts Council. "Memphis Arts Council—Arts Funding." July 1, 2005. http://www.memphisartscouncil.org/AboutUs/News/AllNews/Arts-Funding.cfm (accessed July 30, 2005).

Memphis Chamber. "Memphis Regional Chamber." June 2004. http://www.memphischamber.com/default.asp?contentType=static&browsePath=MemphisFacts,Demographics (accessed July 30, 2005).

Miller, Marilee Hebert. Interview by the author. August 24, 1999.

Miller, Robert L. "Chattanooga, Other Cities, Use the Arts and Culture to Restore Aging Riverfront Areas." In *Cities and the Arts: A Handbook for Renewal*. Edited by Roger L. Kemp. Jefferson, NC: McFarland, 2004.

Mitchell, Sean. "Blueprint for Actors Theatre Not Easily Copied." *Dallas Times Herald*, February 20, 1979.

———. "Louisville Actors Theatre: A Regional Success Story." *Los Angeles Herald Examiner*, February 1979.

Money, Anita-Carol. "Comstock Portrayal Is Strange in *Passenger*." *Louisville Cardinal*, March 14, 1991.

Mootz, William. "*007 Crossfire* Produces More Noise Than Poise." *Courier-Journal* (Louisville), March 14, 1984.

———. "A.T.L. Endowment Campaign Is Aimed at Letting Theater Build for Tomorrow." *Courier-Journal* (Louisville), June 3, 1990.

———. "A.T.L. Festival Produced Challenging New Works." *Courier-Journal* (Louisville), May 29, 1983.

———. "A.T.L. Festival Reflected Unparalleled Creativity." *Courier-Journal* (Louisville), April 3, 1983.

———. "A.T.L. Rated One of the Healthiest Theaters." *Courier-Journal* (Louisville), May 16, 1976.

———. "A.T.L.'s *Courage* Bares a Curious Bloodless Soul." *Courier-Journal* (Louisville), March 2, 1983.

———. "A.T.L.'s *Danny* Is a Wild Voyage through Rage to Love, Salvation." *Courier-Journal* (Louisville), February 25, 1984.

———. "ATL's November Play Festival Boasts Six Never-Staged Works." *Courier-Journal* (Louisville), September 4, 1977.

———. "Actors Theatre's First Ten Years: From Rags to Riches." *Courier-Journal* (Louisville), May 26, 1974.

———. "*Agnes of God*: Another Brilliant Play in a Drama Festival That Fairly Shines." *Courier-Journal* (Louisville), March 8, 1980.

———. "The Art of Beginning." *Courier-Journal* (Louisville), November 20, 1976.

———. "Astonishing New Plays." *Courier-Journal* (Louisville), October 20, 1976.

———. "A Brilliant Season at Actors Theatre." *Courier-Journal* (Louisville), May 22, 1977.

———. "Danger Signs Evident at A.T.L.'s New-Play Festival." *Courier-Journal* (Louisville), March 29, 1987.

———. "Drama: The Season's Most Important Event Won't Even Happen in Louisville." *Courier-Journal* (Louisville), September 14, 1980.

———. "*Early Times* Presents Seven Plays by Beginners Bursting with Talent." *Courier-Journal* (Louisville), February 21, 1981.

———. "Foreign Playwrights Take Jabs at America, but It's All in Fun." *Courier-Journal* (Louisville), February 28, 1980.

———. "*Getting Out* Is a Stunning Achievement." *Courier-Journal* (Louisville), November 4, 1977.

———. "*Gin Game* Endearing, Funny." *Courier-Journal* (Louisville), March 8, 1977.

———. "A Great Experiment." *Courier-Journal* (Louisville), September 19, 1993.

———. "High Drama in the Courtroom: Mann's *Execution of Justice* Places All of America on Trial." *Courier-Journal* (Louisville), March 9, 1984.

———. "How Should New Playwrights Be Nurtured?" *Courier-Journal* (Louisville), November 20, 1976.

———. "Humana Festival's First Play a Bowl of Cherries." *Courier-Journal* (Louisville), February 27, 1984.

———. Interview by Lucretia (Teka) Baldwin Ward. In Ward, Notes on History.

———. "Jon Jory Frets: 'Will Success Spoil Actors Theatre?'" *Courier-Journal* (Louisville), September 10, 1972.

———. "Jon Jory Not Only Survived His Festival, He Thrived on It." *Courier-Journal* (Louisville), February 25, 1979.

———. "Jory and ATL Win Margo Jones Award." *Courier-Journal* (Louisville), March 23, 1979.

———. "Jory Pleased Louisvillian's Play Is Chosen." *Courier-Journal* (Louisville), September 4, 1977.

———. "Louisville's Theatre Fest: An Unimpressive Marathon." *USA Today*, March 31, 1987.

———. "*Medal of Honor Rag* Probes Guilt of Survival with Spellbinding Drama." *Courier-Journal* (Louisville), October 12, 1976.

———. "Monologues by 'Martin' Are Bizarre, Fascinating." *Courier-Journal* (Louisville), March 21, 1982.

———. "Much Ado about Something." *Courier-Journal* (Louisville), September 24, 1994.

———. "Personal Favorites." In Dixon and Crocker, *Humana Festival of New American Plays*, 30–33.

———. "*Sex* Is Clever Cartoon; *Reunion* Oddly Affecting." *Louisville Times*, October 13, 1976.

———. "Society's Waste Viewed in *Food from Trash*." *Courier-Journal* (Louisville), March 27, 1983.

———. "Stretching the Sensibilities." *Courier-Journal* (Louisville), November 13, 1977.

———. "*Thanksgiving* Offers a Feast Fueled by Funny Friendships." *Courier-Journal* (Louisville), March 7, 1983.

———. "That's Entertainment." *Courier-Journal* (Louisville), April 11, 1991.

———. "Theatre Review: 2." *Courier-Journal* (Louisville), March 25, 1990.

———. "Theatre Review: *Blood Issue.*" *Courier-Journal* (Louisville), March 5, 1989.

———. "Theatre Review: *The Carving of Mount Rushmore.*" *Courier-Journal* (Louisville), March 13, 1992.

———. "Theatre Review: *Cementville.*" *Courier-Journal* (Louisville), March 15, 1991.

———. "Theatre Review: *Deadly Virtues.*" *Courier-Journal* (Louisville), March 13, 1993.

———. "Theatre Review: *Glimmerglass.*" *Courier-Journal* (Louisville), February 27, 1987.

———. "Theatre Review: *God's Country.*" *Courier-Journal* (Louisville), March 10, 1989.

———. "Theatre Review: *Keely and Du.*" *Courier-Journal* (Louisville), March 18, 1993.

———. "Theatre Review: *A Passenger Train of Sixty-One Coaches.*" *Courier-Journal* (Louisville), March 7, 1991.

———. "Theatre Review: *A Piece of My Heart.*" *Courier-Journal* (Louisville), March 24, 1991.

———. "Theatre Review: *The Queen of the Leaky Roof Circuit.*" *Courier-Journal* (Louisville), February 26, 1988.

———. "Theatre Review: *Rites of Mating.*" *Courier-Journal* (Louisville). March 2, 1992.

———. "Theatre Review: *Stained Glass.*" *Courier-Journal* (Louisville). March 25, 1989.

———. "Theatre Review: *Vital Signs.*" *Courier-Journal* (Louisville). March 22, 1990.

———. "Theatre Review: *Whereabouts Unknown.*" *Courier-Journal* (Louisville), March 6, 1988.

———. "Thirty Seasons in the Spotlight." *Courier-Journal* (Louisville), August 30, 1998.

———. "*Two Masters* Has Local Premiere at Actors." *Courier-Journal* (Louisville), February 25, 1985.

———. "*Valentine*: Powerful, but Not Yet in Focus." *Courier-Journal* (Louisville), February 2, 1979.

———. "*Very Last Lover of River Cane* at Actors Theatre of Louisville." *Courier-Journal* (Louisville), March 6, 1985.

Mordden, Ethan. *One More Kiss: The Broadway Musical of the 1970s.* New York: Palgrave Macmillan, 2003.

Mufson, Daniel. "Interactive Archive: The Actor's Workshop." 2001–2. http://www.alternativetheater.com/cgi-bin/int_archive/entry_index.cgi?ARC_ID=00019 (accessed August 1, 2005).

Nance, Kevin. "Bogart's *Cabin Pressure* a Valentine to the Theater." *Tennessean* (Nashville), March 28, 1999.

Newmark, Judith. "So Many Plays, So Little Time; But Humana Festival Is Worth It." *St. Louis Post-Dispatch*, March 28, 1999.

"Nonprofit Theaters to Get Ford Aid for New Plays." *New York Times*, July 15, 1976.

Noth, Dominique Paul. "The Louisville Idea Grows." *Milwaukee Journal*, March 11, 1979.

Novak, Hava. "The Guests from Louisville: Professionals of the First Order." *Davar* (Haifa), October 9, 1980.

Novick, Julius. *Beyond Broadway: The Quest for Permanent Theatres*. New York: Hill and Wang, 1968.

———. "Too Much, Too Small." *Village Voice*, March 12, 1979.

———. "What Is This Thing Called A.T.L.?" *Village Voice*, April 23, 1985.

Nowlan, David. "*Blood Issue* Steals the Show at Louisville." *Irish Times*, April 19, 1989.

Nunns, Stephen. "The Rest of the Story." http://www.tcg.org/am_theatre/at_articles/AT_Volume_19/September02/at_web0902_thtrfact.html (accessed June 7, 2005).

———. "Shifting Currents." http://www.tcg.org/am_theatre/at_articles/AT_Volume_19/September02/at_web0902_thtrfacts.html (accessed June 7, 2005).

O'Connor, Bill. "Here are Brief Sketches of Louisville Productions." *Akron Beacon Journal*, March 31, 1985.

Palmer, Tanya. "Risky Business." *Theatre Topics*. 13, no.1 (2003): 63–67.

———. "The Technology Project." In *Humana Festival 2002: The Complete Plays*. Edited by Tanya Palmer and Amy Wegener. Hanover, NH: Smith and Kraus, 2002.

Papatola, Dominic P. "Stage Craft." *St. Paul Pioneer Press*, April 9, 2000.

Pearson, Mike. "Play Havoc: Works Don't Equal Prestige of Festival." *El Paso Herald-Post*, March 28, 1988.

Pender, Rick. "Humana Treatment." *City Beat*. www.citybeat.com/2004–04–07/ onstage2.shtml (accessed June 6, 2006).

———. "Splendid Variety." *CityBeat* (Cincinnati), April 6, 2000.

———. "Taking a Risk." *CityBeat* (Cincinnati), February 22, 2001.

Pervic, Muharem. "Fourteenth B.I.T.E.F. Bitter, Sharp-Tasting, and Documentary." *Politika* (Belgrade), September 22, 1980.

Phillips, Michael. "America, the Bountiful." *Los Angeles Times*, April 3, 2001.

———. "Irrelevant Fest." *Chicago Tribune*, April 10, 2002.

———. "Report from Louisville." *Chicago Tribune*, April 10, 2003.

Pielmeier, John. "Hospitality." In *Program for the Tenth Annual Humana Festival of New American Plays*. Louisville: Actors Theatre of Louisville, 1986.

Pogrebin, Robin. "Offstage Drama at Long Wharf." *New York Times*, June 25, 2001.

Poirier, Richard. Introduction. In *Three*. By Lillian Hellman. Boston: Little, Brown, 1979.

Richards, Lloyd. "Lloyd Richards: Reflections from the Playwrights' Champion—An Interview." *TDR: The Drama Review* 47 (Summer 2003).

Ridley, Clifford A. "Don't Call It 'Regional' Stage." *Detroit Sunday News*, December 11, 1977.

———. "Elusive Possibilities in Two New Fables." *National Observer* (Washington, DC), March 19, 1977.

Riehm, Joan. New Director Wants to Help A.T.L. to 'Run.'" *Courier-Journal* (Louisville), March 11, 1969.

Roberts, Gene. "Integration in South: Erratic Pattern." *New York Times*, May 29, 1967.

Rodgers, Jeffrey. Interview by the author. Louisville, August 20, 1999.

Roudané, Matthew C. *American Drama since 1960: A Critical History*. New York: Twayne, 1996.

Roundabout Theatre Company. "Roundabout Theatre Company: A Short History of Roundabout." September 8, 2004. http://www.roundabouttheatre. org/ history2.htm (accessed September 30, 2005).

Ryen, Dag. "At Actors Theatre, a Great Crop of Drama." *Lexington Herald-Leader*, April 9, 2006.

———. "A.T.L.'s *Encounters* Funny, Touching." *Lexington Herald-Leader*, March 8, 1996.

———. "Maintaining Relevance Is Humana's Challenge." *Monterey Herald. com*. http://www.montereyherald.com/mld/ kentucky/living/5608313. htm (accessed April 13, 2003).

———. "Pair of Plays Takes Creative Look at Rituals of Love." *Lexington Herald-Leader*, March 15, 1992.

Ryzuk, Mary S. *The Circle Repertory Company: The First Fifteen Years*. Ames: Iowa State University Press, 1989.

Sandusky, Dale. "A.T.L.'s *Queen* Proves Mostly a Royal Mess." *New Albany Tribune*, February 26, 1988.

———. "*Carving of Mount* Addresses Issues Not Often Tackled." *New Albany Tribune*, March 13, 1992.

———. "*Cementville* Has Raunchy Opening at A.T.L." *New Albany Tribune*, March 15, 1991.

———. "*Deadly Virtues* Is Unusual Enough to Keep You Interested." *New Albany Tribune*, March 13, 1993.

———. "Excellent Performances Make 2 the Best in Festival." *New Albany Tribune*, March 26, 1990.

———. "*God's Country* Brings Hate to A.T.L. Stage." *New Albany Tribune*, March 10, 1989.

———. "*Keely and Du* Fuels Abortion Debate, Offers No New Insight to Issue." *New Albany Tribune*, March 19, 1993.

———. "Review: *The Gin Game*." *New Albany Tribune*, March 10, 1977.

———. "*Stained Glass* Fails to Deliver at Actors Theatre." *New Albany Tribune*, March 27, 1989.

———. "*Strange Encounters* Fails to Live Up to Its Potential." *New Albany Tribune*, March 4, 1996.

——. "Texas Barroom Play Is Best of the Lot at A.T.L." *New Albany Tribune*, March 11, 1985.

——. "There's No Bolting through ATL's Epic *Glimmerglass*." *New Albany Tribune*, February 27, 1987.

——. "Though Long, Familiar, *Blood Issue* Debuts Well." *New Albany Tribune*, March 8, 1989.

——. "*Train* Only Scratches the Surface." *New Albany Tribune*, March 7, 1991.

——. "Two Plays Differ in Entertainment Value." *New Albany Tribune*, March 2, 1992.

——. "*Vital Signs* Pumps Life into Festival." *New Albany Tribune*, March 22, 1990.

——. "*Whereabouts* Speaks for Homeless People." *New Albany Tribune*, March 6, 1988.

——. "Youth Theme in *Early Times*." *New Albany Tribune*, February 23, 1981.

Saunders, Dudley. "A.T.L. Festival Revisited." *Louisville Times*, February 13, 1979.

——. "At A.T.L., More from the Mysterious Jane Martin." *Louisville Times*, March 22, 1982.

——. "A.T.L.'s *Trash* Stuns the Senses." *Louisville Times*, March 28, 1983.

——. "*Circus Valentine* Too Often Strained, Artificial." *Louisville Times*, February 2, 1979.

——. "Comic Lightning Strikes Unevenly." *Louisville Times*, March 6, 1985.

——. "Confusing Clutter Downs *007 Crossfire*." *Louisville Times*, March 14, 1984.

——. "*Danny* Is Amusing One Minute, Revolting the Next." *Louisville Times*, February 25, 1984.

——. "Despite Flaws, *Execution* Is Compelling." *Louisville Times*, March 9, 1984.

——. "*Doctors* Bubbles with Wit." *Louisville Times*, March 13, 1980.

——. "'Everybody Gained except the Investors.'" *Louisville Times*, January 13, 1973.

——. "Exciting *Getting Out* Wrenches Emotions." *Louisville Times*, November 4, 1977.

——. "Frank Manley's *Two Masters* Visits Southern Gothic Territory." *Louisville Times*, February 25, 1985.

——. Interview by Lucretia (Teka) Baldwin Ward. In Ward, Notes on History.

——. "Lively *Early Times* Captures Youth at A.T.L." *Louisville Times*, February 21, 1981.

——. "*Medal of Honor Rag* Is Haunting Exploration of 'Survivor Guilt.'" *Louisville Times*, October 12, 1976.

——. "Paul Collins Riveting in One-Man *Courage*." *Louisville Times*, March 2, 1983.

——. "Rumors Fly over 'Secret' Production." *Louisville Times*, February 18, 1983.

———. "*Sexual Perversity* Is Good Comedy, but the Language May Disturb Some." *Courier-Journal* (Louisville), October 12, 1976.

———. "*Thanksgiving* Doesn't Live up to Expectations." *Louisville Times*, March 7, 1983.

———. "*Vanities* Is Likable, Somewhat Unbelievable." *Louisville Times*, October 18, 1976.

———. "Vivid, Amusing *The Octette Bridge Club* Opens New Play Festival at Actors." *Louisville Times*, February 27, 1984.

———. "Warehouse Is Theatre for A.T.L.'s Mystery Play." *Louisville Times*, March 18, 1983.

Savitch, H. V., and Ronald K. Vogel. "Louisville: Compacts and Antagonistic Cooperation." In *Regional Politics: America in a Post-City Age*. Edited by H. V. Savitch and Ronald K. Vogel. Thousand Oaks, CA: Sage Publications, 1996.

Savran, David. "New Realism: Mamet, Mann and Nelson." In B. King, *Contemporary American Theatre*.

Schlesinger, Arthur M., Jr., ed. *The Almanac of American History*. New York: Barnes and Noble, 1993.

Schlueter, June. "American Drama of the 1990s On and Off-Broadway." In Krasner, *Companion to Twentieth-Century American Theatre*.

Shafer, Sheldon. "Actors Theatre of Louisville Casts Its Eye on Expansion." *Courier-Journal* (Louisville), May 19, 1990.

Shanley, John Patrick. *Missing/Kissing*. In *Humana Festival '96: The Complete Plays*. Edited by Michael Bigelow Dixon and Liz Engelman. Lyme, NH: Smith and Kraus, 1996.

Sjostrom, Jan. "Festival of Plays a Gold Mine for Regional Theater." *Palm Beach Daily News*, March 30, 2001.

Skolnick, Sara. "Introduction." In *Humana Festival '99*. Lyme, NH: Smith and Kraus, 1999.

Smith, Valerie. Interviews by the author. Louisville, June 18 and August 20, 1999.

Smith, Yandell. Interview by Lucretia (Teka) Baldwin Ward. In Ward, Notes on History.

Speer, Alexander. Interview by Lucretia (Teka) Baldwin Ward. In Ward, Notes on History.

———. Interview by the author. Louisville, August 20, 1999.

Springer, P. Gregory. "The Excitement of Discovering New Plays." *Champaign-Urbana News-Gazette*, March 29, 1985.

———. "Some Promise, No Major Plays at Refocused Louisville Festival." *Variety*, April 6, 1988.

"Standing Ovation from Humana, A." In Dixon and Crocker, *Humana Festival of New American Plays*, 12–15.

Stayton, Richard. "Louisville Festival Is a Hothouse for the American Theater." *Los Angeles Herald Examiner*, March 31, 1985.

Stern, Alan. "Highly Regarded Louisville Is Slipping." *Denver Post*, March 31, 1985.

————. "New York Critics Assail *Octette* in Inexplicable Ways." *Denver Post*, March 28, 1985.

Stevenson, Isabelle, ed. *The Tony Award*. Portsmouth, NH: Heinemann, 1994.

Stuart, Reginald. "Louisville Backing Home-Based Arts." *New York Times*, March 6, 1977.

Sullivan, Dan. "Louisville Picks a Winner." *Los Angeles Times*, November 20, 1977.

Swem, Gregg. "ATL Wins Vaughan Award for Contribution to Theatre." *Courier-Journal* (Louisville), May 31, 1979.

Theatre Communications Group. "A Festival of New U.S. Plays." *Theatre Communications Group Newsletter* 5, no. 10 (October 1977).

————. "Theatre Facts 1999." http://www.tcg.org/programs/ theatrefacts/ tf99_page15.html (accessed June 7, 2005).

Thoman, Nord. "Arts Are Good Business, Leaders Say." *Courier-Journal* (Louisville), October 21, 2001.

Thomson, Lynn M. "Michael Bigelow Dixon." In *Between the Lines*. Toronto: Playwrights Canada Press, 2002.

Traub, James. *The Devil's Playground: A Century of Pleasure and Profit in Times Square*. New York: Random House, 2004.

Victor, Karl. Interview by Lucretia (Teka) Baldwin Ward. In Ward, Notes on History.

Victor, Roanne. Interview by Lucretia (Teka) Baldwin Ward. In Ward, Notes on History.

Victor, Roanne H. Telephone interview by the author, June 14, 2005.

Voss, Zannie Giraud, and Glenn B. Voss, with Christopher Shuff and Dan Melia. *Theatre Facts 2000*. New York: Theatre Communications Group, 2001.

Ward, Lucretia (Teka) Baldwin. "Actors Theatre of Louisville: An Oral History of the Early Years, 1964–1969." Master's thesis, University of Louisville, 1993.

————. Notes on History of Actors Theatre Collection, 1964–1989. University Archives and Records Center, University of Louisville, Louisville.

Ward, Michael. "Jory: Eye of a Dramatic Storm." *Cleveland Plain-Dealer*, April 23, 1979.

Wasserman, Debbi. "Louisville Round-Up: The Third Annual Festival of New American Plays at the Actors Theatre of Louisville." *New York Theatre Review*, April 1979.

Watson, Charles S. *The History of Southern Drama*. Lexington: University of Kentucky Press, 1997.

Weber, Bruce. "A Burst of Energy in the Regional Theater." *New York Times*, December 5, 2000.

————. "Critic's Notebook." *New York Times*, April 11, 2003.

————. "Managers with a Mission to Avoid the Status Quo." *New York Times*, February 22, 1998.

———. "When the Theater Sends Up Itself in Order to Save Itself." *New York Times*, April 4, 2000.

———. "Where Plays Escape the Curse of the Unseen." *New York Times*, April 6, 2004.

Weiner, Bernard. "Louisville Showcases Some Political Scripts." *San-Francisco Examiner-Chronicle*, April 1, 1984.

Weiss, Hedy. "Bernstein, Paris and a Big Mess." *Chicago Sun Times*, April 9, 2002.

Welsh, Anne Marie. "At Humana Festival, Plenty of Themes, but Not Enough Drama." *San Diego Union-Tribune*, April 10, 2005.

Whaley, Charles. "The 29th Humana Festival: 2005." http://www.curtainup.com/humana2005.html (accessed June 6, 2006).

———. "The 30th Humana Festival of New American Plays Celebrates Its 30th Anniversary." http://www.curtainup.com/humana2006.html (accessed June 6, 2006).

———. "The Humana Festival: 2002." http://www.curtainup.com/humana2002.html (accessed June 6, 2006).

———. "The Humana Festival: 2003." http://www.curtainup.com/humana2003.html (accessed June 6, 2006).

"What the Critics Said . . ." 1978. Actors Theatre of Louisville Literary Office.

Wheeler, Billy Edd Wheeler. "Billy Edd Wheeler: Fiction." http://www.billyeddwheeler.com/books.htm (accessed November 2, 2005).

Wibking, Angela. "New Plays Recycle Other, Better Ideas." *Nashville Business Journal*, April 9–13, 1990.

Wick, Nancy. "Making It Work." *Columns Magazine*, March 2002. http://www.washington.edu/alumni/columns/march02/jory1.html (accessed March 2, 2007).

———. "Making It Work." *Columns Magazine*, March 2002. http://www.washington.edu/alumni/columns/march02/jory02.html (accessed June 6, 2006).

Wilson, Edwin. "Humana Festival Returns to Its Roots." *Wall Street Journal*, April 15, 1991.

———. "Playwrights: Three Full Days of Fresh Talent." *Wall Street Journal*, February 23, 1979.

Winer, Linda. "Drama Festival Strays from Innovative Path." *USA Today*, March 28, 1985.

———. "More Is Less at Louisville Theatre Festival." *USA Today*, April 4, 1983.

Wohl, David. "Lots of Legs to Break." *Gazette-Mail* (Charleston), February 25, 2001.

Yahoo.com. "Victor Jory Biography." http://movies.yahoo.com/movie/contributor/1800013598/bio (accessed March 2, 2007).

Yetter, Deborah. "The Emotional War: Women Are Moved by Play They Inspired." *Courier-Journal* (Louisville), April 8, 1991.

York, Julie. "GenX Playwrights Turn Slop Culture into High Culture in Louisville." *South Bend Tribune*, April 4, 1999.

Zeigler, Joseph Wesley. *Regional Theatre: The Revolutionary Stage.* New York: Da Capo Press, 1977.

Zinman, Toby. "Louisville Slugger." *City Paper.* http://citypaper.net/articles/2002–04–25/theater.shtml (accessed June 6, 2006).

INDEX

Johnson, Jory, 49–50
Johnson, Morse, 13
Jones, Chris, 147–48, 158, 162, 216–17n. 39
Jones, David A., 69–70, 72, 149
Jones, Margo, 7–9
Jones, Trish Pugh, 35, 40, 42, 144, 150, 188n. 27
Jory, Jon, 2, 30–31, 35, 58; artistic tastes of, 99–100, 109, 111, 123–24, 151; celebration of festival, 138–43; dictatorial approach, 60–61, 85–86; directing on Broadway, 40–43; effect of critics on, 119–20; establishment, then exploitation formula, 62–63, 165–66; final experiments, 132–38; legacy of, 162–66; at Long Wharf Theatre, 24, 31, 32–33, 46, 65; Martin controversy and, 73–74, 79, 113–15; New Haven theatre, 11–12; personal characteristics, 3, 34, 164; play selection process, 33, 39, 45–51, 90–94; playwriting by, 4, 40–43, 112, 190n. 54; rehearsals and, 61; resignation from Actors Theatre, 138; short-form play and, 56–57; work ethic, 31–32
Jory, Marcia Dixcy, 32
Jory, Victor, 11, 31
Jouét, 153

Kalem, T. E., 62
Keely and Du (Martin), 93, 115
Kennedy, Adrienne, 88
Kennedy Center for the Performing Arts, 60
Kentucky!, 43, 58
Kesselman, Wendy, 64, 79
King, ElizaBeth Mahan, 44, 52, 53, 72–75
Kleiman, Harlan, 11–12
Kushner, Tony, 124

Lamarre, Jacques, 141
Lauro, Shirley, 108, 206n. 34
Lawrence, Jerome, 93
Leatherstocking Tales, adaptation of, 111–13
Leverett, James, 45
Levin, Harold, 40, 42
Lincoln Center, 10, 23

Linney, Romulus, 108, 125, 206n. 33
Listeners (Martin), 159
literary adaptations, 111–13, 208n. 55
literary agents, 93
literary manager, 74–77, 150; Classics in Context Festival and, 96–97, 122, 123–24; experimental works and, 102–3; support of playwrights, 83–84
London, Todd, 86, 113, 114, 127, 145, 210n. 16
Lone Star (McLure), 59, 60
Long Wharf Theatre, 11–12, 24, 31, 32–33, 46, 65
Louisville: citywide celebration of the arts, 123; community leaders, 13–14; community support for ATL, 33–36, 65; media, 13, 15–16, 40–41, 49–50, 144, 185n. 31; playwrights from, 55–56, 103–4, 157; population, 35; urban renewal, 37–38. See also audience
Louisville Times, The, 15, 40–41
"Louisville Tries Noted Authors as Playwrights" (DeVries), 103–4
Louisville Zoo, The (collection), 56, 157
Lowry, W. McNeil, 11
Lucas, Craig, 125

M. Butterfly (Hwang), 105
Machado, Eduardo, 111
malaise, drama of, 60
Mamet, David, 49
Manhattan Theatre Club, 94
Mann, Emily, 87–88, 90, 91, 135
Margo Jones Award, 39, 50, 65, 66
Margulies, Donald, 124
marketing/public relations campaigns, 8, 35–36, 40, 57, 126
Mark Taper Forum, 39
Marsh, Frazier, 52
Martin, Jane, 73–74, 113–16, 124; Anton in Show Business, 139–43, 152; Cementville, 114–15; Flaming Guns of the Purple Sage, 149; Keely and Du, 115; Listeners, 159; Mr. Bundy, 124, 125; Talking With, 74, 79, 114, 149; Twirler, 73; Vital Signs, 114
Mason, Marshall, 84
mass mailings, 35–36
Masterson, Marc, 5, 144–61, 166; audience and, 147–48, 151–55; difficulty

performance space, 10, 23–24, 36–39, 133–36, 157, 189n. 33; car plays, 134–35; 1987–93 phase and, 116–18; off-site, 80–82, 157; phone plays, 133–34; revitalization efforts, 36–38. *See also specific theatres*

Pesola, Robert, 89–90

phases of production, Actors Theatre of Louisville, 4–5; becoming an institution (1980–82), 4, 64–79; exploratory years (1987–93), 99–120; formulaic works phase (1994–98), 5, 121–30, 131, 210–11n. 17; Jory's final years (1999–2000), 131–43; lucky years (1976–79), 4, 45–63; product-to-process phase (1983–86), 5, 80–98, 138. *See also* Actors Theatre of Louisville

Phillips, Michael, 154

phone plays, 133–34, 155

Piece of My Heart, A (Lauro), 93, 108, 206n. 34

Pielmeier, John, 73

Pittsburgh Playhouse, 10, 23

Playfaire 76/77, 50–52, 191n. 25, 196n. 21

Play It Again (Allen), 40

PlayLabs, 129

playwrights, 194n. 70; alterations for, 82–85, 91–94; commissions of non-theatre artists, 101–8, 124, 125, 204n. 4; development of relationships with, 77–78, 91–94; exploration of, 100–107; female, 58–59, 114; in-house, 73; Jory as, 4, 40–43, 112, 190n. 54; Jory's protection of, 68–69; limitations in talent pool, 125–26; local, 55–56, 103–4, 157; Masterson and, 158–59; minority writers, 100–101, 105–6, 148, 151–52; paired-playwright project, 105–6; rehearsal process and, 83, 199n. 13; southern drama, 58–59, 129; university writing programs, 72–73; view of ATL, 53–54

politically themed plays, 48, 59, 90, 201n. 37

press conferences, 90, 101

Princeton University, 11

Public Theatre, 27, 37, 41

Pulitzer Prize for Drama, 52, 53, 114, 115, 121

Pure Confidence (Brown), 158

Pvt. Wars (McLure), 59, 60

Queen of the Leaky Roof Circuit (Breslin), 102–3, 107, 111, 119

Rabe, David, 60

Rambo, David, 136

Rapp, Adam, 154

Rea, Charlotte, 43

Rea, Oliver, 11

Reagan administration, 70–71, 84

Rebeck, Theresa, 154–55, 158

regional theatre, 2, 8–9; 1960s, 7, 23–24, 60; influence of, 65, 163; models for, 7–11; New York bypassed, 92–93; playwrights' criticism of, 46–47; reestablishment of, 23–24; as tryouts for Broadway, 45–46. *See also specific theatres*

Regional Theatre (Zeigler), 8

Rembrandt's Gift (Howe), 154

Reynolds, Rebecca, 134

Reyes, Guillermo, 124

Rhythmicity: A Convergence of Poetry, Theatre, and Hip-Hop, 156

Rich, Frank, 126–27

Richards, Lloyd, 86, 101

Rites of Mating (Hwang), 106

Roads That Lead Here, The (Blessing), 157

Rockefeller Foundation, 39

Roundabout Theatre Company, 24, 71

Ryen, Dag, 156, 158

Ryzuk, Mary S., 93

Samuel French company, 57

Sara Shallenberger Lobby, 132

Saratoga International Theatre Institute (SITI), 136

Saunders, Dudley, 15–16, 20, 22, 185n. 31

Savran, David, 51

Scene, The (Rebeck), 158

Schoenfeld, Gerald, 65

Schubert Theatre chain, 60

Score (Bogart), 154

scripts: difficulties in locating, 72–73; Papp's control of, 53–54; second-production, 91–94, 95; submission process, 75–77, 90–91

Jeffrey Ullom received his Ph.D. from the University of Illinois, where he specialized in contemporary American theatre. An assistant professor of theatre at Vanderbilt University, he teaches theatre history and playwriting and directs the departmental honors thesis program. His published works include articles in *Theatre Journal*, *Theatre Topics*, and *Theatre History Studies* and a chapter in *Angels in the American Theatre*, edited by Robert A. Schanke. Before entering academe, he was a dramaturg at Actors Theatre of Louisville, where he worked with such esteemed playwrights as Tony Kushner, David Henry Hwang, Naomi Wallace, and John Patrick Shanley. His current projects include two books, one about student dramaturgy and the other an analysis of modern pop-artist musicals.